AXIOM OF THE QUEEN'S ARROW

Book Ten in the Pantracia Chronicles

AXIOM OF THE QUEEN'S ARROW

Amanda Muratoff & Kayla Hansen

www.Pantracia.com

For those we've lost.

The Pantracia Chronicles:

Visit www.Pantracia.com for our pronunciation guide
and to discover more.

Chapter 1

Spring, 2618 R.T.

I COULD ONLY WATCH.

My life passed before my eyes, no longer mine, and I only had myself to blame. I welcomed a parasite into my soul. To save my family, my friends, my love. To save my country.

He can't kill Katrin. That would have broken our agreement, which I have to believe holds some kind of power. But he's smart and found a loophole. I never said Katrin needed to be awake. Now she sleeps, my child still in her womb, and there's nothing I can do.

I am damned to be an observer of my actions. His actions as me.

The years went slowly at first, and I fought with every ounce of energy I could muster. I pounded against the walls trapping me within myself.

Uriel.

The sickly greed within him is immeasurable. He has no consideration for life, no conscience. All he seeks is power, and I single-handedly offered him the Isalican throne on a silver, desperate platter.

I won't tell him what he wants to know, though. I won't tell him where the dragons are. No matter how many times he tries.

After a time, I lost motivation to watch for his weakness, and I dimmed. I don't know for how long. I couldn't bear to witness the murder, the bloodshed, and the pain. Inflicted by my own hands and fueled by my power, but not at my will.

Agony ravaged me.

When I emerged, my resolve hardened once again. I learned all I could about him, praying that one day he would slip up and break one of my terms. I needed to be ready, however long it took.

I paid attention to everyone he met, the Shades lusty and wicked in their service. But what held my interest more were the ones who faltered. The ones who'd regretted joining Uriel. I made a list and memorized every feature about their faces, in case I could use the information later to escape my intruder.

I never knew Lasseth Fray before he'd defected, but Uriel thought about him enough that I saw him as an ally until his death. Bellamy had my hopes, too, until I watched him perish at my feet after being delivered by the Shade who'd been meant to suffer my fate.

Kinronsilis Lazorus.

Stolen twin of the prince of Feyor.

He arrived at such a young age, and I screamed at him to run, but he couldn't hear me. Sorrow filled me when doubt surfaced on his face years later. Punishment didn't rebind his loyalty. When he escaped Uriel's clutches, I wept with joy.

Uriel intended to use Kinronsilis as his next host before he stumbled on my ability to jump time and my name. I saw myself in Kin and cheered with every defiance.

Taking the small victories became necessary for my sanity.

At times, I debated letting my mind go, if I even could, but I vowed to protect my country.

My people.

My priestess.

I promised Katrin I wouldn't give up. Even though she couldn't hear me, I trusted that wherever she was, she was with me somehow.

I will stay ready, I promised her.

And so I wait, just under the surface, for the chance to seize my freedom.

Chapter 2

Summer, 2618 R.T.

MATTHIAS'S BOOTS TAPPED OVER THE worn marble floor, the bonfire raging behind him.

I hate this place.

Uriel spent considerable time in the forgotten temple somewhere in the Dykul Mountains. Vines choked the ruins, creating a tangled view of the horrors that happened there. But the worst occurred in the nearby atrium, where the marble was permanently stained in splotches of death. Death by Matthias's own hand, though not his mind.

Seeking solace from the insidiousness, Matthias often distracted himself by focusing on other things instead of what his body did. Twenty-two crumbled benches lined the grand hall, barely visible beneath the overgrowth. Each had an alcove once meant as an altar to the gods.

But this is a godless place.

Dread built in Matthias as a cloaked figure entered the other side of the temple, crossing the space to where he was to stand in exactly forty-eight paces. The Shade dragged a limp body, though it hummed with potential for Uriel's Art, confirming the person lived.

As the Shade stopped, his rain-dampened hood fell from his head.

Kin?

Matthias's mind whirled.

When did Uriel find Kinronsilis? How did I miss that?

"Jarac. Sooner than I expected." Uriel spoke in Matthias's voice, though this time he centered himself on the words.

Right. Kin's twin.

Uriel had claimed Feyor's only prince as a Shade years prior, and the man completed tasks like no other. With the use of his name, he rose in rank faster than any before him.

Each time the identical twin arrived, Matthias struggled to understand until his memory caught up.

"I have completed my task." Jarac let go of the man he dragged, and firelight hit the captive's unconscious face.

Matthias stared at the king of Feyor. The Shade's own father.

King Lazorus.

Uriel's gaze flickered back to Kin, taking Matthias's with it. Again, the dread rose.

When did Uriel regain control over Kin?

"Eager for the throne, I see." Uriel descended the reinforced granite steps, which showed as much wear as the marble floor.

It's not Kin, it's Jarac.

Kinronsilis's twin had never shown the same capacity for empathy as his brother. While Matthias had longed for Kin's redemption, Jarac's soul held nothing but villainy, even before he'd sworn his oath to Uriel.

He'd have been the better twin to steal and shape from the beginning.

Matthias wished he could close his eyes, but the closest he'd ever come was in constructing a tiny, make-believe room in the back of his mind. It housed nothing but a chair, a candle on a little table, and four windowless walls. He could retreat there, hide, imagine he still had a body, but Uriel never let it last long.

Uriel channeled power, and the dense vines along the temple walls shriveled. A wheezing cry of an animal echoed from somewhere unseen, but Matthias could imagine its flesh twisting. Before the scent of death could settle into his nostrils, Uriel jerked Matthias's consciousness, engulfing his Art and yanking them back through time.

The surrounding foliage hummed with revived energy as if Uriel had never drained it. The pool of thrumming shadow within the parasite hovered like a looming thunderstorm at the edge of Matthias's consciousness.

The curious head of a deer lifted behind the broken glass window of Aedonai's altar. Its nose didn't have time to twitch before darkness consumed it, the same echoing cry grating against Matthias's senses as the vines crumbled to dust.

The storm of power doubled.

Then again.

And again.

Uriel jumped through time at a pace Matthias could barely comprehend, blurring each death into a horrid, repeated visage.

When he stopped, everything lived, but Matthias experienced the deaths too many times. This loss was more bearable. He could handle the repetitive loss of wildlife, but it wasn't always animals and plants. When Uriel used people's life energy to fuel him, Matthias screamed within his mind. He witnessed every murder multiple times, when once would have been enough to shatter his sanity.

Uriel's power swallowed the rival king, his unconscious body falling into Matthias's wriggling shadow. "So you shall have another." He stared at Jarac, corruption brewing invisibly through the tether connecting Uriel to his Shade. New threads erupted, entangling and strengthening the existing bond.

Jarac hissed in pain and pleasure as he lifted his sleeve, a black shape rippling from within him to the surface of his skin. Another addition to his tattoo. His power. Inherently, Matthias knew the purpose behind the new rank. It'd grant the Shade the power to shift into a raven.

Is that purposely meant to match Kin's?

"Your task is to take your place as king and declare an alliance with Isalica."

"It will be done, Master." Jarac bowed, placing a fist to his chest.

"How are the new drakes progressing?" Uriel swelled power into his shadow, expanding the darkness behind him.

"Something is interfering with their training. Even with the Dtrüa present, they disobey."

Uriel growled under his breath. "Whip them harder. Go. You will find your father in his bed tomorrow morning. Muster up some tears, won't you?"

"Yes, Master." Jarac straightened, a sinister glint in his eyes as he turned and departed from the temple.

Uriel stole any semblance of Matthias's breath as he disintegrated into shadow, their surroundings blurring and distorting until they emerged in the higher chamber. The atrium boasted concave walls rising to a skeletal glassless frame. Rain pattered on the marble floor, reminding him of the torture he'd inflicted on Kin shortly before his escape.

But wasn't Kin just here?

Confusion clouded Matthias's mind, but he tried to clear it.

It wasn't Kin. His twin.

Matthias fought to remember the moment Isalica's king had approached the Feyorian prince and offered him greater power. Jarac had gobbled up the opportunity, eager to gain access to the Art he'd been denied in his talentless birth. The information Uriel offered about the prince's identical twin only proved to sweeten the deal.

Uriel had needed a new pawn after losing Kin.

How long ago was that?

Feyor's king swelled up from the shadows, consciousness returning after being squeezed out of him by Uriel's power. He coughed as he tried to rise to his knees.

His steel-blue eyes widened, the moonlight shimmering on the silver of his streaked dark hair.

Regret tainted Matthias. This man, his enemy, had terrorized Isalica with war. Sent assassins to kill him and was responsible for the death of his friends. But, regardless of his sins, he didn't deserve to die in such a vile way.

Uriel smiled as a tendril of shadow arched up from the skeletal shadows of the ruined dome above. The jagged edge flicked like a whip and slashed across the king's throat before the man could even gasp.

Blood sprayed, tainting the air with the scent of copper, and Uriel laughed.

The king crumpled, his body twitching for breath that wouldn't come. Blood spattered over his white beard and regal nightshirt.

"Such poeticism in a fast death, no?" Uriel chuckled, speaking to himself. To Matthias. "My favorite part of your power."

Time blurred as it reversed, the king's blood seeping back into his body and his throat stitching closed.

Uriel held his shadow this time.

King Lazorus's eyes widened as he met Matthias's gaze. "King Rayeht? Where am I?" He stumbled backward, his palms brushing over the slick floor, wet with rain rather than his blood. He shivered as his face hardened. "Explain."

Shadow lashed, the razor edge higher than before as it slashed across the king's cheek.

He cried out, his hand lifting to the wound as crimson dribbled into his white beard. More darkness loomed, dancing up from the floor like vipers to sink their fangs into the frightened king. His cries echoed against the stone as he collapsed, his blood flowing through the cracks with the rainwater.

"Please, I'll give you whatever you want." The king crawled backward, hands splashing in puddles on the marble.

"Mmm, begging. So unbecoming of royalty." Uriel strode after him, boots nearly silent. "Your son will be a stronger king."

"King Rayeht, please. I know we've never been allies, but this is insane. We're in a time of peace."

Uriel's victims rarely knew his name. His face. It broke a piece of Matthias each time those who did died, crying out his name for mercy, never to receive any.

Matthias tried to scream at the man to run, that he'd find no empathy in the monster controlling his body.

No sound came out.

It never did.

Onyx shadows burst from the stone floor and lashed at the king, drowning Matthias's senses with the man's endless deaths. Reality altered, and the torture landed on the back of innocents.

Liam. Dani. Micah. Matthias's father. Katrin.

Each time King Lazorus died, his face took on that of someone Matthias loved. The torment pulsed through him, reviving with each jump so Uriel could enjoy the kill again.

Despite all the power Uriel had himself, Matthias's energy to maintain the jumps waned. The one respite he ever received.

Restarting the process one last time, Uriel stretched a hand out before him, and his power eked into Lazorus's veins, seizing his heart. As Matthias's fist tightened, it felt as if it squeezed the soft flesh inside the king's chest, the shadow provoking the vital organ to change its rhythm.

The king gasped, buckling forward.

"It's a shame, really, that I can't leave your body in pieces for your subjects to find." Uriel paced around the choking man, yanking Matthias's consciousness away from his attempts to hide. "But you're old. Your heart is weak." Uriel squeezed, and the king cried out. "But lucky for me, this can be slow, too."

Chapter 3

DANI FOCUSED ON THE FAMILIAR power emanating from Damien.

Ailiena had said there could only be one Rahn'ka.

She must be dead.

Disappointment drooped the Dtrüa's shoulders, and she sucked in a deep breath. "You want to free Matthias? A Rahn'ka can do that?"

Damien's aura pulsed, causing flickers of pale blue light to ripple through her blurry eyesight, though no one else could see it. The power focused near his left arm, curling over his shoulder and the side of his neck.

Ailiena had nothing like that when I saw her.

"Not exactly. I know it's possible to remove the parasite, but I'm unsure how to accomplish it. That's why I'm hoping you two might know something. Micah tells me you were close."

Liam snorted, his boots crunching over the hay-covered floor towards her. "A long time ago. Before everything went to shit." He touched Dani's side, his familiar sign that he was ready to strike if she suggested it was needed.

Dani touched his hand, subtly shaking her head. "Katrin explained Matthias made a deal with..."

Liam gave her a warning squeeze and whispered near her ear. "Are you sure we can trust them with this?"

She tilted her head towards her husband, taking his hand and squeezing him back. "I'm sorry, would you give us a minute?"

"Of course." Damien's energy hummed against her own.

The barn's heavy door creaked as Dani led Liam outside, the exact steps memorized long ago. The chill mountain air refreshed her skin, and she shut the door behind them. "He's like Ailiena. If Micah trusts him, I trust him. Why do you not?"

Liam sucked in a breath. "I don't trust anyone anymore. Especially if they're near our kids. We've dodged Matthias for years. We've been lucky. Why now?"

Dani nodded, sighing. "But if this was something from Matthias, he would have just come himself. It makes little sense for him to use someone to get information about events he's already aware of."

"Unless the thing is trying to assess if we're a threat. Trying to find out what we really know. Katrin—"

"What if this is how we free him? How we finally find Katrin? What if this is our chance to help them get their lives back?" Dani's brow knitted together. "Can you really dismiss them, knowing we may never get another chance?"

His warm fingers tightened. He bowed his head, leaning lightly against her. "And you trust him even if he is whatever a Rahn'ka is?"

"It makes me trust him more." Dani kissed him. "Everything in me tells me to trust him."

"I wish Micah would have warned us." Liam ran his thumb over hers before he started back towards the barn. "I'm getting too old for these kinds of surprises."

Dani chuckled. "Because if Micah had sent us a letter saying he was bringing people here who wanted to talk about Matthias... That wouldn't have seemed suspicious at all, right?"

Liam groaned. "I hate myself for asking if we really want to get involved. We've avoided the thing's attention, and we have a family now. But..." He paused, pulling her back into him. "You really think this is the chance we've been waiting for? To save them?"

"It could be." Dani swallowed. "But we cannot know for certain. I just know that I'd never forgive myself for not trying."

He brushed his hand through her hair, and she touched his face.

"Come. At least hear them out." Dani tugged on his shirt as she drew away. Closing her hand on the barn door to slide it open, she smirked at him. "You know they would do the same for us." She pulled it to the side, entering the warmth again, with Liam close behind her.

"I just didn't think they'd be so... cute." Rae sounded amused, laughing under her breath as a young drake squirmed on the barn floor at her feet.

Micah made a playful growl sound before ushering the creature back outside. "Neither did I until all this." His thick cloak rippled as he stood. "I'll go make sure the kids don't need anything."

"Thank you, Micah. I apologize for the interruption." Dani clicked her tongue, confirming where everyone stood before approaching them again. "We rarely get unknown visitors."

The barn door slid open with Micah's exit before closing again.

Damien approached them. "We apologize for surprising you. We're parents, too, and understand the desire to protect our children, especially when we're discussing things like Uriel."

"Is that its name?" Dani squeezed Liam's hand. "Prior to taking Matthias, it occupied his healer, Merissa."

"And how long ago was that, exactly?"

"Twenty years." Liam let go of his wife. "I'm sure Micah already told you that."

"Seems like a long time to have a single host..." Rae spoke to Damien, but Dani could hear the disbelief in her tone. "Maybe he has a few he alternates between?"

"I doubt it works like that." Dani found one of the barn's support beams and leaned against it. "Matthias agreed to this. He never would again after what the thing did with Katrin."

"Katrin?" Damien spoke her name carefully, as if he could already tell how sensitive the topic was.

Dani averted her gaze, her heart still heavy despite the years. She swallowed, exhaling slowly. "She's in something the auer do called Slumber. We don't know where, but it's underground with no windows or doors. She was to wed Matthias, and..." She cleared her throat. "In the deal, Uriel must keep Katrin safe, so..."

"You keep saying deal. There was an agreement between Matthias and the creature?" Damien's lack of concern for Katrin's situation made her jaw clench.

Rae's scent moved closer, and the woman waited as silence settled before speaking. "You've researched Slumber?"

Dani nodded, a knot forming in her stomach at the tales of nightmares and horrors for those in eternal sleep.

"I'm a quarter auer." Rae drew Dani's gaze. "And I've been in Slumber, though I've never heard of it performed outside

Eralas. It's not like those stories portray."

"Then what parts of it are true? If any of it is, I highly doubt she'll be very much like my sister when she wakes. *If she wakes.*"

"The sleep itself is peaceful, but I didn't know myself when I woke. Damien returned my memories to me." Rae touched Dani's shoulder. "Your sister isn't suffering."

The Dtrüa took a deeper breath. It was a small comfort, assuming Rae spoke the truth. "Thank you." She rolled her shoulders, remembering Damien's question. She recounted the events of that day to him, burned in her memory. How Uriel had tortured Matthias, forcing him to witness the deaths of his friends. The fall of his city. Dani told them all of it, including the terms that'd been required to secure him as Uriel's host.

"What do you mean, he made Matthias see it over and over? He put visions in the prince's head?" Damien stepped closer.

Dani shook her head, debating if she should tell Matthias's secrets.

If it frees him, it will be worth it.

The Dtrüa rolled her lips together. "No. Matthias has the Art. He can jump back in time, but only about a quarter of an hour, and only a few times. His body stays the same, so any injuries sustained remain."

"His body stays the same." Rae's voice rose, directed at

Damien. "That's why..."

"That's why he hasn't needed to change hosts." Damien leaned against one of the barn's stalls, rattling the hinge.

"I don't understand." Liam's stance shuffled. "Because he can bend time?"

"Uriel absorbs life to feed his power. To feed the Shades that serve him. But despite all that, we know it has limits. However, with the ability to jump back, he can undo any destruction his power wrought over and over again, enabling him to continue to build it. That's why he hasn't needed to change hosts. He's not burning through Matthias in the usual way because he just undoes it."

"How are we supposed to free Matthias if Uriel doesn't need to change hosts again? We tried finding ways to break his deal, but he only promised to never hurt us. We can't make him." Liam huffed, pacing. "And yes, he swore to keep Katrin alive, but we have no idea where my sister is."

"The deal Uriel made is what this is going to come down to. It must have purpose and power. Otherwise, why bother making Matthias agree? Which means we need to find Katrin."

"How? I cannot connect to her anymore."

"Connect?" Damien's attention focused on Dani.

She waved a hand in front of her. "Katrin and I could... share a mind when we wanted to. I could see through her eyes, or she could *not* see through mine. Shared hearing, too.

We were connected before she fell asleep, which is how I know what the room looks like."

Damien remained silent for a moment, studying her. "Can you try to connect now?"

Dani nodded, closing her eyes. The sensation came easily, still practiced with her daily attempts. Her Art vibrated with the presence of a visitor, but she ignored Damien's prodding and reached for Katrin.

"Has the ability had a range like this in the past?" Damien's voice seemed to echo within her as well as in her ears, as if his Art spoke as it flowed among hers. It felt so much more refined than Ailiena's had

"Assuming she's still in Nema's Throne, even if she was awake, I wouldn't be able to reach her. She's too far." Dani opened her eyes, letting go of the attempt.

"More and more questions." A smile coated Damien's tone. "But probably best to stay focused on Uriel for the time. He's a greater threat."

"Katrin told us he razed the entire city of Nema's Throne with his power. And that was *before* he had Matthias." Liam's voice hardened. "What's your plan?"

Rae and Damien paused before she spoke. "We stumbled on vague instructions on how to imprison it."

"And that's what you intend to do? How?" The fabric of Liam's shirt flexed as he crossed his arms.

"It's complicated. We're still working out the details."

Dani clenched her jaw as silence settled. She couldn't blame them for not sharing everything.

We aren't, either.

"Well, if you're here, you must need Matthias to accomplish this, no?" Dani chewed her lip, wondering what fate they had in mind for their friend. "We won't let him be freed of one evil just to become a slave to the next."

"It's not like that." Rae's voice softened. "We need him, yes, but we trust he will want to help us."

"And if he doesn't?" Liam's question resounded in Dani.

But we both know he'll do anything to destroy the one controlling him.

"Then we will try to convince him, but you have our word... We won't push beyond that. Just, from everything Micah has told us, he seems like the type to fight back." Damien sucked in a deep breath. "Which leads into another thought. Did Katrin give any indication whether Matthias's mind was still active... aware while Uriel has control?"

Dani lowered her blurry gaze, recalling the last conversation she had with her friend. "Before she fell asleep, she told Matthias she loved him. So she believed he was in there, somewhere, and could hear her."

"So he's been watching a monster live his life for twenty years?" Rae's breath shook. "Gods. I can't even imagine what he's witnessed. That would destroy someone's mind." An unspoken conversation weighed in the air between her and her husband before she continued. "If that's the case, then it stands to reason that he'd need to be aware of the deal being broken."

"What assurance do we have that will even work?" Liam shifted beside her.

"None," Dani whispered. "We could line everything up perfectly, wake Katrin... Kill her in front of Matthias, but if he's not paying attention... If he's not sane, anymore..."

"He won't be able to retake control and jump to save Katrin." Liam sighed. "My sister would die for nothing."

"I can make sure that doesn't happen." Damien's voice. "I can bring her back from the dead if things truly go badly. So..." He paused, likely to exchange a glance with his wife. "It's worth the risk."

Liam grumbled. "I think we get to decide that, not you. Fancy Art powers or not."

Damien huffed. "Fair enough. But consider that the future of all of Pantracia is at stake."

Dani rolled her eyes. "How are we even supposed to get close to Matthias? He's the damn king of Isalica. And we still have no idea where Katrin is."

"Getting close is already taken care of. I have a political conference arranged with the king of Isalica in a week."

Liam's arms dropped to his sides. "How did you manage that?"

"You're not the only ones with royal connections. I'm the

personal advisor to King Jarrod Martox of Helgath. Establishing treaties between our countries is paramount and worthy of the king's time."

Dani stood straight and coughed. "You... Your king defeated King Iedrus." She shook her head. "Are you the deserter? The one who started the rebellion? What was his last name?" She aimed her question at Liam.

"Lanoret," Liam murmured. "Damien Lanoret."

"Nymaera's breath." Dani imagined what the man's life must have looked like over the past decade. "By the gods, you made him what he is, didn't you? The wolf?"

Damien chuckled. "I suppose that is news that would catch the attention of a Dtrüa. But I hope you understand that I am not at liberty to discuss my king's bond with his wolf, though he is not one of you."

"Not sure if this makes me trust you more, or less, Lanoret." Liam's posture changed, minutely enough only Dani would notice him assuming a more defensive stance.

"I'd like to meet him one day." Dani leaned against the post again.

"I'm sure that can be arranged. Stories of Isalica made it to Helgath, too. The legends say you single-handedly changed the course of the Yandarin War, Varadani. When you deserted Feyor. We have a lot in common, you and I."

Heat rose to Dani's cheeks. "I suppose we do." She rolled her lips together. "We have much still to discuss, but you must be exhausted from your journey. I'll have Varin make up a room for you, and we can figure out the next steps. Please don't mention Matthias in front of the children, we try to keep that part of our lives separate."

"Of course. We can relate to the desire not to overwhelm our children."

"How old are yours?" Dani tilted her head, breathing easier with the subject change.

Rae paused, clearing her throat. "Five and two."

Dani's shoulders slumped. "It must be hard being away from them."

"It is, but it is only temporary, and they love Uncle Jarrod." She sounded as if she'd said the same thing to herself like a mantra, reassuring herself her children would be safe. "What about yours?"

Dani smirked. "Nineteen, seventeen, and twelve."

Damien's voice lightened, a smile on his lips. "Teenagers. I'm not looking forward to that age for Bellamy. He's fiercely opinionated as he is at five."

Rae chuckled. "And you think Sarra will be easier. That's cute."

Chapter 4

THE CHILLED MOUNTAIN AIR SET Damien's senses abuzz. The ká sang with the wind as it rushed through the jagged mountain rocks, too sharply inclined to hold the thin layer of snow coating the higher ridges. His left arm ached with the potential power riled through his brief exposure to Dani's abilities while she sought the connection to Katrin, and his own nerves kept them going.

After aiding Jarrod in seizing the kingdom of Helgath, Damien's research into the Dtrüa had started to find answers to help his friend adapt to the long-term effects of his connection to Neco. Learning of Varadani, and her unique bond, particularly with draconi, he'd become fascinated. Though he'd never dreamt he'd meet her. He hadn't known about her before his own desertion, but on hearing stories of her impact on the Yandarin War, he'd become obsessed for a time. Enough so that Rae had teased him about losing her husband to the stories of Varadani.

Heat rose in Damien's cheeks at the thought, but the cold masked whatever color they might have turned. He slipped his hand into his wife's, grateful to have her at his side.

Rae's eyes met his, and a knowing smile crept over her face. "You're loving this, aren't you?"

"Absolutely." He grinned, the cold sharp against his teeth. Liam and Dani had just excused themselves to go into the house, leaving them alone on the porch for a moment while they prepared their children. "But it's more than just meeting her. This might actually be what we've been waiting for to free one of Uriel's hosts."

"It might be." Rae nodded, but apprehension laced her tone. "And Dani seems remarkable. I've read about how Feyor made the Dtrüa and honestly, I'm surprised she's so well adapted. But I worry about what's left of Matthias."

Damien's face hardened, and he squeezed her hand. "We'll figure it out, Dice. One step at a time, remember?"

"Mhmm." Rae lifted her chin, watching him with a softer expression.

Damien recognized the look in Rae's eyes as she glanced down where Bellamy would normally have wriggled his way between them, Sarra grasping at his waist. Flashes of their faces in his memory made his chest ache. "I miss the kids, too." He took both her hands. "You know you didn't have to come. I could have—"

"Wandered alone into a foreign country, intent on sitting face to face with Pantracia's greatest evil? Right. Not something I'd leave you alone for. Besides, this may shock you, but you might actually *need* me, even if I'm not some legendary, animal-speaking war hero."

The Rahn'ka smirked as he leaned in and kissed Rae on the bridge of her nose. "I always need you."

The front door creaked open, and the now familiar voice embedded within Liam's ká rose in Damien's senses. The man was a fighter, through and through. A strange calm echoed in every inch of his soul, but Damien could sense a fiery rage contained beneath it all. If the layers of icy control broke, he'd rather not be the one in Liam's sights.

"Varin just put on some tea." Liam opened the door wider, exposing the front living area. "Come, make yourselves at home."

The front room housed a worn set of couches, a large bear fur rug between them and a crackling fire.

Micah already occupied one couch, a young man beside him showing the retired crown elite sketches in a book between their laps.

A large dining table dominated the open space to the left of the front door, set for an upcoming meal. Someone had already added three additional plates for him, Rae and Micah.

Dani walked across the space, weaving around couches like her vision worked perfectly fine.

She's probably memorized the space.

Her cloudy eyes hovered near Damien's head as she motioned to the hallway. "The room at the back will be yours. Varin put the packs from your horses in there already." Her face showed her age in fine lines near her eyes and lips, her hair as white as the stories told. Even though she must have been around a decade older than him, she still looked like a primed fighter.

Micah never told us why they live here, but they obviously haven't retired.

Liam looked just as broad shouldered as any soldier, his physique similar to Micah's.

It piqued Damien's curiosity, but he refrained from asking their purpose in the mountains beyond the drakes. "Thank you."

The energies of the front room were far calmer than those of Damien and Rae's private chambers back at the castle. The presence of older children caused the more subdued flows, while Bellamy and Sarra's play created a blanket of lingering ká that no one but Damien could recognize. While both his children held the potential to be Rahn'ka, neither had shown any inclination for the Art, yet. With Bellamy's insistence to tell his parents everything that happened in his daily life during their dinners, he doubted his son would gloss over being able to hear voices in his mind.

"The tea just needs a few more minutes to steep." The girl who'd greeted Micah upon their arrival stood in the open kitchen to the right. She wove around the butcher-block table at the center, a long dress-like sweater tight on her hips and over the riding breeches he'd seen her in before. Beaming, she held her hand out towards them. "It's nice to meet you. We don't get a lot of visitors. I'm Varin."

Rae took her hand first as Damien studied the rounder features far different from her mother's. The blond hair also suggested Varin might not be their blood child.

"Rae." The Mira'wyld smiled, releasing her hand. "It's a good thing you have siblings to keep you company."

"Drive me crazy, more like." Varin smirked as she shook Damien's hand, and he introduced himself. "Though having a pair of brothers isn't so bad."

Damien's ká inspected hers as he shook her hand, examining the layers of it and confirming what he suspected. There were no genetic ties, but the familial bond linking all the ká in the room told him they had adopted Varin when she was quite young.

"Do you know where Ryen is?" Liam carried a chair from the far side of the room to the dining table.

Varin shrugged. "He said something about Layla and went out the back not long ago."

"You just got home. What could he be worried about with

that drake, now?" Liam grumbled as he moved to the back door.

The boy on the couch stood, leaving his sketchbook with Micah as he crossed the room. "Nice to meet you, sir. My name is Jaxx. I hope your journey was comfortable, coming so far." Jaxx held out a hand. "Our guest room is quite amenable, but watch out for the window. The frame sticks on the left side."

Varin rolled her eyes. "Don't need to overwhelm them with more information, my little bookworm." She ruffled the young man's black hair, and he frowned as he hurried to fix it. "Do you like sugar and cream with your tea?" She turned before they answered, returning to the teapot and lifting the lid to check the leaves inside.

"Neither for me, thank you." Rae looked at Damien.

"And both for me."

The back door swung open, clattering against the wall beside it as Liam entered, his face sterner than before.

A copper-haired youth followed, his freckled cheeks flushed from the chill outside, but his soft features resembled Varin's. He slipped the fur-lined cloak off his shoulders, tossing it over a storage trunk in the corner. He frowned at his father's back. "I don't need your permission before I make a trip into town. I'm not a kid anymore."

"You're not an adult, either. There are extenuating circumstances now, and it's best if you don't leave. Besides, we have guests." He turned to give his son an unspoken reprimand.

The young man scowled. "They're not *my* guests, and—"

"Boys, that's quite enough." Dani lowered her voice, a growl lacing the undertone. "Ryen, this is Damien and Rae. They've come a long way and will stay with us tonight."

Ryen made a face, begrudgingly looking up at Damien and Rae with a vague nod in their direction.

Rae cleared her throat and stepped ahead of Damien, offering her hand to Ryen. "I apologize if we've delayed your plans."

He looked at her hand, hesitating to offer his own until his father elbowed him in the ribs. With a glance at Micah, who Jaxx had returned to sit beside, Ryen shook Rae's hand. "You're friends of Uncle Micah?"

"Yes. And we've been looking forward to meeting you all for some time." Damien approached, offering his hand before Ryen could step away again.

The young man pursed his lips before he took Damien's hand, and a shock of cold radiated from the invisible force of his ká. A slithering blackness coiled deep within his soul.

Damien steeled his face, turning it into a warm smile as he gently prodded the familiar sensation of power buried within Ryen. His hand wanted to tighten, but he urged his fingers to relax and release their grip.

This isn't the place.

Ryen grunted, retreating towards the back door again, oblivious to what Damien had discovered. As he passed Liam, he mumbled something beneath his breath and disappeared outside.

Dani's jaw flexed, her eyes hovering in her husband's direction as Varin brought mugs of tea to their visitors. The Dtrüa sighed, pouring hot water into a mug for herself. "I'm sorry. He's been having some trouble of late."

"If that's what you want to call it," Liam grumbled as he crossed to the table, gesturing for Rae and Damien to join.

"Is he going to town?" Damien's chest tightened at the thought of the young man slipping away before he could confront him.

"He shouldn't be." Dani's brow furrowed. "Not until next week for the supply run. I don't understand his sudden hurry."

Anxiety boiled in Damien's gut.

He must need to report in. Did he eavesdrop on our conversation in the barn?

"Shit." Dani swiped a piece of parchment off the counter. "He didn't even take the supply list. Liam, can you run this to him? I can't shift with—"

"Let me?" Damien stepped towards Dani. "Maybe I can convince him to stay by asking for a tour of the drake pens."

The Dtrüa nodded, turning the parchment his direction. "He'll be in the eastern barn, prepping his drake."

Rae touched Damien's arm, her unspoken question pulsing through him.

He nearly told her his suspicions in the telepathic way they'd mastered over the years, where he'd speak directly into her ká, but hesitated.

I don't fully understand Dani's Art. She may notice.

He placed his hand on hers. "I'm betting Ryen and Kin have a lot in common." He prayed his wife would understand his vague message. "I've got this."

There's no way his parents know. Not with what they just said about keeping their children unaware of Uriel.

Damien took the parchment from Dani and crossed to the door. "Keep my tea warm? I'll be back, and I'll convince Ryen it's best to stay put for now."

One way or another.

Liam gave Damien a cautious look, but showed his acceptance of the situation by sitting. He rubbed at the corner of his eyes, working the light wrinkles there. "Good luck," he muttered, taking up the teapot. "The kid doesn't listen too well."

Damien paused in the door only long enough to give Rae a reassuring nod before he pulled it shut behind him. Glancing at the parchment in his hand, he stepped over the porch as he folded it and tucked it into his pocket. Letting his senses loose, he soaked in the sheer beauty of the Talansiet homestead.

The ká of the drakes they raised radiated with the natural energies flowing from the mountains and wildlife. The necrotic scar etched within them didn't take long to identify, and Damien approached the smaller barn structure to the east.

As he walked away from the main house, his wife's ká brightened behind him. Glancing back, he sighed at seeing his wife silently hop out the window of their room and jog towards him.

"Didn't trust me to handle this on my own?" Damien kept his voice low, unsure if Dani's hearing might still pick them up.

"Is Ryen a Shade?" she whispered, her aura bright from using her power. Likely to fix the sticky window. "You can't think I'd sit inside while you chase him. You think he overheard what you are? Or could Dani have told him?"

"I have no idea, but if he's trying to leave sooner than anyone expected... that tells me he has something to report to his master." Damien looked at the barn, able to sense not only Ryen's ká within, but also a drake's.

"Then we best stop him." Rae hurried ahead of Damien, her soft-soled boots making little sound on the layer of residual ice.

Damien rubbed the back of his neck as he ran after her, disliking the idea of her being ahead. He quickened his steps, not bothering to silence them like his wife. It'd be better not to startle the young Shade into doing something drastic.

His heart pounded in his ears, but he steadied his breathing as he caught up to Rae.

She gave him a look and motioned with her head to the side before venturing away from him.

He nodded, watching her go before he grasped the big barn door and heaved it sideways. The wheels squealed at first, before the door slid on the rails and sunlight illuminated the barn.

A full grown drake stood in the center, patiently waiting while Ryen fastened its saddle.

The Shade looked up, not masking his sneer. "The hells do you want?"

Troubled is putting it lightly.

"You forgot the supply list." Damien tilted his head, but didn't reach for the folded parchment in his back pocket. "Your mother asked me to bring it to you."

The young man's ká prickled.

"Enslaving the guests, now." Ryen huffed, but returned his attention to the saddle. "I'm not just their errand boy. Let my *father* go play fetch."

Damien frowned, working his jaw at the boy's resentful tone. "Well, I offered." He took a cautious step forward, flexing the muscles in his arms minutely to ready the power within him. "Though I have bigger concerns than who ultimately retrieves the supplies."

"Good for you." The kid spoke in a dry tone, not making eye contact. "I'd wish you luck, but I don't care about your problems."

"You should, since they're your problems, too."

Ryen paused, his hands slowing. "I have no problems."

A wry huff escaped Damien. "That's a pretty thought, but whoever told you that is lying to your face." He resisted the urge to look at the row of narrow windows on the east side of the building, where Rae's ká scaled a stack of barrels towards the thatched roof.

Oh, my wife and rooftops...

"Why are you still here?" Ryen threw down the unlatched buckles of the saddle, whipping them against the drake's hide. It huffed at him, turning its head, and he suddenly looked apologetic as he touched its neck.

"Where are you going in such a rush?" Damien sidestepped to place himself between the teenager and the double door out the front of the barn. He focused on the drake's ká, preparing himself to subdue it as well.

"None of your concern. So leave, and I'll do my whole family the favor of doing the same."

"I can't let you do that." Damien kept his voice even as he sensed the growing tension of the drake, reacting to its rider's intensifying frustration.

Shadows moved above in the hayloft, but not by the Shade's bidding. Rae crouched near the edge, gaze centered on Ryen.

"You can't stop me." The young man finished securing the saddle, lifting a pack to attach to the side. "And I have a hard time believing you want to. Not like my presence makes everyone cheery."

Damien squared his shoulders, flickering his gaze up to Rae before focusing back on the Shade. "Did he promise you anything else? Other than the power?"

Agitation radiated from Ryen's face. "Who the hells are you talking about?"

"You know who I'm talking about. Your master." The Rahn'ka's muscles tightened as the corrosive energies Ryen wielded suddenly grappled at the gaping connection between him and Uriel. Damien looked at the Shade's right forearm, gesturing with his chin. "You can't have completed many tasks, though. You don't have much power, yet. Two, maybe?"

The Shade stilled, hands poised on his pack as his gaze slid sideways to the Rahn'ka. "What right do you have to talk to me about power?"

He didn't overhear what I am, then.

Ryen continued, letting out a dry laugh as he faced Damien. "Though, that doesn't look like a normal tattoo." He touched his neck, mirroring where the navy ink poked out from Damien's coat. "Care to share its origin?"

The Rahn'ka narrowed his eyes, resisting the temptation to flinch at the realization he'd neglected to cover the symbols of his own power. Even if Ryen didn't know what they were, if he could describe them... It only added to the necessity of not letting him leave.

"Let's drop the charade. Do your parents know what you are?"

"I only answer to one, and it's not you." Ryen stepped towards him. "I serve the king."

"A false king. Not the real one your master holds prisoner."

Ryen's eye twitched. "I know everything. Everything my parents lied about. I know Matthias, and I'm important to him. Move aside, you're wasting my time."

"What did he ask you to do? Were your tasks, past and present, really for the benefit of Isalica? I don't know your family very well, but I doubt you're that big of a fool." Damien stepped forward again, flexing his fist as he closed his attention on the drake. He forced himself to keep eye contact with Ryen, even while speaking with the animal to encourage it not to get involved.

"Everything I do benefits Isalica and my king. He deserves to have the full power of the... of all Pantracia has to offer. I'm going to hand it to him, and there's nothing you can do about it."

"I can't allow that to happen, Ryen." Damien spread his

stance, the familiar fighting position etched deep into his muscles.

Ryen drew the short sword from the saddle, spinning it in his grip before advancing. "If you won't step aside, I have no issue forcing you."

"Why not use your Art? It'd be simpler." Damien focused on the blade, the drake behind Ryen slowly stepping away without the Shade noticing.

"My mother's sense of smell is too refined." The Shade arced his blade at the Rahn'ka, striking fast at a downward angle.

The Art answered Damien's hurried call, pulsing into the tattoos on his arm as he lifted his left forearm to catch the blade. The power hummed as it spread in a thin layer across his skin, knitting into the rune-etched blue shield that erupted from his soul, spreading to protect him and redirect the blow like any steel would.

Stepping into the youth's attack, Damien pushed his sword arm up, and his fist found its mark in Ryen's gut.

The Shade huffed, doubling over as he stumbled back. To his credit, he didn't lose his footing, his face contorted in rage.

Blue light burst from the hayloft as Rae summoned her Art-laden bow, aimed for the Shade. "This doesn't need to get any worse."

Ryen gasped, his eyes widening before he followed Damien's gaze to the Mira'wyld. The young man's breath quickened, and the stench of decay rose in the air. The darkness of the barn doubled, surging in from the edges to the Shade. Shadows crawled up his legs in a sinuous rush, absorbing the solid shape of him as they fell like water to the ground. The shadows rippled, bubbling in a rapid crawl around Damien, towards the barn's double doors like a serpent in the grass.

"Fuck." Damien spun, pushing the power of his shield back into his palm as he thrust his hand forward. His muscles strained as if he pushed on a boulder, shaking as his ká manifested into a tornado of swirling blue power. It slammed into the open barn door, cracking bits of the wood as it rolled along the track. Where it crashed into the door frame, the Rahn'ka's power showered sparks to the ground that froze the Shade's shadow in place.

The shadows writhed, rearing back from the doorway. In a wave, the black wriggled through the hay and vanished into the ground.

What the hells...

"Where did he go?" Rae released her bow, and it disintegrated before she jumped to the barn floor.

Damien surged forward, running his boot over the hay where the Shade's shadow had just been. With a flick of his fingers, the shimmering power faded from the doors, and he breathed it back into him.

Several pieces of hay crammed into the creases of a trapdoor, and Damien's fingers found the iron latch, heaving it open in a flurry.

In the basement space, there was nothing but blackness, making it impossible to decipher if Ryen was even still down there.

"Shit." Rae raced to the barn door behind him. "He won't get far. I saw the cellar door when I was climbing to the loft."

"And you didn't tell me?" Damien called after her, but already knew she hadn't had a chance to.

His wife shot him a look, pursing her lips as she heaved the door open. "As long as he doesn't—"

"Help! Mom! Dad!" Ryen's voice echoed over the terrain as he sprinted away from the barn towards the homestead.

Rae closed her eyes, sighing. "This is bad. This looks bad."

"Damn it." Damien glared at the young man's copper hair, shining in the sunlight as he ran for the back porch. He rubbed the tips of his fingers together, urging his ká to prepare for an old, familiar tool. It'd been years since he'd pulled a person's soul from their body. Fortunately, it wouldn't kill Ryen like it would anyone else.

This is getting too messy.

The home's back door opened, and Dani emerged with Liam behind her, a sword in hand.

"What's going on?" Liam called, moving with his wife to the edge of the porch.

Ryen barreled straight for his parents.

"He could hurt them or one of his siblings," Rae whispered, prompting Damien's next movement.

Hopefully they'll listen.

Flicking his wrist, the tether of his power seized hold of Ryen before he could reach his parents. He froze, his body suddenly rigid as Damien pulled the lasso around his ká, yanking on the young man's soul. It separated from his body in a flash of pale blue, hovering just outside himself in an indistinct mist. For a split second, one Damien had missed multiple times before when performing the same action on other Shades, the ká flashed a grey-purple before ricocheting back into the boy. He collapsed in a heap.

Dani launched off the back porch, shifting into her pure white panther form mid-leap. She snarled, pausing only briefly at Ryen's side before hurtling herself towards Damien.

Liam reached his son next and knelt, rolling the young man onto his back.

Panic tightened Damien's throat as he lifted his hands at the charging panther, dropping the rest of his power. "Let me explain."

Rae appeared in front of Damien as Dani's paws left the ground, and the two fell onto the frosty ground in a tumble. The big cat pinned Rae in seconds, teeth gaping near her face as she panted.

The Mira'wyld held up her palms, cringing. "He's a Shade. Your son is a Shade."

Dani balked, and in the open moment, Damien pushed a surge of power into his wife, expanding her ká into a dim dome that forced the Dtrüa off. Fur reshaped until Dani's human form returned, her eyes pinned on Rae, then Damien. "You expect me to believe that?"

"Smell for yourself. Manifesting that power, he killed off all the plant life outside the barn. No way you'd miss it."

Standing, the Dtrüa glanced back at where Liam sat with Ryen before glaring at Damien. "Don't move." She circled them, only making it halfway to the barn before her feet stilled.

Liam, sword still at his side, stood from his son as Varin charged out of the doorway, sliding to her brother. She lifted his head into her lap, looking up in confusion at her father. "Dad?" Her blue eyes were wide as she stared after Dani. "What happened?"

Damien pulled Rae to her feet, quickly examining her. "Did she hurt you?"

Rae shook her head, brushing herself off. "Not a scratch."

The Rahn'ka met Liam's glare. "Let's hope they'll believe the truth."

Chapter 5

LIAM'S GRIP TIGHTENED ON HIS sword, his knuckles near popping. He tackled the boiling rage within him, the desperate instinct to skewer Damien for even touching his son. He didn't understand what had hit Ryen, only that it had emanated from the man because of the thin tendrils of nearly invisible power that returned to him after Ryen collapsed.

Dani strode around their visitors, sight locked on Liam as she approached him.

"This was a mistake." Liam lowered his voice so only Dani would hear. Even Varin wouldn't catch what he said, despite her proximity. "We should never have allowed them onto the property."

Dani's gaze flickered to her son as his sister stroked his hair.

The anger they'd previously held had faded. "We may have made a mistake, but I think it happened longer ago than just today."

Doubt cascaded through him, tearing his gaze from the mysterious Rahn'ka to his wife's misty eyes. "What?" He looked at Ryen, and found his daughter's eyes on him.

"Dad, what is it? What's wrong with him? He's breathing, but..."

"Matthias got to him, Liam," Dani whispered, her voice tense. "The barn reeks of decay, and it explains... so much."

"It explains what?" The strength in Liam's arm collapsed, the blade pointing to the ground. "Dani, what are you talking about? This is our son."

"His anger towards us. Imagine all the things Matthias... *he* could have told Ryen. All the things we never shared with him. Check his forearm. Lasseth had a mark. Said they all did." Dani gulped, reaching for Varin, who took her hand and stood with her mother.

Hesitating, Liam chewed on his lower lip. Every breath felt impossible as he stared down at his unconscious son, bits of dried grass and frost stuck on his cloak and hair.

Damien and Rae stood perfectly still, the Rahn'ka's arm protectively wrapped around his wife's waist. They watched as he crouched and slid Ryen's sleeve up his arm.

Beneath the worn tunic, distinct black etchings ran over the skin near Ryen's pulse. A thin guiding line that divided two shapes, a triangle and a circle.

He couldn't breathe. "What are these?"

"Symbols of his rank and power among the Shades." Damien's voice sounded hollow. "Two tasks completed, and I suspect he was working to complete his third."

"Impossible. He's been on a job for the past two weeks. He only just got back from..." Dani caught her tongue, tilting her head at Liam. "The stars. I need to find his journal." She spun, jogging for the barn. As she neared the two visitors, she slowed, but Rae shook her head, and Dani continued on.

Uriel is still seeking the dragons' location. And he's using our son...

Micah approached Liam and Varin, concern etched on his face.

Jaxx peeked out from the doorway behind him, squeezing past Micah to stare at his unconscious brother with wide eyes.

Liam swallowed, controlling the temptation to shout at Jaxx to get back inside. Lowering his head, he stared at the tattoo on Ryen's arm again before looking at his peaceful face. "What were you thinking?"

"Will someone please tell me what's going on?" Varin stood where Dani had left her, hugging her arms around herself. "Dad, what the hells is a Shade?"

Jaxx cleared his throat. "A Shade is an Art practitioner rumored to cause death in its wake wherever it goes. They have an unknown origin, but have existed for centuries, if you believe the legends." He rattled off the definition like he'd just read it, but the kid retained information better than even Katrin.

He shouldn't be out here.

"A Shade?" Micah put his arm around Varin's shoulders, pulling her closer. "Who is..." His eyes trailed over Ryen again, lingering on the tattoo. "He's not, is he? He's never met Matthias."

"Who's Matthias?" Varin's voice grew more demanding, and she turned to Micah.

"Our king." Micah met her gaze. "He was my closest friend, once."

"Hush, they don't need to know." Liam forced his shaking legs beneath him.

"Everyone knows I was a crown elite, my friend. That is no secret, but—"

"But they're not to know of Matthias." Anger slipped into his tone, and he tried to swallow it through gritted teeth.

"And perhaps that is where we went wrong." Dani drew Liam's attention as she returned, journal in hand. "We should have warned him. We should have warned them all." She tossed the notebook at Liam, and he caught it.

The pages were open in the middle, showing detailed drawings of stars that spanned many nights, with markers showing where the sun had risen and set.

"Ryen said those were important. He worked on them

every night." Varin sidestepped from Micah's hold, moving further from her father. "What should you have warned us about?" She planted her feet in a way that reminded Liam of when she was a youngster taking a stance on bedtime. "Tell me."

The image of the small Varin made Liam flinch at the idea of introducing her to such dangers. But she was nineteen now, older than Katrin was when it all started.

"Your brother made a terrible decision. He's not safe. None of us are." Liam looked at Damien as he snapped his son's journal shut. "Uriel was using Ryen to get knowledge he cannot have."

"What's wrong with him?" Micah looked from Ryen to Damien.

Damien stepped cautiously forward. "He's just knocked out. He'll come to in a few hours. But if he was anything other than a Shade, what I did would have killed him."

A growl rumbled in Liam's chest. "You could have killed him?"

"I knew beyond a doubt that he was a Shade."

"How?"

"You really have to ask?" Damien pushed his sleeve up briefly to show the navy blue of his own tattoo, a glitter of light etching the runes in a shivering pulse. He glanced at Varin, his eyes narrowing as if evaluating what he could continue to say in front of her. "But now that he knows what

I am, and whatever you're concerned he knows... we need to make sure he doesn't return to Uriel."

Liam grimaced, looking at his daughter. "Go inside, both of you." He waved his hand towards Jaxx. "Forget what you've heard."

"We need to tell her, Liam." Dani rolled her lips together. "Maybe if Ryen had known... he wouldn't have done this." Her eyes grew glassy, her brow lifting in the center.

Jaxx hopped down the stairs instead of towards the door, planting himself between his mother and sister.

Dani draped her arm over his shoulders, nearly as tall as hers.

"Dad. I can handle it." Varin touched Liam's wrist, and instinct almost made him pull away. Adrenaline still rushed through his veins, and the inclination to use his sword on something made his entire body ache.

I'm not a fighter anymore, though.

Varin's grip tightened on him, and he relaxed his sword arm, sliding the blade into its sheath on his belt.

"Please don't hate us." Liam looked at his daughter, brushing her cheek to push a strand of blond hair behind her ear. "We were only trying to protect you all."

"Fill them in inside, where it's warm." Dani rubbed Jaxx's shoulder. "We should move Ry to his bed."

Damien and Rae traded a glance, dread building in Liam's gut.

"I don't think keeping your son in your home is a good idea. If he gets desperate enough..." The Rahn'ka dipped his chin. "You need to keep the rest of your family safe."

"Then who will keep Ryen safe?" Dani breathed faster. "We won't leave him outside like an animal."

Damien opened his mouth, but Liam stopped him with a look.

"Shade or not, he is still my son. He will wake up in his own bed, and you can *advise*, but that is all." Liam ignored Damien's astonished look as he faced Micah. "Help me carry him."

Micah pulled one of Ryen's arms over his shoulder, hoisting him up with Liam.

The day brightened, sun peeking through the overcast sky to grant them all distinct shadows.

Rae spoke to Damien, but Liam didn't pay attention as Varin opened the back door for them to carry Ryen inside. They took him down the hallway to his room before carefully laying him on his bed.

Dani pulled off his boots before draping a thick blanket over her son. "Would you get some water, Varin?"

Micah ushered Jaxx out of the room as Varin left, giving Liam and Dani a moment alone.

"You saw what Lasseth could do, do you remember? He disappeared into nearly nothing. What do we do when Ry wakes up? Even if we burn his journal, he might remember enough to lead Uriel to Draxix." Worry weighed on Dani's voice. "We can't let that happen. We need to get our son back."

Liam stared at Ryen's face, examining each freckle he'd memorized over the years. As his son had crossed the threshold into teenage years, he'd grown obstinate, but his gratitude for the home they had given him had always taken the edge off his sharp temper. Thinking back on the last year, Liam struggled to determine if there had been some kind of change in him. Something, anything, that might have hinted at what he'd pledged his soul to.

How did he even get near Matthias?

Closing his eyes, he bowed his head. "I... don't know how." He shook his head rapidly, as if it'd rock some genius idea into him. "We can't restrain him... How did I let this happen?" He looked up, meeting Dani's eyes. "What can we do?"

"I don't know." Dani's jaw flexed with her whisper. "Damien is just outside the door. He might have some options for us?"

A growl bubbled in Liam's chest before he could control it. "I still don't trust him." His eyes drifted to the partially exposed tattoo on his son's wrist, dread creeping back into him. With a glance at the closed door, he lowered his voice. "But Draxix. We feared Uriel might be interested in the dragons, but this proves he is. Why?"

"Power? Same as Feyor's motivation." The Dtrüa sighed

and walked to the door, jerking it open. She glared at Damien, who stood inches from the threshold. "If you're going to eavesdrop, you may as well contribute to the conversation."

The Rahn'ka straightened from where he leaned against the wall. "I assumed you'd rather I stay uninvolved."

"A little late for that, no?" Dani returned to Liam's side. "So tell us what you would do, if it were your child."

Damien stared at Dani, his face hard as he stepped into the room and closed the door behind him without looking at it. "I'd sever him from the power, regardless of his choice. And be ready for what might come after."

"And that is? Beyond further resentment?" Liam stood from Ryen's side, squaring to face Damien. Examining the man's build, he suspected even without his Art, Damien would beat him in a brawl.

I'd think the Art would have made him less focused on muscle.

Damien crossed his arms, his sleeves pushed up to reveal the intricate detail of his tattoo. It was nothing like Ryen's, composed of complex short lines and circles as if letters on the page of a book. But they were a language Liam had never seen.

"We don't possess that ability." Dani squeezed Liam's shoulder, trying to make him hear her words. "Will you help us? We have already agreed to help you free Matthias, thus I have nothing further to offer in return, but…"

Damien lifted a hand and shook his head. "You don't need

to offer more. I know neither of you intended for this to happen. It's just..." He sighed as he slipped a hand into his pocket. "Poor timing. Fortunately for all of us, my wife is paranoid, though she calls it cautiously prepared." He withdrew his hand and held it out, a copper cuff the size of an earring, though thicker, in his palm.

Liam narrowed his eyes. "What's that, and how is it going to help?"

Dani clicked her tongue, her brow furrowing. "May I?" She outstretched her hand, palm up, and Damien tipped the jewelry into it. Running her fingers over the little piece of metal, she swallowed. "An earring?"

"A tool. One Helgath has used for centuries in their capture of Art users. Until recently, that is. It will block your son's connection to Uriel, and will allow us more... traditional ways of keeping an eye on him." Damien met Liam's gaze with a look of empathy.

Dani turned the device over. "Will it hurt him?"

"No. And yes." Damien plucked the earring from Dani's hand. "The initial piercing will hurt, of course. The loss of power will feel like nothing until his withdrawals kick in."

"Withdrawals?"

"Shades have a unique connection to the Art. More like an addiction. They become wholly reliant on the power granted to them by Uriel. The one saving grace is your son is not as heavily connected as the last Shade I severed from Uriel's bonds. They shouldn't be as severe."

"And that other Shade, he's cured? He lives as he did before becoming a slave to Uriel?" Dani tilted her head at the Rahn'ka.

A flinch passed over Damien's face, and Liam touched Dani's wrist to alert her to its presence.

"He's alive. Though his continued cure remains to be seen. It became necessary to put him into Slumber to help recover from his withdrawals." Damien rolled his shoulders. "But Kin served for over a decade. Ryen, I suspect, has been for less than a year. It'll be easier for him. And perhaps we'll convince him to let me fully disconnect him from Uriel's service. But that will take telling him the truth."

"So we keep him here until he recovers." Liam took a deep breath. "And then we can worry about Katrin and Matthias."

Damien shook his head. "We don't have that luxury. My scheduled meeting with the king is in a week. Barely enough time to travel to Nema's Throne and put things into place. Micah was... understandably cautious about bringing us here. And now we have little time to spare."

"We can't leave Ryen here. Even if Micah stayed behind, I can't ask him to confine my son." Liam looked at Dani.

"I can ask Micah to stay with Varin and Jaxx. Ryen will need to come with us." Dani rolled her lips together. "We can fill him in on the way. Maybe being included in what's going on will help him see things clearly."

Damien pursed his lips. "Dangerous, too. If we can't sway him back."

Liam reached for his son's unmoving form, closing his hand around his wrist to cover the tattoos. "He'll see the error of his choice and return to us." He hardened his gaze with the Rahn'ka's. "He's coming with us. This is non-negotiable."

Damien heaved a deep breath with a vague nod. "Very well." He held out the cuff again. "Do you want to put it on him, or shall I?"

Chapter 6

THE BREEZE WHIPPED DANI'S HAIR behind her, blowing streaks of color through her vision. The summer scents danced in an array of hues, brightened by the late afternoon sun. Blurry shapes moved alongside her as they rode the drakes over the plains near the mountains.

The change in altitude brought the season's heat, keeping her skin warm without the need for her furs.

Dani rode alone on Brek, while Liam rode Ousa with their son. They'd let Damien and Rae take Layla, the most passive of them all, having been raised on their ranch.

Her mind wandered to when they'd given Ryen the young drake and how excited he'd been.

Now he hates us.

Ryen hadn't spoken to anyone since waking, brewing in

his rage. She could smell it, the spice of anger on his breath. It made her insides ache.

We should have warned him.

As they reached the edge of the meadow, Ousa's pounding feet slowed, and Liam's voice carried back to them.

"This is as good a place as any to make camp for the night. Terrain just gets rougher as we make our way down the slope towards Nema's Throne."

Brek snorted as Dani brought him to a halt.

She lifted her nose, breathing deep. "Should set up the tarp. It will rain tonight."

"The sky is clear." Rae dismounted, her boots hitting the ground with barely enough noise for Dani to detect it.

"Yes, but humid. Clouds will gather. So, unless you enjoy waking to soaked things, I suggest the tarp." Dani patted Brek and slid to the ground.

Layla whined as Damien hopped down from the saddle. A tangle of blue energy wafted through Dani's blurry vision as he stroked the drake's neck, and Layla lowered her head for scratches around her ears.

Dani strode towards them, focused on the wisps of power. "Do you mean for your energy to be visible?"

"What?" Damien turned, his shape straightening in her vision. "You *see* it?"

"When you use it. When you communicate with the drakes." Dani moved her hand before her, weaving her fingers through the lingering blue haze. "It appears in my sight like a scent."

Damien chuckled. "Jarrod can see scent, too. I thought he was crazy for a while." His attention shifted behind Dani to her son and husband as they dismounted.

"You speak of the king of Helgath so casually. I think Liam nearly fainted when I addressed Matthias's father by his given name."

"Jarrod was my friend before he became my king. Had it been the other way around, I might have been more like your husband."

"From what I've heard, King Martox is a fine ruler. Your efforts to change Helgath ripple through other nations."

"Now I seek a more widespread peace by ridding the world of Uriel. Though, he hasn't outright done anything to damage Isalica from what I can tell. In fact, in many ways, he's been a very just king." Damien patted Layla again, a vague flicker of his power ushering the beast away.

A rock formed in Dani's chest, burning her throat.

The drake sidestepped around them, making her way to Ryen like she had every stop, to check on her usual rider.

Dani clenched her jaw. "A just king who *stole* my friend and put my sister in eternal sleep. A king who never had the right to rule, forcing his way in by taking advantage of Matthias's noble attempt to save the kingdom he cherished."

Damien refocused on her, all traces of his power fading in

the air. "Which is why I want to restore your friend. I'm merely commenting that Uriel could have done far worse to your country, but I do not doubt our decision to free Matthias. Nor our mission to imprison the monster that took him."

My country.

The thought rippled through her with surprising calmness.

When did I stop thinking of Feyor as mine?

The Rahn'ka's words echoed through her, but she kept her anger in check. She exhaled a steadying breath and softened her tone. "Matthias saved my life. All of us, at some point, really. We breathe because of him, which means you have hope in your task... because of him. Show more respect the next time you reference Uriel's performance as a ruler, especially once we have Katrin with us."

Katrin.

Warmth flowed through Dani's chest. She could almost feel Katrin's arms around her, but the sensation blurred to the smell of the dank chamber she'd been put to Slumber in.

The summer grass crunched under Liam's boots as he approached.

Damien's power pulsed against his aura before vanishing. "I apologize. I'll remember that." He turned, speaking over his shoulder. "I'll get the campfire going."

Liam slowed in his approach, and Dani imagined him

watching the Rahn'ka as he walked towards the creaking trunks of the trees, wind rustling through their limbs. "Everything all right?"

Dani sighed. "Everything is fine. As fine as it can be, all things considered." She gazed in Ryen's direction, Rae's scent near her son. "Did he say anything on the ride?"

"Not a thing, and I stopped pushing." Defeat radiated in Liam's voice, and Dani touched his slouching shoulder. "He's so angry, but won't tell me why, or what Matthias told him. What *Uriel* told him. He's only himself in these little moments with Layla."

The drake's purr rumbled at a low frequency in Dani's ears despite the distance between them.

She focused on Ryen's scent as he ran his hands over his drake's scales, whispering something to her.

"You should try talking to him." Liam touched her wrist before sliding his fingers in with hers. "He's always been more open with you." He sighed, leaning his forehead against her temple. "I keep hoping he just didn't understand what he was getting into, and we can help him find the way out of it, but..."

"He's still a kid, but I think he understood what he was doing, at least to some degree." Dani breathed deeply, enjoying Liam's scent. "But whatever he thinks he knows, he only has part of the story. I'll try talking to him, but not yet. He needs to cool down a little first, and spending a few moments with Layla should help."

Layla let out a higher pitched whine as she collapsed onto her side, and the familiar laugh of her son filled the air as the drake rolled onto her back in the grass like a dog, a big blurry shape in her vision. The beast's tail whipped through the foliage nearby, creating a gust of wind.

Dani smiled, swallowing the lump of emotion in her throat. "Are you nervous?" She squeezed Liam's hand. "About finding Katrin? Or seeing Matthias? You were closer to him than I was."

The smell of the campfire drifted into her nose as Damien's shape moved closer to Ryen.

"I don't know what I feel yet. The last few days have felt more like dreams than reality." Her husband wrapped his arms around her waist, pulling her close as he kissed her hair. "I'm afraid of what will happen if we fail. Or what we'll find if we succeed. And I wonder if Katrin will even recognize us. Twenty years..."

"Do I look so different?" Dani tilted her head with a smirk. "Aged beyond recognition?"

Liam ran his fingers over her cheek. "You're far more beautiful. Every day."

Warmth returned to her chest and she smiled, leaning into him. "I love you, you know. In case I haven't said it lately."

"I'll always remember." He lifted her chin with a gentle touch, and his lips grazed hers. "We'll find a way through this.

Together, as we always do." He kissed her again more firmly before his hands slipped away. "I'll get dinner started."

Dani watched his blurry form retreat to the supply packs to gather ingredients. Her breath hitched when the heat of Ryen's anger hit her again, more intense than before. She could feel his gaze on her, but she steeled herself not to react.

Conversation waned through dinner, no one eager to discuss sensitive topics in front of the young Shade. Fortunately, Damien had never suggested physically restraining Ryen while they camped for the night, seemingly satisfied with their rotation of watches to make sure he didn't run. The thought of her son in chains sent shivers down Dani's back, evoking the cold memories of her early days in Isalica after abandoning Feyor.

Worse yet, of the years Feyor spent transitioning her into a Dtrüa.

Per usual, Dani took the first shift, and the others settled for sleep.

Ryen sat with his back to a tree, facing away from the group.

The cooler night air refreshed her, and she still didn't reach for a cloak. Sighing, she rose and clicked her tongue before stepping through the brush to sit against a tree across from her son.

His feet shifted, but he resumed his pretend sleep.

Layla's snores rumbled through the trees, even from twenty yards away.

"When you sleep, you breathe much deeper and slower," Dani whispered. "Though you do not snore, unlike your drake."

A quiet snort confirmed Ryen heard her. He shifted against the trunk, his cloak rubbing along the bark as he straightened. Silence followed until he let out a long breath. "I don't want to talk, Mom."

"What if I want to?" Dani kept her voice soft, not wishing to wake the others.

Ryen's cloak scraped on the bark again as he shrugged.

"We should have told you about Matthias, Ry." Dani bent her knees, resting her arms over them. "He was a close friend until Uriel took him. We wanted to protect you, but I see now that keeping you in the dark had the opposite effect. Is that why you're so angry with us?"

"You shouldn't say his name." Anger smoldered around Ryen. "He is my master and he told me the truth, unlike you."

"The truth of what, my son?"

"I'm not your son." Ryen's voice broke on the last word. "We both know that."

Dani jerked upright and crawled over to him, taking his hands.

He started to pull away, but she tightened her grip, and he gave in.

"You are as much my son as Jaxx is. You and your sister made me a mother. I love you. Your father loves you. You needn't share my blood for that to be true." Dani squeezed his hands. "You *are* my son, and anyone who tells us differently can go meet Nymaera."

Ryen's hands gripped around hers before suddenly going slack again. "Still doesn't change anything." He leaned back, his head thunking against the tree. "I refuse to regret this."

Dani's heart twisted. "Why? Why do you take pride in following the orders of a monster? You're kind and gentle. Remember when Layla hatched, and you didn't even want to help her break her shell in case you hurt her. Whatever Uriel has told you, *convinced* you of, it's not true."

"Don't say his name." Fear lingered beneath his words. "Please."

Dani exhaled slowly. "All right. I won't say it as long as you explain. Tell me what he told you. There's more to your anger than you've confessed."

Ryen pulled his hands from her, crossing his arms. "I know you both knew him before, he told me that much. That you were *friends* with the king of our country but never told your children, even though we were supposedly working to protect Isalica. And he told me what Dad did. How he's a traitor."

Confusion knitted Dani's brow. "A traitor? How did your master justify that?"

"Keeping secrets from the crown. Especially something like the dragons. Draxix." Ryen's voice darkened. "He said he's asked for the truth about their location, to send more troops to protect the mountain, but Dad lied and wouldn't tell him."

"Ry. We haven't told him the location because he seeks to use the dragons for his own advantage, not for Isalica. You know the dragons as well as I do. They aren't beasts for a war machine. They do not want to be found, and we guard that secret. From the king especially. And you know what? Matthias is still in there, in his head, and if he hasn't given in after all these years and told Ur—your master, then we can keep the secret, too."

"You keep talking like they're two people."

"Matthias isn't himself anymore. An Art practitioner came and killed his father. He threatened all of us, and the entire capital city, and wouldn't relent until Matthias gave up control of his body. The thing you serve isn't a person, my love. It's a parasite that's stolen the king's body for his own use."

Ryen's breath stopped, his body rigid. "I don't understand..."

"I was there when it happened." Dani's throat tightened. "Matthias made a deal and saved our lives." Heat welled in her eyes as her voice wavered. "He gave up everything. For us. He let us have a life when he knew he no longer would. Ryen, whatever that *thing* has told you... It may resemble aspects of the truth, but it couldn't be further from it. Your father isn't a traitor. He's dedicated his life to upholding the promise Matthias made to the dragons, to keep them secret, even from his own country."

Ryen paused, lowering his head and muffling his voice among his cloak. "But none of that excuses what he's done to you."

"To me?" Dani rubbed her son's knee. "Liam has been nothing but wonderful to me."

"He chained you. Interrogated you when you first met. Or did my master lie about all that too?"

Dani huffed, smiling despite herself. "Well, I mean... Yes, he did, in the beginning, but I understand why. We were at war, Ry. I was the enemy. He couldn't trust me, but he never hurt me. He never laid a hand on me. His sister offered to free me. I *chose* to stay, because as much as your father didn't trust me, I knew I was safe."

"How do you know all that for certain? Liam could have tricked you, forced you into believing you were choosing it, but really giving you no other choice at all."

Shaking her head, Dani kissed Ryen's knee. "He set me free, once, at the very beginning, because there'd been an avalanche. I still thought he was an arrogant ass at the time, but I still returned to him after I'd done my part to help. I was not manipulated."

Ryen quieted again. "If everything you say is true, and my master really isn't the king at all, then what? Why are we headed to Nema's Throne? You already know what my master is capable of. You should be running the other way."

Do I tell him?

The mistake of withholding information weighed on her shoulders, encouraging her tongue, but their entire plan could fall to pieces if Ryen found a way to warn Uriel what was coming. The fate of Pantracia hung in the balance, and she couldn't risk it just because her heart weakened with her son's words.

"Liam's sister is somewhere in Nema's Throne. We want to try to find her again."

"Katrin? You told me she was dead. Gramma and Grampa said the same thing."

Dani forced a smile. "Letting them grieve their daughter was the kindest choice we could make, but she is not with Nymaera. She is asleep. It's complicated, my love, but we will explain it all in time."

"This Damien person changed your mind about finding her? What is he?" Ryen leaned towards his mother, touching her hands.

"That is not my secret to tell." Dani touched his face, tucking the longer strands of hair behind his ear.

"But why do you trust him? Where did he even come from?"

"Because another, like him, saved me from Feyor. I know things are complicated, but I trust him. He wants to help you."

Ryen snorted. "I doubt it. He made it pretty clear he'd rather kill me early on. You're the only reason he hasn't." He squeezed her harder.

Dani shook her head. "That's not true. No one wants to kill you. Nymaera knows they'd have to get through me, first."

"I've never seen or even heard of an Art like his, though. How do you know he won't just kill all of us when he's done with whatever he's here for? Because we both know he's here for something. Why help Katrin?"

"Don't we all have motives? Why are you helping your master? He may have reasons I am not aware of, but I needn't know it all. I know what matters, and if he was hiding some sinister plan, I would know. I would smell it on him. So would the drakes. You needn't fear him." Dani tilted her head, resting her chin on Ryen's knee. "I will always protect you."

"You can't protect me from everything, Mom. I already proved that by saying yes to becoming a Shade." He shrugged his cloak up, tightening it around him. "You didn't smell that on me, so how can you be sure?"

"Do you not trust me anymore?"

"I don't know who to trust." Ryen's tone quieted. "If you loved me, you'd tell me what he is."

Dani swallowed, straightening. "That's not how love works, sweetheart. I wish I'd been able to stop you from making this choice, and I will forever blame myself for being so..." She huffed. "Blind. But basing my love for you on whether I tell you something only belittles what I would do for you."

"I think your shift is over, isn't it?" Ryen's voice hardened.

Dani touched his hand, but he jerked it away. "I'm sorry I failed you, Ry. I will do everything I can to fix it."

"I'm tired. I'd like to sleep if that's all right with you?"

The lump returned to her throat, and she nodded. "Of course."

Chapter 7

FORCING HIS BODY TO STAY still, Damien debated his best move. Sleep had continued to elude him, and he'd slipped into meditation to calm his muscles and hope for rest. The rumble of voices had pulled him from the state, and talk of things he shouldn't be over hearing.

Dragons. The family is protecting them, and that's what Uriel is after.

His heart raced, and he feared Dani would hear it, but the conversation with Ryen distracted her.

He heard her shift away from her son, standing and making her way around the camp towards Liam, who was next up for the watch.

I've been keeping enough from them.

Guilt inspired Damien to push himself up, and he placed

his hand on a twig beside him, snapping it. "I'll take next watch." He kept his voice low to not wake the others.

Dani paused, staring at him.

How can she do that?

The woman clicked her tongue, stepping over an unlit lantern and approaching Damien. "You *were* awake."

"I was. And thank you." The fear of what Dani could tell Ryen had nearly caused him to interrupt, but she'd kept his secret even though it ended the progress she'd made with her son.

"You're welcome..." Dani whispered, crouching in front of him. "What else did you hear?"

"Draxix." Damien turned towards her, crossing his legs. "We have more to discuss, it seems. You may be able to help me in more ways than our current quest. Though, prying ears make it difficult now."

"Those are things you shouldn't know." Dani glanced in her son's direction. "If the one he serves finds out where they are..."

"I have kept secrets just as dangerous from him before, and this one will be very much the same. And I will tell no one of their continued existence."

"No one?" Dani tilted her head, eyes flickering to Rae's sleeping form.

Damien smirked. "My wife and I are one. I keep nothing from her. I hope you understand that. But beyond her... I will keep it even from my closest friends. Unless I gain the dragons' permission."

Dani fell silent for a few breaths, studying him. "I will wake Liam so we may speak in private." She stood, clicking her tongue again before maneuvering to where her husband slept. Once he sat up and they'd spoken quietly for a minute, Dani rose and looked at Damien. She motioned with her head before walking into the moonlit forest.

Leaving his boots, Damien stepped onto the grass, allowing his power to seep through the green blades and speak with his ká. The whispering voice in his mind told him where not to step on the new budding seeds, and he made his way to the edge of their camp, pushing his sleeves up to his elbows.

Pursuing the Dtrüa, he acknowledged the forest's joy at their presence. This section of the wilds rarely saw travelers, who typically wouldn't be welcome with their destructive ways. But a Dtrüa and a Rahn'ka... And Dani's unique connection that allowed her to speak directly with animals made Damien consider how easily she might kill him if she wanted to. Her persuasion could easily override his when speaking with the drakes. They knew her and trusted her well beyond what his power could convince.

And that's not considering she can turn into a panther and slash my throat.

Damien paused, realizing Dani no longer walked in front of him. A sliver of panic slipped into his gut.

Would she kill me to keep the dragons' secret?

"Fear?" Dani's voice came behind him, and he spun to face her. "Hardly suits you."

Damien urged the instinctive power from his muscles, his tattoos flickering for a breath before he conquered the surprise. He smiled sheepishly as he scratched the back of his head. "I'm not immortal. Powerful, with an extended lifetime, sure. But I can still die."

Dani chuckled. "And you think I'd kill you?"

"I think you would do many things to protect your family if you thought it necessary."

"That is true." She walked past him, weaving through the trees as if she'd walked the path a dozen times before. "But I believe in your honor and your word. Maybe more than I should."

"An Isalican trusting a Helgathian. If our ancestors could see us now."

"I'm Feyorian." Dani smirked at him. "I think that's even more impressive."

Damien laughed with a nod. "Most certainly."

She clicked her tongue again. "You already knew the dragons were sapient."

Damien paused, considering the ancient texts he'd read in Sindré's sanctum. "I suspected. There were clues in the spell meant to imprison Uriel. I hadn't considered they weren't actually extinct like the legends say."

"Definitely not extinct." Dani closed her eyes as she walked next to him. "You haven't truly experienced freedom until you've ridden one through the clouds."

Thrill at the idea mingled with Damien's sheer dislike for heights. Ever since falling from the top windows of the palace during their battle to secure Veralian, he'd developed a strong avoidance. "I'll leave the flying to you, I think. Though there are more important realities to discuss if they're still alive."

"Now, I believe it is your turn to share what you know." Dani looked sideways at him, lifting a dark eyebrow.

Damien nodded, steering them towards the trickling energy of a stream. More ambient sound would only ensure their conversation wouldn't be overheard by any listening ears. "There is much at risk should we try to imprison Uriel again. So much of it can go wrong quickly. One of those aspects I was most concerned about is the actual prison fashioned to hold it. Until tonight, I'd thought the original builders were long gone."

"The dragons built the first one?" Dani tilted her head. "Where?"

"Lungaz. At least that's what I'm guessing based on vague tellings and evidence from its attack on Eralas. Considering the creature's ability to drain the entirety of life around it, Lungaz makes the most sense. The Art cannot exist without life, which is what makes it impossible to channel within Lungaz. I don't believe it was a void before."

"You believe Uriel created it when he broke free?"

"I do. The amount of energy it consumed to do so is what created Lungaz. Hoult, where it transformed into the shadow beast that attempted to attack Eralas, acts and appears exactly the same. But on a far smaller scale because of a different power it used."

"Why do you call Uriel... *it*?" Dani's brow twitched.

The question left Damien more perplexed than her others. He balked, scratching the back of his head. "I don't believe it has a gender, at least not that I can tell. Uriel changes bodies, and I just assumed..."

"He's male." Dani swallowed. "I heard him say it. Another reason he liked Matthias's body."

The Rahn'ka blinked, trying to absorb what Dani suggested. He'd assumed the parasite to have no origin that would grant it such a preference, but...

He might have been something living once. Something... mortal.

Dani cleared her throat, pulling his attention back to their conversation. "I heard there was a crater in Hoult, but not in Lungaz, just the maelstrom. How do you explain that?" She touched trees as she passed them, occasionally clicking her tongue.

Damien paused, considering which direction to spin his answer.

How much am I really willing to tell them?

"Another source of power caused the crater at Hoult, not Uriel. It fueled *him* to take on the form of the beast. And one of the aforementioned secrets I keep from him. As far as the maelstrom, the nearest I can tell is there was a system of tunnels beneath Pantracia there, built by the dragons. They collapsed during the Sundering, which likely led to Uriel breaking free. When the world shattered, so did his cage."

"What was the other source of power? Sounds like something that could be helpful if it could work against him rather than for him."

"And I believe she will, when the time comes. She was trying to kill him when she empowered him."

"She?" Dani whistled under her breath. "A lot of power in one person. Amazing she survived."

"Lucky. And honestly thanks to Rae. That's why Matthias cannot see her. He's likely already seen her face and definitely felt her power. We intended to use the earring to ensure her Art was kept secret while in Nema's Throne."

Dani stopped walking, facing Damien. "What happens now that the earring is in use? What will she do?"

"She'll have to lock down her aura the old-fashioned way. She's just not as good at it when emotions escalate, but she'll be all right. I have faith in her ability to keep a clear head when it comes time." Damien paused as they approached the stream, watching the Dtrüa catch up.

The surrounding forest chirped with life, the breeze

rustling through the canopy above. A fish jumped along the small rapids to the north.

"There's a lot at stake in this for us, but not nearly as much as you and Liam have in it. You must realize there's no way to know what long lasting damage has been done to Matthias. While I can heal Katrin's memories, I don't know if I can help your king."

Dani nodded, a somber expression clouding her face. "Twenty years witnessing a monster do unfathomable evil with his own hands. Victims, staring at his face, thinking he tortured them. Killed them. I have a hard time believing he's still sane, in there. And if he comes back... What kind of king will he be?" Her eyes shone, and she closed them for a breath. When they opened, her emotion had cleared. "After what Feyor did to me, I thought I'd never feel human again, but it pales compared to what he's endured."

"Then it is fortunate he has friends who will be at his side as he rediscovers how to be human again." Damien stared at the milky surface of her eyes in the moonlight. "And while I may not be able to do anything for Matthias, I might be able to help you... if you'd like."

Her brow knitted. "Me?"

"Your eyes. The healing powers of the Rahn'ka are unique. I could..."

Dani scoffed. "A generous offer. I might have taken you up on that, once, but... no. Thank you, but no."

He nodded. "I would have felt bad if I didn't at least offer, but I understand. There are scars my brother won't allow me to heal because they are part of who he is. I suspect you feel the same with your blindness in a way. Though you certainly don't let it stop you, either. You're a legend among soldiers who are brave enough to question."

Dani grinned, a touch of color rising to her cheeks. "That's difficult to believe. I never imagined anyone would hear of me."

"I believe that's true of many heroes." Damien glanced towards their camp, watching the shadows shake with the wind in the trees. "I am sorry about your son. I hope he might come to a place where I truly can help him. But it could become irrelevant if we free Matthias."

"It may. And if we find Katrin and free Matthias, you have my word I will seek permission from the dragons to introduce you."

Damien's eyes widened, a weight he hadn't realized was there, lifting. "That would be very helpful. Thank you. I believe they will be a necessary part of what we're trying to accomplish."

Dani smiled, but a seriousness lingered in her face. "And we will do whatever is necessary."

Four days later...

"You want to leave him with a crime lord?" Damien gaped at how calm Liam looked as they stood on the outskirts of Nema's Throne.

The former crown elites had pulled some strings with old friends, quietly stabling their drakes at the southern barracks outpost. The soldiers posted there remembered them, though gave the Rahn'ka and his wife suspicious glances.

"He's a friend from way back." Liam waved a hand, glancing sideways at where Dani stood with Ryen half a block down the street. "Xavis is the only person we can trust here, since we more or less *gave* him that position."

"But what makes you so certain he isn't loyal to Uriel?"

"Because we stayed in touch." Liam shrugged. "He seemed the most logical ally in keeping an eye on Matthias. He let us know when the king was out of the country on political business. Gave us rare opportunities to visit my folks without the danger of Uriel surprising us."

"And I take it that doesn't happen often?"

"Nah. Last time was when... Well, when he went to Helgath, actually. When you saw him at the palace in Veralian."

Damien nodded and glanced down the alley Liam had led them to in the seedier part of town. Full of dingy gambling halls and brothels.

And all five of them looked sorely out of place.

"What are we waiting for, exactly?" Rae looked far more comfortable than Damien felt, her power locked down and both eyes green.

"Invitation. And a way in the back. Would be better not to be seen if we can avoid it." Liam kept his hood over his head, a shadow covering most of his face. Despite the early morning, gamblers moved in and out of Hillboar Hall's double doors, forcing him to turn from curious eyes.

A young boy slipped out between the doors as they swung open for a pair of hobbling old men. The dark-haired youth blinked wildly at the sun, lifting his hand to shield his eyes. "Follow me."

Liam didn't hesitate, turning on his heels to follow the kid and giving a short low whistle.

Dani led Ryan towards them, trailing behind Damien and Rae.

"Keep half-expecting Jarrod to emerge from the shadows somewhere, along with more Hawks," Rae muttered. "Reminds me of times long ago."

Smirking, Damien focused on the boy as he wove around the corner of the building into a narrower alley. Reaching out, the Rahn'ka could touch both soot-stained walls until they passed through a rickety gate into a more open roadway. Both sides sported large, barn-like doors, which seemed odd for the back of a gambling hall.

A strange tangle of energy knotted against Damien's as he stared at the dirty stone road with deep wagon wheel grooves.

"How *criminal* is this friend of yours, exactly?" Damien eyed the warehouse on the other side of the road.

Dani stood further back, a deadened look on her face while the muscles in her jaw flexed.

Liam ground his teeth. "We... allow certain activities to continue to secure the information necessary to survive. Uriel has done little to quell the more sinister aspects of the criminal guild, which I'm sure have only grown more prominent." He paused, letting the boy rush ahead to one of the large sets of doors.

He rapped on the wood in an offbeat rhythm, and a latch inside clunked.

"But you're sure we can trust Xavis?" Damien studied the soldier's face, trying to read deeper into his dark eyes. But the man's ká offered little in the sea of emotions he already felt just being back in the city.

"As sure as I can be, all things considered. But I don't see another choice. Do you?" Liam met Damien's gaze, and something about his steady glare made the Rahn'ka recoil.

"We can't bring Ryen to the palace." Rae shook her head. "This is the best way. They probably even have an adequate place to... keep him."

The young Shade frowned. "Imprisoning me. I'm surprised you can stomach chaining your own son, Mom."

Dani's tense shoulders hardly reacted. "You left us no choice, Ry. We will be back for you as soon as we can." Her voice lacked emotion, and Liam looked at her.

The boy gave a breathy whistle, leaning out from the entrance and waving his hand.

Liam marched to the door and pushed it further open as he entered.

"Just like visiting the Ashen Hawks, right?" Damien smirked at his wife as he started forward. "Though, this is less dramatic. No pitch black mazes to make our way through."

"They clearly lack creativity." Rae poked him in the ribs before she wove past him, her hand on the string of her more traditional bow which ran across her chest. "Still has a nice homely feel, though, don't you think?"

Damien snorted, pausing at the door to let Dani and Ryen pass first while he scanned the roadway behind them. No voices from outside the room they were about to enter echoed through his mind, confirming they'd remained anonymous.

Good, this is complicated enough as it is.

Moving inside, he blinked rapidly to adjust to the shadows. The room they entered was plain, with green paint peeling off the brick walls and a layer of fresh hay on the stone ground. The old bloodstains couldn't be hidden beneath it all, and a turbulent maelstrom of ká lingered behind by those tortured and killed within the room.

Gritting his jaw, Damien hardened the barrier around his

soul and watched Liam as he walked past a pair of burly men beside a short doorway. He caught a glimpse of the next room, lavishly decorated with wood-paneled walls. The complete opposite of the filthy room they entered.

The wooden door behind Damien snapped shut, and a short woman he hadn't realized was there gave him a sharp smile. Her hair, the same color as the straw, was cropped close to her scalp, and dark kohl lined her eyes.

"My friends!" A big man stood from behind a desk. He dodged the sword display directly behind him, a silver-tipped cane propped in it rather than a weapon. "It's good to see you, even if the circumstances are less than ideal." He approached Liam with an outstretched hand, scars marring the right side of his face.

"Xavis." Liam took the offered hand. "Been awhile. What happened to your face? You piss off the wrong gambler?"

"Nah. Incident with a rat. You don't want to know. But, alas, we are vermin free, now." Xavis's gaze trailed over Dani with a nod before continuing to pass over the others. It settled on Ryen, and he grunted. "Would be easier if you let me use chains. Or rope, at least."

"No." Dani's one word response stilled the room for a breath.

"I know you've got plenty of rooms and henchmen in this place. He won't give you trouble." Liam gave his son a stern look, as if that would make the seventeen-year-old cooperative.

That'll only make the teenager rebel more.

Xavis smirked and jerked his head at one of the men behind them.

The mountain of a man stepped forward, putting his hands on each of Ryen's shoulders. "I'll be keeping an eye on you, pup."

Ryen's eyes widened, his shoulders hunching in as the man squeezed to get his point across. He looked frantically at Dani, who stood with an emotionless expression as he was escorted out of the room.

Liam rubbed his forehead. "He's my son, Xavis, remember that. Hope that man of yours doesn't get overzealous, or you'll do well to remember what happened last time someone in this room betrayed me."

Xavis laughed, unrestrained and loud. "Oh, I remember. I still have you to thank for my station here." The man, who looked more like a soldier than a criminal, dropped back into his chair, putting his worn boots up on the desk. "Sit. Drinks?"

Damien shook his head. "Thanks for the offer, but I don't think we have time for that. Next time."

Xavis's attention shifted to him, a smirk crossing his features. "But I finally have a chance to sit down with the famous Damien Lanoret. Though you're a day early for your diplomatic meeting with our king."

Damien straightened, casting a quick glare at Liam, but he looked equally surprised.

Xavis chuckled again. "Come on. I'm the leader of the most established guild in the city. You really think I wouldn't have heard about a diplomatic visit from the Helgathian king's personal advisor? And one as famous as Damien Lanoret."

"He loves it when people know his name." Rae smirked, sarcasm lacing her tone. "It makes him extra comfortable."

The crime lord shifted his attention to her, not hiding his slow gaze up and down her.

Damien growled, his fist tightening.

"And you're Raeynna Lanoret. Leader of the Ashen Hawks and also an advisor to the king of Helgath. Pleasure to meet a fellow guild leader." He bowed his head to her before meeting her eyes again.

Rae gave him an exaggerated curtsy.

"I assume your reasoning for flaunting your knowledge is to let us know you've caught us at a disadvantage?" Damien remained still, his senses whirling about the room to evaluate their next move if the visit turned sour.

"Not at all." Xavis waved a hand to dismiss the idea. "Just enjoy having powerful people owe me favors. Is there anything else I can do for you while you're all in town? Need rooms for the night?"

"That's unnecessary. Thank you for your courtesy, but we must be going." Rae kept her even gaze on Xavis.

"Big plans? You seem eager to leave."

Liam stepped between them and Xavis, forcing the crime lord's eyes to him. "I trust you can keep our visit here quiet?" While a question, the tone suggested otherwise.

Xavis grinned, leaning further back and putting his hands behind his head. "Damien who? I have no idea what you're talking about... Helgath diplomats? In my hall?"

Damien rolled his eyes but gave an affirming nod to Liam. "Let's go."

Dani stepped around Xavis's desk, and the man stiffened as she leaned to whisper in his ear.

The crime lord's jaw flexed, but he nodded, and she straightened.

Liam frowned but followed Dani as they crossed back through the straw-strewn chamber.

The woman who'd closed the door behind them still stood there, and dramatically bowed as she opened the door, allowing them all back onto the street.

I can't believe Liam and Dani trust this Xavis enough to leave their son here. But what other choice is there?

Damien loosened his aura, allowing his senses to reconfirm they were alone on the street. "There's no time to waste. We should get started."

Dani exhaled slowly, tension still radiating from her.

"Right. Katrin." She blinked before closing her eyes, rolling her shoulders. As she focused, her Art seeped from her skin in a haze of pale blue ká.

At first, it drifted aimlessly, but then it soared east like a ship's harpoon, leaving a line connected to Dani. The energy left behind a thin trail that glittered like minuscule snowflakes dancing in the breeze.

"Is it working?"

Damien ignored Liam's question as he stepped towards the stream, allowing his ká to connect and follow the flow.

It tugged at his chest, as if his physical body needed to go, too. It paid no heed to the streets, cutting sharply north towards the city center.

The Rahn'ka's lips twitched. "This way."

Dani let out her breath, and the connection disappeared from the air. "Do I need to maintain that the whole time? It's harder with her unconscious."

"No, we have a direction now." Damien pointed, ignoring the fact that it was directly into one of the large empty warehouses beside them. "I trust you both might know the city better than us, though."

Liam followed Damien's point. "How far in that direction?"

"Not sure. We'll have to double check as we go. But at least half a mile.

"Then we better get moving." Liam brushed by Dani,

touching her side before he led them out of the narrow alley, returning to the colorful Hillboar Street. But they turned north, headed towards the city center.

Rae leaned into Damien as they walked. "She said there were no windows or doors. How are we going to get to Katrin if there is no path?" Her tone held an air of hesitation, as if she knew the answer.

"It depends on what's between the surface and her. We won't know until we're closer. But between the two of us, I'm sure we can figure something out." Damien allowed Liam and Dani to move ahead, as they'd agreed on before, crossing to the other side of the street to follow less conspicuously.

"I just don't know how well I can use my power while concealing it." She rolled her shoulders, running a hand over her braided hair. "Being this close to Uriel makes me nervous."

Damien slipped his hand into hers. "He might not have even seen your face in Hoult. As long as you keep your power hidden, everything will be all right."

"What if I need to use my power for us to get to Katrin?"

"We'll find another way. Or I'll try to help shield you. Either way, we need to do this. It's our best chance." He walked closer to her, transferring the cloth-wrapped bottle in his pocket into Rae's cloak. "I finished that this morning, just in case. And it should work."

Where Uriel was concerned, Damien had no shame in

developing as many contingencies as possible, and the guardians had cooperated in helping create another weapon they had at their disposal.

It'd been years since Damien had even heard whisperings of the secret faction responsible for protecting the Berylian Key, as if they'd vanished when their ward went into Slumber. But their gift, delivered by the Key's brother, held the possibility of making all the difference.

Jalescé and Sindré had pooled their ká to aid in using the blood Deylan presented to Damien. They'd begun turning it into a tonic that would, theoretically, stun Matthias. And Uriel by proxy. The guardians hadn't been able to complete the salve, leaving it to Damien to finish in the early morning hours, when the sunrise and its effect on the energies of Pantracia could aid in its potency. Yet, there was no guarantee.

We don't even know if it really is Matthias's blood.

Stripping what he could of the man's ká from the dried blood had been painstakingly slow, and part of the reason for delaying so long before attempting anything like they would tomorrow. And now that the time was near, Damien's stomach wouldn't stop twisting.

He squeezed Rae's hand. "I'm nervous, too. But this is it. If everything Liam and Dani said is true about Matthias's abilities... He's the reason Uriel has grown so powerful. This could change everything. It's more than just gaining access to an abandoned host, now."

The Mira'wyld nodded. "I know. No pressure, right?"

He smiled as they crossed onto one of Nema's Throne's main roads, leaning to give her a quick kiss on the cheek. "None, whatsoever."

People filled the streets, horse-drawn carts making their way up and down the center while the people stuck to the edges. Little merchant carts had colorful roofs and drapes to attract customers, along with the sweet smells of morning pastries.

Dani and Liam paused ahead and stood off to the side. A breath later, the energy erupted from the Dtrüa again, cutting through the air towards the city center.

How can Katrin be hidden in the middle of Nema's Throne?

Damien looked up over the two-story buildings comprising most of the city. Piercing into the azure sky, the glass pinnacles of the country's largest temple glittered, casting spectrums of light over the rooftops. With the importance of the gods in Isalican culture, the temple marked the true center of Nema's Throne, and the threads of Dani's connection to Katrin flowed directly towards the three monstrous towers.

Damien kept walking, Rae next to him watching Dani.

The line of energy dissipated again, and the other two resumed their pace.

"Where is it pointing us?" Rae glanced behind them before

taking her husband's hand. "It's getting crowded."

"Hopefully that means we can blend in even more. But I think it's just going to get more crowded the closer we get." Damien tapped her chin gently to encourage it up. "When was the last time we visited a temple?"

Rae's eyebrows rose. "Probably not since Brynn's naming ceremony. Jarrod and Corin both cried that day." She smiled, a look of longing washing over her face.

He brushed a stray hair back over her braid. "I think they were both just happy to be fathers. And I think we might get a chance to visit one of the most famous temples in Pantracia. Maybe the gods, if they're actually real, will bless us." The irony of his own disbelief in the gods made him smirk, considering all he knew about ká and how it functioned. But the more he experienced, the less he believed in supernatural entities being responsible for all.

"Katrin is in the temple?" Rae's gaze shot to the giant structure. "Or under it?"

"We'll find out." He tugged her into the street, crossing to hustle in front of Dani and Liam towards the grandiose road that led to the front gates of the temple's property.

Flowers lined the streets in crystalline vases the size of horses. Each tier grew more complex as they neared the open gates. The intricacy of the glass shards, weaving like a massive ice sculpture, were surely crafted from the Art by those living within. Beyond the archway, the temple grounds opened into sprawling fields of hedges and flowers.

As they entered the luxurious green space, the crowds thinned and quieted, drawn into the reverence of the temple grounds. The energies altered, the air shifting as they spread in an invisible web across the sky. It stretched between parapets of stone and glass, like awnings of power, designed to maintain the temperatures around the temple grounds. Despite being open to the sky, each region of the gardens was strictly controlled to best service the major god they were dedicated to, and the season they represented.

To their left, summer's entrance was in full bloom beside an odd juxtaposition of autumn. The gradients of green made way into the lush yellows and pinks the trees were forever locked within.

Each square section of the gardens spanned at least fifty yards across, and each with a huge cottonwood at the center. In the distance, Damien spied the barren branches of winter, icicles still hanging from the boughs despite the hot sun above. But his attention turned towards Eamane's corner, where the brilliant green of the cottonwood rustled in an unfelt summer breeze.

Damien's soul buzzed with the ká all around him, but he fought the instinct to interact with it.

"She's here?" Liam adjusted his hood as he came close enough for them to speak quietly. "You're sure?"

"Somewhere in the compound, yes. But I'll need Dani to

focus again so we can pinpoint it."

The Dtrüa closed her eyes, keeping her white hood over her hair. Energy drifted from her, moving slower as it pulsed through the air into one of the closer sections of the garden. It rippled towards the outer wall of summer, disappearing in the lush foliage within.

Dani opened her eyes, letting go of the attempt. "Are we close?"

Damien studied the direction and stepped onto the path, crossing under the vine-covered arch. He glanced back, making unintentional eye contact with a priest, but the man only gave him a subtle nod.

"This way," Damien whispered, starting down a narrow stone walkway between low slung lemon trees. Beyond, the garden opened to a grove of banyan trees also out of place in the Isalican climate. Their roots wove into dense patterns, blocking the rest of Nema's Throne from view. Wild grass sprang up between their roots, offering a soft place for passersby to sit.

With a glance behind them, Damien reached to his boots and began untying them. He'd never considered the importance of the banyans the auer built their Slumber chambers beneath, but now it seemed too obvious.

Dani wandered deeper into the garden, but Liam stood on the path between them and the entrance.

When his toes touched the grass, he loosened his aura

enough to feel the whispers of the banyans' ká.

They energetically responded, filled with the power fed to them by the priests' careful maintenance. But there was a tone of concern among them, eager to share news that no one else could hear or understand.

"Uriel's definitely been here." Damien crouched, running his fingers along the petals of a sunflower waving in the contained breeze. "But... not for a while."

Everything around him blurred as he focused on each voice, silently asking them his questions, hoping one might understand what he sought. It was one particular banyan tree near the outer edge that spoke the loudest when his fingers glided onto its smooth bark.

The banyan greeted him, though its voice vibrated with weariness. Flickers of memories buried within the roots spoke of the shores of Eralas, but they were overshadowed by a drain on the tree's energy.

"She's here," Damien whispered, unsure if they were even close enough to hear. He followed the trails of the banyan's ká to the chamber below, where its roots ebbed with sacred power to sustain an unconscious soul.

It has to be Katrin.

In a rush, he sought answers from the tree as to how to enter the chamber. But the ká had nothing useful to aid them.

He ran his fingers over the tree's roots, following their energy with his. "There's no direct entrance to the chamber...

but, the ground is thinnest over here." He gestured his head around the south side of the tree.

Rae glanced around them. "I can't just upturn the ground. Someone will notice."

Dani walked to the other side of the banyan, crouching and touching the grass. "There's a burrow." She touched the tree, and Damien strode around it to see what she'd found.

A hollow at the base of the banyan must have once been the home of an animal, but it'd long since been vacated.

"I can dig here." Dani lifted her gaze. "It might go deeper and get me closer."

Liam stepped to his wife, peering into the burrow and looked at her skeptically. "I don't think a panther is going to fit gracefully down there."

"I can try to give us some cover, if you can reinforce a hiding aura around me." Rae looked at Damien. "To be safe."

Damien nodded as he reached out to touch her familiar ká. Sending waves of his into her, he focused on her aura, hardening it like a shell.

Rae lifted her hands, blinking slower as she focused.

The surrounding greenery shivered before sprouts erupted from the ground, growing up in vines, reaching for the tree branches above. Brush followed, thickening their cover with luscious rose blooms and sunflowers.

The Mira'wyld's chest rose faster as she used her power without letting any slip away from her. She continued the growth until they could no longer see the original path, encapsulated within the new foliage and the banyan tree's wide trunk.

Letting go of the power, Rae bundled it away and ran a hand over her braids. "I don't think any got out, did it?"

Damien smiled and shook his head. "You didn't even need me. You would have been fine."

Rae smiled, pride glimmering in her eyes.

"I can fit." Dani shifted, white fur spreading over her skin in a pearly coat. She lifted her maw, cloudy eyes looking over the three of them before she focused on the burrow. The panther form doubled her size, preventing her from fully entering the hollow. Extending her claws, she dug, quickly making progress through the soil.

"Where's Neco when you need him?" Rae whispered, quirking an eyebrow at Damien. "Though, she'd give him a run for his dinner."

"Not if dinner is involved. My bet is on the wolf in that case." Damien brushed past Rae towards the burrow to crouch and peer after Dani as she wedged into the tight hole.

Dani kicked a mound of loose dirt, splaying it over Damien's head and shoulders.

Bet on the wolf. Dani's scoffing voice entered his mind, laced with disapproval. *I beat a damn bear.*

Damien smirked as he brushed dirt from his tunic, and Liam chuckled at him as he sidestepped away.

"I don't think she liked that comment." Liam flicked a speck of dirt that'd landed on his shoulder before he pulled back his hood for the first time since entering the city. The sunlight pressing through the trees shone on the single strands of silver nestled throughout his black hair.

Dani disappeared within, but the sound of her digging continued.

"How deep is it?" Rae crouched beside Damien.

"Ten feet or so. I think." The Rahn'ka touched the tree's roots again. "Trees don't really think in measurements." Damien leaned over the burrow, shouting down after Dani. "Be careful, I think you're getting close. Try not to disrupt any of the roots if you can. It might... complicate things."

The sound of digging slowed before it stopped. Silence hung for a breath before a thump followed it.

Dani's voice came from the hollow. "I'm inside. Careful when you're coming through, there's a bit of a... drop, at the end."

Pausing just long enough to exchange a glance with his wife, Damien slid into the hole feet first, thankful for the size of Dani's panther form or he might not have fit at all. Wriggling down came in tedious increments, but when his boots touched empty air, he sucked in a breath and channeled his ká lower.

The muscles of his legs and knees readied before he dropped, and he landed comfortably on his bare feet.

A faint green radiated through the contained space, and a ripple of power shivered up his body at his beckoning. It surged into his fingertips, the blue glow rising into a marble sized ball.

"I'm down!" Damien turned around and stilled.

Dani stood over a woman who laid on a stone bed. The Dtrüa's eyes flooded with tears, reflecting the light he'd summoned. "Katrin," she whispered, touching the woman's cheek.

Art flickered over Katrin's skin, shimmering over her peaceful face and down her body. It kept her pristine, contrasting with the surrounding space.

Spiderwebs and roots crowded the corners of the room, vines poking through the walls. Dead insects lay bound and forgotten in the webs, and a cockroach scurried across the floor.

Dirt shuffled loose from the hole behind him, and Liam plopped to the ground with a grunt.

The Rahn'ka focused on the hum of power dripping from the tangled roots of the banyan tree.

They hung like a chandelier from the center of the room, drooping towards Katrin's slumbering face. Little specks of green marched down the spirals like ants, gathering into a raindrop at the tip of one root before falling onto the woman's forehead. Each pulse renewed the flickering aura around her that kept her asleep.

Dani sniffed before touching Katrin's hand. "I can't believe we found her."

Rae dropped into the chamber, landing in a crouch before rising. Her eyes wandered to the mess of spiderwebs in the ceiling corners. "Whoa, there's a lot of—"

"Roots? Yeah, there are tons down here." Liam gave her a deadpan look and shook his head.

"Roots. Yes, lots of roots." Rae furrowed her brow, looking at Damien with a tilted head.

Damien swallowed his laugh as he met Liam's gaze, and the soldier's look said enough.

Bugs? Really? Dani's afraid of bugs?

"How do we wake her?" Dani lifted her chin, drawing the others' attention.

The Rahn'ka stared at the drop of power as it gathered again and held out his hand. Turning his palm upward, he channeled his ká into a miniature shield. When the hazy energy dripped, it collided with the power of the Rahn'ka in a sparkling display like lightning. It radiated through the shield, which reacted by raising its walls higher. The energy dissipated in a ripple and the aura around Katrin dimmed.

"Just remember, she won't have memories right now. So, best to be gentle." Damien looked at Dani, then at Liam as he stepped closer to the stone table.

Gazing down at his sister's face, Liam's eyes turned glassy. With his touch to her hair, the green aura melted. It faded up her limbs, and Katrin's fingers twitched against Dani's.

A deep inhale came first, as if waking from a dream, and Katrin's eyes flickered open. They looked like dark pools in the pale light of the chamber, just like her brother's, a glitter of tears in the edges as if they'd been trapped there for twenty years.

The young woman breathed again, more rapidly, as she looked around her in a sleepy daze. "Where am I?"

"You're safe," Dani whispered, lifting Katrin's hand. "It's all right."

"Oh, Katy girl. I've missed you." Liam ran his hands through her loose black hair again.

Katrin blinked. "Do I know you?"

The hurt in Liam's eyes, even knowing this would be the case, made Damien's chest ache at the memory of Rae's lost memories so many years ago.

"You don't remember us, but we can fix that. What's important is that you're safe." Dani helped Katrin sit up, a gentle expression on her face as she withheld her tears. "My name is Dani, and this is your brother, Liam."

With the woman clear, Damien dismissed the little shield stopping the drip. It resumed, radiating onto the stone table and soaking into the rock. He didn't know how closely Uriel monitored the chamber and couldn't risk stopping the flow entirely.

Katrin squinted through the dimness at Liam, searching his face.

"I can help you remember." Damien stepped towards the stone altar where she still sat.

Flinching, she shirked back from his touch. "Who are you? And no one has told me where I am." Her voice, while calm, held a dignified strength that exceeded her years.

"Everyone take a breath." Rae approached, motioning for them to take a step back, which they obeyed. She centered her gaze on Katrin. "You're in a Slumber chamber. Once, many years ago, I woke within one, too. I didn't know my name or remember a thing."

Katrin scooted to the edge of the table, her light blue dress dancing around her ankles. The toes of her linen flats barely scraped the dust-covered ground. "Slumber?" She touched her forehead before sweeping a long strand of her black hair over her shoulder. "I think I've heard of that. Something... the... auer do?"

"Yes." Rae held the acolyte's gaze. "Your name is Katrin."

"Katrin." She nodded, speaking slowly. "Why did the auer put me in Slumber?"

"The auer didn't do this to you. That is where our stories differ. You've been kept here to prevent you from saving the man you love. I know you have no reason to trust us, but you must. We've come to free you."

Katrin's dark eyebrows knitted together as she shook her

head. Her lips parted before they closed again, and she glanced at the others before returning to Rae. "Did you get your memories back?"

"I did. Damien..." She motioned to him. "Gave them back to me. He can do the same for you. You just need to let him."

"Uhh..." Dani paced across the space. "We may not have time for that right now." She looked at the Rahn'ka. "I hear a lot of activity approaching. Can you confirm?"

Shit.

Damien had focused his Art on the chamber around them and Katrin, and had missed more ká entering the garden above. He might have suspected priests out for a stroll, if it weren't for the size of the group and the direct path they took towards the banyan trees.

Closing his eyes, Damien allowed the voices of the ká above ground to paint the image of ten soldiers hesitating at Rae's wall of overgrown foliage, confusion rippling through their souls.

"Dani's right. We have company. Apparently this place wasn't so unguarded." Damien met Liam's eyes as the man stepped beneath the tunnel they'd entered through.

The soldier's hand moved to his sword hilt, pushing his cloak out of the way as he peered upward.

"Trust us?" Rae offered Katrin her hand. "Please?"

Katrin stared, her eyes flickering to Liam's sword before she swallowed. "All right." She took Rae's hand and hopped down.

Never would have believed she's been laying still for twenty years...

Damien joined Liam, looking up into the dank tunnel. "You first. They haven't made it through Rae's barrier, yet, but I don't think it'll take them long to figure out a way around." He interlaced his fingers and gestured up.

Liam didn't hesitate, placing his boot in Damien's hands and jumping up to the hole. His hand closed on an exposed root, using it to hoist himself up.

Dani followed him, clicking her tongue before leaping and grabbing Liam's forearm.

The man lifted his wife, and they disappeared above.

"Me next. I'll lift Katrin up." Rae nodded at the acolyte before entering the tunnel above, the roots bending to support her while she reached down for Katrin.

Damien gestured to the woman, who hesitated again as he approached. "I promise I'll restore your memories as soon as we're away from here. You can trust us."

Katrin bit the side of her bottom lip and looked up at Rae. "I don't see much of a choice right now." She accepted Damien's help as she jumped for the opening.

"You'll be glad later, I promise." Rae caught Katrin's arms, hoisting her up into the opening. "Go, I'll be right behind you."

Wriggling past her, Katrin disappeared into the tunnel, and the Rahn'ka met his wife's eyes.

Damien smirked. "You sure you can lift me? I'm pretty heavy."

"Shut up and jump." Rae smiled. "And use your power to help me if you don't want me to drop you on your ass."

Pooling as much energy as he could into his legs, the flow aided his muscles in increasing his jump. His hand closed around her forearm, but he used it to pull himself further up to grasp a root. Funneling more power into the banyan tree, he reinforced the limb so he could scale past Rae. Following the stream of his energy up to the tree's trunk, he realized its anger at the encroaching guards as they cut the foliage blocking them.

"Better hurry. These things are never simple." Damien spoke over his shoulder before crawling out from the animal burrow, Rae behind him.

Liam stood with his sword drawn, facing the wall of plants.

Their ká wailed as the steel tip of a sword cut through, and the voices of the soldiers behind became clearer.

"This way." Dani led them away from the advancing soldiers and through the thick brush, some crafted from Rae's

Art. "No one is over here, yet." She paused, pulling foliage to the side so Liam could exit first.

Rae went next, using her Art to encourage the greenery to stay out of the way for the rest of them.

"Who are we running from?" Katrin kept her voice low, despite the suspicion in her eyes. "Why are they after us?"

"Oh, you know. No one important," Dani muttered.

"In the name of the king! Surrender peacefully!" The shout echoed from the other side of the foliage wall, and Damien cringed.

"King?" Katrin's voice rose in pitch as she spun to look at Damien. "You're running from royal guards?"

"Technically, you are. We're helping you." Dani motioned with her head. "Please. There are more guards coming. We need to go."

Katrin spread her stance, crossing her arms. "No. I want answers. I don't remember a lot, but I must trust my instincts. And my instincts tell me the king is not my enemy."

"The king himself isn't, but he's not making these choices. Someone else is, and I can't explain it all right now, but..." Dani stilled, listening.

Damien's gaze darted to Rae, who stood with Liam out in the open. "You need to—"

"Halt there!"

Liam and Rae's heads whipped to the side, their bodies stiffening.

The Mira'wyld made eye contact with Damien.

Don't even think about it...

He opened his mouth to dissuade her from the wild idea she'd already settled on.

She minutely shook her head and snapped the foliage back into place.

He lost sight of them, but their footsteps took off towards the summer garden's entrance, stealing the guards' attention.

Damn it, Rae.

Chapter 8

"RUN!" RAE TUGGED LIAM'S CLOAK as she took off towards the entrance archway of the gardens. His footsteps thudded behind her, but she didn't look, her heart racing at how close the guards sounded behind them.

"Stop! In the name of the king! You're under arrest!"

"Fuck. That means hurry up." Rae glanced at Liam before the unnatural scorch of a southern summer disappeared in a wave of cooler Isalican air.

That's better.

Priests stumbled out of their way, shouting their complaints as Rae and Liam banked around the sharp corner towards the temple grounds' glass gate.

"What about the others?" Liam slowed, looking back the way they'd come.

"We need to draw the attention away. It will keep them safe. Trust me." Rae grabbed his arm. "Your family is safe with Damien. And I'm sure he's telling Dani you're safe with me, so let's make that true, shall we?"

Liam hesitated before his pace returned. With a burst of surprising speed, he cut in front of her and turned sharply once outside the gates, forcing Rae to slide on the worn stone to follow.

"You know somewhere safe we can hide?" She turned sideways for a stride to fit between two pedestrians.

The strangers yelled, their annoyance mirrored by others they barreled past.

Liam nodded but didn't speak, jerking his head down the narrow alley that ran along the temple's garden wall and the two story residences beside it.

Rae looked up, then behind them.

The guards trailed farther behind, forced to funnel one at a time into the mouth of the alley.

"Alleys are a little predictable." Rae huffed, leaping over a fallen crate after Liam. "I've always had better luck with rooftops."

"Temporary," Liam breathed. "Your turn to trust me."

"You think rain would help our escape or hurt it?"

"Help." Liam abruptly jogged sideways, scraping by a tight corner before following the oddly angled house to another narrow side street.

Rae took a deep breath, finding the courage to access her Art without Damien's extra wall of protection preventing the energies from leaking from her hiding aura. She skidded after the soldier, steadying her breathing.

Clouds gathered thicker above the city, darkening with each step they took before bursting with rainfall.

Sealing her power away, Rae let go of her control to let the weather maintain itself.

"That skill would have been so convenient back when I used to break the law," Rae muttered, holding her breath when Liam slid off a one-story retaining wall to the ground below.

His boots hit metal, echoing hollowly. A grunt preceded the scrape of the rusty metal hinges, and the drain cover clanged against the cobblestone as he dropped it.

She paused at the top of the wall before leaping, falling with the rain for a breath before landing next to Liam. "Sewers?"

"Why? Don't tell me you're as squeamish as my wife." Liam gestured with his head to the dark hole. "It's about a fifteen-foot drop. After you." His chest heaved, a slight flush in his cheeks from the run.

"Not squeamish." Water ran over Rae's face, dripping off her chin. "Just takes me back." She crouched at the opening, bracing one hand on the edge as she dropped inside. Her eyes adjusted to the darkness, light filtering in through the grates deeper in the sewer tunnels.

I wonder if there are tunnels beneath this capital city, too.

Above, wood scuffed along the stones as Liam positioned a stray barrel lid against the iron grate. He slid to the edge of the hole, slipping his fingers between the iron bars to tug it closed behind him. He swung down with a jolt, still hanging onto the iron as it clanked into place, bits of light streaming through as water dribbled from the street above.

Dropping, he landed in a crouch, holding his sword parallel to the ground before he stood with a wince. "Haven't done that in a long time," he whispered, but pointed down the tunnel.

"Me, neither." Rae smiled. "Feels good, though, doesn't it?" She wiped stray hairs back from her face, slicking them over her braids.

Liam chuckled. "Feels like I'm going to be sore in the morning." He shrugged his cloak up on his shoulders as they started forward.

Rae laughed, walking behind him. "If it makes you feel better, I probably will be, too."

Rainwater flowed through the sewer tunnel back towards the main road. The walkway widened slightly, mossy arches just high enough that she didn't need to duck when passing beneath. The roar of the rainfall above echoed through the stone tunnels, drowning out their footsteps as a thin stream of water rushed past their boots.

Liam paused roughly one hundred yards away from where they'd dropped inside, looking back up the tunnel to ensure they hadn't been followed. With a sigh, he leaned against the curved wall. "We can stay down here for a little while. The rain will wash away our scents so the tracking hounds can't find us." Smirking, he met her eyes. "Quite the handy trick."

Rae huffed a laugh. "It can be helpful. Fog, rain, snow..." She shrugged. "Fire. At least this should give the others plenty of time to get out of there."

He nodded, leaning his head back, the rim of his hood falling to expose his face. "All those tricks must be pretty useful for an Ashen Hawk. I heard the rumors that they were working within the law now, but certainly didn't expect someone so... close to King Martox to be the one leading them."

Mirroring Liam, Rae leaned against the cold wall. "I'm not sure I'll ever get used to people calling him King Martox. You know we were a couple for a while?" She grinned. "Jarrod has always been my closest friend and, for a long time, I never knew his bloodline. I took over the Ashen Hawks after my... I don't know what to call her, but she died, and so I stepped down as political advisor to the Proxiet to run the Hawks. It's been a bit of an... adjustment period, but we're becoming something Sarth only dreamt of."

Liam studied her face, his dark eyes evaluating everything she said with a collected calm before a smile crept across his lips. "It was quite the upheaval King Martox caused down in Helgath, wasn't it?"

Rae snorted. "You have no idea." She motioned in the air between them. "Makes this all look like a regular day."

Liam's brow quirked. "I hope you're referring to the running... Not the bit about freeing Matthias from the control of an evil infestation and waking my sister up from twenty years of Slumber."

"Well..." Rae shrugged. "No, not exactly, but this isn't the craziest thing I've seen, either." She let out a long breath and evened her tone. "I really hope we can free your friend. I can't imagine what it's been like to have lost him for so long."

The soldier's face hardened as he nodded. "We mourned them both, in a way. Honestly, I doubted that I'd see either of them again."

"But your sister is awake. That's a good start, right?" Rae tilted her head.

His gaze drifted to the wall beside her. "I'm glad to see her, but it's still strange. She hasn't changed at all since that day he locked her away." He chewed his lip before looking back at Rae. "Damien can really restore her memories?"

"He restored mine. He will do the same for her."

Liam nodded, crossing his arms. "I still have a lot of questions, but it seems ungrateful of me to ask them, considering all you've already done and promised."

"What questions? I can't promise answers, but maybe I can ease your mind."

"Dani trusts Damien inherently because of whatever power he has, and that's the part I don't understand the most. What is a Rahn'ka? And how is it that the famous Damien Lanoret has access to the Art but no one has ever talked about it?"

Rae smiled, rolling her lips together. "Because it is imperative no one knows what he is. There is only one. I met him before he had the power... He didn't get it until after he deserted. You cannot share this information with anyone. We keep it from the kingdom, too. I can't *tell* you what exactly he is, but what he does has to do with the souls of people, animals..." She made a face. "Rocks, even. It's really confusing, but he's an honorable man and wants to help you. You, Katrin and Matthias. And Ryen."

A flinch flickered across Liam's features as he angled his head down. "I can keep secrets. Too well, sometimes." He rolled his shoulders and dropped his arms to his sides. "And I hope he's as good as he seems to think he is. We could use some luck." He looked down the tunnel at the closed grate they'd entered from, then up at the one closer to them. "As an Ashen Hawk, you got any tricks to find the others?"

Rae scoffed. "Sure do. We'll go to the easternmost tavern and ask for their recommendation for an inn. We'll meet the others at that inn."

He lifted his eyebrows. "Sounds like you've done this before. Dare I say, a few times?"

The Mira'wyld smirked. "Perhaps."

Chapter 9

KATRIN PULLED HER ARM FREE of Damien's grasp, backing towards the now sealed hedge.

He looked confused. And she wondered if it was a look she'd seen on him before. If she'd known him before.

What if they're all lying to me?

Lifting her hands in front of her, she tried to recall if she knew how to defend herself. But the man in front of her was easily twice her weight. She wouldn't have a chance.

"Relax," Dani whispered, her milky eyes hovering near Katrin's face. "You needn't fear us."

"I think it's well within reason to not be relaxed right now." Katrin felt oddly out of place in her own body, distracted by her fancy dress. She ran her hand down the intricate stitching, unsure how she could afford such expensive attire.

"Fair." Dani crouched before sitting cross-legged in the grass. "But the guards are gone, and we're alone... Let's all sit and figure this out."

Katrin stared at her, heart pounding in her chest.

Damien stood a few feet away, still poised to tackle her if she ran.

"I think I'll stand." Katrin crossed her arms.

"Damien, sit down." Dani didn't look at him, and Katrin wondered how good the woman's sight was.

He glanced at Dani, but Katrin could tell his attention never truly left her. It made the pit of her stomach twist.

"I'm not lying to you." Damien sounded calm, despite the obvious tension in his body. "I just want to restore your memories. With the guards distracted, I can help you understand all of this." He strode to Dani and lowered himself to the ground, crossing his legs and tucking in his bare feet. He lifted a hand out to Katrin. "Please. Let me?"

Katrin stared, reminding herself to keep breathing. Her stomach churned, and an inexplicable wave of nausea threatened everything within her. She rubbed her fingers against her clammy palms, her head heavy.

How do I know I want my memories back?

Damien waited, his hazel eyes pressing a calming weight on her like wool blankets wrapping around her in winter.

A flicker of a memory stabbed in her mind. Shivering cold, somewhere dark, but with someone's arms around her. Her fingertips chilled as they brushed along the memory of a wall made of snow.

An avalanche?

Katrin flinched as she sat, still out of reach of the strange man offering to help her. Her eyes moved over the woman, examining her face. "I do know you, don't I?" she whispered, the memory of warm fur tickling her palm. "But I remember something odd. Like..." She closed her eyes as flashes of fur and fang filled the inside of her eyelids. "A big cat?"

"I can shift." Dani nodded. "I am a Dtrüa, and I can choose to be a white panther when necessary."

Katrin nodded, licking her lips as she recalled watching a white panther slink through the trees of a snowy forest. New flakes coated the creature's fur and Katrin's face. She breathed, swallowing the lingering nausea. "And I can trust you."

"I am your friend. Your sister. I would never betray you."

Katrin turned slowly to Damien, who sat with his spine straight and a curious look on his face.

"We don't have time to consider why you remember any of this, but I'll take it as a stroke of luck. Please, Katrin. Trust Dani's faith in me. I won't hurt you." Damien held out his hand again, palm up. They were scarred and callused, like those of a warrior.

Like her brother, or...

Why can't I remember his name?

The sudden feeling of loss made her feel hollow, and she gulped. "What are you going to do?" She lifted her hand and scooted close enough to lay her palm on his.

"It's hard to explain, but close your eyes. And try to clear your mind. I will guide you." Damien's fingers closed around hers, his skin warm.

She nodded and greeted the darkness of her eyelids, urging herself to take a steadying breath.

The man's energy collided with hers like waves cresting on shimmering sand.

Why can I sense his Art so well?

She gasped as her eyes snapped open, yet didn't move. Within her mind, wisps of light blue wrapped around her in a tornado, rushing out to form the shapes of people she knew.

Mom? Why are you crying?

Her mother brushed her hair from her face, placing another heavy kiss on her forehead. Katrin's own face felt wet, and she glanced behind her at the old priest, who waited patiently to take the thirteen-year-old for a life within the temples.

Her hands pushed down on the bread dough, a flour-dusted table in front of her. Then the dough became a man, writhing as she twisted the threads of the Art and stitched his gash closed.

Ash burned her eyes, but Matthias's face hovered above her, contorted in agony as he prevented the bookshelves from crushing them both.

Matthias.

The fire wreathed up into the trunks of trees, ash turning to snow. A woman with an arrowhead in her arm looked up at her with milky eyes, the white of her leathers stained red.

A panther erupted from the snowbank, and fresh air rushed into her lungs as Matthias stepped in front of her, the warm feeling of his lips still sweet on hers. Then the anger at him for the secret he'd kept.

Then love.

Pain.

Her body screamed at her, and her hands flew to her abdomen as she looked down at blood-covered sheets. Dani's touch banished the fear as the Dtrüa held her.

A lie spoken to the man she loved on a grass-covered hill outside the encampment, then parapets of stone rising to the sky with snow falling into the courtyard.

Matthias before her on a bent knee. Her heart pounded yes, and he kissed her.

Wings drummed through the air, pushing her hair from her face. She touched her abdomen again, as if she could feel the life within her. Zaelinstra's all-knowing eyes watched her as she lowered her scaled head to reveal the collapse of the towers. The crumble of ash and shadow. The glory of the city, lost within a suffocating wave of decay and destruction, and Matthias tugging her back in time with him to face Merissa.

Then Matthias...

Tears filled her eyes as the familiar dirt of her tomb encircled her, and she stared at the face of the man she loved. But he was nowhere in those obsidian eyes.

Katrin gasped as the warmth of the summer garden grounds flooded her senses. Birds chirped, oblivious to the horrors she'd just remembered, as tears streamed down her face.

Damien sat before her, his eyes softer as he withdrew his hand from hers and pulled on his boots.

Unable to control the sob, Katrin lifted her hands to her mouth to stifle it in case any of the guards remained nearby. Turning to Dani, she threw herself at her friend and wrapped her arms around her waist as she collapsed onto her lap. "Oh, Dani." Katrin urged herself to breathe, to calm. She didn't have time for emotions, not now. Not with all that'd happened, all that could happen.

Water soaked her clothes, dripping from the canopy above, but it hadn't been raining before she'd closed her eyes.

"You're safe, now." Emotion roughened Dani's tone, and the woman embraced her.

Katrin sat up and gripped Dani's shoulders. She searched for signs of age, finding the small creases on her friend's face barely visible. Wrinkles.

Her heart leapt. "How long?" She could hardly speak, the words hoarse. A raindrop brushed down her cheek with her tears.

Dani tilted her head, swallowing, and whispered, "It's been twenty years, Kat."

The nausea she thought she'd controlled returned, and something broke within her chest. "Twenty years?" The words didn't feel real. She looked at Damien, now certain she'd never met him before, yet grateful for his calming presence. "Matthias?" Her hands moved instinctively to her abdomen as she met Damien's eyes. "The baby?"

Dani took Katrin's hand and squeezed. "Matthias is still... that monster."

"But your baby is fine." Damien touched her knee. "It appears Slumber affected him the same as you. He's in exactly the state he was when you were put here. And everything seems perfectly normal with his energies."

Katrin stared at Damien. "He?" The knot in her stomach tightened even more as she pressed her hands along her stomach. While not understanding who or what Damien was, she knew enough about the mysteries of the Art to not question it. But the pain lingered as she imagined Matthias's face, his irises still black and gold.

Tears threatened her eyes again.

"My son will not grow without his father." She turned a determined look to Dani. "We need to figure out a way to free him."

The Dtrüa smiled, specks of rainwater in her eyelashes. "We have a plan."

Damien stood, brushing grass and mud from his breeches, his blond hair sticking to his forehead. "But we should reunite with the others, first. The guards might come back. Or whoever our little spy was that alerted them to come." A flicker of blue light radiated at the back of his eyes, and Katrin could sense the Art at work within him. "We're still alone for now, but that might change quickly."

Katrin nodded as she picked herself up, shaking out the skirt of her dress as she did. Her hand found Dani's, entwining their fingers. As Dani stood, Katrin moved close to her, pressing up against her arm. "Thank you," she whispered. "I can't imagine what all this has been like for you."

Dani shook her head, tears brimming in her eyes. "I told you I'd find you one day. But we couldn't have done it without our new friends." She gazed in Damien's direction. "How do we find them?"

"Getting separated like this isn't exactly uncommon for me and my wife. So we head east, which is fortunately... away from the palace and likely any further trouble."

Katrin's hand tightened on Dani's. "Tell me everything while we walk?" She started towards the branches that the guards' swords had cut, but Damien beat her.

He pushed the branches aside, holding them open for Dani and Katrin to climb through.

Dani nodded as she walked out of the foliage with Katrin. "Liam and I live in the mountains, protecting the secrets they hold. We have three children, who—"

"Three children?" Katrin squeezed, a smile crossing her face despite the fog still in her mind. She shook her head. "But in twenty years, I suppose that makes sense. I'm glad you and Liam found some happiness."

Dani's head bowed as they exited the summer garden, and the rainfall chilled. "We looked for so long. Years. I'm sorry, I wanted—"

"Don't." Katrin shook her hand. "I know you did whatever you could. None of the time matters. We have now."

Except Matthias has been trapped the entire time I've been asleep.

"Micah introduced us to Damien and Rae. They're advisors to the Helgath crown, and they're here to help us free Matthias. Though, from what I understand, this is their endeavor rather than their king's."

"Helgath?" Katrin faced Damien. "I'm surprised Helgath let an Art user out of their sight, let alone an advisor, especially for a personal quest."

Damien smirked with a shrug. "Helgath isn't the same country from twenty years ago. We had a bit of a... rebellion, and a new Dannet family rules."

Katrin squinted, mind whirling.

Helgath changed?

She'd thought it more likely for Liam to take up knitting.

A ray of sunlight shone into her eyes as it reflected off the brightly paned windows of a clothier.

They started down the east road leading away from the temple, but she paused to look back at the glass spires stretching towards the sky. Spots of sun broke through the rain clouds to shine rainbows between glass peaks.

May the gods guide me.

For the rest of the journey to the eastern-most tavern that Damien instructed them to, Dani filled Katrin's mind with new stories.

History.

The Dtrüa talked about her children. How they'd adopted two siblings after years had passed without a child of their own. And then, shortly after the adoption, how she'd become pregnant with Jaxx. Dani's voice lowered when she spoke of the dragons, as if still trying to keep some of the information from Damien, or perhaps just listening ears. She never called them by name, referring to them as the secret they protected. It brought some comfort to know that the creature within Matthias hadn't found the ancient beings.

When Dani spoke about Damien and Rae's arrival on their homestead, Damien slowed to walk beside them and told her the monster's name.

"So, this Uriel, whatever he actually is, can be removed?"

"We believe it must be possible, since an abandoned host is required to imprison him."

"And you had the right idea, before, when you tried to harm yourself." Dani's voice held regret. "Though we think Matthias must be aware of the broken deal for it to work."

"But if Matthias must know, then Uriel will, too. And he will always stop me by bending time."

"Unless Matthias can wrestle control first, then he's the one who jumps back to stop you, instead." Damien slowed as they neared the edge of the city, the streets growing less crowded and the buildings more spread out.

"Sounds like a lot of risk. How do we know Matthias is still..." Katrin swallowed the lump in her throat. "Still..."

"We don't. But this is all we've got." Damien touched her shoulder. "Based on your memories of Matthias, though, I believe he's still fighting."

Katrin nodded, rolling her lips together as she looked at the familiar, yet entirely different, street.

"I'll be right back." Damien jerked his head towards the swinging sign of a tavern. "Then we'll find Liam and Rae."

Liam.

Katrin squeezed her eyes shut, envisioning the hurt on his

face when she hadn't remembered him.

"He's looking forward to seeing you, too." Dani wrapped an arm around Katrin's shoulders.

"I've missed so much," Katrin whispered, leaning into Dani's touch. "My head is still spinning."

"I can only imagine." Dani sighed. "Your parents are well. Your sister, too."

"Izi," Katrin breathed, calculating just how long it'd been. "Gods she'd be... twenty-two, twenty-three? Older than I am." A shiver passed down her spine.

"The last time we visited your parents, Izi and Varin were inseparable. Our daughter... Your niece is nineteen, now." Dani smiled, gazing up as the clouds thinned and the rain subsided. "You'd like her."

Katrin nodded slowly, blinking after Damien as he disappeared through the tavern door. She considered the Rahn'ka's aura as it faded further away, her own Art still tingling from the interaction of her memories returning. She wondered how much he'd seen, how much he knew of her now. Of Matthias. It sent a raw shudder down her spine as she leaned more heavily into Dani, forcing the Dtrüa to spread her stance to support them both. "You trust him?"

"Do you remember the woman who helped me escape Feyor? The one who broke my bond to the other Dtrüas?"

The old conversations seemed blurry in her mind, but the events hadn't been so long ago.

No. They were over twenty years ago. Even if it feels like months.

She swallowed as she nodded. "You told me there were no other Art practitioners like her."

"There weren't. And there are none like him, now. The one who helped me died, but his power is the same as hers."

Katrin grimaced. "And he wants to help us? To help Matthias? You really think he can?"

"He and his wife want to imprison the creature controlling Matthias. I don't know if they can, but part of the process requires Matthias's help. So they're motivated, at least, and as long as that man of yours is still in there, it should work." Dani's head twitched as the door to the tavern opened, and Damien exited. The Dtrüa's cloudy gaze hovered near Katrin's face. "He has brought you back to us, so I must believe he can help us accomplish the rest."

Katrin slid her hand into Dani's. "I pray he can. And that Matthias is still whole in there." Her chest felt hollow even as she said it. "Though I wonder if death would have been more merciful."

Dani swallowed. "I think you'd be right on that one."

Damien made eye contact with Katrin and motioned with his head as he approached. "This way."

Katrin studied the Rahn'ka as he turned down the street, his shadow stretched out in front of him. It made her stomach twist, and she clasped harder to Dani, images of the walls around them crumbling within depths of black. Uriel's dark shape rising above it all, his eyes still Matthias's.

She squeezed her eyes shut, trusting her footsteps beside Dani's. The sensation of the stone beneath her thin soles became her only focus until Matthias's face returned. But Uriel still tainted the look in his eyes as he caught her hand and pulled the shattered ceramic plate away from her throat.

I'm the only one who can free Matthias.

Katrin's spine straightened as she urged herself from the comfort of her friend. She could no longer be the frightened acolyte with a prince to rescue her. A strand of her loose hair tickled her cheek as she brushed away the tears filling her bottom lid and looked to the eastern sky.

Like rows of an orchard in fall, the strips of clouds shone with orange and red, welcoming the coming night.

"We can do it," Dani whispered. "It might be messy, but we can free him, too."

Katrin bit the corner of her lower lip. "Whatever it takes."

Chapter 10

LIAM PACED, COUNTING THE TAPS of his boots along the wooden floor of the inn. His eyes flitted to the window, where the sky changed shades with the setting sun.

"You'll wear your boots out, you know." Rae's gaze flickered to him, but she didn't rise from her spot laying on the room's bed.

"I don't understand how you're so calm." Liam rubbed his jaw, his foot twitching the moment he paused. He glared at the tip of his boot, urging it to be still.

Fidgeting won't make the time go by faster.

"They'll be here soon." Rae looked at the ceiling again, hands behind her head. "Enjoy the calm. It won't last."

Liam groaned as he grabbed the back of his neck and glared at the ceiling. Raising three children had been anything but calm, but he suddenly longed for the chaos of their household instead of the memories the city held. "You left a die on the steps outside. How is that supposed to help him?"

Rae smirked. "I left it with the five on top"

"So?"

"We're in room five."

"And he's supposed to make that connection from a random die that a drunk could have dropped on the doorstep?"

Footsteps echoed outside their room. More than one person.

Rae sat up, falling silent.

A sharp ting struck the wooden door, echoing through the room.

Three knocks, then one.

A radiant smile broke across Rae's face. "Let them in."

Liam crossed the room in two long strides, hastily unlatching the door and pulling it open.

Damien stood in front, the die Rae had left behind in his right hand and still raised as if he'd just knocked with it. He met Liam's eyes only briefly before he focused on Rae behind him. Relief colored the Rahn'ka's face as he stepped aside, ushering the two women behind him inside first.

Katrin's hair hung loose around her shoulders, draped over the delicate fabric of her dress. Her dark eyes looked stronger than before and knocked the breath from Liam as they met his. Her mouth parted, as if to say something, but stopped as she lunged at him.

Catching her, Liam sobbed as he wrapped his arms around his sister and felt her return the embrace. He pushed a kiss to her hair as she burrowed her face into the collar of his cloak.

Dani gave a half-hearted smile, leaning against the wall as Damien closed the door and crossed to his wife.

"You remember?" He touched her cheek as Katrin looked up.

She nodded furiously and burrowed her head again. "Oh, Liam. I'm so sorry."

Liam's heart thudded, and he squeezed her harder. "You have nothing to be sorry for."

Katrin wriggled free of his grip, pinching his chin. Stepping away, her hand brushed Dani's again as she moved to the window. Leaning against the sill, she looked about to open the panes for more fresh air as she normally would have, but paused as her palm pressed to the glass. She tugged the curtains shut to hide the view, plunging the room into darkness.

No one spoke, but a shimmer of light bubbled up from the area next to the bed, and Damien transferred a little flickering ball of azure flame into the lantern on the bedside. Once he closed the lamp house, the light doubled and grew white.

"So." Rae's hand rested on Damien's, and all eyes turned

to her. "Who needs a drink?"

Liam gawked at how relaxed the two of them seemed as Damien smirked and crossed to the desk which held the bottle and glasses Rae had insisted on collecting from the innkeeper before coming into the room.

As Damien popped the cork, Rae quirked an eyebrow. "No one? After all that? Katrin wakes from eternal slumber. We have a chase through the city, and now we need to plan how to take down Pantracia's most notorious evil, and no one needs a damn *drink*?"

Katrin broke the silence first. "A little might help take the edge off, I suppose." She crossed to Damien as he poured a small amount into a glass and held it out to her.

"Probably shouldn't have more than that, anyway, all things considered." Damien's eyes darted down towards Katrin's stomach and her cheeks flushed.

"Should I not...?" She touched her abdomen, and a flood of relief echoed through Liam's body.

She didn't lose the baby.

"You're pregnant?" Rae stood.

Katrin's face flushed further as she nodded and lifted the cup to her lips. "I was before... Slumber, and Damien confirmed I still am."

"Congratulations." Rae's tone tightened, her gaze meeting Damien's as they had a silent exchange.

Dani clicked her tongue, accepting the offered drink from

the Rahn'ka as tension filled the room. "Will that change something?"

"Maybe." Damien didn't look up as he poured another drink. He held it out to Liam, who shook his head. He shrugged and lifted it to his own lips.

"You haven't told me the plan yet, but my son might change it?" Katrin moved to the bed, sitting as she nestled the glass in her lap.

"Well..." Rae sighed. "We probably need to kill you. Temporarily, of course."

Liam's gut clenched, but Katrin only nodded in understanding.

"Once he's in control, Matthias will jump back and change it." His sister spoke with certainty.

Damien frowned. "*If* it works. I had planned to bring you back myself if it failed, but I'm not entirely sure what my method of resurrection will do to the baby in your womb."

Liam gritted his teeth. "Then we're not doing it that way."

Dani took his hand and squeezed. "It's Katrin's choice."

Katrin met his eyes, her lips pursed, and he knew her answer before she said it.

"Katy girl..." Liam stepped towards her, lowering to his knees before his sister as he took her hands. "We can find another way."

"This is the only way we can get Matthias back. It's worth the risk." Katrin brushed a lock of hair from his forehead.

"And I'm not saying this out of some love sick need of not being alive without Matthias. This needs to happen to protect Isalica from Uriel. And the rest of Pantracia." She looked up, meeting Rae's gaze, then Damien's. "There is no way to seal away Uriel without Matthias restored to his own body, correct?"

Dani had crossed the room, standing by the window as she watched Rae, too.

"Technically, we just need any old host of Uriel's. But we've never found one living after he was done with them." Damien took a slow gulp of the liquor in his hands.

Rae nodded. "Matthias is our best shot."

"And Uriel will not abandon him willingly." Katrin turned back to her brother, touching the side of his head. "He already called Matthias his favorite host."

He might have said it to her twenty years ago, but if Uriel was still within the king, it had to be true.

Liam sighed, taking Katrin's hand from his face. "You're sure? The baby..."

"Will have his father." Her face hardened. "Please don't make this any harder than it already is, brother."

He kissed the back of her hand as he stood, eyes flickering to his wife. She reached for him, and he took her hand once more.

"All right. What's the plan?"

Chapter 11

"WHAT DO YOU MEAN, SHE'S *missing*?" Uriel slammed his fist onto the table, overturning the goblets on top.

Tension radiated through Matthias as he watched through the creature's gaze.

Katrin's awake? Matthias channeled his thoughts more directly to Uriel. *You lost her. You failed.*

Alana flinched, turning her emerald green gaze down to the lavish carpet of the dining hall. It seemed wholly unbecoming of the wicked auer, but Matthias had seen her do it so many times in his presence.

"Master, I don't how it happened, but she's... no longer in the Slumber chamber. I sensed something amiss and sent guards—"

Uriel crossed to Alana, forcing her gaze up by gripping her

throat. "But your useless guards didn't find her. Tell me she at least remembers nothing."

Uriel's growl made Matthias inwardly cheer.

Run, Kat.

Alana gasped through the choke-hold, the feeling of her hand gripping Matthias's wrist distant. "She won't remember. I wove that into the Slumber spell." A strand of her straight black hair fell free, brushing across Matthias's skin. The shock of a long ago memory rippled through him as he pushed Katrin's hair behind her ear.

"Your failure reeks of incompetence." Uriel shoved her away, heat flowing through his veins. "And this is the second time you have failed, Alana. My patience is not infinite. Find her. I don't care what it takes. Don't return until you have better news."

She will stay far away from you. Matthias pushed the thought louder.

"Shut up!" Uriel picked up a fallen crystal goblet and smashed the end off on the table before holding the sharp point to his own chest. "I have no tolerance for your opinions, so stop trying to antagonize me."

Alana's eyes flashed in knowing, but she smoothed the satin fabric of her gown. Her tanned hand closed around Uriel's on the broken goblet, but instead of pulling it away, she pushed it closer as she slipped her seductive touch around Uriel's waist. "I may need to use the Hollow Ones, but we'd need to get them here first. And I could aid in a distraction once they are dispatched." Her hand slipped lower on Matthias's hips, making him cringe.

Uriel's grip returned to Alana's delicate throat. The purr in his body changed from anger to a far more loathsome feeling.

"Not now." He squeezed, despite the lingering desire in the auer's eyes, and pushed her away.

Alana detangled from him with a sharp inhale, wincing as shadow lashed down her wrists, drawing a maroon line of her blood. She clasped her hand around the wound, bowing her head once more. "Please forgive me, Master."

"That remains to be seen, and wholly depends on your success today." Uriel snapped the remaining bits of crystal in his palm, and pain shot through Matthias as it made deep cuts in his hand. "Perhaps I will enjoy killing you again later today."

Alana glanced up. The look of her dead eyes returned to Matthias's thoughts. He'd seen her die so many times, but Uriel always jumped and brought her back. It seemed no matter the depth of his anger at her, he was more determined to keep her. The same could not be said of so many others who had betrayed Uriel. The ones who had been his Shades and failed to hide.

The worst had been Lasseth. A death that Uriel had delighted in many times over, and in so many horrible ways.

Thankfully, the dead man would not remember all the deaths. But Matthias did.

Memories blurred between Lasseth and Kin, and he panicked.

Is Kin dead? He retreated deeper into his own mind, finding solace in the small room he'd crafted to keep to himself. The walls rippled with movement before dissolving into falling snow. He looked up, finding the dark sky above him.

The courtyard. Matthias clenched his jaw, wishing he could return to the moment he'd proposed to Katrin at the palace. *She doesn't deserve Slumber.*

His mind jarred.

Katrin isn't in Slumber anymore. She woke up. Who woke her?

Matthias strode through the delusion of snow, watching flakes melt as they hit his palm. *Dani. Liam. They must have found her. If they have her...*

Shadow crept across the snow, onyx serpents curling around the path's edge until they rushed to the frozen fountain at the center. They tangled together, swelling upward into the shape of a man. But not a man. His arms were too long, and legs bent the wrong way. He towered over Matthias, black pits where his eyes should be framed by ridges of spikes and obsidian scales.

"Your monster shape does not frighten me." Matthias

found his voice, wishing the beast would grant him a moment of peace.

A wicked smile, too wide and filled with black glass teeth, spread across the creature's face. It melted into another, more human appearance, and Matthias stared at himself with empty black eyes.

"Somehow, that's no better." Matthias frowned, controlling his breath. "Shouldn't you be, you know, busy with my body? Who controls it while we're both here?"

The imposter never slept, never stopped. In turn, neither did Matthias. Without rest, his mind never ceased plaguing him with memories and images, not all based in reality.

"I can multitask." Uriel's slithery voice hissed over the air, not at all fitting from Matthias's lips. "I found it necessary to remind you why I allow you this..." The man looked distastefully at the snow falling from the sky. "Sanctuary." He scowled. "If you continue to interrupt, I will take it away."

Uriel held his hand out in front of him and shadows boiled from his palm towards the painted tiles of the path, covered in a thin layer of new snow. The pool wriggled to Matthias's feet, but the king refused to move.

"Fuck you." Matthias kept his voice even. "You and all your threats."

The parasite chuckled, walking calmly over the tar-like coating towards Matthias. "But my threats are exactly what got you here, did they not? You seemed to give them plenty of credence before."

"And I won't make that mistake again."

"I only needed the one." The shadow chased after Uriel's heels like a cloak, wrapping up his body before vanishing among his pitch-colored attire.

But Katrin's awake.

Matthias huffed. "We'll see about that."

Uriel leapt at him, his power like whips as they shattered into his flesh. Claws ripped at Matthias's throat as he met the black depths of Uriel's eyes, only inches from his own. "You're mine." His grip tightened, and pain seared through every inch of Matthias's soul.

Matthias yelled, tugging at the tendrils at his throat. "For how long, *Master*?" He twisted the word with sarcastic delight, chuckling through the agony. "For how long?"

More. More rage and acid broke through the shadow, dropping Matthias to his knees. He forced his vision to focus through the black flowing in from the edges, tinged with red as if his own blood still occupied his veins.

Uriel retook the grotesque form, his face more doglike with writhing vines and spikes along his body. He roared as he threw Matthias to the ground, and shadow swelled over his body. It wrapped around his limbs, pinning him to the hard tile of the courtyard. Metal chimed as the shadow turned leaden, iron encompassing every part of him.

Panic shot through his mind as he struggled to move. "What the hells is this?"

"Enjoy your precious courtyard. It's all you'll see until after I've cleaned up this mess." Uriel slunk away, a sinister smile on his ruddy lips.

"No. This is impossible. You can't trap me." Matthias held his breath, pushing against the iron. But it wouldn't budge.

Snowflakes still fell, turning his vision into a flurry as he stared at the sky. The flakes rushed past him as if he soared through the stars themselves.

"I already have." Uriel's voice slithered around Matthias, even though he could no longer see him.

A door slammed shut.

Chapter 12

RAE HELD A SMALL BALL of fire in her hand, creating an eerie glow on Katrin's face as the woman led them through hidden walkways within the palace. "And you're sure this leads to the meeting room?"

The idea of Damien sitting down, alone, in a room with Uriel made her skin crawl.

If that creature catches any hint of what we're planning... or what Damien is....

Rae gulped, pushing the thoughts from her mind in time to hear Damien's voice enter it.

We're meeting in his private study. Panic tainted his tone, despite it being his Art that carried it into her mind.

Katrin glanced back, studying the tunnels. "Assuming he's still using the same meeting room as twenty years ago, then yes."

"Hold on." Rae stopped, waiting for anything else from her husband, but his voice didn't come. "They're meeting in Matthias's private study."

Katrin's eyes widened as she faced Rae. "What? How do you—"

"Doesn't matter. Just something we do. Is it normal for him to take meetings in his personal chambers?"

Her gaze became distant before she turned and wriggled past Rae in the tight corridor. "This way."

She continued onto a set of dark stairs, holding her skirts up around her ankles. The young woman moved with more certainty in her step, as if she fully accepted what was about to transpire. She showed no fear of the death that threatened her should they fail.

The hem of her skirt dragged through the thick layer of dust on the ground, which confirmed the passageways likely hadn't been used through the duration of her Slumber.

"We haven't quite figured out how to get you in close to where we're meeting without the palace guards spotting you." Damien had confessed the night before after finishing a glass of whisky. "We think they'll protest a cloaked figure, companion of a visiting advisor or not. And we don't want to risk you being recognized."

"It's been twenty years. I doubt any of the guards are the same in the palace. Besides, wouldn't Uriel have changed his crown elites to people he'd trust?" Liam had accepted the second offer of whisky Damien made, but nursed it.

"Even more reason to avoid the hallways." Rae lounged against the wall at the head of the bed, bouncing her foot where she crossed her legs.

"Then we don't use the main halls." Katrin looked up, meeting Rae's curious look. "I know another way in."

"The passageways." Dani straightened. "Gods, it's been so long, I forgot they were there."

Katrin's face had hardened at the comment, and Rae could only imagine what it was like for her with all those lost years. At least the auer had only put her in Slumber for a day or two to erase her memories.

"I can go with you." Dani sat beside Katrin.

"I think it would be better if you stayed with Liam. You two are former crown elites. If you walked into the palace, that would garner some attention, no?" Rae crossed her arms. "While you distract everyone, I'll be with Katrin, and I don't miss."

Rae stifled a cough as dust stuck to her lungs. She followed Katrin around another bend, maintaining her flame without loosening her hiding aura.

They'd climbed at least three sets of stairs, and woven around so many corners that Rae felt more lost than she ever had in the maze leading to the Ashen Hawks' headquarters.

"You're sure we're going the right way?"

"This is the passage I probably know the best." Katrin glanced at her, her tone quieted by the heaves for breath after the rapid ascent of stairs. "If they're meeting in his private chambers, that means Uriel must be nervous about something. It's not traditional unless there's a need for further security."

"Probably that his walking deal-breaker is loose," Rae grumbled. "If we succeed and Matthias jumps back, how are we going to know?"

Katrin brushed a cobweb aside, shaking it from her fingertips. "I'll know."

"Good. Cause I'd rather not kill you twice."

"You won't remember the first time if you have to do it again."

This is so confusing.

"Right." Rae rolled her shoulders.

Katrin lifted her finger to her lips in a quick signal as they turned another dusty corner. She reached for Rae, a trickle of her energy passing through the air towards the flame Rae held. It tugged gently on the Art, and the little flame hopped to Katrin's waiting palm. Lifting it ahead, she stepped over a jut of stone into a more narrow passage that forced her to turn sideways.

Rae slid through the narrow space with Katrin, voices

murmuring from the other side of the wall. Specific words were lost, but she recognized Damien's tone.

Making eye contact with Katrin, she lifted a finger and tapped her temple. The plan required the acolyte to connect with Dani, giving the Dtrüa and Liam the signal to approach the palace and hopefully draw Uriel temporarily from the room.

Katrin's chest swelled with a deep breath, the bubble Rae could sense around her Art hardening as she closed her eyes. After what felt like an eternity, her eyes fluttered open, an odd milky sheen flickering across them before restoring to her umber irises. She met Rae's gaze and gave a quick nod.

Now we wait.

Rae flexed her hand, feeling the familiar click of her rings against each other. A spark of Damien's energy reverberated through the space with them, still contained beneath her aura. She shrugged her weapon from her shoulder, closing her hand on the leather grip of her old short bow. Reaching over her shoulder, she ran her thumb along the thicker fletching of the two arrows she'd prepared with the poultice crafted from Matthias's blood.

A knock came from the other side of the wall, and Damien's voice disappeared.

Murmuring came from multiple people, and an annoyed timbre tainted the king's voice.

Rae squeezed her bow, her palm heating against the leather.

The door closed again, silence settling.

Now. Go up. Damien's tone tensed.

Rae nudged Katrin and snuffed out her flame.

The acolyte moved quickly, pushing her boots against the seemingly solid wall ahead of her. She braced her back against the stone behind her as she shoved with her legs, her skirts tucked into the sides of her belt.

The stone groaned as it slid over the threshold for the first few inches, then Katrin caught herself as it moved easier. She glanced at Rae, light brightening her determined face. The look told her not to hesitate, no matter what.

Rae nodded, and Katrin turned from her, slipping out into the vibrant light of the study.

The Mira'wyld followed, taking in the large room full of books and a second-story balcony lining the upper wall. She glanced at Damien, who stood near the only door to the room, before leaping for the bottom of the thin iron railing and pulling herself up underneath it. She rolled onto her side, steadying her breath as she watched the others, and drew one of the spelled arrows from her quiver.

Stone ground again as Damien heaved against the bookshelf displaced by their entrance, while Katrin's soft footsteps rushed towards the two-story window that overlooked Nema's Throne.

The temple spires shimmered in the summer sun, a distant thunderstorm looming on the western horizon.

The acolyte hopped onto the bench seat nestled beneath the window, wrapping herself in the thick navy curtains.

Rae met Damien's eyes as he smoothed the fabric of his fine silk tunic and checked the sleeve button that concealed the tattoos that might have revealed to Uriel what he was. She'd gotten used to seeing him in high collared shirts while in the courts of Helgath, always hiding the runes of the Rahn'ka she loved to trace.

His jaw tightened, his face taking on a look similar to the one he always had before needing to make a large formal address in the palace. He gave her one quick nod, and it conveyed everything to her without him needing to speak in her head.

Be smart, be safe. And run if I tell you to.

Rae's heart raced, but she nodded, rolling onto her back and out of sight as footsteps approached the study door again.

This is it.

They'd discussed killing Katrin before Uriel re-entered the room, but the chance of someone returning other than the king himself kept that off the table. Matthias needed to see her, not his guards.

The footsteps, at a fast pace, reached the door, and it swung open with greater force than necessary.

"Please tell me you're there. You're alive. Katrin?" Matthias breathed hard, and Rae furrowed her brow.

Did we already succeed?

Rae didn't move, her palm sweaty around the bow.

"Your majesty?" A tinge of panic tainted Damien's voice, too genuine to be his acting.

The thick material of curtains rustled.

"You jumped already?" Katrin's voice. "Matthias?"

"It's me." The king, unconcerned with Damien, rushed across the room, and Rae tilted her head to get a glimpse of him embracing the acolyte.

She pushed against his chest, pulling back from his embrace and staring up at him.

Damien paced behind the king, the look of confusion on his face changed to suspicion.

Unease eked through Rae's chest.

This doesn't feel right.

Katrin touched the king's cheek.

"King Rayeht?" Damien prompted, his knuckles flexing as he prepared to break the hold on his power if necessary.

Matthias ignored him. "How are you in the palace? How did you get free?" He finally glanced at Damien, and Rae shifted out of sight again.

He doesn't know I'm here. Which means I never killed her. That's not Matthias.

Katrin didn't speak, cupping his face with her other hand. "None of that matters. I came for you."

Rae peeked again, grateful Katrin kept Matthias's gaze away from the balcony. Sucking in a deep breath, she rolled over and nocked the arrow. Pulling it taut on her bowstring, she aimed for Matthias's back.

The stun will only last a few seconds.

Barely able to hear over her pulse, she loosed the arrow.

Uriel cried out as he buckled forward into Katrin, but she slipped free of his grip.

Darkness boiled up beneath Uriel's hands as he caught himself, but they twitched feebly, strength sapped by the toxin on the arrowhead now wreathed with wriggling shadows.

Rae yanked another arrow from her quiver, taking aim at Katrin.

"You!" Uriel's gaze found Rae's face. "You dare interfere again? Where is Amarie?" His voice boomed through the room, rattling her bones.

A commotion rose outside of the room, but Damien had moved to the door, sliding the lock into place as thunderous knocks rained down with shouts of concern.

Peeling her eyes off the king, Rae looked at Katrin as the acolyte turned to expose her chest to the Ashen Hawk. The subtle nod encouraged her hand to release the arrow.

"Death is too merciful. I will destroy you all!" The voice

that came from the king was not his own, tainted by the timbre of a more sinister tongue.

The arrow cut through the air, sinking into Katrin's heart.

Chapter 13

MATTHIAS STRAINED AGAINST THE IRON holding him on the courtyard ground. Snow piled around him, but he couldn't feel its cold. He squeezed his eyes shut, heaving imaginary breath.

This isn't real.

Images played through his mind of all the wickedness Uriel could inflict with him unaware. The damage he could cause Katrin.

If he jumps, I'd never know.

The king shouted, struggling against the iron. "Let me out!" He flexed against the bars, maintaining the pressure as he held his breath before collapsing again.

Somewhere on the gloomy horizon, he swore he could hear Uriel's twisted laughter.

"Asshole," Matthias muttered, closing his eyes. He gritted his jaw, piecing together the day and when Uriel might have an opportunity to find Katrin.

How long has it even been since he ensnared me here?

He recalled the sun setting before Alana had come with the news of Katrin's escape. The shadows cast along the rugs through his private chambers. The next day had been packed with meetings, but with the news of Katrin... Matthias betted he would move all his meetings to his private study. One meeting was with a foreign diplomat, the name etched in his memory from his venture to greet Helgath's new ruler.

He'd met King Jarrod Martox years before, but the meeting here in Isalica would be with his personal advisor, Damien Lanoret. Images of the man's bearded face jumped into his mind, despite the years, having felt a kinship with the rebels.

The two had overcome immense odds to reclaim a kingdom under a just leader, and Matthias had basked in their success. The bond between Martox and his wolf had reminded him of Dani.

"Rumor suggests you can speak with your namesake, wolf-king." Uriel had grinned at Martox, glancing at the black wolf resting by the ornate throne.

The beast's amber eyes opened to peer across the ballroom at him, tongue flicking over his lips before he placed his head back on his massive paws.

Jarrod laughed, but his matching amber eyes gave nothing away. "It would sure make combat more interesting. Nothing quite like having drakes, though. And a few wyverns, if I remember correctly. Impressive, and plenty of rumor still surrounds how your country accomplished to sway the creatures after Feyor held the monopoly of their kin."

Uriel chuckled, rolling with the deflection like any good politician. "Much easier to fight alongside them than against. I can't imagine a more daunting enemy."

The Helgathian king smirked, eyes flickering to the wolf again. "I don't know. If it has blood that can spill, or a head it can lose, then killing it is straightforward. I believe the most daunting would be the one up here." He tapped his temple, his voice lowering. "I find we can be our own worst enemy. Yet, this is the place of our own greatest power." He lowered his hand, the chandelier light flickering off his gold wedding band.

Uriel tilted his head, but before he could speak, another man joined them.

He looked similar to Damien, but with his hair closer cropped and thin laugh lines at the corner of his eyes. The king consort stepped close to Jarrod, the movement intimate even though the men didn't touch.

"I apologize for interrupting, but I need to steal my husband from your company, King Rayeht." Corin had been introduced earlier, even though neither Matthias nor Uriel had needed it. He was as infamous a Lanoret as his brother.

Jarrod gave Uriel an apologetic smile, nodding to his husband. "Excuse me."

Matthias's memory faded, King Martox's previous words resounding through him again.

This is the place of our own greatest power.

The Isalican king suddenly wondered what experience Martox had in fighting the Corrupted of his mind.

The words echoed again.

Our own greatest power.

Matthias stilled. "This isn't real." He slowed his breath and touched the iron. "This is *my* mind. I can control it just as much as he can." Gritting his teeth, he imagined the cage turning to dust.

The iron shivered, then crumbled. It disintegrated before his eyes, floating away like snow on an invisible breeze.

Gasping, he stood, wiping the remnants from his clothing. He closed his eyes, willing them to open to reality. He tried to blink, but his body still wouldn't respond beneath the invader's control.

Uriel's glare held steady on a vaguely familiar woman laying on the upper level of his private study with a bow aimed near him.

Who is that? I know her from somewhere.

Pain pulsed from his back, and he realized an arrow had already hit him.

Why isn't Uriel moving?

Confusion muddled his awareness as he tried to place the woman's face.

"Where is Amarie?" Uriel's shout shook Matthias's memory.

The woman from Hoult. She was with Amarie.

He inwardly smiled at the person who'd saved the Berylian Key from a most undeserved fate.

But why...

Uriel's vision followed the woman's next arrow as it sliced through the air and sank into Katrin's chest.

"Katrin!" Matthias made the yell, and for the first time, the word echoed from his lips.

Nothing else moved.

Katrin didn't fall, her body frozen with the arrow jutting out of her torso. Wisps of her hair floated as if underwater with the start of her collapse, a peaceful expression on her face.

The king side stepped, looking at the other two people in the room also frozen in time. His eyes settled on the man with his hand on the door's lock.

King Martox's personal advisor. Damien.

His shoulder screamed where the arrow protruded from his upper back, waves of pain undiluted by the parasite who controlled his body. Matthias spun, suddenly able to move his own feet, and stared behind him.

Where he'd stood, the fiend heaved as if desperate for air, blackness vibrating outside of his body. The gangled form of shadow shifted in and out around him, as if he couldn't control it.

Matthias looked again at Katrin and the frozen splash of crimson around the arrowhead. He reached over his own shoulder, fingers wet with his blood. He winced and yanked the arrow shaft from his body, gritting his teeth.

He whirled back to Uriel, fists tight. "Our deal is broken."

The beast panted, long, shadowed limbs unable to claw at the blue glow of a ghostly rod protruding from its shoulder.

The arrow. I know that Art.

"Get out." The words felt as powerful as the energy emanating from whatever held Uriel in place.

Runes danced along its shaft, a halo searing Uriel's black form.

Matthias glanced from the arrow to the woman who'd loosed it. The Art it contained vibrated in a way that reminded him of the pulse lingering at ruins Uriel visited in Feyor.

How does she wield that power? And how is it keeping him frozen?

Matthias returned his gaze to the monster, his back hunched and exposed. The king thrust the bloody arrow into his blackened flesh. "I said get out!" He grabbed Uriel by the shoulders and heaved him across the study.

The charred beast slammed into the study door, barely missing Damien. The door broke from its frame, sending Uriel rolling down the hallway.

Wood splintered, and the guards who'd been on the other side froze mid-air in their collision.

Matthias gaped at his hands.

How did I do that?

Uriel lay still for a breath, and the vibrant blue light of the Rahn'ka winked out. His body convulsed, claws raking gashes into the carpet. Darkness writhed around him as he rose to his feet. The endless void of his gaze pierced through Matthias, and he took a slow step forward.

He surged back into the study. His tendrils lashed along the walls, displacing books. They slithered like vipers, dancing along the deep shadows before shooting out of the gaps towards Matthias.

Razors lashed.

They tore into his skin as he lifted his arm to protect himself. The black vines wrapped tight, yanking him off balance as Uriel charged like a bull.

Specks of black flecked to the carpet. The beast's thick shoulders sprouted spines, tar dripping from their tips.

Tar that reeked of rotten flesh.

Fuck.

Matthias braced himself, but the monster plowed him backward into his mahogany desk.

Thunder rattled around them as the furniture crashed to the floor, scattering the maps and parchment. Wood groaned, cracking as Uriel pushed Matthias down.

The king's neck screamed as the back of his skull impacted the floor. Urging his muscles to respond, he slammed his legs into the creature's concave chest.

Uriel reeled back, his shadows grappling at his wrists to cease his tumble. The power wriggled from his fingertips, seething up to the shelves surrounding them. More wood shuddered as the cases collapsed beneath the weight of the tendrils, raining books and debris on them.

The king grunted and rolled away, bracing on the broken desk to stagger to his feet. "You can't be here anymore!"

"You're nothing." The creature lumbered forward, claws scraping along the floor. His body twitched, mouth transforming into a forlorn scream before reforming the wicked grin. Different forms flickered, unable to coalesce solidly within the daylight streaming through the window. The beast's shadow behind Uriel convulsed, shrinking with a high-pitched whine around the halo of blue still emanating from the arrow.

"I am king!" Matthias charged, grappling Uriel backward until a squelch of flesh ruptured through the beast's body. The king stepped back, eyeing the giant splinter skewering the monster's torso.

Uriel glanced down at the wood impaling him, his chin

slowly lifting as the voids of his eyes met Matthias's. A jagged claw traced the edge of the wooden shard before he stepped forward. The flesh tore and rippled around the wood, but no pain showed in the creature's face.

"You're weak. Incapable and unworthy. I am eternal." The parasite's taloned hand reached out, snatching Matthias's throat as he jerked free of the wood.

Matthias struggled against his grip, wheezing for air as the beast walked them backward. Debris crunched under Uriel's feet, but Matthias's boots barely touched the carpet.

"Accept your fate. You're mine."

The king abandoned trying to free himself, eyes returning to the arrow shaft.

He lunged.

Grasping the shaft protruding from Uriel's shoulder, a spark of lightning ruptured down the king's spine, but he refused to let go. He tore the arrow free before plunging it into the creature's side. It sank into his flesh, and he thrust it deeper under Uriel's ribs. "I am yours no longer."

The creature howled, grip slackening as he recoiled. Black oozed from the wound on his side, dribbling to the carpet. Uriel lowered his head, baring wicked obsidian fangs as his body morphed further. A flash of shadow echoed a dog-like shape, curled horns erupting from his forehead. Massive wings beat in the study's air, shaking the few books still upright free of their resting places.

Matthias's heart thundered, and he spread his feet into a fighting stance. "You're done. It's over."

Sulfur mixed with decay as Uriel's shape condensed, the shadow of wings wrapping around his gangly limbs. Head turning, he focused behind Matthias before lunging. He twisted past the king, claws pointed at Katrin, still frozen in time.

Charging, Matthias landed a heavy kick to Uriel's midsection. "Get out!"

The beast lurched, stumbling, and staggered sideways over the windowsill.

Glass shattered as Uriel toppled through, shadows flailing in the air. His body and power vanished as it plummeted.

Matthias ran to the window, panting as he searched the ground for the fallen creature, but found nothing. He scanned the sky, but it, too, hovered hauntingly empty. As if it all had been a dream.

With a whoosh, life resumed in the courtyard below, and Matthias spun to face the room.

Katrin fell, and he spurred his feet forward, catching her before she hit the floor.

"What the hells..." Liam's voice echoed through the room as he stepped over the shattered bits of the study's door, glancing at the thrown guards in the hallway.

Damien groaned as he rocked to his feet, blood welling from a quill-sized splinter in his shoulder. He tore it from his flesh with a huff.

His former crown elite froze as his eyes met Matthias's, a hand moving back to touch Dani and stop her from entering the room.

Two more guards pushed past them, staring at the destruction, then their king. "Your majesty..." One guard turned to the other. "Send for the crown elites. And the king's personal healer."

"No." Matthias looked away and stared at Katrin's face, touching her cheek as his eyes heated. "Stand down. Leave us."

"Sir?"

"Leave us!" Matthias's voice rocked through the room.

The guards remained only a breath longer before scurrying out.

Silence descended, as all seemed to wait for another to break it.

"Don't move." The woman on the balcony pointed another drawn arrow at him, and he shook his head.

"Uriel's gone." Matthias swallowed, looking at Katrin again. "I need to jump. I must save her."

A hand closed on Matthias's shoulder, and he gazed up to meet Liam's eyes. He looked older, yet still just as strong as the crown elite he'd promoted so many years ago.

Liam's eyes drifted to Katrin, a deep sting echoing through them. "Not yet. We have time. Prove it's you."

Matthias breathed hard, scouring his mind for what proof he could offer. "How?"

Damien stepped forward, the collar of his shirt displaced just enough to expose a navy tattoo along the left side of his neck.

I know those markings.

Damien pressed his fingers to the wound on his chest. "We suspect there are things that Matthias never told Uriel. Name some of those things that Liam would know."

Matthias narrowed his eyes at the personal advisor, suddenly far more curious about Damien's role in all that had happened. He looked far too put-together considering the room around him had imploded and a woman lay dead on the floor.

The king cleared his throat. "Katrin is pregnant. I never told Uriel that. I never told him about Zaelinstra, either." He laid Katrin's head down, rising to his feet as the archer's arrow tracked his movement.

"And Uriel? Can you say something of him you learned that he'd never share?" Damien stepped calmly forward.

Matthias eyed the advisor. "I've seen his true form. We fought, just now, here. I... I kicked him out the window, but he disappeared."

"Not exactly what I was looking for." Damien faced

Matthias, looking up to meet his eyes.

Throwing his hands up, Matthias stalked closer to Damien. "What do you want me to do? Recount each evil he committed with *my* hands just to prove I've witnessed everything he's capable of?"

"Not a step closer!" the woman on the balcony shouted.

"What are you?" Matthias motioned with his chin to the exposed tattoos. "High collars in summer. You want to hide that, Rahn'ka?"

Damien winced, touching the collar. "Shit. How..."

"I saw the body of a woman who had similar markings. Uriel despised her.. Hunted her like a deer because he feared her. But..." Matthias closed his eyes, and flashes of horrible memories made his chest ache. Gritting his teeth, his neck twitched and knuckles popped. "She killed herself before Uriel could question her. I am not your enemy."

Damien's body stilled, every muscle tensing as he studied the king's face. "We'll see." The Rahn'ka's hand shot out and gripped behind Matthias's neck, pressing his other to the man's chest. A sudden wave of heat entered him, scorching through every vein as a strange tingling sensation poked and prodded.

Matthias's vision flashed pale blue, etched with runes like those that'd been around the arrow in Uriel's back. He blinked them away as Damien's eyes met his, and the Rahn'ka's shoulders loosened.

"It's true." Damien's arm fell to his side, his voice hovering in disbelief, and he glanced up at the woman on the second level as she lowered her bow. "Uriel is gone."

The tension in the room vanished as if everyone inside let out a collective exhale.

"Katrin?" Liam stepped closer to his sister, looking at Matthias. "We hoped you could..."

"I need to jump, but I should take one of you with me." The king looked between Damien and Liam. "Who's it going to be?"

"Me." Damien held out his hand, ignoring Liam's scowl. "It'll be easier not to convince me again."

Matthias grasped Damien's forearm. "Brace yourself." He flooded his veins with the Art and yanked on the threads of time to pull them backward.

Chapter 14

KATRIN'S HEART POUNDED, HER BREATH echoing in her ears as she angled her chest towards Rae. She closed her eyes, already welcoming the pain that would come when the arrow struck her.

"No!" Matthias's voice snapped her eyes open as his arms encircled her, spinning her sideways with him as Rae's arrow shattered the window behind her.

Katrin fought to free herself of him after they collided with the window frame, but his grip held strong.

"Rae, break off!" Damien's shout echoed through the room and thunderous knocking started on the door.

Matthias abruptly let go of Katrin, his eyes meeting hers. He panted, holding up an empty hand as he leaned on the frame. "Gooseberries," he whispered, cringing and glancing over his shoulder at his back. Blood smeared over the wood as he staggered.

Hope radiated, and Katrin forgot how to breathe. "Matthias?" She touched his chin, encouraging his gaze back to hers. Heat rose in her eyes. "Please, tell me it's you."

"It's me, Kat." The king gestured to the Rahn'ka. "Damien?"

"He's free of Uriel." Damien nodded as Rae stood from her hiding place on the balcony. He eyed the door where Liam's voice now echoed through the wood, demanding to be let in. "Think you can get the guards to leave again?"

Matthias nodded with a pained expression.

Katrin sobbed as she threw herself against him, avoiding his injury.

Burying his face in her hair, Matthias breathed deeper. "Gods, is this really happening?"

The door to the study burst open, Liam and Dani rushing in first, followed by four guards.

"Your majesty!" One turned to the other guard. "Hurry, fetch the crown elites and the king's personal healer."

"No. Leave us. I have a healer here." Matthias didn't move, his hands shaking where they touched her sides. "Do not question my order. Go."

The guards hesitated but backed out of the room, shutting the door behind them.

Liam looked at Damien in silent question, and he nodded.

Damien strode closer, putting a hand on Matthias's injured shoulder. He pushed his palm to Matthias's back, making the king grimace.

Katrin slid her hands up to join his, reaching for her Art.

"I've got it." Damien assured her, and Katrin watched as blue flickered down Damien's fingertips and rushed into Matthias. The surge of the Rahn'ka's energy felt so different from her own as it started the healing process.

She tore her eyes away as she reached for Matthias's jaw again, cupping his face in her hands and staring at him in wonder. Brushing a hand back through his thick hair, she brought her lips to his forehead and kissed him. His skin had never tasted sweeter. "I'm so sorry," she whispered.

Matthias shook his head, growling as the healing continued. "None of this is your fault." His eyes met hers, laced with deep sorrow. "You freed me."

A relieved sob escaped her as she pressed another kiss to his cheek, then to his lips.

The king broke the kiss quickly, the muscles at his jaw flexing before he examined the others in the room.

Damien stepped away as Liam and Dani approached.

"I owe you all the greatest debt." Matthias looked at Liam and let out a breath. "I'm so glad you're safe. There's something I need to tell you, though."

Liam interrupted whatever he might say next by pulling Matthias into a rough hug, emotion welling in his tired eyes.

"Later," he gruffed. "But if it's about Ryen, we already know."

Matthias let go of Katrin's hand to embrace Dani at the same time, squeezing them both.

The Dtrüa's eyes gleamed with tears as she pressed into Matthias, a quiet sob shaking her shoulders.

Katrin watched Matthias as his body tensed. She expected him to grip Dani tighter, but he withdrew from them, his face grim.

The king stepped back and looked up at Rae as she put a foot over the railing above. "Who *are* you?"

Rae jumped down from the balcony, her bow again over her shoulder. "I'm Rae. A Mira'wyld and Damien's wife. I recognized you at the palace in Helgath when you... *he* visited a year after Jarrod's coronation."

"Damien's wife... You were pregnant, yes? Too ill to attend the evening." Matthias's voice held a thoughtful air, and he shook his head. "You saw me first, didn't you? And recognized him... me, from Hoult?"

The Mira'wyld nodded. "I didn't know if Uriel had seen my face, and I couldn't risk him seeing me in the palace."

"He did. He saw you when you saved Amarie. You made a good choice." Matthias ran a hand through his hair, cringing. "Thank you, for what you did. For me, for Katrin... Amarie. Is she safe?"

"She is." Rae glanced at Damien.

"She's in Eralas. In Slumber. With Kin." Damien crossed his arms.

Matthias's gaze shot to Damien. "They're together?"

Katrin furrowed her brow, squeezing Matthias's wrist.

The king flinched and looked at her hand, his body stiffening.

"They don't know it, but they are together." Rae sighed.

Katrin recoiled from Matthias, the knots in her stomach growing tighter.

Does he not want me to touch him?

"We don't need to talk about this right now." Damien stepped closer. "How are you feeling, King Rayeht?"

Matthias drew a shaky breath, squeezing his eyes closed before looking at the Rahn'ka. "I don't know. And you've more than earned the right to call me by my name."

Lingering nausea rumbled in Katrin's stomach, and she touched where she prayed her child still grew.

I'll ask Damien to check again later.

Looking up at Matthias, she stared at the tiredness in his eyes but resisted reaching for him. "Perhaps some sleep?"

Clearing his throat, Matthias shook his head again. "No, I don't think so. I have too much to do. Starting with—"

"With all due respect, it can wait." Something in Damien's stance added to his confidence. "You *must* rest and take some time. Your ká is... in tatters. It will take time for you to return to old routines. You'll have to be patient with yourself."

Matthias crossed to his desk, opening a lower drawer, and retrieved a handful of shiny objects. Tossing them on the desktop, he looked from the two steel crown elite insignias to Dani and Liam. "I need both of you. If you want them."

Liam tensed, casting his gaze to the floor. "We hardly deserve the offer with how long it took us to free you from that thing. And..." He looked at his sister, shame in his eyes. "Wake Katrin."

The king's gaze lowered, his breath coming faster. "Are you declining?"

"No." Dani's soft voice preceded the click of her tongue as she advanced, nudging Liam before she passed him and took the insignia. "I'm honored to serve at your side once again."

Liam nodded as he approached behind his wife. "It's good to have you back."

Katrin watched Matthias as he leaned against his desk, weariness radiating from every inch of him. She frowned as she crossed the lush carpet to return to his side. She hesitated with her hand on the desk beside his. "Come. Let's at least get you some tea in our chambers. Give you some time to... adjust."

"Our chambers..." Matthias sounded confused at first, but he backed away from the desk. "No. I don't want to go in there. Not until..."

"I can have the room cleaned," Dani offered. "The bedding changed, and the wardrobe replaced."

Matthias nodded. "Please ask the staff to arrange rooms for yourselves, as well."

"We'll take care of the details." Liam pinned the insignia to his shoulder, patting it like it was an old friend.

"You can use my chambers in the interim." Damien stepped aside. "But you must rest. When was the last time you slept?"

Matthias looked up, his eyelids fluttering as his mouth opened. He paused, swallowing. "Twenty years? Give or take."

Katrin winced, stopping herself from reaching for him again. While it had been merely like falling asleep for the night to her, it'd been so very long for him. So many years of torture and destruction that he'd surely witnessed.

His skin probably doesn't even feel like his own anymore.

Katrin looked at Dani, then met her brother's stern gaze. "Can you please have some tea sent up to Damien's chambers, but tell the staff to leave the cart at the door. I think it's best if we all give Matthias some time to adjust." Her hand hovered over his shoulder, her entire body aching to take him into her embrace. She gestured with her chin towards the door. "Come. I'll walk with you."

Matthias nodded, straightening from the desk and taking a deeper breath as he walked towards the study's exit.

Liam followed, but froze when Damien lifted a hand.

"May I have a word, before you go?" Something in the Rahn'ka's gaze suggested the seriousness of the coming conversation, but Katrin ignored it as she guided Matthias past.

They can worry about everything else. Matthias is my focus now.

Dani opened the study door, pausing when a guard took a step towards her, and tapped the emblem on her shoulder.

The guard fell back into position and saluted, a puzzled look on his face.

Matthias followed her out and looked at the guard. "Crown Elites Varadani and Liam Talansiet will take command of the crown guard. All other crown elites are hereby dismissed. My former personal healer, Alana Di'Terian, is now wanted for treason and is to be killed on sight. She is extremely dangerous and should not be approached alone. Do you understand?"

"Your majesty." The guard lifted his fist to his chest in salute, but the look of confusion deepened. "For such orders, you will—"

"I will see to it." Katrin hardened her gaze, not recognizing the young man's face. He'd likely been a child when she last set foot in the palace. The thought made her dizzy, but she squared her shoulders. "Send the king's advisors to me in Lord Damien Lanoret's chambers, or they may report to

Crown Elites Varadani and Liam. We thank you for your discretion in this."

Matthias kept walking, his stature rigid, yet weary as he rounded a corner ahead.

Dani touched Katrin's shoulder. "He will need time. I will take care of the rest of his wishes. You go with him."

Katrin closed her hand over Dani's as she nodded. "I know. And thank you. We'll get through this." She began down the hallway after Matthias, but paused as a thought entered her mind. Turning back, she saw the guard disappear into the corridor. "Did he really convince the kingdom I was dead?"

Dani hesitated. "He did."

Katrin frowned, straightening her skirt as she looked at the guard who remained, a quizzical look on his face as he looked between the two women. "Then it shall be interesting to reveal that Katrin Talansiet is very much alive."

The guard's eyes widened.

Good, let him spread the word.

Katrin turned, stepping loud enough for Dani to hear her.

Matthias had disappeared towards the guest chambers.

So much of the palace still looked the same. Tall glass windows dominated most of the walls, extra thick to resist the winter storms and support the structure. From a distance, the upper levels of the palace resembled shards of crystal, white marble making up the lower portion.

Katrin slowed to watch the storm clouds from the west roll

in over the city. Her city. Nema's Throne remained the jewel of Isalica, and the sun pushing through the grey sky shone on the glazed clay roofs of the various districts. The roads wove like spiderwebs, only identifiable because of the break in pattern between the buildings. Smoke rose from the eastern district where the tradespeople worked, despite the rush of wind that rattled the trees along the promenade to the palace steps.

The beauty made her chest ache, grateful for the moment to appreciate what she'd almost lost.

But I almost lost so much more.

She heaved in a deep breath, banishing the memory of Matthias's face when it hadn't been his. Pursing her lips, she breathed again.

We will fix this. All of this.

She turned from the window, determined steps carrying her down the hall at a quickened pace after Matthias. She rounded the corner down the lofty hallway that housed the palace guests, spying Matthias as he paused at the distant door.

A sunbeam streamed through the window on the opposite side of the hall, casting his strong shadow over the paneled door. He stared at it, his body tense.

A royal staff member stood behind him to the side, talking too quietly for Katrin to hear.

She hurried her step, near skipping along the decorative ice-blue rug. "Matthias?"

The king jumped, making the staff member flinch, too. He looked at the uniformed woman as if seeing her for the first time. "Leave us."

Katrin gave her an apologetic smile. "The king would prefer to be undisturbed for a time. Please, go." She slid in beside Matthias, careful not to touch him as she went for the knob on the door and twisted. Pushing it open, she looked at the room beyond, where natural light flooded in from the row of windows that led to a grand terrace. Several stood ajar, the wind rustling the sheer white curtains as it rushed towards the new channel of escape.

Matthias strode inside, tugging at the collar of his formal coat. Crossing to the open windows, he stood before them and touched the glass. "This feels like a dream."

Katrin guided the door shut as quietly as she could, never taking her eyes from Matthias. "I promise it's not." She leaned against the door, her knees weak. Looking at his face, it seemed as if far more than twenty years had passed, and yet no time at all. "Matthias..." She breathed his name, trying to find the right next words. "Tell me what you need. Anything."

"I don't know how to live," the king whispered, his voice rougher than normal. "This is no longer my life."

"Then we'll make it yours again." She stepped forward, despite how unstable her feet felt. "It is yours. It's not too late for us, either. None of this was your fault."

"Of course it was." Matthias's tone hollowed. "I agreed."

She stepped around him, placing herself between him and the window. Lifting her hand, she made sure he saw it before she pressed it to his cheek. "You didn't have a choice. You couldn't have done anything different. It was an impossible situation."

His jaw flexed. "You don't know what my hands have done."

"They weren't your hands." Katrin reached for him, entwining their fingers.

Matthias pulled away, stepping backward as he shook his head. "Tell that to the man who died, over and over again, begging for mercy from the benevolent *King Rayeht*." He bowed his chin, cringing as his voice lowered. "Or the people before him. Or the people after."

Katrin watched the shadows on his face, wishing she could wipe them all away. "I cannot imagine the hells you've been through. But they're over now. You're you, and we have a chance to fix all this. To make Uriel pay for all the suffering he's caused." She held her breath as she ran her hands down over her abdomen. "We have a chance to be a family again."

His brow knitted. "I'm not the same person, Kat."

"I don't expect you to be, but please... you can't blame yourself for all of this." She dared a step, but paused when he mirrored the movement away. Her heart cracked. "Will you try to sleep?"

"I missed you." Matthias tilted his head, and a lock of hair fell over his forehead. "Every moment. I longed to see your face."

"I'm here," she whispered, lifting her hands.

"I know." The king's jaw worked, and he took a step closer to take her hands. "But I'm afraid I'm not."

She furrowed her brow as she closed her fingers around his. His skin felt warm, and a flutter of relief washed through her. She took a careful step into him, still holding on. "Damien said the creature is gone. I trust him."

"Oh, he's gone." Matthias studied her hands. "Assuming that was all real, he's definitely gone."

"This will take time." She rubbed her thumb along his.

"Don't make me sleep."

She met his eyes, unable to hide her sadness. "You're sure it won't make you feel better? It's been so long..."

"I'll lie down, but only if you stay, and I can't promise I'll sleep."

She nodded, reaching to brush a strand of his hair behind his ear. "I'll stay." She tugged gently on his hand, urging him to the four-poster bed. White satin drapes hung at the edges, the rich blue bedding inviting. She released Matthias, sitting on the bed first and patting the spot beside her. "I've missed holding you."

The king's chest rose faster. "I can't."

Katrin pursed her lips, wishing she knew the right things to say. "What do you need? What will make you comfortable?"

Matthias gritted his teeth, taking a steadying breath before answering her. "If I knew, I'd tell you. But all I know is I can't hold you. I can't touch you. These aren't my hands, and I can't..." He looked away, emotion glazing his eyes. "Uriel, and all the death, and Alana... I can't..."

Katrin shook her head and scooted further back onto the bed to make more room. "Then I'll just sit here beside you. You don't need to touch me until you feel ready. But whatever Uriel might have done, it wasn't you. And they weren't your hands that did it."

Approaching the bed, Matthias touched the silk sheets before sitting. He looked at her, pain clouding his eyes. "I'm sorry," he murmured, letting out a breath and lying on his side to face her.

"You have nothing to apologize to me for, Prince." The old nickname slid off her tongue.

The hint of a smile twitched his lips. "I've been demoted?"

Her cheeks heated. "Of course not. It's just... still new to me as odd as that might be."

"It's new to me, too." Matthias reached across the bedding and took her hand.

She smiled, brushing her thumb along his skin. "I love

you," she whispered. "I've loved you every moment."

Matthias closed his eyes but squeezed her hand. "And I, you, Priestess."

Her heart thudded.

A light rap sounded against the door, and she jumped, but Matthias didn't. His breathing came in even slowness, his grip on her hand slack as he slept.

Thank the gods.

Katrin lifted her hand to her mouth, studying his face, finally peaceful. Emotion tightened her throat, and she rolled her lips together, exhaling a shaky breath. Moving her hand to his face, she hesitated over the vague lines at the corners of his eyes. They weren't as noticeable as Liam's, proving that Uriel had used his Art to keep the king young.

But he's aged in so many other ways. I'm the lucky one.

Her hand hovering over him, she withdrew and forced a deep breath. Heat rose in her eyes, despite all she'd done to hold in the tears. Her shoulders quaked as she fought to hold in the sob while slipping her hand from Matthias.

Scooting to the edge of the bed, she gripped fistfuls of the blankets, hoping to pull strength from them. She swallowed, forcing herself to her feet. Her hands brushed over her cheeks, wiping away the tears as she approached the door.

The smooth surface of the door cooled her fingertips as she lingered there, contemplating the pounding in her head.

Opening the door a crack, she met the Rahn'ka's warm

hazel eyes and saw the knowing in them.

She leaned to look behind him, relieved to see him alone as she sniffed. "He's asleep."

Damien looked over her head into the bedroom beyond and nodded. "I can help keep him that way. And..." He rubbed at the back of his neck. "We should talk. Privately."

A rock dropped in Katrin's stomach, and she fought to lock away remaining emotion. She nodded and opened the door wider.

Damien gave a grateful smile and picked up a tea tray from the table in the hall beside the door. The ceramic set looked so delicate in his calloused hands, hard worked for someone in his position.

There'd been so little time for her to ask questions about Rae and Damien, or their presence. Too many questions seemed an insult to all they promised to help with.

And what they've given back to me.

Damien moved silently across the room to the nook arranged with chairs and a small table for taking breakfast. He slid the set onto the surface without a single clink, his attention on the slumbering Matthias.

With her slow push, the door latched, a click echoing through the room. Katrin eyed Matthias, realizing how odd he looked sprawled on the bed.

He must be cold.

She bustled to his side, tugging the blanket free from the

base and draping it over his body. Her hands shook, but she didn't know why. Her knuckles brushed his shoulder before she could realize how close she was.

Matthias didn't move, his breathing even and deep.

"He won't wake while I'm here." Damien's voice was quiet, but not a whisper. "We can speak freely."

Katrin turned, staring at the Rahn'ka, and loosened her aura to investigate the man.

A thin string of energy ran from him to Matthias, which she suspected accomplished what he suggested. The power held no malice, but a comforting sensation.

"Can you help him?" Katrin blurted the question before she could talk herself out of asking more of the man who'd already helped so much. "He's... suffering."

Damien shook his head. "Not much. I can help him sleep, but his ká... his soul, is in turmoil. Beyond my ability to heal. He needs time to do it himself. And twenty years of damage... could take awhile."

Lowering her chin, Katrin stared at the rug. "I... just don't know how to help."

"Just be patient. Understanding. Those are the biggest ones. Your love will help." Damien stepped closer, drawing her gaze. "But there is no way for either of us to understand the horrors he's been through."

Heat rose in her eyes again, and Katrin stepped past Damien as tears welled. She rushed to wipe them away and crossed to the tea, lifting the lid to inspect the leaves in the pot before pouring a cup.

"You sound like you've been through a similar situation?" Katrin poured a second, offering it to Damien.

"I'm from Helgath. My country has had trying times in the past. And my wife and I were part of some tumultuous moments. There were... emotional repercussions for us as well. More for her, though, as she was held in Lazuli's prison for months enduring interrogation and torture." Damien came up beside her, accepting the offered cup. He moved to one chair, settling into it.

"They tortured her? She seems so... balanced."

Damien chuckled. "She puts on a good show. But she has healed over time. It took years, and in some ways, there are still pieces to put back together." He rested his cup on the arm of his chair as his other hand unfastened the buttons at his high collar.

The fabric parted, and Katrin stared at the navy tattoo that wove up the side of his neck. "Speaking to her might give me a better idea of how to help Matthias. Do you think she would mind?"

"No, she and I already discussed the possibilities of what the king might be facing. She's willing to help in any way she can, including sharing her own experiences." Damien tapped his thumb against the rim of his cup. "But Matthias's mental health is not the most pressing problem we should be discussing."

Katrin glanced at the chair she couldn't bring herself to sit in. Relaxing seemed impossible. Instead, she looked at the grand glass windows and doors that led to a small balcony.

The city lay beyond, the view as stunning as the one she'd enjoyed in the hall. Thunderclouds hid the sun, casting a dark shadow over the city districts.

"You think he'll attack, don't you? Uriel?" Katrin's stomach clenched, and she sought to calm it with a slow sip of her tea. It heated her body, but did little to comfort.

"We have to expect it." Damien spoke behind her, far too calm. "He'll try to make good on his threats to Matthias. The ones that made him say yes in the first place. We just have to hope that he's slowed down enough for us to prepare."

Katrin touched the window, running her finger along the spires of the temple. "He'll need a new host, first. Someone who will say yes, and has power of their own?"

"Seems a safe assumption. When Matthias reappointed Liam and Dani, he included an order to capture and execute someone named Alana. Do you know who that is?"

Katrin rested the rim of her cup against her lip, letting the steam from the tea soak into her senses. The memories of the moments after Matthias had been taken by the creature felt only a day away.

"That's the name of the auer Merissa... Uriel then, I suppose, brought into the palace. She was responsible for King Geroth's death and put me in Slumber. It seems she stayed in the creature's good graces for all these years." She turned, meeting Damien's inspecting gaze.

"An auer? That's a curious companion. Hadn't expected one of their kind to be helping him." Damien rubbed at his short blond beard. "She's logically our greatest threat, however."

"I'm sure Matthias knows more." Katrin glanced at the sleeping man, her shoulders drooping. "Uriel will want him dead if he can't have him back."

"I'll be surprised if Uriel doesn't put together what we're planning. He's been imprisoned before and will probably recognize the pieces coming together. He won't refrain like he has in the past." Damien drank from his cup, emptying it in one long swig. He leaned forward, placing it on the table before him. "The true battle for Pantracia will begin soon. And I hope we're all ready for it."

Katrin's body felt leaden, barely able to remain standing.

Damien stood, bowing his head to her briefly.

"Wait." Katrin rolled her shoulders, placing her half-full teacup on the table.

The Rahn'ka paused, meeting her gaze.

"We've been in a rush since you woke me in that chamber beneath the temple grounds. There are pieces to this I'm missing. If this is to be a battle for our world, isn't it best if all parties involved understand what is coming?"

Damien hesitated, taking uneven breaths. "There are a lot of complicated elements. Secrets..."

"They seem hardly fair for you to continue to keep, all things considered. If this is truly for all of Pantracia, Helgath cannot be the only ones—"

"I am not here on behalf of Helgath. It might have been a convenient way to gain an audience with the king, but all I've done here is as the Rahn'ka." Damien's eyes hardened.

"Can I trust if something arises that I should know, or that impacts Isalica, you'll tell me?"

"I will share all I can." Damien's jaw twitched. "You can trust me."

Katrin huffed. "I'm fairly certain there are children's stories about trusting Helgathians."

"Much has changed." Damien smiled. "And we are to be the instruments of more, if all goes as planned." He glanced at Matthias, an odd blue light flickering in his eyes. "I'd keep a physical distance from him while he's sleeping. I can only do so much for the dreams."

Katrin looked at Matthias, guessing at the turmoil in his mind, despite the peace on his face.

He's suggesting Matthias might hurt me.

She sucked in a breath and nodded as he paused beside the door. "Thank you. I don't want to seem ungrateful with all the questions... I mean it. Thank you."

Damien gave a charming smile. "Your understanding is thank you enough. Be ready, in case Uriel's strike comes. I'd suggest getting out of the city, but..." He looked at Matthias again. "I suspect that would cause greater complications."

Katrin nodded, knowing there would be enough gossip around her return. They didn't need the king mysteriously vanishing from the palace, too.

And he and Micah probably don't look similar enough anymore, even if he was here.

"I'll be ready."

Damien gave another bow before he silently slipped out the door. Beneath his gentle touch, the door hardly made a sound.

The room suddenly felt empty, despite the soft breaths from Matthias. She turned, catching her reflection in the mirror beside the armoire. Pausing, she examined herself.

Dark circles hung beneath her eyes, a smear of dust on her cheeks from the secret passageways. The tears she'd sought to hide had run a clean trail on her right cheek, and she loathed to know Damien must have seen.

She wore the same fine dress she'd donned on returning to the palace after finding the dragons. It didn't look worn by the years that'd passed, only dirtied by her excursion through the hidden passages.

A splattering of red ran over her left shoulder, and she

reached to touch the dried blood she hadn't realized was there. It wasn't hers, though. The arrow had never been loosed at her because of Matthias's jump. It was his... from when he'd been hit before being freed.

And it worked.

Fingers trembling, she went to the water basin beside the mirror and poured just enough to soak a silk cloth. Despite her rubbing, the blood remained, refusing to allow her to forget the events of the day.

There will be no forgetting.

Matthias twitched in her peripheral vision, and she turned to see his eyebrows furrowed, eyes rolling beneath his closed lids.

Every muscle in her body longed to go to him, to hold Matthias through the nightmare that plagued his sleep. But she wetted the cloth again and set back to scrubbing.

She abandoned the attempts to clean the outer layer of her dress, removing the surcoat and draping it over a chair to dry and passed the hour with a book in her hands near the window. She couldn't recall what she'd actually read, her mind swimming with each word to something entirely different. Her eyes flitted up to the city with each shift of cloudy shadows, the distant rumble of thunder cascading over the mountains.

No one had come to her with any paperwork to sign or see to. Liam and Dani had likely intercepted it, and she wished she could thank them.

Lightning flashed, brightening the evening sky.

Street lanterns glowed with life, and the light from the temple reflected off the grey clouds. Nema's Throne lay perfectly at peace, unaware of the chaos that could very well be coming.

Katrin set her book on the armrest, pulling down the light blue sleeves of her dress from where she'd shoved them to her elbows, and let out a long sigh.

Movement in the corner of her eye made Katrin's heart leap. She twitched, bumping the book, and it clattered to the floor.

Matthias jerked upright, eyes wide and breathing fast. "We need to go."

Katrin gasped. "What?" The mounting fear settled as she stood, but her body remained rigid.

The king swung his legs out of bed, throwing the blanket aside. "We need to get to the front courtyard. Right now." He approached her, holding out a hand.

"Matthias, you were dreaming." She squeezed his fingers. "Why do we need to go to the courtyard?"

"Let's go, Kat. No time. Gooseberries."

Chapter 15

Fifteen minutes earlier...

"WE NEED TO FIND ALANA." Damien glared at the obstinate guard, who stood with his arms crossed.

"Beggin' your pardon, my lord, but this ain't Helgath." The man's brown mustache twitched, his eyes darkening. "I don't take orders from you and don't understand why we're hunting down the king's personal healer."

"Because she's committed treason. Gods, aren't you listening?"

The heavy wooden door to the palace's military conference chambers flung open, and Dani strode through holding a scroll. "Listen up!" Her voice cut through the air and silenced the room in a rush. "I have the signed order. Alana Di'Terian is a traitor to the crown. She is to be killed on sight. You..." Dani squared her shoulders at the guard Damien struggled to reason with. "Search her chambers for any clue to where she might be."

"Ma'am." The guard saluted, casting a wary glance at Damien. "Are we to—"

Liam cleared his throat, drawing gazes. "These are unprecedented times. Our king is in distress and he needs those he can trust. Our Helgathian visitors, Damien and Rae Lanoret, are hereby granted emergency authority. If they give you a command, perform it as if it comes from my mouth. Or our king's."

The guards shuffled, their armor clattering as they exchanged looks.

Liam's face hardened. "You have your orders. Go. Find the auer."

Damien rolled his eyes as the guards spurred into action, including the one who'd refused to listen to him.

"Rae fill you both in?" Damien tugged on the tight collar of his shirt. No matter how many years he'd worn the style, it still felt constraining.

"She may have mentioned they were giving you trouble." Dani crossed the space like she'd walked the room a hundred times before. "We posted extra guards at all the entrances to the palace, including the hidden ones."

"Good, don't know what Uriel learned from Matthias regarding those." Damien met Liam's concerned eyes and sighed. "Look, it's going to take time…"

"We have other concerns right now. Like Alana. What do you know about her?" Liam touched Dani's hand as he walked past her, surveying the room for any listening ears.

"Nothing really, beyond her apparent role here and with your previous king's death. Matthias was asleep when I went to visit. It seemed... cruel to wake him, so I didn't."

Liam grunted. "Rae implied we don't have that kind of time, is that true?"

Damien nodded. "If I were Uriel, I wouldn't let us get our feet under us. He's going to strike as soon as he can. All the more reason to let Matthias sleep. We will need him."

"Doesn't even get a day to rest," Dani murmured, touching the hilt of the bone-carved dagger at her side. "As soon as he can... Does that mean minutes? Hours? Days?"

"I doubt we have days, and it's already been over an hour. It's impossible to say." Damien's attention returned to the door as it opened.

Rae paused in the doorway, her quiver full. "I swept the healers' chambers and found nothing. Has the crew finished searching Alana's room yet?"

"Just started."

"I'll go help them." Rae turned on her heel, disappearing again.

Liam never altered his gaze from Damien. "What's the plan, then? How do we fight something that can destroy the city?"

"We fortify what we can. We are evacuating as much of the city as possible back to the palace. Then it's up to me to create a barrier." Damien hid the anxiety of the idea from his face, remembering how draining the last shield against a Shade had been. He'd needed to pull excess energy from Jarrod just to maintain it and knock out Kin on that street in Lazuli.

And now we're talking about stopping his master.

Damien's muscles flexed as Liam nodded and turned to his wife, her face grim.

"I should go get Ryen," Dani whispered.

Damien winced, having forgotten about the young man in all the chaos. "You should. In the meantime, I need a place here in the palace with lots of life. Preferably nature."

Liam's brow furrowed. "What for?"

"I don't have time to explain the intricacies of my Art right now," Damien growled. "But I'm going to need a lot of energy."

"The front courtyard should work. It's practically a garden, and just in front of the palace." Dani crossed to the door. "It will take me at least a half hour to get to Ryen. I'll contact Katrin if I have problems."

Liam nodded as he stepped in close to her, placing a kiss on her temple. "Be safe."

The Dtrüa closed her eyes for a breath. "Should we use the talisman?"

"Not yet." Liam touched her cheek. "But depending on

how bad it gets out there, use it."

Dani nodded, giving him a kiss before vanishing into the hallway.

The crown elite watched the doorway even after she disappeared.

"Thank you. For trusting me with command." Damien resisted the urge to tug his collar loose again.

"Saw little choice." Liam didn't look at him, his eyes still lingering on the door. "Feels like I have less and less of those each passing moment you're around."

Damien flinched. "Not intentional. But rest assured I know how to handle command."

Liam's dark eyes flickered to him. "They say your rebels fought the impossible fight and won. Let's hope that luck carries to us today."

"Not luck. Just competent people at my side. So I have full faith in what happens next."

A hint of a smile curled Liam's lips.

"What were you and Dani talking about? The talisman?" Damien watched his smile disappear as Liam shifted.

"A gift. From the dragons." The crown elite met Damien's eyes, a gravity within them. "In case of emergencies."

Damien swallowed the jolt passing through his body. "What kind of emergencies?"

"This kind. Zaelinstra entrusted us to make the call if there was ever a time it became necessary for the dragons to become involved in the human world again."

"That's a big choice and a lot of trust."

"It is. Need any weapons? Armory is over there."

The crown elite already had a pair of swords strapped to his back, and Damien could sense the calm radiating through his ká at the concept of battle. A veteran soldier's focus.

Damien looked at the doorway, clenching his left fist where he'd typically summon his spear.

But I've kept the secret from Uriel thus far. Best to continue.

He nodded before jogging across the room and opening the door to the weapon storage.

It'd been mostly emptied, a handful of weapons strewn on the floor in the hurried rush out of the assembly hall. A single short sword leaned against the far wall, and Damien could tell its hilt was loose before picking it up.

He turned it over, honing into the surrounding energies. The palace, while mostly stone, still held enough life for him to silently request aid. The ká of metal in his hand hummed as he pushed power into the loose gaps around the hilt, a flicker of blue running along the sharp edge of the blade.

Liam's footsteps crossed the threshold of the storage room. "There are others in the—"

Damien didn't hear the rest of what the man said, drowned out by the sudden howls of pain reverberating against the barrier that barred the voices from his mind. Even at a distance, their fear penetrated every bit of energy in the area like a shock wave.

Death. Decay.

Damien's heart leapt as he spun to Liam. "He's coming."

Liam stiffened. "Uriel?"

The ká screamed, forcing Damien to harden his protective barrier.

"Shhh." Damien lifted his hand, gaining a glare from Liam. He ignored the soldier as he dove back into his power, allowing his vision to shift to the hues of the Rahn'ka. Tentatively stretching his ká towards the city, invisible beyond the thick walls of the palace, he balked at the familiar corruption.

Wisps of darkness flicked against his senses like a snake's tongue, clawed feet tearing through the cobblestone streets.

The hair on Damien's neck stood, and he reached blindly in front of him. His hand closed on Liam's wrist as his vision returned, and the soldier already had his hand on his sword.

"Corrupted." Damien's tongue stuck to the roof of his mouth. "And not just a few."

"Say again?" The deadpan look in Liam's eyes confirmed he'd heard of the deranged beasts.

"Remember what I'm about to tell you. Sever their spines. The Art doesn't work on them. I need to find Rae." Damien hurried to the door, but it opened before he reached it.

Rae walked inside, looking down at a sheet of parchment

as she spoke. "It looks like Alana fled, and the crown guards can't find her. Do you want to expand the search into the city? The evacuations into the palace are making things complicated, but Uriel could take her as a host." She looked up and met his gaze, straightening. "What is it?"

"Evacuations are about to get more complicated." Damien hurried to unfasten his belt and add the sword to it. "Corrupted are advancing through the streets, headed this way."

Liam spun, running towards the door.

"Wait, where are you going?" Damien pushed authority into his voice, and the soldier paused.

"Dani's out there. I need to catch up to her." Liam tore the door open and it ricocheted off the wall. "Don't try to tell me I can't go."

Damien shook his head. "Just... send as many citizens to the palace as you can. And remember... the spine. I think that talisman might become a necessity very soon."

Liam gave a quick nod before he disappeared into the hall at a run.

Rae chewed her lip. "How bad is it?"

Damien met her eyes, the dark pulses of power still cascading against his ká. He pursed his lips and shook his head. "I need to know where Uriel is centering his attack from. Or I risk erecting the barrier in the wrong place. I have to assume the Corrupted are just the beginning." He brushed his fingers over hers, their wedding bands clinking. "How does he have Corrupted?"

Squeezing his hand, Rae tugged. "He must have a summoner in the city. Come. Let's get a better view." She let go of him and darted out the door, racing to the front courtyard of the palace.

He funneled the Art into his muscles, sprinting down the unfamiliar halls. Faces blurred as they rushed past staff and guards searching the palace, shouting after them in surprise.

The massive front doors were already open, the wind of the thunderstorm howling through the front foyer. Rae and Damien hopped down the tiered entry, two steps at a time, to the courtyard.

The stone sloped down the hill towards the elegant bridge that led into the rest of the city. The two dragon statues on the far end faced the streets, roaring at the stormy sky. A crowd of people surged from the wide boulevard beyond.

A pair of guards stood near the open silver gates on the palace side of the bridge, eyeing each other as a crowd of people continued over the moat below.

"Open them both!" Damien shouted at the guard standing beside the one closed gate, allowing them to search the faces entering, in case Alana hid among them. "No time for that anymore. Get the civilians on the palace grounds as fast as possible."

AMANDA MURATOFF & KAYLA HANSEN

"Sir?" The guard looked at Damien, his eyes wide as Rae rushed past him.

She looped her bow over her head, ignoring the guards as she passed through the gate. Deftly, she jumped onto the stone railing, continuing towards the city side.

She's heading for the tower.

"We're escalating the evacuation of the city. Get out there and coordinate." Damien shoved the guard towards the bridge, and it seemed to be all the encouragement the man needed, despite the quiet still dominating the streets.

Damien dodged a group passing through the silver gate, pulling himself up onto the same railing Rae had used to bypass them. He looked ahead as Rae leapt for the tower beside the dragon statue, scaling her way up the outer wall.

Screams rose from the city, distant, but clear enough for Damien to turn his attention east.

All heads turned to follow his gaze.

"Move!" Damien waved his arm towards the palace. "Faster!"

His encouragement, and the rise of terror in the city streets, sped the people forward once more.

"Can you tell where they're coming from, yet?" Rae's voice barely reached him over the commotion of fleeing civilians.

She pulled herself onto the top of the tower. A basic roof enclosed the top, but the sides were open aside from the support beams.

"Check near the temple!" Damien looked up, debating joining her.

But if I do, it'll take me longer to get to Matthias if we need to go back.

Rae shrugged her bow off her shoulder, peering east. "The temple is dark." She drew an arrow, looking down at him. "Go. You should be almost close enough to feel it. I'll cover you in case they advance."

He nodded, hopping off the railing and pushing into the crowd. The pressure against his aura threatened a headache with all the terror.

Breaking free from the crowd, Damien gasped as he reached the entrance to the main thoroughfare that connected the palace to the temple.

Garlands of flowers draped between buildings over the street, their leaves rustling in the roaring wind. Lightning flashed behind the temple, but the writhing power wrapped around the glass spires swallowed its light. Blackness wriggled like a python consuming its prey. It breathed with each gust of wind, surging over the stone until there was nothing but tar covering the magnificent structure.

A wretched howl shook the stones at Damien's feet, drawing his sight back to the street. An arrow whizzed past his head, thunking into the skull of a small Corrupted slinking towards his boots.

Rae's bow twanged again, but he didn't see where the arrow soared.

Defying his instincts, Damien closed his eyes.

The power of the Rahn'ka soared into him with his beckoning as he loosened his hiding aura. Pantracia answered his request, and his veins lit with pale blue sparks.

The city reformed in front of him beneath his black eyelids, the ká of each brick and stone echoing into his soul to paint the images. He followed along the streams of energy until they faded. The blackness consumed everything, and as Damien raised his Rahn'ka sight to the temple, only flashes of ká remained, guttering like a dying candle. He latched as quickly as he could onto the fleeing energy of a sparrow as it took to the sky, and the city of Nema's Throne lay before him like a blueprint.

The outer edges remained intact, their shapes still visible. But the center...

The temple.

A yawning void circled the temple grounds, a maelstrom pulling in whatever remained of the living. The gardens were dead, shriveled and decayed. Black ash swirled with the wind like snow.

A horrible shape, indistinguishable as anything but teeth and spikes, struck the sparrow, and its life sputtered as Damien's ká fell to the street.

Rae shrieked in pain, jerking Damien from his trance. He spun.

An onyx, matted mass clung to the side of the tower, razor claws already flecked with blood. She pinned its foot, drawing another arrow that she buried into its skull a breath later.

He met her eyes and could read the urgency without her needing to speak.

Damien hurled back towards the bridge, civilians forced into the tight bottleneck. A group of guards had taken up position behind them, their swords drawn and pointed at the sinister black pack racing down the road.

The Rahn'ka's heart thundered, and he looked back for his wife.

A Corrupted soared at Rae from the dark sky, but she couldn't raise her bow before it collided with her. It clutched her, wings flapping as it propelled her backward into the moat.

"Dice!" Damien sprinted to the stone railing, his stomach churning at the red clouding the crystal water as a struggle continued below its surface.

Matthias. Get to Matthias.

A frustrated cry escaped him as Corrupted leapt the moat, skipping the bridge entirely to cut the civilians off.

Rae broke the surface, growling as the creature splashed with her. "Go, Damien!" She fought to pull herself out of the moat, the thing chewing into her leg. "Get him to jump!"

He tore himself away, despite the feeling of her ká already fading from the blood loss. It made every inch of him ache.

She won't die. She won't die.

He pushed through the throngs of people, channeling more of his power to propel him faster. Centering his attention on Katrin's ká, he locked eyes with the woman who had come out onto the guest room's balcony in the chaos.

She stood with her hand over her mouth, black hair whipping around her in the wind. Movement shuffled behind her as Matthias crossed through the glass doors, eyes wide. The king hurried back inside, and Katrin followed.

No time to go through the palace.

The tattoos on Damien's arm blasted to life with a mere thought, and his fist closed around the shaft of his spear. He spun it without losing a step and plunged the spearhead into the stone, vaulting himself up.

The second-story balcony's railing collided with his chest, and he grunted as he forced his hands to close on it.

Katrin shouted as she spun back towards the door. Fear turned to relief in her eyes as Damien hoisted himself over the rail.

"Matthias!" Damien called as the king tore open the bedroom door. "We need to jump. Now!"

Matthias faced him, hesitating. "How far?"

"Far as you can, but you have to take me with you. We need all the time we can get."

The king let go of the door and approached Damien. "I won't get many tries at this, taking you with me."

"Then we better make the first one count." Damien held out his hand. His chest tightened, heart still screaming at him for abandoning Rae. "Quickly, or my wife will have died for nothing."

Matthias's jaw flexed, and he grasped Damien's forearm. "You'll return to where you were. Where do we meet?"

Damien quirked his head at the balcony. "Front courtyard. Go!"

The Art scorched through the Rahn'ka, invading him without asking permission. It blurred his vision, and the king's grip tightened until it vanished. The world sped by in reverse, retracing through Damien's movements until he landed with startling force back in the armory with Rae.

Damien gasped, panting.

You'd think it would be less jarring the second time around.

Rae stared at him. "Did you hear me? I said it looks like Alana fled, and the crown guards can't find her. Do you want to—"

"Stop. That doesn't matter now." Damien instinctively reached for her, closing his hand in hers. The warmth of her skin did little to banish the memory of her fading ká. He shook his head, trying to sort the memories. "We don't have time. Corrupted are coming, and Uriel is mounting his attack. We have to go... now."

His wife's eyes widened. "Go where?"

"The front courtyard. We need to position archers before the Corrupted leap the moat."

"There are towers out there. I can take one." Rae spun to the door.

"No!" Damien caught her wrist. "You stay on this side, and keep your eyes on the sky."

Liam rushed to the door.

The Rahn'ka shouted after him, "Tell the guards to encourage the civilians to take shelter on the city side of the moat. The bridge is a deathtrap."

Liam gave a terse nod as the door bounced off the wall. "I'm going after—"

"I know. Sever the Corrupted's spines. And tell Dani to use the talisman." Damien ignored the glare from Liam before he took hold of Rae's hand, tugging her to follow as they ran.

"Did you jump with Matthias?" The Mira'wyld kept pace, her eyes narrow on him. "What happened?"

"Uriel is at the temple. In fifteen minutes, we'll be overrun with Corrupted. And you'll die, but not this time." He squeezed her hand so hard his ached.

Rae's pace faltered. "I die?"

"Keep your eyes on the sky, all right?"

"Eyes on the sky. Got it."

Chapter 16

"LET'S GO, KAT. NO TIME. Gooseberries." Matthias hurried for the door, jerking it open.

Katrin followed him, her hesitation diminishing as she pulled up the hem of her skirt and tucked it into her belt as they started down the hallway.

"What's happening?" Katrin tried to catch his eyes.

"Corrupted are attacking from the city. They will overrun the palace soon."

"Corrupted?" Katrin's voice shook in understanding. "There's never been a summoner in Isalica before... The temples—"

"When Helgath eliminated the summoners, Uriel used Alana to train more here. With the aid of a new alliance with the arch priest at the temple here in Nema's Throne. Turns out, he's not a good man like everyone believes." Matthias led her down a curved stairway, glancing back at her.

Katrin grew silent, her eyes distant. "What can I do?"

"Stay in the palace where it's safer." Matthias reached the bottom and set off towards the courtyard.

She caught his hand, pulling him to a stop with surprising strength. "Oh, no. Absolutely not. I will not sit back while *our* palace is besieged. What do you want me to do? Or shall I find something on my own?"

The king's veins heated. "Katrin, you're pregnant."

"And my child will have a home to grow in. Here." She squeezed him harder. "With *our* people."

"*Our* child. Rae died, Kat. An advanced Art user with impeccable fighting skills, and she died! I need you to stay safe. I need you and our baby to stay in the palace where those beasts can't tear you to shreds." Matthias's heart thundered in his ears. "You asked me what I need. *That's* what I need."

Katrin pursed her lips, pulling back from him. She stared into his eyes before looking over his shoulder at the doorway to the guard chambers. "I just got you back." Her grip tightened. "Don't you dare let me lose you again."

"I'm not going anywhere." Matthias shook his head. "I'll be right here, with Damien and Rae, helping defend our people. You don't have to stay inside, but can you at least stay with me?"

She narrowed her eyes at the compromise, but nodded, and relief washed through him.

Damien's voice came from behind him. "Liam is ordering the civilians to take shelter in the buildings near the moat on the other side. Archers are on their way to the ramparts to defend the courtyard."

Matthias spun to face the Rahn'ka. "Uriel will operate out of the temple, and—"

"I know. I already saw. We have little time." Damien gestured, and he and his wife joined Katrin and Matthias in passing through the open front doors.

Matthias turned to a guard stationed there. "Gather all the crown guards in the courtyard. We're going to need every sword."

The guard nodded and left her post, rushing to carry out her orders.

Thunder rumbled across the courtyard stone, a flash of lightning near the northern edge of the city.

"He will have taken Alana as his host." Matthias finished his sentence with a frown as they walked. "But he's working with the arch priest."

Good thing the Hollow Ones are too far away for Uriel to use tonight.

"Do you know who summoned the Corrupted? Easiest answer would be to take out that person." Rae hopped down the steps first, her bow already in her hand. She looked up, scanning the sky above the moat.

At least these two have experience fighting them.

"Alana." Matthias snarled the name. "Without a doubt."

"We won't be able to get to her, then. We'll have to defend where we are... and I'll have to adjust the barrier." Damien rushed across the cobblestone to the trickling fountain

"The barrier?" The king rolled his shoulders. "You can protect the city?"

"In theory. The best way to protect it from Uriel's power is to make it so he can't absorb anything's ká. Problem is, my power is finite." The Rahn'ka turned back to Matthias, his body stiffening as his eyes paused on something to the left.

Matthias followed his gaze, finding a spear, its head glowing pale blue, sticking out of the ground near the balcony to the room he'd just slept in. "That yours?"

Damien held out his hand in the weapon's direction, despite the thirty-foot distance. The light in it pulsed, then of its own accord, it tore from the stone and lanced through the air into the Rahn'ka's waiting hand. He ran his other hand over the shaft, eyes dancing up and down it. "We don't have time to consider all the theoretical reasons, but this confirms one thing..." He met Matthias's eyes. "I might be able to save more of the city if we keep jumping."

A rumble of discomfort stirred in the king's stomach. "How would that benefit you?"

"My power depends on the souls of everything around me. They give of their ká to fuel mine, which I can shape with the Art."

"Sounds an awful lot like how Uriel used my power." Matthias looked at the spear, suspicion souring his tongue.

Damien frowned, his eyes flashing blue. "I'm not like Uriel. I seek permission and am gifted the power by life. Uriel consumes and destroys."

"You don't kill the things you take from?"

"No. Never. I preserve life. I scratch the surface of what a ká can hold."

"He can't even eat meat." Rae elbowed her husband, but kept her eyes up.

A weight lifted off his shoulders. "If you gather what you can and we jump, you can gather it again, but the jumps are limited. I'll only be able to do a few, and only if they're short."

"Then we push it as much as we dare, and I take as much ká as the living energies here will give me. They will understand it saves them in the end."

"To what end? Uriel won't stop. Alana's power has limits, but once the creatures are summoned, it takes none to maintain them." Matthias glanced at the bridge, but no Corrupted entered the courtyard yet.

"We must hope that if I can absorb enough, it will dwindle Uriel's reserves as well as protect those within the barrier. I'll adjust it to prohibit the Corrupted from entering.

Fortunately, their souls are nothing like ours. We'll have to send troops to pick them off and hope I can maintain the barrier long enough to see it done. Some aid from above wouldn't hurt, either, if Dani and Liam follow through."

Crown guards emerged from within the palace, swarming down the front steps and past the small group towards the bridge. They assembled in rows, weapons drawn.

"Where are they?" Katrin looked from Matthias to Damien.

"They went after their son." Rae's tone hung with dire finality.

Damien winced as he met Katrin's eyes. "My barrier will never reach that far into the city. We have to save who we can and trust they can save themselves."

Katrin's hand slipped into Matthias's as she faced the bridge to the city, and the king followed her gaze.

The temple darkened on the horizon, tendrils of black stretching up into the sky. The storm's wind doubled, rushing into the courtyard and bringing the howls and screams with them.

How are we going to survive this?

Damien sat on the cobblestone, placing his spear on the ground in front of him. "Katrin, can you ask Dani if she's used the talisman?"

"The what?" The acolyte looked at Matthias.

The king shrugged. "I don't know." He watched Damien close his eyes. "What are you doing?"

"Getting ready to save as much of the city as I can. Are you ready to jump?" Damien looked up at him, his face hard set. "And did you contact Dani?" He glanced at Katrin, who gave Matthias another confused look.

"Not yet. You said to ask about a talisman?" Katrin closed her eyes after he nodded and rolled her shoulders. The familiar calm that came with her connection to the Dtrüa settled into her face. Her brow furrowed, and her head tilted. "She's fighting. She can't answer until she shifts."

As Katrin opened her eyes, hazy white covered them like Dani's.

"I'm ready," Matthias muttered. "But remember, they're limited. So use them wisely."

Damien tugged his boots off, throwing them aside before unbuttoning his tunic. As he stripped away the fabric, the entirety of his tattoo became visible, light already pulsing across the runes. The navy tattoo cascaded from his neck, down his left shoulder, and onto his toned chest before rolling down his arm. He stretched out his hand to his spear, and it vanished in a wisp of light fading into his skin.

A phantom breeze pushed up over them as the ground beneath Damien rumbled. Trails of his power seeped into the crevices between stones, dancing up like blue sunbeams.

Civilians rushed past, giving the group a wide berth as they sought shelter inside the palace. Shouts and screams rose louder in the city, getting closer.

"Dani says she already used it and nothing happened." Katrin hurried the words, her breathing faster before the clouds disappeared from her eyes. "And she's fighting again."

"We're on our own, then." Damien spoke, but his voice sounded different. As if others spoke over him in a whisper. He closed his eyes as the tattoos on his skin glowed brighter. "This is the moment you need to return to, Matthias."

Matthias shifted his weight between his feet, feeling exposed without a weapon. "I need a sword." His muscles twitched with anticipation.

"No, you don't need to waste your energy with a blade."

"You've gotten too comfortable in the way you speak to kings," Matthias mumbled.

A smile danced across Damien's face, but his eyes remained closed. "It's worked out well for Jarrod Martox. Wait until the absolute last moment you can to jump."

"Funny, King Martox hardly seemed like the kind of man who'd put up with that when I met him."

Howls reverberated across the courtyard, black shapes cresting from the city streets onto the bridge. A dark shadow rose in the sky from the eastern horizon, the horrible beat of bat-like wings echoing with screeches.

"Fuck, I hate Corrupted." Rae nocked an arrow and side stepped, her weapon raised.

"Stay back," Matthias whispered to Katrin. "Just in case."

As the first Corrupted bounded closer, chaos erupted. The crown guards jumped into action, creating a cacophony of metal clashing and flesh squelching.

Rae loosed her first arrow, followed immediately by her second, into the sky.

A vulture-like Corrupted plummeted from above, thudding to the ground before them in a mess of wings and claws. Two arrows jutted out of its thorny spine, but its limbs still twitched.

As the cries of soldiers joined the roar of beasts, the king faced Katrin. "I was wrong. I need you to do something."

Katrin's chest rose sharply as she reached for him. "Name it."

"I'll tell you next time. For now, get inside. Please."

The acolyte narrowed her eyes, but gave a curt nod. She turned, running up the stairs two at a time while a flurry of wings rushed in like a tornado towards the palace entrance.

"Kat! Down!" Matthias's heart leapt into his throat as Katrin immediately obeyed, throwing herself to the marble stairs. Her hands latched behind her neck as Rae's arrow found its mark in the creature, small claws tearing at the waistline of Katrin's dress. The thing squealed, its impish body tumbling onto the stairs as another whirled back at the acolyte.

A high-pitched ring sounded as the ingvald struck a glowing blue barrier, bouncing off like a bird hitting a window.

Alana used the creatures as messengers, but the mass of them was a tempest of teeth and claws. They flung themselves at Katrin again as she peeked out from beneath her hands, the swarm colliding and falling back off the domed barrier.

As the ingvalds fell, the barrier swelled, growing around them before it flickered out as if it'd never been.

Katrin stumbled up, racing for the double doors that slammed shut after her, crushing one unfortunate Corrupted between them.

Matthias breathed easier as he turned back to Damien, who hadn't moved at all.

Rae stood in a protective position beside him, an arrow nocked, studying the sky.

A shadow lifted from the city, and Matthias's chest tightened.

Tendrils of power rippled from the city center, slithering through the buildings like the limbs of a great sea creature of legend. Wood cracked and stone crumbled, the structures of the city falling to ruin in the black wave's path.

The memory of the utter destruction of Nema's Throne, first wrought into his mind during Uriel's compulsion to say yes, brought bile into the king's throat. The horrible images mingled with what he saw now as the beauty of the capital fell.

Damien's barrier flashed into existence as a serpentine Corrupted lunged, lashing at the protective bubble with wicked claw-like arms.

Matthias looked at the courtyard beyond the fountain and saw a mess of blood and bodies. The gates at the side of the courtyard had been thrown open as more crown guards rushed into the battle. Their battle cries echoed with the snarls of the Corrupted as the forces met.

The wind whistled through the trees at the edge of the courtyard, lightning flashing. Tar poured over the roofs of the houses as it flowed across the city.

The barrier pulsed again, pushing outward. It surged over the crown guards in the courtyard's front, pushing the Corrupted atop them back like a tidal wave. The soldiers gaped as they stared at the monsters tearing at the translucent field.

The ringing grew louder, making Matthias cover his ears.

Shadow rolled over the lip of the moat, surging past the roaring dragon statues at the end of the bridge. The garlands crumbled to ash, and a fleeing civilian stumbled as it overtook him. His body withered from the ankles up, his skin shrinking against his bones until he collapsed into the darkness.

"We need to instruct them to fight at the barrier edge when we go back." Matthias stepped closer to the sitting Rahn'ka. "Ready to go?"

Uriel's power struck the barrier, breaking like the sea on a wall. It rolled up, blocking the city from view.

Damien hissed as if in pain, his muscles twitching. He panted. "Go."

Matthias closed his hand on the Rahn'ka's shoulder, an odd buzzing tickling through his fingertips near the glowing tattoo. "So demanding." He pulled from his well of energy, the power searing through him as it usually did. When it entered Damien's body to take him back, too, it lit up, brighter than before. The sensation turned electric, snapping at his skin as he dragged the Rahn'ka's power back in time with them.

But his power doesn't destroy. Not like Uriel's.

The scent of death trickled into his nose as the trees at the edge of the courtyard, just outside Damien's barrier, withered.

Matthias sucked in a deep breath, his legs quaking as they came to a stop seconds after the moment Damien had requested. "Close enough, boss?"

The glow of his tattoos appeared more vibrant than

before, and Damien rolled his shoulders with a smirk. "Good enough."

The air hummed, the ringing returning as the Rahn'ka's power flicked through the air like a mirage in the desert.

"Katrin." Matthias turned to her, meeting her eyes. "I need you to gather the healers remaining in the palace. Bring them here, so we may hold the line longer this time."

Her hand closed around his as she nodded. "How many times so far?" She locked her eyes with his as howls rolled into the courtyard.

The beat of wings signaled the ingvald's arrival, and they screeched as they bounced off Damien's barrier.

"Only once out here." Matthias panted, his body aching from taking the second person with him and the knowledge he'd have to do it again.

Katrin squeezed before she spun and ran up the stairs, vanishing into the foyer and leaving the doors open behind her.

"Fuck, I hate Corrupted." Rae nocked an arrow and side stepped, her weapon raised.

The Corrupted only made it halfway across the bridge before they collided with an invisible force. A wave of power rippled through the air around them as the crown guards twitched in surprise and held their position.

Matthias banished the images of their corpses. "Fight at the barrier's border!" he commanded the guards, his blood pounding faster when they shouted their obedience. "Sever their spines!"

The crown guards charged, but none stepped past Damien's barrier, slashing their weapons through the force field and keeping the beasts at bay.

Rae loosed her first arrow, followed immediately by her second, into the sky.

The vulture-like Corrupted plummeted from above, striking the domed barrier before it slid off into the moat with a splash.

The ground shook as tendrils lashed at the clouded sky, lightning crackling behind the shadow of Uriel's power as it rose from the temple. The spires snapped, falling out of sight in a shower of glass.

Matthias bowed his head, closing his eyes to the decimation of the city.

The Corrupted howled, their claws scraping along the stone as the barrier pushed them back. Black shapes launched from the far side of the moat, sharp pings echoing through the barrier as they latched onto the Rahn'ka's power. Their deformed jaws gnawed at the bubble even as it continued to grow.

"Dice, get to one of the towers." Damien's voice was strained, sweat coating his skin as his body shook. "Be my eyes."

Rae looped her bow over her shoulder and took off across

the courtyard.

"This is the new moment." Damien huffed, lowering his head slightly. His knuckles were white where his fists rested on his knees.

"How long do you need? The jumps will be shorter each time."

"Can you do a few very short ones? Like ten seconds each?"

"I can try. Say the word."

Damien heaved a breath, his tattoos pulsing. "Now, and go until you can't any more."

Matthias closed his hand on Damien's shoulder again, ushering his power into his veins.

The world spun as he jumped back those few moments, watching Rae's position in the courtyard bounce backward once she reached the base of the tower.

The shimmer of the Rahn'ka's barrier rolled into the streets of Nema's Throne. Corrupted struck its surface, and the air rang.

"Again."

Matthias gripped Damien's shoulder harder, dropping to one knee.

Matthias gasped, his heart pounding in his ears and his vision swimming.

The barrier pushed another twenty feet, and the temple's spires shattered again.

"Again."

"Fuck off."

The king let go, his palms meeting the ground as he cringed. Pain burned through him, and Rae reached the tower once more.

Lightning struck the far reaches of the barrier as it swelled over the roofs Matthias had seen Uriel's power destroy, but couldn't recall how many jumps ago.

The spires of the temple crumbled on the horizon as Uriel's power overtook them. The barrier flashed again with another strike of the storm above, the lightning dancing trails across its surface. Uriel's power curled, whipping back on itself as it slithered around the barrier's edge.

Damien inhaled loudly, his spine straightening as his power seeped up from the surrounding ground. "Now, we hold out." He opened his eyes, and they blazed with pale blue. "And hope for a miracle."

Chapter 17

DANI'S CHEST HEAVED AS SHE struggled to catch her breath. Darkness suffocated her, not a hint of light disrupting the shadow. She'd made it halfway to Hillboar street, and although the Corrupted were scarcer, several kept trailing her.

Katrin had asked about the talisman.

Dani had blown the whistle, as Zaelinstra had instructed, but the expected hum of power never came.

Maybe Uriel's power is disrupting the fabric.

She'd hidden in a dead end alleyway to communicate with her friend, but staying in one place wasn't wise.

Finding her Art, she channeled it for only a breath before halting.

"Dani!" Liam's bellowing voice echoed through the streets, bringing both terror and relief with it.

"Liam!" The Dtrüa stood, jogging towards the origin. "I'm here!"

Boots pounded against the ground, followed by the scrabbling of claws. The scuffle of Liam's feet told her he'd spotted the Corrupted, and metal rang with his even breaths. Flesh split, and bone cracked as something wet splatted onto the road.

Another roar burst between them, and Dani rolled backward over a crate as a stinking shape landed where she'd been moments before.

Liam's sword broke through the creature, and its angry howl turned to one of pain.

"These gods' damned things are everywhere." Liam moved to her, taking a defensive position, and she imagined him scanning the streets. "Where's Ryen? We don't have much time."

"I never reached Hillboar Hall." Dani winced, touching her side where one of the Corrupted's claws had met her flesh. The warmth of her own blood felt like a distant memory with how little fighting they'd done over the years. "And I tried to call Zaelinstra, but nothing happened."

"Shit." Liam moved towards the flapping of wings, but Dani beat him to it.

Her Art ran through her veins as her body changed. The scent of the Corrupted struck her stronger as her massive paws pounced on it, tackling the screeching bat creature to the ground. Its feathers tasted vile as she tore at its throat, snapping its spine.

Liam stepped back, turning as another closed in from behind, heavy paws scraping the cobblestone. He lunged, but his blade struck stone instead of the creature's hide, and it barreled down the alley at Dani.

She threw herself at the wall, claws scraping into the brick as she bounded around the beast, burying her teeth into its shaggy back. It rolled, throwing Dani into a pile of splintering wood.

The Dtrüa let out a yeowl, shuffling to free herself of the broken crates when another joined the fight. Ryen's scent found her, and she climbed free, flanking the Corrupted with her son on the other side.

"Ryen, heads up." Liam's voice. "Aim for the spine."

Metal whizzed through the air, and Ryen caught the tossed sword as if they merely practiced in their training arena at home.

Dani growled and lunged, tackling the big creature to the ground next to her son, who slashed and severed its head.

The thing's reeking blood filled Dani's nose, followed by the more pungent decay of further death beyond the alley.

"Looks like we have a moment." Liam breathed hard, moving closer. "Dani, where's the talisman? What do you mean, nothing happened?"

Dani shifted back to her human form, blood sticking her

clothing to her side. She reached into her neckline, producing the bone whistle on the leather tie. "I tried it a few times, but there was no hum of power like when we tested it with Zaelinstra."

Liam took the trinket from her fingers, pulling the thong from over her head. "What a time for it not to work."

"What's going on?" Ryen panted, his voice lower as he leaned over his knees. "Xavis evacuated Hillboar Hall. I slipped away when he wasn't watching."

Liam growled. "It's not safe. You should have stayed with Xavis."

"Fuck that, Dad. I came to find you." He moved to Dani, his hands gentle as they brushed aside the bit of torn tunic to look at the injury on her side.

"I'm fine." Dani touched his hand. "Uriel is destroying the city."

"He's pissed, and I'm guessing it was something you did with that Damien guy?"

"Without a doubt." Dani took a deeper breath and winced. "We freed the king. Now he wants revenge. I tried to call the dragons, but the whistle did nothing."

"Can you sense anything about what Uriel is doing, since you're one of his..." Liam's voice grew strained as it faded.

"No." Ryen sounded weary. "Not with this thing." His fingernail clicked on the metal of the cuff earring he still wore. "But we need to get out of the city. Everyone here is going to be dead soon if the master wants it."

"No. We should get back to the palace. We can't outrun this and we have a better shot with Damien's barrier."

"What the hells is that guy?" Ryen touched Dani's arm.

"Our only hope, at this point."

"Unless we call the dragons..." Her son's voice softened.

"We tried that. I just said—" Dani paused when Ryen pushed something into her palm. She ran her thumb over it, her breath quickening. "Ry... Is this..."

"Can we gloss over the part where I stole it and replaced it with a forged one and just be grateful I gave it back?" His tone held the lilt of humor, but a current of shame ran beneath it.

Liam grunted, his hand brushing Dani's, that now held the talisman gifted to them by the dragons. Even in the brief touch, she sensed the tension in him. The hesitant hope.

He might end up all right, after all.

The growl of Corrupted vibrated the air, and Liam spun as Ryen stepped past Dani to join his father.

"I hope you know you're going to be grounded after this."

"Right, for the rest of my life, probably." Ryen sidestepped as something the same size as Dani's panther form prowled forward, letting out a hiss.

It lunged as Dani lifted the whistle to her lips and blew.

Chapter 18

RAE REACHED THE BASE OF the tower and jumped to catch a handhold partway up. She climbed, her hands faltering as a flash of light blinded her and Damien's barrier expanded over the city. Blinking, she stared as the Rahn'ka runes flickered on the translucent wall, large enough to cover the three blocks of the city closest to the palace.

He can't maintain this for long.

Reaching the top, she pulled herself up and onto a knee. Her gaze settled on the city, and her stomach lurched at the destruction.

Voids of blackness claimed several districts. Every tree and flower drained of life.

So many people out there are dead.

Guilt weighed on her shoulders.

Because of what we did.

Checking her quiver, she counted her arrows. Not enough to fight off an army, but enough to cover civilians in their rush for shelter.

What does it look like? Damien's voice echoed through her thoughts, and her fingers twitched in surprise.

She peered at where the largest temple she'd ever seen had dominated the eastern skyline and saw only a mound of blackness. The sphere of Uriel's power bubbled, its surface continually shifting. It looked so much like the shape he'd taken in Hoult as Amarie fought him, only this time, the shadowed orb was the size of a building. A shiver cascaded down her spine.

At least he can't take that beast form without Amarie's power.

Tendrils lunged at Damien's barrier, lashing between the Corrupted that still attacked the surface. Every living thing the shadow passed over crumbled to dust.

Rae shut her eyes, focusing her thoughts to reply to her husband. *Just keep the barrier going, and don't worry about the rest.*

Damien sounded exhausted already. *Do you see any civilians outside the barrier I can extend to?*

Forcing her eyes to open, she scoured the remnants of buildings as far as she could see, but only Corrupted moved through the streets. She almost replied to Damien, but a glimmer of white fur drew her eyes deeper into the city. *Shit. I see Dani.*

Rising to her feet, Rae stepped to the edge of the tower and squinted. With the aid of her Art, she summoned a lightning strike that briefly illuminated the area where the Dtrüa fought.

How far from the barrier's edge?

Rae shook her head. *Too far. She's with Liam and Ryen. They're getting overwhelmed.*

Swinging herself over the side, she started her descent, tapping the rings on her left hand together. The Art-crafted bow hiding within wouldn't do any damage to the creatures, but the power still provided her with a semblance of comfort.

I'm going to help them. Rae pushed the notion at Damien, knowing he'd hate it.

No, stop. I can't... Damien's voice faded, an echo of an exasperated growl shuddering through the connection.

Rae's boots hit the ground, and she glanced back at where Damien sat within the center of the barrier. *I have to. I'll bring them back to the barrier.*

Lightning rippled across the Rahn'ka shield, casting an eerie glow through the darkness. Everything around her hung in a dim blue light from high above.

Damn it, Rae. Be fast. I will need to collapse the barrier to a more constrained size to last longer. I can't give you much time. Just until they evacuate the nearby buildings to the palace.

Rae sprinted between the buildings, hesitating when she reached the edge of the barrier.

Corrupted crawled all over it, gnawing at the invisible force.

I'm insane. I'm actually insane.

Rae found the thin connection to Damien. *I'll be fast and keep my eyes up. I love you.*

The glowing ceiling of the barrier dropped, and in a flash the outer wall surged out, launching the Corrupted into the nearby buildings, where their bodies broke against the stone.

"Thank you," Rae whispered, and rushed outside the protected area. She drew an arrow as she ran, pulling her bow off her shoulder.

Rounding a corner, she spotted the others on the next street over and nocked her arrow. Taking aim, she loosed it, then another, dropping a bear-wolf Corrupted to the ground.

Liam's gaze lifted and met hers. "Nice shot."

Black blood oozed down the length of his sword, more coating his clothing, along with specks of red where his arm bore a gash.

Dani emerged from a side street, her fur matted and glossy with onyx.

Rae looked at Ryen but held back her suspicion. "Let's go! The barrier is about to shrink and we need to get within it."

The white panther hurried towards her, and hot air touched the back of Rae's neck.

The Mira'wyld ducked, and Dani launched over her, tackling whatever beast had snuck up from behind.

Rae spun, eyes wide on the enormous leathery wings flapping on the cobblestone as Dani crunched the creature's thin neck in half.

Liam shoved Ryen forward, the young man heaving for breath and covered in blood, similar to his father. "We've summoned the dragons. We just have to hold until then."

Rae gulped. "No kidding, hey? A dragon. Real in the flesh. Totally normal." She loosed another arrow into the sky. "I thought the talisman didn't work?"

"Well, I—"

Liam's face hardened as he interrupted his son. "We had another."

"All the more reason to take cover. I don't imagine your winged friends can control where their breath goes. Assuming the legends told the truth of that ability." Rae's stomach flopped.

Normal fire couldn't hurt her, but she'd never tested her abilities against a dragon's scorch.

Liam nodded, spinning to catch a lizard-shaped Corrupted on his blade, the steel cutting through the monster's jaw before his son sliced its neck. The thing's head hit the ground with a wet flop as another launched forward.

A distant drum drew Rae's attention to the east, expecting another Corrupted, but the sky remained fathomless.

The beat continued, but her gaze found nothing until a lightning strike illuminated the sky.

"Shit. Shit." Rae ran backward, eyes locked on where she'd seen the giant draconi's silhouette only seconds before. Turning, she snagged Liam by the arm and tugged. "Run!"

Chapter 19

THE SKY TURNED ORANGE AND crimson, a roaring unlike any creature blasting through the streets as they ran.

Liam's body ached in muscles he'd never felt before, and his boots soared over the stone. Relief encouraged him to push himself harder, seeing Dani running ahead to clear their path of Corrupted.

With her in panther form, there'd be no keeping up, but she remained within eyeshot, lunging between Corrupted as they emerged from dark alleys. Their black oozing blood coated her fur.

A humming blue light hung on the air ahead of them. Behind him, a sea of fire bloomed, heating the air.

"Faster!" Rae ran next to him and Ryen, bow still ready.

A glimmer of red scales reflected a lightning flash, thick

wings whirling through the sky above the Rahn'ka's barrier. Razor teeth shone as Zaelinstra opened her jaws, a torrent of flame spewing over the city towards the blackness of the temple.

The meteor of fire sank into the shifting surface of shadow boiling to consume the city, and it shrank back. Black tendrils writhed like the twitching legs of a dying spider. Something bellowed, deep and sinister, making Liam's skin crawl.

A boom shook the ground, an arm of Uriel's power tearing through the buildings.

Liam's knees protested the movement of the ground, but he gritted his teeth.

Ryen went down, losing his footing as the cobblestone street ruptured.

Dani skidded to a halt, turning back for them, but a shadow crashed down from above. The building fell towards them, bricks raining like snow flurries in winter.

Shifting his weight, Liam dropped and slid along the rough ground. His arms wrapped around his son, sheltering him as debris buried them. The battering of the stone seemed like nothing to the pounding of his heart.

Dust plumed around them, suffocating and thick. Most of the fire's light dimmed, small gaps in the fallen bricks creating dusty rays through the darkness.

Ryen's coughs shook beneath him, and Liam met his son's startled eyes.

Voices shouted beyond the rubble, but he couldn't make out the words.

Footsteps pattered on the road, diminishing into the distance.

Liam pushed himself up with a groan, the ache in his body confirmation that nothing was broken. "Are you all right?"

Ryen coughed again, nodding. He looked up, but his eyes focused somewhere above his father. His entire body suddenly tensed, and he jerked his arm sideways, breaking Liam's support. At the same time, his knees pushed into his father's abdomen.

Despite being the one to teach him the maneuver, Liam tumbled to the side, thrown clear as another wave of stone and glass rained down.

The ground buckled, a dark chasm beneath swallowing them and the debris. The fall only took a few seconds.

Liam landed hard, covering the back of his head with his hands as chunks of the building pattered over him. A cough rattled his chest, everything quiet despite the chaos beyond his awareness. He pushed his hands beneath him, rolling over and peering into the dark space. His back twinged, but he could move. The thought of his son sent a chill along his spine, banishing all sensation but fear.

"Ryen!" Liam choked, staring at the mound of debris his son had flung him clear of.

He slid through the dust, rushing to the only part of his son he could see.

Blood coated Ryen's hand, protruding from the rubble.

Liam tore at the stone, no longer feeling the strain as he cleared the way to Ryen's head. His son's raspy gasp for air made his heart clench.

Why did he do that? If I'd shielded him...

Movement shifted the debris above him, and his head snapped up, expecting the mangled shape of a Corrupted to crest the opening above.

Wood snapped and a section of sky reappeared as a form fell into the rubble's hollow with him.

He scrambled for his sword, his hands shaking and bleeding.

Rae groaned, coughing as she crouched, skulking towards them. "Just me."

"Shit." Liam breathed. "Where's Dani?" At Ryen's pained, wet cough, he spun back to his son, falling to his knees. "Hold on, Ryen."

Fire raged above, mingled with the howls of the Corrupted.

"Your wife is safe." She pulled stones off Ryen, tossing them across the cellar floor. "Hurry."

Ryen cried out as Liam pulled a stone from beside him.

Rae paused, hands hovering over the next piece of rubble. "Liam," she whispered, motioning to the spot he'd just exposed.

The bellowing of the dragons above overpowered every sense as he beheld the blood. The shattered bone. And the iron rod protruding from his son's ribcage.

The world blurred as Liam stared, his heart denying what his mind already knew.

"Bad, huh?" Ryen grimaced, his face pale. "I know that look, Dad."

As a soldier of the Isalican military, Liam had seen plenty of death to know it far too well. But looking into his son's eyes, he shook his head. "We'll figure this out. You'll be all right." He looked up at the glowing sky, a rim of blue meeting the blazing red clouds. His gaze flickered to Rae. "Fire's coming. You better go."

"Nope. I told Dani I'd keep you alive." She sucked in a deep breath, her right eye shifting hue to a bright yellow. "And something tells me you're not leaving. So let's hope dragon's fire behaves like other fire." She tilted her chin up, abandoning her efforts to free Ryen and rolling onto her back to face the sky.

"It's hotter." Liam looked down at Ryen, eyeing the blood flecking his lips. He touched his son's blond hair, pushing the long locks from his eyes. "We'll hold out. We just need to wait for Katrin, and she'll fix you right up."

Ryen shook his head, eyelids heavy as he blinked. "You should go."

"I'm not leaving." Despite his attempt to use authority in his tone, it cracked. "What were you thinking?"

Ryen's bloody hand fumbled for his father's, and Liam squeezed.

"I was thinking I've screwed up enough in the last few years. And that Jaxx and Varin need *you* way more than they need me." Ryen grimaced as he wheezed a shallow breath. "I'm sorry. For everything."

Liam's throat tightened, his eyes betraying him by looking at where the iron broke through Ryen's flesh. His bleeding had slowed, but his face was ashen.

Zaelinstra howled, and the fire struck.

Liam welcomed whatever might come with it for a moment as he watched his son struggle for another breath. "Just hold on."

The chamber heated like a furnace, but Liam hardly noticed, even as Rae yelled at the effort of keeping the flames at bay.

"I'm sorry, Dad." Ryen's brow upturned in the center, his voice breaking. "Please don't hate me, I—"

"Shhh." Liam touched Ryen's chest. "I don't hate you. I never could. You are my son. And I will always love you. Always forgive you."

"Tell mom..." Ryen choked, coughing.

"You know damn well she feels the same way." Liam tightened his grip. "But you can tell her yourself. You're going to hold on." Even as he said it, the elongated blink Ryen gave spoke otherwise as the air heated further around them.

Liam glanced at Rae.

The Mira'wyld's hands shook, her head tilting back as she fought to keep the inferno away. Fire swirled at Rae's fingertips, like a blazing windmill that pushed it around them. It grew brighter as the roars from above intensified, the beat of Zaelinstra's wings shaking the stone.

As Ryen's body shifted with the stone, he made no sound, and his grip on Liam's hand weakened. The young man's eyes glazed over, peace overtaking his expression as his breathing ceased.

A sob broke from Liam's chest as he touched Ryen's face once more. He couldn't breathe, his vision blurring as he closed his son's eyes.

Chapter 20

FIRE RAGED, AND DAMIEN GRIMACED as sweat ran down his spine.

He'd needed to abandon his attention on Rae, unable to maintain the tether between them while adjusting the barrier for the flames. The shape of the dragon on the horizon had sent a rush of terror and excitement through him.

Its wings spread as large as the palace, and Damien doubted it'd even fit within the courtyard he fought hard to protect.

"The Corrupted are dying!" Matthias's voice came distantly, as if he spoke through water. "But I still can't see Liam or Rae."

Damien panted, nodding his head. He'd pushed his body to the absolute limit, and already felt the power of the barrier waning despite collapsing it to only encircle the palace. He'd seen Dani plow through the barrier in her panther form before shifting. Rae had almost joined her, but they exchanged quick words before his wife raced off again.

And then the fire hit.

"Uriel?" The Rahn'ka cringed, hands braced against the stone in front of him.

"The temple has fallen." Matthias took a deeper breath as the orange in the sky diminished, the flames dissipating as the dragons ceased their assault on the Corrupted.

The courtyard lay empty behind them, except for the rush of healers working in a triage area to the west. Katrin and the guards had funneled the civilians inside.

Still no Rae?

He wanted to ask, but Matthias would have said something if she'd made it inside the barrier. Maintaining his concentration with his eyes open had become impossible. He'd taken everything he could from the ká around the courtyard, their lethargy adding to his own. And he couldn't ask any more of the king, who sagged with his own exhaustion.

A hesitant calm washed over the courtyard, and Matthias touched his shoulder. "You can stop, now."

Damien paused, forcing his back to straighten as he urged his power to confirm the king's words. But he could sense nothing beyond the barrier or the blurry sensation in his head.

Trust him.

Damien breathed as he released his hold, and cold washed through his limbs. He gasped, collapsing forward.

The king caught his upper arm and righted him. "I'll go ask Dani about Rae and Liam."

Damien gripped his arm, grateful the king paused instead of overpowering the feeble resistance. "Thank you."

Matthias squeezed him before letting go, footsteps echoing away.

The chaotic sounds of the courtyard rushed into Damien's ears, and he focused on the distant cries of the children within the palace foyer. The city loomed with desolation, still aflame or in piles of rubble.

Pressing against his knees, he sat up as much as he could, watching the fire as dragon wings flashed in a distant lightning strike.

The king's steps returned, hesitating in their approach. "Dani is leaving to search for Liam and Ryen. She said a building collapsed on them, and Rae went back to protect them from the fire."

Damien nodded, his heart pounding at the thought of Rae being beyond the barrier when the dragons took to the city. There'd been two of the monstrous beasts for certain, though it seemed as if only one would have been required to lay waste to the city if it'd wanted to.

Someone gripped beneath his arm as he stood, and he looked to see Katrin hoisting his arm around her neck and pulling him to his feet.

"Let's get you somewhere more comfortable to rest." She urged him to turn, but Damien protested. Despite it, the small woman guided him towards the palace doors, still propped open.

Guards helped civilians up the stairs, leading the injured inside.

"No, not until I know we're truly safe. And Rae…" Damien got a foot ahead enough to stop them. "Not yet."

Katrin's brow furrowed. "You're as stubborn as Matthias."

Damien gave her a weak grin, but it felt hollow. "I'll take that as a compliment?"

Shouts erupted from the east side of the courtyard, accompanied by the rhythmic drumming of wings.

Twisting free of Katrin, Damien wavered on his feet as he beheld the burning city beyond the bridge. The flames roaring on the collapsed buildings near the moat edge guttered like candles under the onslaught of wind brought by the dragon's wings.

The remaining regiment of guards shifted towards the silver gate at the courtyard entrance, arranging in their rows despite the futility.

"Stand down!" Matthias stepped towards his troops, who cast wary glances over their shoulders as the ground shook beneath the dragon's bulk. "She is our ally. Zaelinstra is no threat."

The dragon's red scales glistened in the dying firelight. The image of her with the shattered temple on the horizon looked like something from a nightmare, but the king approached.

The crown guard hesitated until Matthias reached the back line and proceeded through them, forcing the guards to move or unceremoniously bump into their king.

The dragon's serpentine neck swung down, a canine shaped head the size of a large horse dropping near the entrance to the bridge. Spines framed her face like a sun, cat-like eyes narrowing, and Damien sensed her studying him.

She crawled over the rubble on four legs, moving like a slender feline with her wings tucked against her back.

In awe, Damien watched as the dragon shook, the fires gleaming on her shining scales. The spines along her jaws continued down her back, some as large as he was.

His feet carried him on, despite the lethargy.

She's a terrifying beauty.

Zaelinstra shifted again, circling around Matthias. Her claws bit into the stone road, and she studied one of the dragon statues at the end of the bridge, her head tilting. Gradually, her gaze returned to the humans before her, slitted pupils focused on the king.

Matthias kept his voice low as Damien and Katrin joined him. "Isalica is deeply in your debt... I am, too. Thank you."

"I believe I also owe you, King." Her voice rumbled like the echoes of the storm above. She surveyed the three of them and gave a low snort. "Your friends left out some details in our conversations about the state of the kingdom."

"I kept your secrets as I promised." Matthias's tone held strength, but his eyes were hollow.

Zaelinstra's head angled up to her companion, who still circled in the sky. "I knew the situation would be dire when Liam and Dani summoned me, but didn't expect... this." She lifted her head, looking over the razed city behind them. "Zuriellinith."

"He was one of you, wasn't he?" Matthias glanced at Damien. "He was a dragon."

Damien's heart jumped into his throat. "What?" He gaped at the king, then back at the dragon as her wings twitched.

"I was not yet hatched when he committed his great atrocities. But we use him as a tale of caution for our hatchlings to this day." She lowered her head, wicked jaws only a foot from Matthias's chest. She huffed in a deep breath, and the exhale blew the king's hair back. "You are fortunate."

Damien couldn't hear Matthias's quiet reply.

"Can we go back to the bit about Uriel being a dragon?" Damien flinched as the dragon's focus turned to him, head moving like a serpent.

"I know what you are too, Rahn'ka."

Damien clenched his jaw, looking around them, but all the guards and civilians only stared from the other side of the courtyard. "Then I suspect we have a great deal to discuss." He swallowed, steeling the lingering fear from his face.

Zaelinstra snorted again, lifting her head over them. "In time. Perhaps when you can stand without wobbling." She stepped gracefully between Damien and Matthias, walking over them. Her tail swooped stone aside as if it was a tumbleweed, missing them by inches.

As she cleared Damien's view of the courtyard bridge, silence settled.

Gazes drifted to the figures emerging from the city, breath stilling in Damien's chest.

Rae strode onto the bridge, entering the courtyard. But his relief was quickly overshadowed by the limp teenager in Liam's arms.

His ká had faded, except for the thin thread still connecting it to his body while he traversed the Inbetween.

Dani ran towards Damien, her soot-covered face streaked with tears. She ignored the dragon as she barreled into him, hands meeting his forearms. "You can bring him back, right?

You said you can bring someone back." Her voice shook, eyes bright and bloodshot.

The Rahn'ka could follow the thread, but the mere thought made everything in him shudder. He sucked in a breath and loathed himself. "I can't."

Dani shook him, eyes darting sideways to the king, who hurried to her. "Then jump. Please. Jump back. We can save him!"

Matthias shook his head as his shoulders sagged, his breath faster. "Dani, I did. I tried. I can't go back more than seconds right now."

The Dtrüa wailed and dug her nails into Damien's forearms. "You said you could save someone! Help him! *Please.*"

Damien embraced the pain and closed his eyes. "I'd never make it back, Dani. I can't. I'm so sorry."

Liam halted a few yards away as Katrin strode over to him, and they laid the boy on the cobblestone.

Dani shoved him away, anger sparking in her face with a new flood of tears. "You would try if it were your son," she whispered, turning from him.

The truth of what she said ripped through him, but Damien shook his head. If he risked it all to go into the Inbetween and died, too, it'd jeopardize everything.

The dragon lowered her maw close to Dani, and the Dtrüa leaned on her, silently sobbing.

"I will send Zelbrali to get your other hatchlings." Zaelinstra spoke in a quiet tone. "It is best to keep them close, now. The shadows will be hunting."

"Thank you, Zael," Dani whispered as Liam pulled her into him instead.

"I must carry word to the Primeval. But will return by morning." The dragon turned to Damien and Matthias before looking at the sky, where the other dragon circled, the fire shining on its golden scales. "He will remain to ensure you may rest in the meantime. I believe we are well beyond keeping our existence secret from humans any longer."

Matthias nodded as Zaelinstra's wings spread. Lightning flashed behind the thin membrane of her wings before they pounded down, and a rush of wind nearly knocked them off their feet. Her shape darkened the sky as she soared near the golden dragon, then turned west for the mountains.

Rae joined Damien, her face also marred by tears that had since dried. "I couldn't do anything for him. He saved his father."

Damien leaned against Rae as his knees weakened, unsure which sensation caused it. "A bitter way to gain redemption." He breathed slowly, touching his wife's hair. "May Nymaera welcome him into her arms."

No one spoke as they shuffled around the long meeting table, gathering coffee and breakfast food.

Matthias sat at the end of the table, eyes vacant as he stared at his coffee.

A thin canvas tent shaded them from the sun, set up in the garden so Zaelinstra could join them when she arrived.

The thunderstorm from the night before had left the ground soaked but cleared away the remaining smoke from the smoldering city. The palace itself blocked the view, but the bright morning did little to erase the memories of the night before. Everything around them hung quiet, devoid of even birdsong.

Damien reached for another loaf of bread, his stomach still rumbling even though he'd already eaten four times the usual meal amount. The strength in his muscles had returned, and he forced himself to slow as he spread cheese over his bite.

Rae side-eyed him but kept quiet as she added an unusual sugar cube to her tea. Her palms donned no scars from the blistered burns Katrin had healed, but she hadn't slept well, and exhaustion slowed her movements.

Liam stood, his arms crossed and his focus impossible to discern from the glaze in his dark eyes. Despite pleas from his sister, he'd insisted on being present.

Dani hadn't emerged from their chambers, and Damien didn't want to ask why Liam wasn't with his wife.

Guilt still flailed his insides at his inability to save their son.

At the Dtrüa's desperation. Her nail marks still marred his arms.

The acolyte pinched herbs from a tin one of the staff had brought her into a teapot, then added something else. Her eyes were bright, her movements steady, a sharp contrast to how the king looked.

Did he even try to sleep?

Damien set his bread aside and opened his mouth, but stopped when the flap to the tent behind Liam brushed aside.

"Sir." The crown guard saluted Liam and extended a bundle of papers.

Liam took them and tilted his head towards the door.

The guard didn't hesitate, refraining from looking at the exhausted bunch before he left again.

Liam unfurled the parchment, examining the writing. He flipped to the next page, his lips tightening.

"How bad?" Matthias's tired voice sounded as if he already knew the answer.

Liam glanced at the others before clearing his throat and lowering his raspy voice. "An estimated fifty-five thousand casualties among the population. About twenty-two percent, though they're still finding survivors."

Matthias's jaw flexed, his eyes briefly closing. "And the city?"

"The destruction consumed approximately thirty percent of the city's infrastructure. The outer districts are mostly

unscathed, but the center of the city around the temple..."
Liam cringed as he walked to Matthias, holding out the
bundle.

The king swallowed and nodded, taking the parchment. "I
have already sent word to Omensea, Icedale, and Undertown
that we require their aid in recovery." At a movement from
Katrin, Matthias continued. "I would have sent word to
Ziona, but they're in the middle of a military uprising. Our
alliance is no longer solidified."

Katrin touched his wrist, her eyes widening. "How long?
Seiler? And Kelsara? Are they all right?"

"Both safe. They relocated to Undertown when Ziona's
monarchy collapsed shortly after our treaty. They have two
children." Sadness lurked behind the king's deep voice.

He's probably never met his brother's children.

Katrin's shoulders slumped as she looked back at the
teapot, stirring the herbs with a spoon, her eyes distant.

Rae bowed her head, looking sideways at Damien again.

"Helgath will send what aid we can, but we must look out
for our own, too." He reached for his wife's hand beneath the
table. "Uriel recognized Rae, and if he connects her to me...
we have to expect he may set his sights south."

Matthias met his gaze. "Of course. I can provide you with
an escort on your journey home, if you wish."

"Thank you." Damien watched as Liam returned to the
doorway, assuming his unfocused stance again. "I'm... sorry

for the destruction this all brought on your country, Matthias." He looked at Liam, clutching Rae's hand beneath the meeting table. "And for the lives lost. I wish there was more I could do."

"Many of those who survive have you to thank for it." Katrin brushed the king's wrist again. "You and Matthias saved countless lives yesterday."

If only I could have saved one more.

Damien gave a weak smile, but nodded. "Still, I regret I must ask you for another favor."

Rae squeezed his hand beneath the table.

The king gestured with an open hand. "What is it?"

"Uriel will know a Rahn'ka was present in the city yesterday. Hopefully, he doesn't know for certain who it was, but all the same, he'll start putting pieces together. He's been imprisoned before..."

"You're implying he will become more desperate." Katrin poured hot water into the teapot over the herbs she'd added. The ceramic lid clicked as she twisted its lock into place.

Damien nodded. "We had the advantage of him wanting to remain secret before, but with an attack of this magnitude... It's a question of if he's abandoned that ruse entirely, or if he'll return to the quiet workings like before. But if he feels threatened..."

Matthias rolled his shoulders. "He lashed out because of the opportunity. Proximity and our awareness already established. But... if I had to guess, I would say that he will hide, now. Lick his wounds. Give us the illusion of victory while he rallies strength. What is the favor, my friend?"

Damien pursed his lips, studying the king. "Rae and I need to begin the journey home tomorrow. We have our own family to protect if you're wrong. But there are other duties that need to be attended to here. Things that need to take priority..."

"The prison." Matthias sat straighter in his seat. "You want me to oversee its construction."

"I know it is a lot to ask, but I believe the dragons will respond better to working with those they are familiar with rather than two strangers from Helgath. And... they are a necessary part of this. More so now than before, learning the truth of Uriel's origin."

The king remained silent for a moment, his gaze moving to Liam. "I may be Isalica's ruler, but my power is worthless without the right connections. So I must defer to my crown elite. What do you think, Liam?"

The crown elite straightened. "Assuming there truly is no way to just outright kill the bastard, then I don't see another option. We'll work with the dragons in securing a location for the prison and the construction itself."

The king met Damien's gaze. "It will be done."

The Rahn'ka nodded, a wave of relief loosening his chest. "There are other components that must still come together to make imprisoning Uriel a reality. But it became fairly clear that maintaining energy is going to be the greatest hurdle."

"You need Amarie for that." Matthias tilted his head, a look of knowing underneath the exhaustion. "Don't you? That's why Rae was with her."

Damien hesitated, his eyes darting to Katrin briefly as he considered the weight of the information.

"There's no point in hiding it from her. I'll tell her, anyway." The king tapped his fingers on the table in front of him.

The Rahn'ka shook his head. "You must understand, only Rae and I know the full details of the situation. I didn't even tell Jarrod when he asked."

"Fair. But this is unprecedented. I know everything he's done in the last twenty years, and I know that when he emerges, it will be to kill me. I must not keep secrets, just in case." Matthias sipped his coffee for the first time, his brow furrowing as he set it down.

"If you die, it may already be too late." Damien eyed his untouched coffee before looking at his wife.

"Perhaps the shared knowledge will be the determining factor in keeping me alive. I will remember more, I'm sure." Matthias's tone was grave. "Things you'll need to know. I will write these things in depth whenever I think of them and address the letters to you. We cannot have any secrets among us."

Rae gave his hand a gentle pat beneath the table. "Tell them."

Chewing the edge of his tongue, Damien reached into his ká and pushed a weave of energy out around the tent, sealing it from prying ears.

Katrin shifted, her attention centering on Damien.

"The story of Uriel's first imprisonment is... convoluted. It's millennia old, far before even the Sundering. The guardians speak of the event as if it was the entire reason the Rahn'ka came into existence. The spell itself is something I'm still working to understand, and I have been getting little help from the resident guardians. Even they seem hesitant to talk about Uriel or his Shades." Damien recalled the arguments with Sindré, who refused to even help sort through the ancient tomes in their sanctum.

"And what, exactly, is a Rahn'ka?" Katrin watched him.

Damien glanced at Rae. "Supposedly, an Art practitioner meant to balance the forces of our world. The Rahn'ka ceased to exist after the Sundering, but the guardians used the sanctums to preserve and channel the power to support one. Sometimes the power drove the person they chose mad, sometimes they were just a little crazy. Ailiena was the last successful Rahn'ka before me."

"Our children will eventually inherit the power, too, once they mature." Rae took a deep breath. "But this won't fall on their shoulders."

Damien closed his hand on her knee. "No, it won't. We've already started gathering what is necessary to imprison Uriel, and it's closer now than ever."

"What else is necessary?" Katrin leaned forward against the table.

"Well, a Rahn'ka." Damien pointed at himself and then gestured to Matthias. "An abandoned host." He glanced at Rae, and she gave him a subtle nod. "A Mira'wyld, a Shade redeemed, and... the Berylian Key."

"So you have everything." Matthias tilted his head. "Except the prison itself."

"Yes." Damien nodded, his stomach tumbling at the realization that what Matthias said was true.

We really have everything. One day, this might be over.

Liam stepped forward, making everyone pause as he approached the table. He grunted, dismissing the concerned look from his sister with a wave and focusing on Damien. "If I'm going to be working with the dragons, I need more than a list. I only see the three of you. Who's the other two? And what's a Mira'wyld and the Berylian Key?"

"A Mira'wyld controls the elements. Water. Wind... Fire." Rae blinked at him with a sad look.

Liam's brow lifted in understanding as he nodded slowly. "And the Key?"

Damien swallowed. "It's an old conductor of ancient ley lines from before the Sundering. When it broke, the power pooled into a single source, which is *believed* to be infinite."

"It sure feels that way, too." Matthias leaned back.

Katrin turned to Matthias, confusion in her face. "You've seen it?"

"Not it. Her. Amarie got Uriel's attention on the coast of Helgath, and he almost captured her. Probably would have, if not for Rae." The king looked at Rae again. "You can't imagine how much he detests you."

Rae gave a wry smile and shrugged.

"Hoult. That destroyed fishing village? That was Uriel and this Key?" Liam plopped into one of the chairs, pushing the plate of breakfast meats further from him.

Rae rolled her lips together. "It was."

"Who's the Shade?" Katrin's voice held an air of hesitance. "You said you have one already, which is good, right?"

Matthias sighed. "And it's fortunate it is who it is. Even in the current situation, Uriel would never release Kin from service entirely. He's become a point of pride."

Damien's brow furrowed. "Why would Uriel release any shades from his service? My understanding is he just kills those who betray him."

"Despite what we witnessed, there is a limit to Uriel's power, especially now that he no longer has access to mine. One of the first things he did when I became his host was bolster the number of Shades he had. Before... he could only maintain..." The king shrugged. "Five or six reliably. And that depended on the natural power of his host at the time. He's going to cut his ranks."

"That means this potentially was an even more substantial blow to his power base." Katrin's face brightened as she met Damien's eyes, but a frown came a moment later. "What kind of retaliation are we expecting?"

"There's no way to know." Damien rubbed at the back of his neck. "But we have some advantages. Do you remember any other Shades of note, Matthias? Ones he'd keep?"

Matthias's gaze shot up. "He'd still try to keep Kin, but... he also has the other one." The king shook his head. "Jarac. Fuck. Feyor will attack. And my brother is in Undertown."

"What?" Liam's chair shifted back, grinding on the stone. "What does Feyor have to do with this?"

"Prince Jarac. Kin's twin. He's a Shade." The king grabbed a piece of blank parchment from a stack on the table. "I sent a letter to Undertown redirecting forces to the capital, but they need to stay there and prepare for war."

Damien's eyes widened, his entire body suddenly rigid.

Kin has a twin?

In all the time Kin had been inside Sindré's sanctum, he'd never mentioned such blood ties.

"Son of a bitch..." Damien grumbled.

"Jarac isn't just a prince, anymore, either. He's king now." Liam cast a confused glance at Damien before focusing back on the king. "Word came of Hendrick Lazorus's death months ago."

Matthias's quill paused. "Yes. I killed him." He swallowed, stretching his wrist before he continued writing.

Katrin put her hand atop his. "Not you. Uriel."

The king glanced at her with a subtle, solemn nod. "Uriel always meant for Kin to take the throne, but he settled for the brother. Kin was supposed to be Uriel's host before he found me."

"Kin?" Damien caught himself imagining Kin's face with obsidian eyes. It sent a shiver down his spine. "He was going to be Uriel's path to a kingdom. Before, he'd been playing smaller games."

Matthias nodded. "He altered his plans when he learned about my Art and my blood."

"Certainly worked in his favor." Damien's mind whirled, trying to piece together the fragments of information. He heaved a deep breath. "Kin left out those details when he came to me to help break the bond. I feel like being the twin brother of a royal would have been pertinent information." His hypocritical irritation tainted his tone. "Do you think Uriel will use Jarac as a host rather than keep him as a Shade?"

"Unlikely. Jarac has no connection to the Art and wouldn't maintain Uriel for long unless he cut all strings to his existing Shades, and he won't do that. Jarac is better as a Shade. Isalica's arch priest, though... That's who I'd target."

Matthias's features twitched in a brief cringe before he hid it.

"Why not stay in Alana? Isn't that who we believe Uriel to have taken now?" Katrin urged the cup of tea she'd made closer to Matthias, replacing his coffee cup with it.

"His terms with her were likely time restrictive. I doubt he's still using her. The attack on the city would have taken a toll on her already." The king's upper lip twitched in the hint of a sneer.

Katrin's brow knitted, and she opened her mouth, but stopped when the steady beat of wings filled the garden courtyard. The ground trembled as the massive shadow of a dragon landed beside the tent.

Liam exchanged a look with Matthias as he moved to the canvas panels on that side of the tent, lifting them as a pair of guards scurried to help secure them aside.

Zaelinstra lowered her head, her long teeth sending a twinge through Damien.

She could devour any of us whole.

"Apologies for the delay." The dragon settled onto the ground, her belly scales scraping the cobblestone. The ká of the flowers and bushes beneath the dragon squealed in surprise, crushed beneath her.

Damien winced, but hardened his aura against the voices, and Zaelinstra gave an apologetic, knowing look.

"Not necessary." Matthias folded the paper before him and handed it to one of the guards. "Send this to Undertown immediately."

The guard nodded with a salute and hurried off, steps quicker than the situation warranted.

"Welcome back, Zaelinstra. Do you bring word from the Primeval?"

Chapter 21

"YOU SURE YOU DON'T NEED anything?" Liam stared at Katrin as she leaned against the doorframe of the temporary bedroom for Matthias. Her brother's gaze flitted over her head towards the king behind her, who strode into their room.

Katrin gave Liam a weak smile. "I'm sure. The tea I asked for has arrived, and I think Matthias could benefit from some quiet."

Pursing his lips, Liam touched her wrist. "What about you?"

She brushed his touch away. "I'm fine. And I shouldn't be who you're worried about." She cringed. "I'm sorry."

"No, it's fine." Liam shook his head as he stepped back. "But I don't think she wants me around."

"Liam, you're her husband…"

"And right now I only remind her of our limp son in my arms." Liam closed his eyes and shook his head harder. "I'll stay close in case you need me."

Katrin tried to banish the knot still lodged in her gut, unsure if it was the death of a nephew she never knew, or the lingering tension clouding Matthias. "You should try again."

Liam sighed but nodded. "I'll go check on her." He leaned forward and kissed the top of her hair. "I'll either be here in the sitting area, or just in the chamber beyond." He gestured with his head behind him. "If you need anything…"

"Thank you. Same goes for you." Katrin gave a half-hearted smile. She opened her mouth again, but closed it with a sigh.

This is all insane. How do we move forward from here?

Liam gave her a brief, understanding nod before he turned, and she closed the door gently behind him.

The iron handle's chill permeated through her palm, but she couldn't bring herself to let go right away. Her fingertips brushed over the intricate carving of the door meant to belong to one of Matthias's crown elite. But they had removed all from service, and there were many to sort through to replace the king's most trusted.

"There are plenty of rooms if having your own would be more comfortable for you." Matthias's deep voice lacked emotion as he stared out the west-facing window, giving a view of the mountains rather than the devastated city.

Katrin paused, contemplating the thought. She turned slowly from the door, her skirts whispering across the grand rug before the room's hearth. "I'm not sure how much comfort is readily available right now. But I can't stand the idea of being in a different room." She stopped several feet away. "Would you rather...?"

Matthias shook his head, rolling his shoulders. "How are you? How is the baby?"

Before she realized what she was doing, her hands ran over her abdomen. "I was getting a little worried because I wasn't as tired as before, but Damien assures me the baby is perfectly fine."

The king let out a breath, but his posture didn't relax. "And you?"

Katrin met his stormy eyes, wishing she could understand everything going on in the mind behind them. "Handling all of this, mostly." Her knees weakened as visions of the destroyed city flickered in her head. She strained to keep the devastation from her face. "I'm here, with you. Liam and Dani..." She tried to block the images of Liam carrying his son's body from the rubble. She swallowed. "I just wish there was more I could do. But I'm grateful to be with you right now."

Matthias's eyes bored into her, seeing straight through her veiled answer. But he didn't press for more. "I don't know how I feel about having you close. There will be attempts... and I don't want you caught in the middle."

The sharp pang in her chest felt like a knife, stirring her step closer to him. "I'm not leaving you, so don't even suggest it." She circled away from him, hoping he wouldn't see the pain on her face, but he caught her wrist.

The king's chest rose faster as he tugged her into an embrace.

The warmth of him encouraged her arms to wrap around him, burying her face against his tunic. His heart raced in her ear as she fought to keep in the tears she'd restrained all day. Her fists tightened on the fabric at his back, and she breathed his scent deep.

It remained mostly the same as she remembered, though the decay of the city's destruction still lingered. The image of Uriel's shadows curled around Matthias made her mouth dry, but she squeezed her eyes shut and buried her face harder against him.

"Kat, you need to understand something," he whispered, his mouth against the top of her head. "And it's important you hear me."

She nodded against his chest as she opened her eyes, staring out the window at the mountains as his arms tightened around her.

"I am... I'm not the man you—"

"Stop." Katrin lifted her head, pressing her hand to his

chest where it'd been. Peering up, she met his dark-rimmed eyes. "You don't have to explain... any of that. I know I won't ever fully understand what...." Her throat tightened, and she swallowed the emotion. She pressed her hand against his heart, feeling the beat against her palm. "You are still *my* prince. *My* Matthias. However changed you are..."

Matthias tilted his head, patience prevailing in his expression. "I need you to listen, Priestess. I am not. As much as I want to be, I am *not*. I will not hold you to previous—"

"Matthias, stop." Katrin pushed from him, suddenly cold in his absence. She wrapped her arms around herself as she walked back into the room. "Please, look at this from my perspective, too. For me, we were together only days ago. We were in the Yandarin Mountains on the backs of drakes, returning home with the news of a child on the way." She stared beyond him at the mountains, so unchanged despite the years. It made her ache. "We're... both going to have to take this a day at a time. I know it's not the same here." She gestured at her head, even as she shook it. "But in my heart you're still *mine*. Despite everything."

Emotion shone in Matthias's eyes. "I wish it were so simple, but you must realize that to me, you're a memory. A wonderful, blissful memory, but I can't be the same person you loved. I can't be a father."

Katrin stepped towards him again, touching the sides of his jaw. Her fingers ran through his beard as she tugged his face down closer to hers. "Do I seem like a memory now?" She brushed her hand through his hair. "I'm not going anywhere, Matthias. Even if you're not the same person, I will continue to love the memory and that will be my guiding light to love you again as you are now." She gripped the back of his hand, encouraging it to her belly. "And you will be an even more wonderful father. *Because* you worry about all this. Because of who you are at a level that Uriel could never destroy."

The king's jaw flexed, and he withdrew his hand from her abdomen. "You're not listening. I could hurt you. Hurt our child. My mind... it's... not right." He bowed his head, a pained expression crossing his features. "Even before I... came back. I don't remember things. I don't... I don't know what's real all the time."

Stroking his hair back from his forehead, Katrin shifted to catch his eyes. "Then I'll help you with that." Her touch moved back down his jaw. "This is real, right now. I'm real. And there's nothing you can say that will make me walk out that door. I know the danger, but I'm still here. And that's my choice."

A shadow passed over Matthias's gaze as his breath quickened. "I pray you never know the true depth of the danger." He stepped back, cringing. "You should rest."

Studying him, Katrin narrowed her eyes. "What just happened?"

"Nothing." He paced away, rubbing his hand.

"Bullshit." Katrin hardened her tone. "I thought we'd agreed to be honest with each other in these situations. If you want me to understand, then you have to tell me."

Keeping his back to her, Matthias stretched his hand. "I lost my temper."

Pursing her lips, she eyed the marks on his knuckles that hadn't been there before. "Was it the wall or the armoire?"

"The wall."

"But not me. That's how I know." Turning to the short table in front of the fireplace, Katrin knelt to sort through the pouches of herbs she'd requested. "I'll make you some more of that tea. It helped earlier, right?" She'd encouraged him to drink the entire cup during their conversation with Zaelinstra, despite him insisting he'd rather have more coffee.

Matthias's tone softened. "Maybe. But it tasted like feet."

Katrin rolled her eyes. "It's not supposed to taste good. It's supposed to help you relax." She untied the drawstring on the mint and threw extra leaves into the tea strainer within the ceramic pot. "Did it make you feel sleepy at all? Or cause anything to go numb?"

"Numb?" Matthias finally faced her, an eyebrow quirking. "Not that I noticed. Are you tranquilizing me?"

"It's helping, isn't it?" Katrin pinched more laquoa flower petals into the mixture.

"Well, I didn't punch the dragon, so maybe."

Katrin snorted despite herself and shook her head. "I somehow doubt that would have gone over well." Lifting the pot of hot water, she poured it over the tea mixture. "At least the dragons will help, and they're not angry about Liam and Dani bringing them into all this."

Matthias stared at her, the same intense look he'd given her many times since returning. "I know this is difficult for you, in a way I can't understand. It must be... cruel, and I'm sorry."

"You don't need to apologize." Katrin's brow furrowed. The lines of his face were different than she remembered when he had that look, and it left a hollow pit in her stomach. "Why do you keep looking at me like that?"

The king averted his gaze, rolling his shoulders. "I don't know what you mean."

The sudden inclination came to wrap her arms around herself and curl into a ball near the fire.

But that won't help either of us.

Katrin smoothed the fabric of her skirt. "Matthias, you can talk to me." Her throat tightened, but she swallowed. "No matter how you push, I won't go anywhere. You might deny it, but I know you need someone right now."

Matthias sighed. "It helps, all right?" He watched out the window, hands in his pockets. "You haven't been here for two decades. Uriel never looked at you, so sometimes it just... helps to focus on your face, because it separates the past from..." He gestured with his hand.

Her chest ached. "Then look at me. We don't even have to talk if that's better."

As he faced her, the king's expression held a hint of surprise. "You always want to talk."

Katrin scowled, the acrid scent of the tea turning her attention to the pot. "I can *not* talk." She lifted the strainer from the teapot, and the lid clinked as it locked into place.

The room grew eerily silent except for the slosh of tea as she poured it into a cup. The ceramic tinking as she lifted the saucer and held it out to Matthias, lifting her eyebrows.

He accepted it, but turned and set it on the small table. When she opened her mouth, he quirked a brow, and she closed it. Stepping closer, he touched her face.

Pursing her lips, Katrin met his eyes. Unable to stop the inclination, her hand slipped to his waist.

Matthias's thumb passed down her cheek and over her chin as he studied her face. His jaw flexed, a sea of emotion warring in his irises.

Her tension ebbed away with his touch, the back of her eyes aching as tears she didn't fully understand wanted to form. Pushing her tongue to the top of her mouth, she urged it to remain quiet as she ran her fingers over his beard. She wanted desperately to kiss him, and her eyes deceived her by flicking to his warm lips. Her stomach twisted as she silently cursed herself and met his eyes again. Her lips parted, but she stilled her tongue just in time.

Matthias played with her hairline at her neck, his chest rising faster. The corner of his mouth twitched before he dipped his chin and kissed her.

A fire roared through her at his gentle affection, a soft moan whispering against his lips as she returned it. The pressure at the back of her eyes grew, so she closed them as her hand slipped into his hair, and she silently begged him for more.

The king's kiss renewed with greater intensity, stealing her breath for a moment before he broke it. A growl rumbled from his chest, and he took a deep breath. "I, uh..." He gave her a sheepish half-smile. "I'm trying."

She smiled back at him, feeling the glisten in her eyes. "I know." She stroked his hair from his forehead, pushing it behind his ear. "Drink the tea, and we'll just sit here... together... all right?"

Matthias nodded, tension returning to his posture as he stepped away and they sat. Unspoken thoughts danced through his eyes, bringing a look of sadness that he hid with a sip of tea. Cringing, he gave a sideways nod. "Better than this morning, at least."

"Good." Katrin fished the little notebook from her pocket, plucking up the lead pencil wedged between its pages. She scribbled the addition to the tea down, tapping the tip of the writing tool on the page. "I'm hoping the other changes help, too."

"Can I make suggestions?"

She quirked an eyebrow. "Of course, but no promises. Sometimes it is how the herbs work together in certain proportions."

Matthias eyed the tea. "Would be easier to cover the taste with whisky."

A sharp laugh escaped, and it lightened everything on her shoulders, but she shook her head. "Better not to mix that with those particular herbs. I'm sorry." She touched his knee before leaning back into the crook of the couch, tucking her feet underneath her. Her lips held the pencil as she turned the page and jotted down the word 'whisky' and stared at it, as if it'd encourage inspiration for what the alcohol might work with.

Setting down his empty teacup, Matthias closed his eyes. "Bottle might help with sleep."

"The tea will do that just as well." Katrin glanced up at him, hoping he'd see her worry, but he didn't open his eyes. "You should try lying down."

His eyelids flickered up, and he huffed. "If I lie down, I'll pass out. And sleep is a different kind of torture."

"Because of the dreams?"

Matthias nodded. "I slept a few moments last night. Exhaustion is preferable."

"But you can't continue to function like this. You're still human." Katrin reached forward, touching the back of his hand. "I'm hoping the tea helps you sleep deep enough to avoid the dreams all together."

His eyes met hers, his hand turning to hold hers. "There is no respite from the nightmares. Not yet, at least." He glowered at the bed before eyeing the couch. "Stay?"

She squeezed his hand. "I'm not going anywhere." Releasing him, she lifted her arm to the back of the couch, brushing his shoulder. With gentle encouragement, she trailed her hand across his back as he leaned closer to her, his head settling into her lap.

His dark hair stood out against the still unfamiliar pale yellow fabric of the new dress. The dark circles beneath his eyes were so much more apparent in the sunlight from the window.

She traced her thumb up his cheekbone, running it beneath his eyes. "Please remember how much I love you, Matthias," she whispered, still stroking his skin.

He hummed, resting his hand on her knee as his eyes closed. "You put something in the tea that wasn't there this morning."

Katrin smiled, twisting a lock of his hair. "Just trying to find the right combination to help." She watched the muscles in his face relax as she rubbed his temples. "I'm a bookworm, remember? I've studied cases of soldiers back from war with symptoms like yours, though their experiences can't compare, I know."

"You drugged me," he mumbled, his breathing slowing to a deeper rate.

She watched the last of his stress leave his face as sleep took him. "Only a little."

Chapter 22

WISPS OF BROWN AND GREY clouded the breeze, making Dani's hair tickle her neck.

Decay. Destruction.

Death.

A glorious numbness filled her chest, trapping a scream she couldn't let out. Her cheeks felt tight from repeatedly drying tears, her eyes swollen.

She stared at the bright sky, at the shifting rays of sun through the clouds that Ryen would never see again. A breeze he'd never again feel.

The drum of wingbeats echoed through the distant wind, and she gritted her teeth. She knew the cadence of Zelbrali's flight.

That's Varin, Jaxx, and Micah arriving.

Her heart broke with a new dagger of grief as she imagined her daughter's agony once she learned of her brother's death.

I cannot tell her.

Pushing that burden onto Liam hardly felt fair, but she doubted she could form the words.

A tear hit her wrist, and she looked down, surprised, touching it, and then her face.

A knock sounded on the door, making her jump, before Katrin twisted the latch.

Zelbrali landed in the courtyard below, Jaxx's shout to his father telling her Liam was already there. Already prepared to tell them without her.

"Can I get you more tea?" Katrin's skirts brushed along the worn rug as she made her way towards her friend.

Dani shook her head. The previous cup still sat untouched on the side table, where its heat had slowly diminished.

"You need to eat or drink something at least." Katrin kept her voice low, touching Dani's wrist.

A pained cry echoed up from the gardens below. A sound Dani had heard before, but the depth of Varin's sorrow now far surpassed all loss she'd suffered before.

Dani squeezed her eyes closed, fresh heat springing from her eyes. Her throat closed, but a sob escaped, and she collapsed forward with her face in her hands.

Katrin crossed in front of her, reaching the window. The hinges squeaked as she sealed it shut, locking away the echoing sobs from Dani's daughter.

She could imagine Liam holding Varin, stowing his emotions as he had since it'd happened.

Why doesn't he hurt as much as I do?

"I want to be alone," Dani whispered, pulling her feet up onto her chair in front of her and wrapping her arms around her knees.

Katrin didn't move from the window, and Dani felt her gaze. "I don't think that's been helping, so I'd like to try something different." She approached, putting her hands on Dani's forearms before kneeling. "I'm getting better at the *no talking* thing. So we can just sit here, and I can just be here. I need to make up for the time we lost."

Dani blinked as more tears fell, centering her gaze near Katrin's blurry face. "You never even met him." She cringed, blinking faster and biting the inside of her cheek. "My son is dead, Kat. My *son*. Nothing will help."

Katrin's grip tightened. "No, I suppose nothing will." She brushed a strand of Dani's hair behind her ear. "I'm so sorry. There aren't even words to convey how much."

Dani gripped her legs harder until her nails sparked pain beneath them. "I never even got to see him. Say goodbye. I wasn't there. I wasn't with him..." She bowed her head, hiding it behind her knees. "He thought I hated him."

Katrin shifted, sitting on the arm of the chair and embracing her. "No, Liam would have told him the truth, you know that. Just like I know Ryen loved you, regardless of all the chaos in the end." She pressed her lips to the top of Dani's head. "You must forgive yourself, just as he would forgive you. It wasn't your fault that you weren't there in the end."

Giving into the ache in her chest, Dani cried into Katrin's dress.

Only minutes passed before she heard the tap of Varin's steps. Righting herself, she swiped the wetness from her face. "I cannot let Varin see me like this," she muttered.

"Like what? Grieving?" Katrin squeezed her hand. "Don't be as stubborn as that husband of yours. Let yourself feel, Dani. Maybe sharing it will ease the pressure, even if just a little."

The door clicked open, and Katrin stepped back as two sets of feet hurried through the room towards their mother.

Jaxx reached her first, barely giving Dani time to scoot forward in the chair before he embraced her, Varin quickly behind him. Her face was wet as she buried it against her mother's neck, collapsing against the side of the chair.

Even as she tried to control her reaction, a betraying sob shook Dani's body. She gripped Jaxx, pulling him closer with one arm and the other around Varin. "I'm so sorry, my loves," she whispered, kissing her younger son's head.

Varin's grip tightened as fresh tears touched Dani's neck. "I'm glad you're safe. When I didn't see you with Dad in the garden, and the look on his face…" She squeezed her mother tighter.

Dani cringed. "I'm sorry I wasn't strong enough to be there."

She shook her head against her mother's neck.

Jaxx was the first to release her from the embrace, but Liam approached behind him.

"I'm sorry. They wanted to see you right away. I tried…" His voice was the usual gruff tone it'd maintained the last several days, hiding all signs of his own remorse.

"No. I want them here," Dani whispered, a pained smile crossing her face. "I need you all."

Katrin's soft steps crossed the room before the door closed gently behind her.

Liam stepped forward, caressing Dani's wet cheek before kissing her temple. "Then we're all here."

Jaxx moved behind, wrapping his arms around Dani's shoulders briefly before standing to emulate his father. He sucked in a short breath, and Dani swore she could hear his mind reeling.

"Are we really going to be staying here? In the palace?"

Dani sniffed and nodded. "We are, for now."

"I always thought Uncle Micah was making up the stories about you all being crown elites." Jaxx's voice remained strained, hiding the emotion with his disbelief.

Dani silently applauded his attempt to lighten the haze of

grief clouding the room. "They were all true."

Varin finally loosened her grip, pressing her forehead to Dani's before sniffing and standing up. "Who was that woman who was in here? She reminds me of Aunt Lind, if she was thirty years younger."

Liam scoffed. "Not far off from the truth. That was Katrin, my younger sister."

"I thought she was…" Jaxx trailed off, unable to say the word.

"We have a lot to explain." Dani reached for her son behind her, taking his hand. "Because there will be no more secrets."

Dani walked over the grass, the voices of her family murmuring around her, but she hardly heard them. Their scents calmed her nerves. But one was missing.

One would forever be missing.

Her heart ached, constantly threatening her eyes with tears, but she bit her tongue to keep them in.

I wish I had something of his with me.

She opened her mouth to ask Liam where Ryen's cloak was, but her intention faltered when she heard her husband's chuckle.

How can he laugh right now?

A part of her whispered he was trying to ease the burden of

grief off their other two children, but her mind refused to accept it. The haze of her pain continued to drown out their conversation, blurring her senses.

Dani didn't even try to stop herself when her foot caught on an uneven bulge in the grass, landing on her knees with an exhale.

"Mom!" Jaxx crouched beside her, touching her arm. His head turned in her blurry vision as he exchanged a look with his father.

Liam had already lowered himself to her, grasping her arms to pull her to her feet.

The Dtrüa tensed, shrugging him off to remain on the ground. "I'm fine," she whispered, letting her shoulders droop.

"Dani." The way he spoke her name made her ache more like something else had broken. He crouched again, but stopped when Varin spoke.

"Go ahead with Jaxx, we'll catch up." The sun turned her daughter's hair into a gold shining spot in Dani's vision.

Hushed words passed between Jaxx and Liam as they walked away, but Dani closed her eyes, shutting them out.

"Mom." Varin knelt in front of her.

Dani opened her eyes to blink at her daughter's shape. At a face she'd never seen clearly. While the possibility reawakened with Katrin, it would never be an option with her older son. Not with his pyre set to light the next day.

"I don't know what life will look like without one of my brothers, either..." Varin's voice shook. "But he saved dad's life, and I will... *forever* be grateful for that. He died a hero, and I..." Her words broke, and something inside Dani snapped.

The Dtrüa leaned forward and embraced her daughter, pulling her tight. "I love you both so much. A piece of me is missing."

Varin shifted to pull away, but Dani tightened her grip and shook her head.

"But I am grateful, too. He is... *was* a fighter." The words tore through her chest, taking the pieces of her heart she attempted to stitch back together with the truth. "And I am so proud of him. I wish I'd told him..."

"He knows, Mom," Varin murmured into her ear. "He knows, I promise."

They remained for a time, and Dani steadied herself with her daughter's even breaths.

Dani drew away first, and Varin stood, pulling her mother to her feet with her.

"I miss him, too, Mom, but he's here." She moved her hand from her chest to Dani's, inhaling a shaky breath. "And here."

Dani touched Varin's face, swiping her daughter's tears away with her thumbs. "Where has my little girl gone? All I see now is a smart young woman, who I cherish so much."

She pulled her into another hug, breathing her scent. "I'm so glad you're here."

"I'm not going anywhere." Varin sighed. "We'll get through this together."

Holding hands, they walked after the boys, and Dani used the back of her free arm to wipe the tears from her face. "How were things with Uncle Micah while you three were home?"

"Exhausting." Varin huffed. "He was so keen on keeping us distracted, I don't think Jaxx ever had time to even pick up a book. He even tried to bake cookies." She paused, and Dani could hear the smirk. "Even the drakes wouldn't eat them."

Dani's lips twitched in a smile, and she swallowed. "Did he come to the palace with you?"

"He did. He's here, somewhere. Probably looking for... King Rayeht. Wow, that's still weird to say. Will we meet him?"

"Of course." Dani nodded. "He's practically your uncle, too."

"Because he and aunt Katrin..." Varin's voice trailed off, waiting for her mother to complete the thought.

"They were... *are* engaged, last I knew. Though it has been a long time."

They neared a familiar decline towards a terrace along the palace moat.

"I still don't understand where Katrin has been all these years. Dad doesn't want to talk about it."

"It's a sore subject," Dani whispered. "But she was asleep for a long time, and the Art kept her young. She wants to know you, though." She cleared her throat. "Both of you."

Varin's steps slowed, her gentle touch encouraging Dani to do the same. "I feel like I hardly know anything about her. You and Dad never..."

"And we should have." Dani put her arm around Varin's shoulders. "We should have told you more."

"You were trying to protect us." Varin circled in front of her mother, stopping her descent towards where Liam and Jaxx's scents hovered near the railing overlooking the dry moat. "But we should probably stop talking about Aunt Katrin."

Faint yellow tinted Dani's vision, and she let out a breath. "Where is she?"

"She just came through the archway of magnolias behind us." Varin always used familiar scents to tell Dani the location of things. "She looks... tired."

Empathy relaxed the Dtrüa's shoulders, imagining the stress her friend coped with amid everything.

Katrin was trying to be there for not just her, but for Matthias and Liam, too. Not to mention the darkness she probably battled for herself, for missing two decades of her loved ones' lives.

"Come. You should meet her." Dani guided Varin around, approaching Katrin at a leisurely pace.

"Dani." Surprise laced Katrin's voice, along with the exhaustion her daughter mentioned. "I'm glad you're getting some fresh air, finally."

The Dtrüa nodded, swallowing the rise of tension in her throat. "I'd like you to properly meet my daughter, Varin." Letting her arm fall to her side, she nudged the teenager.

"Hello." Awkwardness hovered between the two as footsteps approached from behind.

"Hey Katy girl." Liam brushed his hand against Dani's, and her shy son stepped cautiously beside her. "Sorry, I need to get to that crown guard induction I mentioned. I'll see you at dinner?"

Dani clenched her jaw, keeping her gaze averted to the side. She said nothing as Liam leaned to kiss her and Varin's heads.

"You can come with me next time, Jaxx." Liam rustled their son's hair, hesitating before taking off towards the palace.

Forcing a smile, Dani let out a breath and motioned to her other child. "And this is Jaxx. Jaxx, this is your Aunt Katrin."

"A pleasure." Jaxx shifted in a formal greeting, extending his hand. His voice held steady, but she could still hear the undercurrent of grief.

What were he and Liam talking about?

"I'm fairly certain the pleasure is all mine." A light smile returned to Katrin's tone as her hand met Jaxx's. "Though I'm still getting used to being an aunt to more than just Izi."

Varin turned to her mother. "Will we be able to visit them soon, you think?"

"Maybe..." Dani nodded, wondering if the farm would be a safer place for their children than the palace.

Jaxx groaned. "Grampa always makes us work in the cow barns, though. And cows are way grosser than drakes."

Dani smirked. "I'm sure Gramma's pies make up for it, no?"

"That's actually one of the few things I do know about you, Aunt Katrin. Your pies. Gramma always said yours were better." Varin paused, hesitation entering her tone. "Maybe you could teach me, sometime?"

"Aunt Lind burns everything," Jaxx mumbled.

"Your mother tried to teach me, once." Dani rolled her shoulders. "Not one of my strengths."

Katrin huffed. "I'd be happy to teach you, even if your mom is a lost cause for baking. Have you seen the kitchens here in the palace, yet? They're certainly an excellent place to learn."

"I haven't." Varin's tone relaxed. "But I look forward to it."

"As do I and your father. Been awhile since we had pie." Dani tried to smile, but it made her chest ache. "Then you can show off the next time we visit Gramma and Grampa."

Chapter 23

MATTHIAS STARED AT THE GROUP of crown guards waiting for him to speak with unwavering patience. Silence weighed on the air, all eyes on him.

The king cleared his throat. "You all may believe you know me." He exhaled slowly. "You don't. I am not the ruler who has presided over this country for the last twenty years. I am forever changed, and I humbly request your patience as our country undergoes this transition. I cannot explain the depth of the cause, but my loyalty is stronger than ever."

A few of the guards exchanged glances, but Matthias rolled his shoulders and continued. "Most of you find yourself in an unexpected position. Our city has suffered an unprecedented attack, taken irreparable damage, and endured... unimaginable loss. Your friends, your family. What you were before this attack no longer matters. Whether you sat at a desk, organized the armory, or handled training at the barracks. You have been chosen... called to a higher duty because amid all this chaos, it has become clear that I can trust you. I have removed the traitors from the palace, but it will take time to reestablish ourselves as a unit. As a unified force."

A door at the side of the room quietly opened, and Liam slipped inside before carefully closing it so as not to draw attention.

Matthias smiled, gratitude filling his chest at his and Dani's renewed support. "Training will resume at a deeper level to prepare you all for the roles you've taken on. It is no light matter, and believe me when I say you have my utmost respect. I—"

The door at the back opened, and Micah's gaze met his.

The king's chest squeezed.

His oldest friend returned the smile, eyes bright.

"I look forward to serving with you all." Matthias sucked in a breath. "Crown Elite Liam Talansiet will give you your orders." He looked sideways at Liam, who nodded.

The guards saluted, raising their fists to their chest, and the king stepped down while Liam moved to take his place. He found Micah again, and motioned with his head to exit through the side door to the armory hallway.

"Our priority is still finding more survivors. First regiment to the..."

As Matthias closed the door, Liam's words faded, and he turned to face his friend.

The sunlight pouring in through the open windows on the opposite side of the hallway lit the silver in Micah's beard, for a moment looking more the part of Matthias's father than his double.

Micah shut the door he'd used, eyes flashing towards the ruins of the city beyond the window. Black mounds of stone and splintered wood, the shattered spires of the temple like a broken bottle piercing the sky.

His friend tore his eyes away, turning again to Matthias. His face softened, and he gaped. "It's really you."

Matthias smiled, emotion tightening his throat as he nodded. "It is. How are—"

Micah jerked forward and pulled him into a rough hug, which Matthias happily returned. "Gods, it's good to see you again." The former crown elite withdrew, studying the king's face. "You hardly look different from the last time I saw you."

"I don't think you can play the part of my double anymore." Matthias smirked, his shoulders lighter. "Not with all that's going on there." He motioned to his own temples, where Micah had greyed over the years.

Micah grinned and shrugged. "It makes me look more refined. Always difficult getting the guards to listen to someone younger than them, so maybe it'll help earn a little more respect at last." His eyes flickered to the city again, sadness filling them. "I'm glad you're back."

"I am, too." Matthias sighed, shaking his head. "Are you? Back, that is. Will you take your old position again?" His stomach twisted at the idea of ruling without the man he'd never led without.

"Liam just reinstated me." Micah smiled, and something in Matthias relaxed. "And I sent word to Stefan. I assumed you wouldn't mind having him back, too. Might take a bit more finagling for him, since he'll be moving the family, too."

"He has a family now?"

"Wife and three little Stefans. Terrors."

Matthias grinned, but his insides ached. "That's wonderful. What about you?"

"I enjoy being Uncle Micah." The man ran a hand through his thick hair. "You know me."

"That I do." The king took his shoulders and shook him. "I can't believe you're real. And already reinstated... Thank you, brother."

He nodded, patting Matthias on the shoulder. "I hope this familiar face helps. How are you holding up? I don't know how much..." He trailed off as he met Matthias's eyes.

Lowering his arms, Matthias wondered how much Micah knew. "I was a passenger in my life for two decades, and I saw the wickedness my hands inflicted. Just trying to take it a day at a time, and Katrin is helping me sleep."

After she'd dosed him with tranquilizers in his tea, he'd

slept the entire night, but it hadn't been entirely without dreams.

"I saw her briefly in the garden. She... looked the same, too." He chuckled. "I guess not everything changes."

Matthias looked up as noise echoed through the hallway, the guards all leaving the address chamber to follow their orders.

Liam arrived through the side door, appearing next to them. "We're due to speak with the city liaison now, if you're ready."

The king nodded, looking at Micah. "Join us for dinner later?"

"Of course."

Matthias patted his friend on the shoulder one more time before watching him walk away, disappearing around the corner.

Liam gestured down the hall, and they strode in the opposite direction. "I think we're making real progress. Change is good."

"Changes are the *last* thing the people need right now." Holbert's white hair looked more tangled than usual, like puffs of clouds on either side of his balding head. "Stability is what they need."

Matthias groaned as he rubbed his thumb and forefinger

over his eyebrows. "I think any semblance of stability is gone at this point."

A young woman frantically scribbled on a piece of parchment, her smooth black hair constantly reminding him of Katrin's. Her lips pursed into a thin line and fingers covered in splotches of ink. She looked far too young to be the city's planner, though her promotion had been sudden.

"We must rebuild, but to do things the same as they were only sets us up to make similar mistakes. The city must be reinforced, and the temple..." Matthias frowned, resisting the urge to glance out the window at the destroyed spires.

The woman looked up, her eyes panicked. "What about it? You don't want to change it, do you?"

"I want to change its hierarchy. It needs new leadership. A new arch priest or priestess." The king leaned back in his chair.

"Absolutely not." Holbert lifted a pair of thin spectacles to his face, peering down at the parchments laid out before him. "In fact, we were very fortunate that High Priestess Delacour was away when the temple..." His gaze turned blank for a moment. "Shattered. She will be here to help organize within the hour."

Images flashed in Matthias's head of the high priestess's vow to follow Uriel by whatever means necessary. Whether she knew the truth of the imposter remained irrelevant to her moral compass.

"High Priestess Delacour will be arrested on sight." Matthias tapped a finger on the table. "High Priestess Amelina will take the position instead. "

"Delacour is Amelina's superior by nearly twenty years..." Holbert glowered down the shining oak table.

"And she's as corrupt as they come." The king steadied his heart rate.

"Your majesty, High Priestess Amelina is dead. She didn't escape the temple." A mousy, grey-haired gentleman spoke from the end of the table, rifling through another set of papers. "As is High Priest Kol. Delacour is the only High Priestess within the city."

Matthias stood, bracing both hands on the table. "Then we will find another. I don't care if we promote a priestess over Delacour. Did you not hear me? She *will* be arrested. Have other options for me by tomorrow. This is not up for discussion."

"The entire city is in turmoil, and a deviation from the temple's designated hierarchy like this will throw everything into further chaos. Corrupt or not, she should—"

Matthias slammed his fist onto the table. "Advisor Holbert, you are dismissed."

The air grew taut in the room as everyone stared.

"Pardon, your majesty? I just—"

"The king told you to leave." Liam stepped forward from his protective position behind Matthias. "Go, or I will remove you."

Holbert sputtered, standing and gathering his papers.

"Leave those." Liam instructed, and Holbert balked.

Everyone remained still, as if a predator stalked the room as the advisor shuffled out the door, glancing back at Matthias with wide eyes.

Only Liam's footsteps sounded as he moved to where the advisor had been, and slid his paperwork down the long table towards Matthias.

"Permission to speak candidly, your majesty?" The mousy man smacked his lips together.

Matthias tried to remember his name, but could hardly recall seeing him around the palace. "Granted, Mister...?"

"Telvesh, your majesty." The man nervously made eye contact before looking back down at the table. "Advisor Holbert should not question you, but the matter of replacing the arch priest is still a delicate one. The people are desperate for someone to guide them, and are looking to the temple."

"I appreciate the fragility of the situation." Matthias sat. "But I refuse to hand the seat to someone undeserving. Do you have a suggestion for me?"

"I regret I am not familiar enough with our religious structures to be any guidance in such matters. But, you should know, there are outcries that *you* are the problem, your majesty. The... *corrupt...* one."

Matthias hummed. "That makes sense."

Telvesh straightened, and the room hovered in stillness again. "Your majesty?"

"I wasn't myself." The king took a deeper breath. "Those closest to me can attest to that, but that time has ended. Things will improve now. Return to the way they were under my father's rule. Perhaps it would increase favor to turn a portion of power over to the citizens and have them elect a new arch priest or priestess for the temple. Delacour won't be an option, but I will find others."

"Are the other rumors true?" The woman who resembled Katrin suddenly looked embarrassed, as if she hadn't expected herself to speak. "Apologies, your majesty."

Matthias lifted a hand. "What rumors?"

"That the woman you were to marry is back from the dead? The shelters are abuzz with talk about her."

"Katrin was never dead. Only held in an Art-induced sleep while her body recovered from the illness that killed my father." Matthias sighed. "She is well, now, and will make a public appearance soon."

"Do you still intend to wed her?"

Nerves fluttered in his gut, and the king softened his tone. "If I could ever be so lucky."

"How is this relevant?" Liam crossed his arms, making the woman sink back into her chair.

"I imagine Ermine asks because Katrin Talansiet is a popular subject of the rumors she mentions. Specifically relating to the king and Acolyte Katrin's connection to the temple. Some believe that the gods, themselves, were involved." Telvesh smoothed his silver hair back. "That she truly returned from the dead to help right the misdoings of a corrupt leader."

Liam grumbled. "Ridiculous."

Ermine's eyes darted up to him, color rising in her cheeks. "Some also believe the king is the one responsible for her disappearance, after realizing it would bring the influence of the temples into the palace at last."

So close to the truth, yet I can't tell them any of it.

"You're saying it's in my best interest to wed her, then?" Matthias hated thinking of his relationship with Katrin as political, but losing control of his country was a threat he'd imagined may come.

"And the people need to see you together as frequently as possible." Telvesh laced his fingers together in front of him. "Lady Katrin should be heavily involved in the temple's reconstruction, both in building and administration."

Matthias scoffed. "I doubt I could stop her even if I wanted to."

Ermine's face relaxed, but she didn't look up. "Good," she whispered.

Telvesh tapped the papers stacked in front of him. "Change is inevitable, but we need to hold on to what traditions we can. Midsummer is coming, and with it, we should plan a celebration."

Liam lifted his eyebrows. "Now? We hardly have enough food to feed everyone, and you want to do the Midsummer Feast?"

"There are other traditions of the holiday we can focus on. The dragons, for example..."

"He makes a valid point." Matthias leaned back in his chair. "We could request Zaelinstra join us for the Midsummer Festival and hold the tournaments we normally would. Food is scarce now, but aid from Undertown and Omensea should arrive within the week."

"You believe a dragon would actually attend?" Ermine's eyes lit up.

"I can't make any promises, though I think Liam would have a better idea if that's possible." Matthias looked at the man who'd spent the most time with the draconi.

Liam snorted. "Zaelinstra will enjoy the reverence, I'm sure. But it seems an interesting use of the new treaty with Draxix."

The king shrugged. "Our alliance with the Primeval will only strengthen with a show of economic support. Puts words to action and could restore confidence in our monarchy."

"Then it's settled." Telvesh looked to Ermine, who scribbled the numbers he started spewing at her regarding how many people would attend and where they would host the festival's events.

"Think now is our chance to escape?" Liam muttered, casting a wary glance across the table to where Ermine and Telvesh hunched over a pile of papers together. "This should keep them busy at least for the rest of the day."

"It is. If we leave quickly," Matthias whispered and stood, turning for the door. "I need to find Katrin."

Liam followed him out, quietly closing the door behind them. "I should check on Dani and the kids."

Matthias started down the hallway with his crown elite. "How are you all holding up? Is there anything I can do?"

Liam's jaw twitched. "No."

The king tilted his head. "You can talk to me, you know. It's been a long time, but I'm still here for you."

"I know. It's just..." Liam tensed, cringing as he touched his jaw. "I don't know what to say or do myself. He's gone, and my wife hates me right now. And I don't blame her."

"I doubt she hates you." Matthias swallowed the lump of guilt. "You did everything you could. I can't imagine what you feel... I'm sorry."

"Don't." Liam stopped, turning to Matthias. "I don't need

any more of that. Dani doesn't understand, but I just need to keep moving. Keep busy." His voice snagged as he looked down. "It doesn't hurt as much when I do."

Matthias huffed and nodded. "I understand that better than you might think." He motioned back the way they'd come. "As much as I'd love to claim this is all to improve my country, it's also... the only way I can cope, right now. So whenever you need to be busy, you just let me know."

His crown elite nodded, swiping his hand beneath his eyes. "I better go find my family." He cleared his throat and patted Matthias's shoulder. "See you at dinner?"

"See you then." Matthias watched Liam disappear around a corner before he started for his chambers, but Katrin wasn't there. He checked the library next, then the secondary dining hall on the off chance she'd gotten hungry. After finding no sign of her, he stopped in the hallway and debated seeking Dani to ask her to connect with her.

She wouldn't have left, would she?

He hadn't seen her since that morning, when he'd left for his meetings while she slept. Digging through his memories, his brother's face came to mind, and he smiled with a scoff.

The archery range.

As he approached, the thunks of arrows striking their mark echoed through the open doorway. He strode through the bow room to the range's door, pausing to lean on the frame and watch her.

Katrin drew back on another arrow, aiming with a steady breath the way Seiler would have taught her. She'd dressed in a long tunic and pants, a look he rarely saw on her, but it reminded him of their more adventurous days. A knot kept her black hair tied at the base of her neck, short wisps dancing against her temples she shook out of her face. Smoothly releasing the string, she let out a soft exhale.

The arrow sank into the target, finding the ring around the center mark.

"Been practicing? Or perhaps our mutual archer friend gave you some pointers." Matthias smiled, crossing his arms.

Katrin smirked, glancing at Matthias before looking at the target twenty yards away, tilting her head. "Little too low, still."

They had constructed the range for Seiler when he'd taken an interest as a teenager. Considering Isalica's harsh winters, the indoor location was a necessity their mother had insisted on. Matthias couldn't remember the original purpose of the long stone-lined space, though if it'd had doors he might have thought it a hallway.

"A proud shot, regardless." Matthias eyed the flat bow in her hand and the others on the wall behind him. "We could have that one adjusted to fit you better. The handgrip looks too big, and the string a tad tight. You should have one that's just yours. Seiler knows this stuff better than I do, though."

Katrin shrugged, looking down at the bow and running

the string between her fingers. "I've gotten used to it."

Narrowing his eyes, the king studied her slouched shoulders. "Are you all right?"

Reaching for an arrow from the quiver she'd left slung on the wall beside her, the acolyte spun the shaft in her hand before nocking. "I'm fine." Spreading her stance, she drew back for her shot, aiming for one of the further targets.

Definitely not fine, then.

Matthias chewed his lip, wondering what her reason would be for not telling him the truth. He held his tongue until after she'd let her arrow fly. "Should I give you some space?"

Her arrow went wide, sinking into the lower outer edge of the straw-filled target, and she frowned. "I still haven't figured out the longer shot." Her shoulders sagged as she dropped the bow to her side, and she turned more fully to Matthias. "Any advice?"

Straightening from the doorframe, he accepted her invitation to stay and entered the range, closing the door behind him. "Seiler is better at this." He approached her, standing behind.

"That truly sounds like an excuse." An air of teasing joined her half smirk. "You've already said that. Just show me." She shifted her back towards him, stepping into his touch.

Matthias scoffed. "Fine. But when I can't help you much, don't say I didn't warn you." He guided her hands up into an aiming position. "Wind isn't a factor here, but gravity is. Aim higher so you don't need to pull so hard on the string. It will give you greater control of your side-to-side aim." He quoted his brother, though the instructions hadn't made the king much better of an archer.

"Last time I did that, I hit the ceiling." Katrin glanced back at him, only catching his eyes for an instant.

Matthias chuckled. "Your arrows aren't the first to land there."

"It'd be easier if I was just stronger and could pull the string back further..."

"Force may work in many aspects of fighting, but this isn't necessarily one of them. This takes finesse and patience, both things you have in abundance beyond me. The strength will come with time."

She dropped her arrowless aim, leaning back into him. "I don't feel like I have the time."

Matthias wrapped his arms around her and lowered his mouth closer to her ear. "Are you planning on going somewhere?"

She shook her head, her hair tickling his neck. "That's not what I meant. It's just..." She sighed, turning into him and nuzzling into his chest. "I feel like I've already missed too much."

"I understand." Matthias rested his chin on her head. "But for clarity's sake, which part is bothering you at this moment?"

She shook her head and pulled back. "You don't need more." She slipped from his hands, adding the bow to the hook that held her quiver.

Matthias frowned. "I don't need more? What does that mean?"

"More worries. More regrets. You have enough, and I don't want to add any more."

Resisting the urge to hold her again, he leaned against one of the posts dividing the range. "So you've decided not to share your problems with me, rather than having us try to find peace together?"

"Let's focus on one bit of peace at a time. There's no fix for the time I lost, only more time for me to cope with it. You're the one who still can't sleep through the night. The one trying to rule a country that just suffered unfathomable loss." Katrin stepped closer, touching his wrist. "Don't worry about me. I'll be all right. We need to focus on you because without you, everything falls apart."

Matthias fell silent, letting his thoughts settle for a breath before speaking. "If I am so fragile that being there for your pain will be too much, then I shouldn't sit on the throne. Beyond that, what if your healing just happens to heal me a little, too? What if your happiness is so entwined with mine that the only way to find light is to do it together?"

She winced, looking down.

Using a finger, he lifted her chin. "Tell me why you're

upset. Not the generalized bit about losing time. I know that, and I know it hurts, but what is making it *sting* right now?"

"I met the kids. Dani and Liam's... Varin... she's almost the same age as me. And Jaxx... Twelve, and apparently an avid reader, who I never got to share my favorite childhood books with. And Liam.. Dani... I never got to see them become parents. Have our children play together, grow up together. And Ryen, I'll never..." Her voice cracked, and he pulled her into a tight hug.

"There is no getting those lost moments back, I know." Matthias kissed the top of her head. "But think of it as a trade. It's hard now, because you've missed out on the last two decades, but that means you'll get two extra at the end of your life. Think of what more you'll see of the young members of your family and their children. It's what I always told myself while I couldn't be a part of my family. I know it does little to ease the hurt of missing out on seeing your nieces and nephews grow up. I missed mine, too. It's not too late, Kat. We will make memories now, teach them things and read books. Our child may not grow *with* them, but they'll be together. It will be a different kind of future, but still beautiful."

"How do you do that?" Katrin touched his jaw.

"Do what?" He tilted his head.

She smiled. "See the bright side, despite everything."

Matthias huffed. "I've had a *lot* of time to think. And

believe it or not, I didn't spend all of it wallowing in darkness."

Her fingers ran over his cheek, brushing into his hair. "Thank you."

"You can share these things with me." He ran his thumb over her bottom lip. "I may not be in a good place most of the time, but if I can help you, it gives meaning to what sometimes feels like a futile existence."

She shook her head. "Don't talk like that." She moved in closer, their hips touching. "And you can confide in me, too."

"Mmm." Matthias's blood heated, and his goal of speaking to her about politics slipped away. "What if I don't want to talk?" He dipped his chin, brushing her lips with his.

Her eyes flashed with excitement as her fingers tangled in his hair. Their lips parted, and her breath tickled his skin before she pulled his mouth back to hers. The heat of her tongue traced his as she lifted to her tiptoes against him.

Matthias walked her backwards, his heart picking up speed as his body reacted to her taste.

Something clattered to the floor, and her back met the wall.

Her hands roved over his shoulders as she wrapped her legs around him, her weight shifting into his arms. The kisses grew deeper, more desperate, as he felt the buttons at his collar come loose.

He pressed against her, pushing up the sides of her long

tunic to touch the thin fabric beneath. Breaking from her mouth, he kissed her neck, and she hummed into his ear. A sharp inhale followed by a moan as his hips instinctively rocked.

Flashes of his hands running through black hair appeared behind his closed lids. But it wasn't Katrin he touched. The memory of Uriel's use of his body overpowered his senses, temporarily replacing Katrin's scent with Alana's.

Matthias balked, pulling from Katrin and meeting her gaze. His hands stilled, one supporting beneath her, the other just below her chest. Her wet lips encouraged him back, and he kissed her harder, cupping her breast. He found her stiffened nipple and rolled it between his finger and thumb, making her gasp.

Her teeth grazed his lip, grip tightening on his tunic before her touch found his skin, sending sparks through him. Her legs tightened around him, urging him closer.

Desire's inferno surged into his veins, making his hips rock again.

The bitterness of Alana's mouth reignited on his tongue, and he broke the kiss again, heaving for breath. He stared at her, but her eyes flickered jade in the lantern light. Alana's eyes. The image kept fluttering to the auer, and he lowered her, keeping her at an arm's distance as he stepped back.

"What's wrong?" Katrin moved forward, but paused. Her cheeks rosy, her chest rising in rapid breaths.

"I can't," he whispered, running his hands over his face. "I'm sorry. I can't."

Katrin's brow furrowed, and she tugged at the bottom of her tunic to put it back in place. "Can't?" She leaned against the wall, crossing her arms. "Why?"

Matthias lowered his hands and stared at them, remembering all the things they'd done. Anger seeped into his chest, and he cringed. "These aren't my hands. This isn't my body. It's done things I never would have." He looked at Katrin, trying to see her clearly through his cruel imagination.

She moved faster than he could anticipate and caught his hand. Lifting it to her cheek, she held it there. "It's me, Matthias." She pressed her hand to his chest. "And this is all you. None of what he did with your body was you."

"But I felt it." Matthias shook his head, instinct telling him to push her away, but he pulled her closer and breathed her scent. "I love you. I always loved you. Forgive me, please."

She wrapped her arms around his middle, hugging him fiercely. "I love you, too. And I'll always forgive you, even if there's nothing to forgive right now." She pulled away to look up at him, cupping his face. "This is you, and we don't need to rush."

Will it ever feel like it's me again?

Matthias closed his eyes, the progress he felt like he'd made that day slipping away.

Why am I even here?

He took her hands, lowering them from his face. "I'm sorry."

Katrin shook her head, turning her hands in his. "Stop apologizing. What did you come down here for? You had a serious look on your face, the one that usually means you've been dealing with politics."

"I needed your advice on a delicate matter. But we can talk later." Defeat echoed through him, and he clenched his jaw.

She didn't look away, studying his face in silence. With a deep inhale, she nodded and stepped back. "We can talk now, if you'd rather."

Matthias focused on a long bow hanging on the wall to the side. "Many of the temple's followers believe I'm corrupt and that I imprisoned you." He scoffed. "Ironic, how close to the truth that is. Anyway, I must select candidates so the people can elect a new arch priest or priestess to run the temple here."

"I'm assuming the local high priestesses aren't available?" Katrin tucked a strand of hair behind her ear.

"Delacour was working with Uriel, and Amelina is dead. I have no other knowledge, and I could use your help selecting a few for the people to choose from. They have also suggested that you make a public appearance and discuss your illness."

The long-term sickness had been her idea, and he glanced at her.

She nodded. "That will help, at least for a time. I'll write some letters to the temples in the south. Moving one of the high priests or priestesses from Lyon or Mecora may disrupt things for a little while, but it assures they might not have been corrupted by Uriel." She chewed the inside of her lower lip. "What kind of public appearance?"

"Preferably one where you don't claim to have been trapped by the king for twenty years?" Matthias met her gaze, but couldn't hold it. He turned, striding to the door. "You should talk to Liam, I think he will have some ideas."

"If the people think you imprisoned me, wouldn't it make sense for us to be seen together, too?"

Stopping, he stared at the woodgrain of the door and buttoned his shirt. "Ideally."

"Then come with me to visit the shelters tomorrow." Katrin walked after him. He expected to feel her reach for him again, but it never came. "No excuses this time."

Matthias nodded once. "I can do that." He opened the door, walking into the bow room. "I should deal with a few other things now, but I'll see you at dinner?" He looked back at her, the heat from their exchange no longer in her face.

"Sure." Katrin pursed her lips. "You're certain you don't want to talk about this more?"

"Most definitely." The king swallowed and walked away, exhaling a steadying breath as he opened the hallway door.

I'll never be who I was.

Chapter 24

Three weeks later...

ZAELINSTRA SAT PATIENTLY, THE WOODEN wreath woven with sprigs of summer ivy still perched on her head like a crown. She'd lavished in being the center of attention during the city's midsummer celebrations, and even a week later still wore her gift. Her cat-like eyes focused on Katrin and Dani as they stood hand in hand near the center of the garden.

Liam hovered near the waist-high oak table, which looked bare with only a meager tea setting near the edge. When it became clear the king and his companions would spend their morning in the garden, the staff had filled their meeting tent with platters of food. But Matthias had stopped them, much to the displeasure of the head cook. Instead, the king commanded the food be sent to the shelters, where his people needed it more.

Katrin dropped her hands, a bead of sweat glistening on her temple. "I can't."

Dani let out a breath and ran a hand through her hair. "This isn't working."

The dragon huffed as she lowered her head. "The channel of energy was correct that time. I sensed it ready to form, but there is a disconnect between you two." Her gaze shifted to Dani. "You must be perfectly aligned to—"

"We know." Katrin sighed, brushing the sweat from her forehead. "You already explained."

"Well, I still don't get it." Liam smirked as he poured water into a pair of glasses.

Zaelinstra narrowed her eyes at Liam, and it sent an odd shiver down his spine despite the history he had with the dragon.

"Maybe Katrin would have an easier time doing it without me?" Dani took a deeper breath, and Liam evaluated each subtle movement. Her shoulders were still far tenser than he'd ever seen, her face tired.

I don't even know if she's sleeping.

Liam had taken to sleeping on the couch in the common room between crown elite chambers, unable to stand the silence between them. She acted almost normal in front of others with him, but when they were alone, they hardly spoke. It ate at his insides, but he had no idea how to fix the growing rift.

Zaelinstra snorted. "Impossible. A single being cannot bend the fabric to forge a new path. Even I require my other bonded half to create one. You are fortunate. Humans rarely receive an élanvital, let alone meet them."

"That's another thing I still don't get." Liam held out one drink to Katrin, and she took it with a grateful smile. Moving to Dani, he lifted her hand and pressed the cup into it. "This whole, bonding thing..."

"It has to do with the winter solstice." Katrin waved her hand before taking a long drink. She sighed as she lowered the cup. "And I'm guessing it's more common among the dragons because they hatch together, even if they don't have the same parents."

"So, you're soul mates or something?"

"We weren't even born in the same country." Dani sipped her water. "I mean, based on what they told me. I'm Feyorian."

"Distance matters not." Zaelinstra's tone tightened with annoyance. "Must we return to this conversation? The élanvital bond is required for folding the fabric, just as it did on the day and time of your birth."

"We don't even have the same birthday." Katrin put her glass aside. "How can you be sure we're one of these bonded pairs? Maybe that's why we can't do this."

Zaelinstra chuffed, and her claw twitched against the cobblestone. Both Katrin and Dani went rigid in an instant, surprise lighting their faces. In unison, they shivered and relaxed.

"That... is how I know." Zaelinstra turned, her massive body curling around the center of the garden. Her tail brushed by the trees, shaking their leaves.

Katrin rubbed at the back of her head, shivering again. "That felt like..."

"Being struck by lightning?" Dani rolled her shoulders, stretching her neck.

"I merely prodded at the bond." Zaelinstra settled back to the ground, rolling onto her side like a big cat. "You'll recover. And hopefully feeling it that way will help the two of you properly channel it for this purpose."

Matthias appeared next to Liam, having disappeared inside to give instructions for the castle's kitchen staff. "Going well, I see." The king hardly interacted with Katrin, tension radiating off him.

I guess Dani and I aren't the only ones having issues.

Dani set her water down on the table before returning to Katrin. "Perhaps a different location would help? It's been a long time since I was at Undertown. Honestly, I hardly remember anything there but the prison."

"If your thoughts are not perfectly aligned—"

"Yes, yes," Katrin scowled as she took Dani's hands in hers

again, ignoring the dragon. She turned so her back was to Matthias, as if seeing him would disrupt her.

They'd chosen Undertown to communicate faster with Matthias's brother.

The dragon's spines rippled along her back, showing her own annoyance with the acolyte.

Katrin's impatience is certainly new.

"Maybe we can try your parents' ranch? It's only been a few years since I was there, and shorter for you." Dani softened her tone, glancing in Liam's direction.

"Home?" The word sounded painful from Katrin. She swallowed, her previous defiance seeping away.

"Unless you'd rather not... They'd love to see you."

"I..." Katrin lowered her gaze, and Liam's chest ached.

"It's Ma and Pa, Katy girl."

"Yes, and they're twenty years older than last time I saw them." Katrin glared at her brother, and her eyes flickered to Matthias for just a moment.

"If this is a location the two of you can hold better in your minds, then it is the best choice." Zaelinstra prompted Katrin to turn back to Dani. "Try it."

Katrin blew out a slow breath and bobbed her and Dani's hands up and down. "All right. Behind the house. By the flower bed."

"I remember." The Dtrüa closed her eyes in concentration, her breathing even.

"Maybe I should go," Matthias whispered to Liam.

"No." Katrin turned sharply without letting go of Dani. "Stay."

"Focus." Zaelinstra hissed, tapping her claw again.

Liam crossed his arms as he leaned against the table. "What's going on with you two?" He eyed Matthias, and while the king looked more rested, he still had dark circles under his eyes. "Even I can feel whatever is hovering in the air between you."

And focusing on someone else's problems means I don't have to think about mine.

At the dragon's glare, Matthias just shook his head and muttered, "Nothing."

"Liar." Liam pursed his lips.

"Quiet!" Zaelinstra blew a gust at them, kicking up garden debris from the recently trimmed foliage.

Silence settled, attention on the women. Their breathing quickened, light sparking between their grasped hands.

"Something's happening." Dani stared at the gap between her and Katrin. Her jaw flexed, a breeze pushing their hair from their faces.

Liam stood straighter, his shoulders dropping as he watched.

Katrin closed her eyes, her hands shaking as her fingers twitched against invisible threads. Her arms tensed as if she pulled on an impossible weight, Dani's doing the same.

Matthias exchanged a glance with him but said nothing.

Dani panted, and prismatic colors danced to life between them. Her hands gripped into fists, and she pulled the opposite direction Katrin did, straining.

"Yes," Zaelinstra whispered. "Pull harder and it will stabilize."

The Dtrüa stepped back, leaning into the effort, and sweat beaded on Katrin's forehead. Dani bared her teeth, and they both growled as the colorful light between them brightened and snapped wider.

It blew the wind back, whipping Liam's hair from his forehead.

Nymaera's breath.

Katrin doubled over, heaving a deep breath as she grasped her knees, nearly toppling backward.

Matthias strode to her, catching her by the elbow to support her. He whispered something, and her hand closed on his forearm as she righted herself with his help.

Dani stared at her hands, her eyes wide as they flickered back to the portal rippling with power. She smiled and looked at Liam before seeming to remember herself.

Hovering in the air between the two woman, the portal swelled, the outside edges shifting like waves on a beach. There were threads in the air between where he stood and the palace gardens beyond the portal, as if he looked through a torn cloth. Each fray pulsated, drifting on a phantom breeze.

Prisms shone along the edges, dancing in and out of his vision as he looked at Dani, her eyes now on her creation.

I wonder what she sees.

"Well done," Zaelinstra purred, watching as Matthias released Katrin before studying Liam.

"Will it actually work?" Katrin rubbed her palms on her dress. "How do we know?"

"Should we throw a rock or something?" Liam looked at Zaelinstra, who kept her eyes on the portal as if she could see something the rest of them couldn't.

Dani strode for the rippling light, lips tight.

"Dani, wait." Liam stepped forward to catch her hand, but the prisms brightened as she stepped through the shattered hole in the fabric without hesitation. Panic rose in his chest, and he jogged around the portal, but Dani was gone.

Everyone hung silent for a tense breath, staring at the rippling surface.

With sparks of light, the Dtrüa reemerged, a deadpan look on her face. "It works."

Relief loosened Liam's chest, but only briefly. "What were you thinking? What would have happened if it wasn't working properly?"

Zaelinstra snorted. "She'd have become trapped in the fabric, and wouldn't have been able to emerge again."

"Then good thing it works," Dani murmured, walking away towards the palace.

Katrin exchanged a glance with her brother before calling after her friend, "Where are you going?"

"Varin and Jaxx wanted to visit their grandparents," Dani called without looking back.

Matthias approached Liam. "So. Things aren't better, yet?"

Liam winced, crossing his arms. "No." He didn't look at his king, staring at the portal Dani had so recklessly entered. His stomach turned, trying to comprehend what would have driven her to such actions. Ryen's death weighed on her. But Varin and Jaxx were evidently on her mind.

But she still risked dying.

Katrin's gaze remained on his wife until she disappeared into the palace. Her shoulders heaved up in a sigh before she turned back to the portal and squinted at it. "I didn't think we'd actually do it. Does this mean we can open a portal straight to Draxix as well?" She looked at the dragon, who'd lumbered to her feet.

"Yes, and no. The Primeval are the only beings capable of lowering the wards and allowing a portal to connect. I would not advise entering a portal to Draxix unless you gain a clear welcome in." Zaelinstra eyed the horizon, her serpentine head lifting above the foliage of the garden. "You have earned rest at your parents' ranch, young ones. But I must return to see to my kin's planning of the prison." Her eyes shifted to Liam, boring into him. "Your mate is suffering, and while she may push you away, you must be the stronger and push back."

A growl bubbled in Liam's chest, despite the size of the creature lecturing him. "I'm trying."

"Try harder." Zaelinstra looked unimpressed while she spread her wings.

Liam opened his mouth to respond, only to get a mouth full of dust that the dragon kicked up with her sudden departure. Coughing, he glared at the massive silhouette in the sky and shook his head.

"Is that it?" Jaxx's voice came behind him, the boy breathing hard as he gaped at the portal.

Liam moved quickly to stand between his son and the portal before Jaxx could leap straight in like his mother. "Hold it. We're going to make sure we step through together so nothing crazy happens. Just like we did the first time into Draxix."

Varin huffed as she came to a stop next to her brother. "Mom and Aunt Katrin made that?"

"Not without considerable effort." Katrin gave her niece a warm smile, but tension lingered.

Dani loped towards them in her panther form, stopping next to Varin.

What can I even say to her when she clearly doesn't want to talk?

"Can we go, yet?" Jaxx looked up at his father. "Why are we just standing here staring at it? We've all seen portals before."

"Yes, but ones made by the dragons. And hopefully your mother and aunt will forgive me for still being a little leery of the first human-made one."

Katrin wrapped her arms around herself, chewing her bottom lip. "You four should go first. Maybe warn Ma and Pa before Matthias and I come through?"

Dani chuffed something indistinguishable and padded ahead, entering the portal again.

Liam glared at the spot her pale tail vanished from as Jaxx motioned with his head. "All right. Go on."

Entering the portal felt like a wave of temperate water rushing over him. He'd forgotten the bright flash of light that came the instant he stepped through, stars painting the black of his eyelids while a whoosh of air wrapped around him. For only a moment, he felt weightless, and then a country breeze brushed past his face. The familiar scent of his family's farm filled his nostrils, instantly relaxing his shoulders. He blinked the white from the edges of his vision, forced to release Jaxx as the boy darted ahead.

His son bounded over the steps to the back porch in a single stride, his hand moving to the iron handle without any consideration to knock.

A startled yelp echoed from the kitchen, one Liam knew

well from all the times he'd startled his mother.

"Jaxx!" Yez's shout turned into excited squealing as she rushed to her grandson, standing in the doorway. She pinched his cheeks, which the boy valiantly bore, before smothering him with an excited hug. "What are you doing here? You've grown!"

Dani stood a few yards away, still a cat. She lifted her maw, ears pinned back, and sniffed before turning. She loped away, head and tail low.

Am I failing her?

Varin appeared from the portal, making his mother's eyes widen.

"What in all Pantracia is happening?" The grin remained on her face as her granddaughter embraced her next. The grey-haired woman's gaze locked on Liam with a look of joy, and he braced himself for her question. "Where's Ryen?"

Something in Liam's face must have told his mother, because she sobered, clinging tighter to her two other grandchildren, who hugged her just as fiercely.

"There's a lot to explain." Liam's chest ached as he looked after where Dani had gone. He couldn't follow her. Not yet. "We better sit down, though. Where's Pa?"

"I need to clean," Ma murmured, rising with shaky legs and heading for the kitchen.

He hadn't held back, finally filling them in on where Katrin had been all this time and why Matthias had never visited. The toughest part came with recounting his son's death, and neither of them had listened with dry eyes.

They don't need to know he was a Shade, though.

Pa leaned back in his chair, the same one he'd always used, though it'd been reupholstered, likely by Izi, sometime recently. He rubbed at his eyes, still red rimmed. "We should warn Lind and Storne, too. They're due for dinner tonight."

Liam's older sister lived with her husband on the farm as well, though they'd built a separate home on the far side of the fields.

His body ached, but Liam pushed himself to his feet with a nod before his father quickly gestured for him to sit again. "I'll go. I need the walk, anyway." He stood, the age in his joints making the motion slower than Liam remembered.

Varin sat quietly near the fireplace, while Jaxx had jumped to go help his grandmother. She met her father's eyes, hers still shining with tears for her lost brother. "Should I go back to tell Katrin and Matthias they can come through?"

Liam nodded without fully looking at her, his mind still whirling with all the things he'd told his parents. All the insane details of their lives from the past twenty years. Events and situations he never could have imagined for himself when growing up in the very living room he now sat.

His daughter brushed her hand over his shoulder as she walked to the back door, but he missed catching her fingers by a fraction. As she left, her footsteps paused in the doorway before resuming, but the door didn't swing closed.

The summer breeze kicked inside, bringing the scent of the porch honey blossoms in with it.

"Oh, sweetheart." Yez stared at the back door, her chin wobbling all over again.

"Can we just..." Dani's shaky voice came from behind him. "Can I just..."

His own grief and shame made movement impossible as Liam ran his hands around the back of his head, lowering it to his lap. He'd done everything he could to hold in the emotions over the past weeks, especially when the funeral pyre had been lit. Yet, suddenly, sitting on his mother's couch, every defense weakened.

"Of course. Yes. We can." Yez nodded, wiping a counter. "Will you help me? I... was just cleaning. Apparently a king will be visiting." Her tone was uncertain, as if she only wanted to do exactly what Dani needed, whatever it was.

The sounds of their cleaning and Dani's footsteps blurred in Liam's senses, everything around him suddenly consumed as if beneath depthless waters. His shoulders shook without his permission, a well surging up out of control as his eyes burned.

Something closed on his shoulder, a touch he instantly knew.

Dani stood behind Liam and squeezed. She leaned over him, touching her nose to the top of his head.

He reached to his own shoulder, touching her skin, and it burst through the hollow. Sucking in a breath through his nose, Liam straightened, bidding everything back down beneath the heavy shroud of restraint.

I have to be strong.

He swiped quickly at his eyes as her touch left him, steeling his face into the serious expression he'd mastered while in the military. When he turned to say something to Dani, the back door rattled shut with her departure.

Chapter 25

KATRIN STARED AT THE PORTAL as Varin disappeared within it for the second time.

"Ready?" Matthias stood next to her.

"Does it make me a bad daughter to say no?" Katrin looked down to where their hands seemed far apart, both unwilling to touch despite how close they stood.

Matthias hummed. "A terrible daughter. They won't even be happy to see you, back from the dead."

Katrin frowned, focusing on one of the wavering threads in front of her. "You don't have to be so damned sarcastic all the time." Her stomach flipped at her frustration with him, and she silently hated herself for saying anything aloud.

The king took a deep breath, letting it out slowly. "I'd give anything to see my parents. They love you. Nothing will ever change that."

"But with everything Liam told them. If I were in their place, I wouldn't even know how to act." Katrin wrapped her arms around her abdomen, touching the part of her belly that had swelled so subtly only she'd be able to tell. "It feels wrong. To be happy and grateful. I've been far luckier than so many others."

"Well, I can't see a purpose in my presence other than to make them uncomfortable." The king rolled his shoulders. "You should go be with your family. It's not every day parents get to see their lost child again."

Katrin's hand lashed out to catch his as he turned. She locked her fingers with his as she shook her head. "You are the father of their future grandson." Meeting his stormy eyes, she tried to remember how to breathe. "Besides, I need you."

Matthias stilled, studying her with somber eyes. "I doubt that."

She squeezed his hand harder, making her knuckles ache. "I need *you*."

His stance relaxed, and he glanced at the portal. "Together, then."

Nodding with a breath, Katrin focused on the shifting air. She stepped forward, refusing to let go of Matthias. She blinked when they emerged on the other side, squinting into the sunlight over the pine mountains to the west. The scent of tulips came first, before the sweetness of the rhododendrons Lind had planted.

Her mother appeared in the window next to Varin, mouth agape. The door ricocheted open, and the woman rushed down the steps. "Katrin. My Katrin. It's really you." She hurled herself at her daughter, ignoring Matthias.

The king released her hand as she embraced her mother, stepping back to give them space.

She touched her mother's coarse hair, so much greyer than it'd been the last time she'd seen her. She smelled the same, though, like herb gardens and fresh dough. When she closed her eyes, her mother hadn't changed at all, but when Yez pulled back to touch her face, Katrin couldn't help but stare at the wrinkles on her face.

Tears ran over the grooves, the age that had taken root. It made Katrin's heart crack, but she smiled anyway. "Hi, Ma."

The woman sobbed again as she threw herself into Katrin's arms. "You truly haven't aged at all." She ran her fingers through Katrin's hair as the rhythmic thunk of wood announced her father's arrival.

His warm arms encircled her, too. Pushing a kiss to her hair, he didn't speak. His steady breaths worked to calm not only Katrin, but also her mother.

Yez pulled away again, her husband following suit. She ran a hand through Katrin's loose bits of hair, tucking them behind her ear. "I've missed you."

Katrin nodded, unsure how to respond.

It doesn't feel nearly as long to me.

Her father moved from beside her, a cane she'd never seen before supporting his uneven gait as he approached Matthias.

"Sir," the king's formal greeting matched his palace attire, and he extended a hand.

Pa took his offered grip, shaking it hard. "Welcome home, son."

Matthias's face finally relaxed, and he nodded. "Thank you. It's good to be here again." His voice came softer than she expected, lacking the burdens he carried at the palace.

"Can I help make dinner?" Katrin met her mother's gaze, which still hadn't strayed from her. "Where's Lind and Storne?"

"They ran to town to fetch Izadora." Pa reached into his pocket, plucking out his pipe. The familiar scent of his unlit tobacco drifted to Katrin and made her smile. "Join me on the front porch, Matthias?"

Maybe being in a place where things haven't completely changed will be good.

The king nodded again. "It would be my pleasure." He glanced at Katrin, his eyes shimmering as he smiled.

Katrin watched the men enter the house on their way to

the other porch, her heart leaping into her throat when she heard Matthias chuckle at something her father said. Tears brimmed in her eyes as she looked at her mother. "I'm here, Ma."

Ma wrapped her arm around Katrin, leading her towards the same old back stairs. "I was thinking of meat pies for dinner."

Chapter 26

THE GROUND VIBRATED, AND DANI slid her hand across the fence, focusing on the frantic beat of hooves.

Zaelinstra won't eat any of you.

She smirked at the thought of the dragon snacking on a cow, reminding her of her argument with Ousa the first time they'd been there.

The wing beats grew louder, lowing echoing from the cattle rushing to take cover in the barn.

Dani's hair whipped back, a gigantic blurry shape blocking the brightness in front of her. "You know, you could have landed much further away, and I'd still have heard you." She angled her head up, listening to a second set of wings descending. "Is that Zelbrali?"

Her insides twisted at the unexpected visit, and she

debated connecting with Katrin before dismissing the notion.

They'll have heard the cows, anyway.

Zaelinstra huffed her confirmation, her warm breath blowing Dani's hair back from her face again as she lowered her head. "Next time, I will. The stench here is... impressive."

Dani chuckled despite herself. "You get used to it. Eventually."

The ground shook as the second dragon landed behind Zaelinstra, their wings catching the evening breeze before tucking on their back.

Zelbrali gagged. "I was better off in the air. Terrified farmers be damned." The younger dragon lifted his wings again, beating them against the air to push the scent of the cows away.

"Not that I'm disappointed to see you, but..." Dani waved her hand in front of her face with a roll of her eyes. "Why are you here?"

The silence between the dragons grew palpable, and she imagined them exchanging a glance.

"I'm afraid we come with... complicated news." Zael snorted.

The Dträa sighed, her nerves already as ruined as they could be. "Out with it."

"Out with what?" Liam's voice startled her enough that she rocked backward on the fence, grabbing the post next to her.

Dani gritted her teeth, realizing the dragons' attempts to reduce the smell must have blown her husband's scent away, too. "Zaelinstra comes with *splendid* news." She tilted her head, listening more intently to identify who else had joined her without her awareness.

Katrin stood with Matthias near Liam, while everyone else remained on the homestead porch, whispering to each other.

Liam grunted. "Is the Primeval changing their mind about helping with the prison?" His tone mirrored Dani's concerns. They had never actually met the Primeval, but all experience with them had proved them to be overly cautious.

"No." Zaelinstra's blurry mass shifted in front of her. "But we are missing a vital piece in its construction."

"Well... You made the prison last time. Can you not make this piece again?" Dani resisted the urge to glance at Liam.

"No."

Getting sick of that word already.

Zael huffed a warm breath at her, as if able to read her thoughts. "We cannot craft a new lock, because the weaves of the Art require Zuriellinith's blood. As his original body no longer exists..."

"No more blood to use." Liam let out an exasperated breath. "So it's impossible."

"Where is the original prison, now?" Katrin finally spoke, her voice still foreign in Dani's ears. "Is the piece you're missing still there?"

Another long pause made Dani's insides twist harder.

She's taking a long time to get to the point.

"Somewhere a dragon cannot reach. Which is why I came here. I will need your human hands." Zaelinstra's voice shifted as she lifted her head towards Matthias. "And unfortunately, it is not within your lands, King. But in your enemy's."

"Feyor has the original prison?" Matthias groaned. "But that... Wait. Lungaz. Uriel hated that place. Feared it. Is this connected to the maelstrom?"

Zelbrali's wings shuddered with an amused breath. "Smart human."

"You think Uriel was afraid of Lungaz because it was his original prison?" Katrin's voice.

"No." Matthias's voice softened as he addressed the acolyte. "He feared it because there is no Art in Lungaz. No access to the fabric. He would be ejected from his host immediately."

"Fuck, seriously?" Liam leaned against the fence near Dani, making it tilt beneath his weight. "That would have been good to know twenty years ago."

"And how do you suppose I could have told you?" The king sounded annoyed.

Zael made a sound Dani imagined was the dragon equivalent to clearing her throat. "The missing lock. We must retrieve it before we can even begin rebuilding the prison.

Which will be a lengthy process I don't believe we want to delay any further."

"How lengthy are we talking?" Matthias's tone took on a political nature.

A pause.

"At least a decade."

All were silent for several breaths.

Dani gaped at the dragons, her chest heavy.

At least a...

"Shit." Liam pushed away from the fence. "Damien probably would have liked to know that before we went and pissed Uriel off."

"Better he didn't," Dani mumbled to him under her breath. "Otherwise he may have wanted to wait. And then Matthias would..." Her shoulders slumped as her mind connected the dots.

Ryen would still be alive.

She swallowed, exhaling a controlled breath through her mouth to ease the tension in her throat.

He'd also still be a Shade.

The conflicting emotions rattled around within her, dizzying her until the soft inside of Zaelinstra's wing brushed by her arm.

"Quiet those thoughts, Varadani." The dragon's voice took on a comforting tone, quiet enough she doubted even Matthias and Katrin would hear.

The air grew thick with tension, as no one spoke as if all lost to what possibly could come next.

Dani centered herself with a nod. "What must we do?"

"You don't seem nervous," Zaelinstra's voice rumbled over the wind as they flew, Dani on her back and Liam a hundred yards away on Zelbrali.

"We're retrieving an ancient Art-laden lock from the middle of a deadly maelstrom in a place I cannot shift. What's there to be nervous about?" Dani couldn't help the dry tone, not an ounce of fear tainting her chest.

I spent too much time being afraid.

"One slip into the water..." Zael's warning weighed no heavier than it had the first time at the homestead hours ago.

They'd reopened the portal to Nema's Throne before leaving, making sure Matthias and Katrin made it home. Even the king's Art would have been useless where they were going. With Katrin pregnant, Liam and Dani were the best options, while the other two worked on finding a suitable location for the prison.

"Inevitable death. Yes, I understand."

"Humans generally fear death."

"And, yet, it finds us, anyway," Dani whispered.

Zaelinstra quieted, letting silence reign as they flew higher, banking between clouds.

They sparkled in her vision, mist dappling the air with the scent of water and sun. For a self-damning moment, she wished she could see.

"Your mate is worried about you." Zael's scales vibrated with her voice under Dani's hands, the warmth permeating through her body to banish the cold of their elevation. "And aches for the loss of your hatchling as well."

"Liam wants nothing to do with me." Dani leaned forward, avoiding most of the wind's resistance. "Not that I blame him, with how uplifting my company must be."

"While I do not have full confidence in speaking for him, I believe that isn't true. I can see how much he longs to be near you with each glance, even if you can not."

"Yes, I am blind. I haven't forgotten." Dani took a deep breath, clenching her jaw.

Why am I incapable of having a simple conversation?

Zael huffed, her body wobbling on the wind as she turned her head back, displeased with her response. She righted herself again, and the steady beat of her wings resumed.

"I'm sorry," Dani muttered. "I'm just trying to keep breathing, and it's easier if I... you know." She ran a hand over her braids, a habit she'd formed after too many hours spent combing wind-blown hair. Liam had often helped, and she shirked away from the memory of his fingers in her hair.

"I lost a hatchling, once." Zael's tone lowered. "Many, many years ago. It is not easy, and most do not understand the pain you will carry for the rest of your life."

Dani cringed and let go of the rope around Zael's neck. She flattened her hand on the dragon's scales. "How did you... heal?"

"Time, but... There is no true healing from such a loss. Only learning to cope and keep them with you in other ways. Keeping their memory alive with those who knew them helps."

As they descended through the clouds, the glittering ocean far below emerged as a great expanse of blue.

Dani peered sideways at the blurred form of Zelbrali, sun shining from his golden scales.

Am I wrong about Liam?

"I cannot... *feel* anything. Unless I think about Ry, then it's just... agony." She breathed the last word, swallowing the lump in her throat. "Sometimes I almost forget, and I think of the time he and Varin had a flour-fight in the kitchen a couple years ago." She almost laughed, but it stuck in her chest. "Will I ever laugh again? Or not feel guilty for smiling?"

"You will. And it will be because one day, memories of him will bring joy instead of sorrow. Because there will be other flour-fights that will form new memories and help you hold on to those old."

"I saw his face," Dani whispered into the wind, not even sure if she spoke loud enough for Zaelinstra to hear. "I borrowed Katrin's sight for the funeral, and... I saw his face for the first time."

And the last...

Zael's body rumbled beneath her in a comforting purr. "I am glad your élanvital could grant you that. But I'm sure it makes it harder in other ways. There is no shame in mourning, Varadani. But it should not stop you from living, not forever."

The horizon line darkened as land approached. But the ocean below grew rougher, with turbulent water rising into crashing waves. They descended until the water was only twenty yards below, the sting of the salty air embedding deep in Dani's nose. Approaching Lungaz from the north had been Zelbrali's idea, avoiding curious human eyes.

"I miss him," Dani breathed.

"And he must miss you. He is at peace. All the ache you feel, that's love. That's the love inside you with nowhere to go. Let it flow into others, and it will ease the pain."

The Dtrüa nodded, even though the gesture would go unseen. "Thank you."

Zaelinstra slowed as the wind shifted with their approach to the northern coast of Lungaz. The scents dimmed, wind ripping sideways as a low roar rumbled in the distance.

"How deep is the maelstrom?" Dani glanced at the other dragon, still out of earshot. "How low can you get?"

"It will be a rough landing, but there is enough space for

both Zelbrali and I." The dragon hovered closer to Zelbrali, wings working hard to keep them in place despite the pull of the storm. The air grew thicker with water as a dense mist settled in around them.

Dani's skin prickled with the absence of her power, her veins eerily silent.

A silent conversation must have occurred between the dragons before Zelbrali's wing beats changed, shifting lower as he dropped into the gaping hole beneath them. Even in Dani's vision, the maelstrom looked like the maw of an ancient monster. White swirled around the edges, blending into the azure of the sea. At the center, a sickly grey stone.

The moments from earlier flashed through her mind. Varin's scent as they hugged farewell, and Jaxx's scoff that she'd be fine.

I must do this for them.

Dani rolled her lips together, gripping Zael's scales tighter as they descended after Zelbrali. The darkness of the surrounding ocean made her claustrophobic, and suddenly the sky seemed so far away.

Zael bobbed in the air as she carefully maneuvered above Zelbrali, a horrible chill rushing in around them.

The smaller dragon landed with a scrape of talons on stone, Zaelinstra landing a breath later. The ground quaked, walls of angled water rushing around them in a cyclone. It blocked most of the daylight, the sun too low to penetrate so far down.

"Step with care, Varadani," Zaelinstra warned as the Dtrüa slid from her back to the uneven ground.

The ocean's vibration rippled through her whole body, making her feet tingle. "Liam?" The speeding water stole her husband's scent, muting her senses.

"Here." Liam's boots scuffled across the stone to her left.

Instinct filled her to embrace him, but she resisted. Her heart pounded, adding to the roar in her ears.

Barely audible against the raging sea, Liam grunted as he lifted the rope Zelbrali had shaken from his neck.

"Where is the fissure?" Dani focused on the dragon, already dreading the coming darkness.

"Twenty paces to our right, on the other side of me." Zael wrapped her body around Dani, her neck brushing against the Dtrüa's hair.

"This sounded like more fun in theory," Dani muttered, patting her winged friend. "Wish us luck." She ducked beneath the behemoth, keeping a hand on her scales.

A bright spot burst to life before her with the huff of Zelbrali's breath.

Liam coughed, holding the torch away from himself. "A little close, there, friend."

Zelbrali responded with a throaty laugh, whistling between his teeth. "I never miss."

Dani stepped further, breathing deeper when the scent of decay touched her nose.

"Careful," Liam's voice shifted closer behind her. "The rock is slick, and the drop inside doesn't look survivable."

"Did you tie the rope to Zelbrali?" Dani approached the edge, a rock clicking off the toe of her boot and falling within the fissure. No clattering echoed back at her.

"It itches." Zelbrali's claws scraped along the stone as he took a slow step. The rumble of the rock beneath Dani's feet seemed to deepen.

"Be *still*," Zaelinstra growled, and another silent conversation took place between the great beasts.

"Let's get this over with." Dani held her hand out to Liam. "Give me the rope."

"I got it." Liam's tone showed his disapproving frown. He gave her the glowing torch before maneuvering around her. He heaved the hemp over the black rim of the fissure into the prison below. "I'll go first."

Dani caught his forearm. "I'm smaller."

Liam grumbled. "No, I'm first. Please don't fight me on this."

She opened her mouth to argue, but his scent finally found its way to her. The teal made her resolve weaken, and she chewed her lip. "I cannot lose you," she whispered. "Be as careful as you can." Forcing her hand to release him, she stepped back.

Liam paused, his scent lingering for a moment before the maelstrom's wind swept it away. "I will." He crouched near the edge, the rope creaking as he wrapped it around his leg. His blurry shape disappeared from her sight as he dropped over the edge and into the darkness.

Chapter 27

MATTHIAS STACKED THE PARCHMENT AND slid it to Telvesh, rising from his seat. "We will adjourn there, then. I like the options you've brought forward for replacing the temple's leader. I will ask Katrin to meet with them both once they've arrived in Nema's Throne."

Ermine smiled and stood with everyone else. "There was one last matter I hoped to ask you about, your majesty."

"Yes?" Matthias lifted his chin, his shoulders relaxed.

"Lady Talansiet's involvement in your rule and public appearances has aided your reputation greatly, but a wedding might be the morale boost our city needs."

"That doesn't sound like a question." The king resisted the urge to retreat, his relationship with Katrin still unsteady.

Ermine cleared her throat. "Well, I suppose... *Is* there to be a wedding, my king?"

"That remains to be seen." Matthias rolled his shoulders. "And once we have decided, I will notify you." He nodded at the others around the meeting table. "You're all dismissed until tomorrow. I apologize for the late finish."

Once everyone had shuffled from the room and shut the door, he sighed and sat down again. Eyeing the map of Isalica hanging from the wall, he tapped his fingers on the table. He stiffened, looking at his hand. Lifting his fingers, he tapped them down one at a time.

Still my hands.

The king swallowed, flexing his hand before rising and approaching the map.

A knock came at the door before he had much time to study it, and he sighed. "Enter."

The latch clicked open, and his eyes met Katrin's.

"Oh good, I was hoping I wouldn't be interrupting." She stepped inside, her lilac skirts brushing past the door before she gently closed it. She held a scroll, tapping it against her palm as she approached. Pausing on the elaborate rug of the meeting hall, she eyed him. "I'm not, am I? Interrupting?"

Matthias looked at the map, realizing he still touched Nothend's map marker, and dropped his hand. "No. Of course not. Do you need something?" He studied her expression, but deciphered nothing.

She'd schooled her face since returning from her family's

home. He'd hoped it would fade, since she'd certainly put it on to hide her anxiety from her parents. But she still looked at him with those unfocused eyes, so unlike the sharp acolyte when they first met.

The scroll tapped on her palm again before she held it out. "This just arrived from Undertown." She moved closer, the chandelier light from above dancing over the wax seal. "I think it's from Seiler."

A spark of nerves ignited in his chest, and he took the scroll. Running his thumb over the royal seal bearing his brother's initials, he broke it open.

> *Matthias,*
>
> *How am I supposed to properly convey all I feel in a letter? You're back. I can hardly believe it. I would have written sooner, but after your letter all I could think of was sending as much aid as we could spare. With your warning, we've decided to accept your offer and return to Nema's Throne. This letter will precede our arrival by some weeks, but I am pleased that Isalica has its true king once more, and we can again embrace as brothers. I have missed you. Please give Katrin my adoration. We will meet again soon.*
>
> *Seiler*

Matthias smiled, letting out an exhale. "Seiler and Kelsara are returning." Excitement to see his brother flooded him. "Will probably only be a few weeks before their arrival."

The stoic appearance on her face cracked, but only briefly. "It will be good to see them. I'm relieved they're both safe."

Her lack of enthusiasm made his brow twitch. "Are you feeling all right?" He glanced out the window, dreading the end of the day.

Perhaps that's why the meeting ran so late.

They'd relocated his belongings that day to his royal chambers, the ones he'd only ever used while Uriel corrupted his body.

The royal chambers had been redecorated, cleaned, and gods' knew what else, but his chest still ached at the thought of stepping inside those rooms.

Katrin shook her head. "Just tired. And a little disjointed. Seeing Izi..." A forced smile made its way onto her lips as she shook her head harder. "I'll be fine."

"I know. She's all grown up, living on her own. Well, with her husband, at least. Perhaps they'll have children soon and the littles can grow up together." Matthias approached her, putting a hand on her shoulder. "Have you... felt anything, yet?" His gaze flickered to her abdomen, which had rounded over the past weeks as she neared the middle of her pregnancy.

Katrin followed the look, her hands running over the loose dress she'd changed into after returning to the palace. She frequented the less restrictive attire when in the palace, but the bump of their growing child was still slight enough she could hide it when she wanted to.

"Not yet, but the midwife says it's still too early." She chewed her bottom lip as she looked up at him. "Come to bed?"

Matthias hesitated. "In the king's chambers?" He wished he could sleep in the crown elites' wing forever, but it would raise suspicions higher than they already were.

"Yes, in *your* chambers."

He looked at the map before nodding. "I suppose I can't avoid it much longer, anyway."

"I can stay with you until you fall asleep if it'll help." Her fingers closed lightly around his forearm. "I'll make you tea, too."

Matthias touched her chin, lifting it so he could better see her eyes. "Maybe you should stay with me. The whole night, I mean... If you want."

Her grip tightened on him, a brightness flickering in her dark brown irises. "Stay?"

He nodded. "Unless you..."

"No." Touching his hand, Katrin brought it to her cheek. "I want to. I just know you've been worried... But of course I will stay with you."

Warmth filled his chest, and he leaned forward, tentatively closing the distance between their lips until he nearly touched her.

She didn't close the final distance, but her eyes fluttered shut in anticipation. Yet, everything within her remained stiff and in control. Her nails bit lightly into his arm, sending a jolt through him as her lips parted, a light breath tickling his mouth.

Matthias brushed his lips against hers, sliding his arm around her waist.

She moved naturally into his touch, eagerly accepting the kiss with a subtle movement. Her hand brushed back into his hair, tangling among the strands.

Take small steps.

His heart swelled as he breathed her scent before pulling away. "Lead the way, Priestess."

The king's chambers had been completely redesigned at Matthias's request under Katrin's instruction.

The flooring had been replaced, walls painted, and even the chandelier was new. Ice blue drapes hung by the windows, complementing the navy bedspread.

After drinking Katrin's tea, sleep came easily, aided by having her next to him.

With nothing to distract his mind, the nightmares set in.

A mix of memory and fears, they devolved to a mess of shadow and blood. Somewhere, Katrin screamed. He ran through muck, but his boots stuck to the tar and slowed his pace. Shadowed vines writhed around bodies, laced among the trees. Their faces twisted in silent cries as Corrupted tore through their flesh. Alana's laugh mingled with his as his hands pulled the darkness tighter.

"Katrin!" Matthias shouted, but his voice sounded lost in the thickening fog.

Someone clung to his ankle.

He looked down, his stomach lurching at the gold crown shimmering on the man's head.

"Please, I'll give you whatever you want." Lazorus stared up at him as the shadow ate away at his eyes, his skin melting to reveal the white of his skull still stained with blood.

"I didn't kill you," Matthias breathed, trying to back away. "It wasn't me."

Lazorus's decaying body grappled for Matthias's wrist, shaking his arm as he tried to climb up him. "We're in a time of peace." His voice turned raspy as he grabbed harder, pain spiking in Matthias's bicep as the Feyorian king pulled him down towards the mud. Tendrils slithered up the corpse's limbs, cutting into Matthias as Uriel's low chuckle made his head ache.

"No." Matthias breathed quicker in his panic. "No!" He struck out, his fist colliding with the dead king's jaw.

The man stumbled back, and something crashed.

Ceramic shattered, skittering across the new wood floor of his bedroom.

Matthias sat up, breathing fast as he blinked in the dark room. Only a single lantern provided any light, and pain erupted from his hand. He grunted, looking at his fist, and dread built in his gut. "Katrin?"

Her groan drew his eyes to the floor beside his bed, where she sprawled on her back. A dark bruise already formed on her face, and his heart seized.

"Gods, I... I..." Matthias shirked away, shaking his head. He squeezed his eyes closed, finding the Art and yanking time into reverse.

Matthias's eyes flew open, and he sat up, throwing the blankets off. Standing, he pulled his tunic on, breathing hard.

"Matthias?" Katrin shifted, rolling onto his side of the bed and brushing her hand against his thigh. "What's wrong?"

He flinched and spun to face her, taking several backward steps from the bed. "Everything." He stalked away, looking for his boots.

She pushed herself up, running a hand through her messy hair. "Did you have a nightmare?" Her nightgown had ridden up her body to expose the soft skin of her legs as she slid to the edge of the bed. "I can make you more tea."

"No. No more tea." He growled when he couldn't find his boots, even if he still wore his sleeping pants. "This was a bad idea. It's never going to work. I need to work."

"Wait, slow down." Katrin stood, stepping over the very spot he'd seen her laying moments before. "What happened?"

The feeling of his fist meeting bone rippled through him, and he cringed. "Nothing."

"Don't lie to me." Katrin glared in the darkness. "Tell me what happened."

The king clenched his teeth, shame echoing through his body as his hands shook. "I can't."

Katrin sighed and lifted her hand. "Well, since we're both awake..." Fire sparked in her eyes, reflecting from the orb that rippled into existence in her palm. She bobbed it upward, and it hopped from candle to candle on the chandelier.

At the brightness, Matthias tucked his injured fist behind himself, swallowing.

But Katrin's gaze on him suggested she'd already seen. "What did you punch this time?"

His throat burned, and his pulse raced. "I didn't mean to." He stared at her, flexing the fist behind his back. "I was having a nightmare, and I didn't know. I didn't know it was you."

Her eyes flickered down to where he hid his wrist again, a knowing passing across her face. "I must have tried to wake you. I shouldn't have done that. I know better." She took a single step closer before pausing. "I thought we'd promised to tell each other everything, especially with jumping." She studied him, crossing her arms.

Matthias frowned. "All the more reason to do things differently," he whispered. "This isn't working."

"I knew the risks when I accepted your invitation to stay here with you. One accident hardly constitutes it not working."

"You knew I could knock you unconscious?" He gaped at her. "Really? What if I'd used more than just my fist?"

"Yes! And I knew if it was serious, you'd have jumped to fix it. But I refuse to be afraid of you, Matthias." Katrin moved again, stepping closer to him.

"No. No. I won't be the kind of man who hits the woman he..." Matthias stepped away, keeping the distance between them. "I'm not the husband you want. I'm not..." He glanced at her midsection, wincing. "I'm not the father you want for your son." He crossed the bedroom, entering the adjoining study and grabbing a candle on the way.

He strode to his desk, flipping through pieces of parchment to find the documents he'd started to draft the day before.

Nema's Throne is done.

"You don't get to decide what *I* want." Katrin followed, her steps confident as the lantern in the study sprang to life at the will of her Art. "What in hells are you doing?"

"Fine. I don't know what you want, but I don't want that child of yours to grow up with a father like me, and—"

"Of *ours*." Katrin's voice rose. "He will not have any father but you."

He met her gaze. "Then he will have no father."

"Will you listen to yourself? You can't mean that."

Matthias shook his head. "I do mean it. I want better things for you, for him. I will give you both everything you ever need, but I won't be part of that."

"Stop." Silver glistened in her eyes. "Stop. You don't get to just walk away like that. Not from me, not from our son. These nightmares, these accidents do not define you."

The king's eyes burned. "I hit you. I *hit* you, Katrin. And it will *never* happen again."

"Even if you hadn't jumped, and I still bruised, it wasn't you who hit me, Matthias. It was that blackness inside you're still learning to deal with. The things *he* put you through. Not you. I won't let you punish yourself for something you are not responsible for. You will be a wonderful father to our son, and you—"

"No. Don't you hear me? I get to make my own choices now, right? This is the choice I'm making, and everyone will be better off for it. Especially once we get out of this place." He returned his attention to the parchment, picking up the quill and scrawling without sitting at the desk.

"Out of this... What are you talking about?" She moved

closer, her tone softening. "Matthias, please just sit for a minute so we can talk."

"This place." He motioned with his hand. "Nema's Throne. I'm moving the capital."

"What?" Katrin gaped. "Nema's Throne has always been the capital, for over a thousand years, and you want to move it?"

"Nothend will be the new capital. And once I'm finished with this document, I will reciprocate Feyor's declaration of war."

"War? Matthias." Katrin moved so quickly he didn't have a chance to stop her. She grabbed his writing hand, pushing it to the table. "Stop, you're not in the right state of mind for any of these decisions."

The quill left a black streak across the document he'd been working on, and he snarled. "This is my only state of mind, no matter how I hide it." He looked at her, muscles flexing.

"Then hit me." Katrin gripped him tighter, her nails biting into his skin. "If you have only one state of mind, it's the same one that would do so... so do it again." She shoved hard on his shoulder, and he turned with it, facing her.

"What?" He gaped at her, imagining the bruise on her jaw as it'd been before.

"Hit me. If you want me to fear you as you believe I should, then do it. Hit me, and I'll let my son grow up without his dad."

"That's not fair." Matthias stepped closer to her, searching her eyes.

"Neither is this." Katrin squared her shoulders as she stepped into him, forcing him back against the desk.

He bumped against it with a thunk, the glass vial of ink toppling to its side before rolling across the desk to where he braced his left hand. The ink slicked between his fingers before the jar toppled to the floor.

Matthias lifted his hand and stared at the black dripping down his wrist towards his elbow. The edges of his vision blurred as he watched it, lifting his other hand to smudge the drip across his skin.

My skin.

The king's eyes flickered to Katrin, and he admired the fire in her gaze. Taking her arm with his ink-stained hand, he pulled her against him and kissed her.

Katrin let out a startled gasp as she fell into his arms, her breath heavy against his before her scowl melted into another kiss. She pressed against him, making the desk dig into his thighs. Sucking in a rapid breath, she pulled back, a hand on his chest. "What are you doing?"

Matthias watched her, touching her face before running his hand through her hair. "What I should have done weeks ago."

Katrin's brow furrowed, and she brushed her hand over his cheek, specks of black on her fingers. "You're going to have to be more specific." Her eyes flickered between his and his lips.

"I was trying, but you stopped me," he whispered, a smirk twitching the corner of his mouth as he watched hers.

Her lips quirked in a smile before forming a silent 'oh'. The room blurred as she pushed harder against him. "I apologize, Prince. Please, do continue."

He tightened his arm around her waist, lowering his face towards hers, but paused before they could kiss. "I don't want to hurt you," he murmured, his other hand trailing to her abdomen.

"You won't." She laced her fingers with his on her belly. "I trust you, entirely." Katrin closed the distance this time, rising to the tips of her feet as she pressed her mouth against his. As it renewed, the lightest flick of her tongue brushed his lower lip, making Matthias's spine tingle.

He gripped beneath her backside and lifted her from her feet, growling as he turned and set her on the desk. Sliding his hand up her waist, he cupped her breast as her legs wrapped around him. Their mouths met in a flurry, a whimper emerging as he pinched her nipple through the lacy top of her nightgown.

Matthias barely noticed as she unbuttoned his tunic, shrugging it off his shoulders to let it fall to the floor. His lips parted from hers for only a heated breath before another passionate kiss. He pushed his hands up her thighs, taking the silky fabric with them. Caressing over her abdomen, his touch lowered until his thumb stroked the bundle of nerves between her legs.

Moaning into his mouth, Katrin ran her hands up his bare back and rolled her hips to grant him better access. She encouraged his tongue to mingle with hers as she gripped the back of his head. She broke the kiss with a breathy whimper, humming as she ran a finger down his chest and abdomen. "Take off your pants."

The king kissed her neck and chuckled. "As you wish, Priestess." He pushed his sleeping pants down, and they fell to his feet. His thumb pressed harder in another circle, eliciting a twitch from her legs and a breathy cry.

Heat rushed through him, and he tugged her to the edge of the desk. Kissing her neck again, he eased his length into her in one smooth motion. Her tightness surrounded him, making him groan into her skin as his thumb maintained its steady rhythm.

Running her hand through his hair, Katrin gripped his head close, her lips forming a kiss near his ear. Her breath echoed through every inch of him, the pitch of her voice rising with each movement of his thumb. Teeth grazing his earlobe, she dug her heels into his thighs.

Matthias rocked his hips back before plunging deeper, making the desk hit the wall and sending a vibration through them both. He breathed in the lavender smell of her hair and thrust again as his breathing sped.

Her entire body tightened around him as he thrust harder, the knock of the desk against the wall becoming a rhythm to match their pitched moans. She buried her face into his shoulder, mouth moving against his skin as her legs shook and ecstasy rocked through her.

Her warmth tightened around him, but he didn't slow, pushing her into a second wave of euphoria as her nails dug into his back.

He panted, his control slipping at her cries, and he moaned into her skin. Pleasure tore through him, heating his body as he pushed deep, holding her against him. Finding her mouth again, he kissed her, picking her up off the desk.

Wrapping her arms around his neck, she clung to him as he strode from the study back to the bedroom. He put a knee on the bed before laying her back, hovering over her.

Her eyes sparkled in the candlelight, and she touched his cheek. With another stroke of his hair, she tangled her legs with his and rolled him to his back. She nuzzled into the crook of his arm, kissing his skin with a happy sigh.

Matthias smiled, pulling a blanket over them before looking at his hand again. Ink stained his palm, wrist, and forearm, dappled all over in a haphazard abstract painting. He huffed and draped his arm over her, pulling her close. "I'm an idiot," he whispered.

"Yes, you are." Katrin smiled against his skin, kissing it again.

He kissed the top of her head before pulling back to look at her face. "Forgive me?"

She tilted her chin up, looking at him. Touching his chin, she smiled. "Always." A playful look lighted her face. "Except in this case, only if you agree not to move the capital."

"I won't move the capital," he murmured.

"And no more silliness about not being a good dad?" She ran a finger over his lower lip.

Matthias let out a breath. "I can't be a good dad, unless..." When she opened her mouth, he placed a finger over her lips. "*Unless* I can be a good man, first. A good husband. If someone will still have me."

Katrin pushed herself up with her elbow, looking down at Matthias as she ran her hand along his beard and into his hair. "Are you asking me to marry you, Prince?"

"I'm asking you to be my queen." Matthias tilted his head, touching her cheek. "To be my wife. To marry me. Pending no more interruptions."

"And my answer is still yes. All interruptions be damned." She leaned down, kissing him slowly. She drew it out for a lovely moment before pulling back and looking at him again. "I will marry you because of who *you* are. And for no other reason."

Chapter 28

PLUNGING INTO THE BLACK, LIAM could barely hear over his pounding heart. He blinked rapidly, trying to force his eyes to adjust to the shadows, but it only made them come to life.

Uriel isn't here. Zael would know.

The rope hung loose beneath him, where it ended impossible to see. He kept the rope taut as he moved down a slow foot at a time, the dripping of ocean water in the cavern beyond growing more pronounced.

He jolted when his foot touched solid ground, and a steadying breath rushed in as he slid his boots blindly against the damp stone. His chest tightened, and he imagined some great monster lumbering through the darkness towards him. He peered up, the fissure above glaringly bright.

"I'm down!" His voice echoed back at him, hollow in the shadows.

"Can I toss the torch?" Dani crouched at the edge, holding the flame just within the fissure.

"I think so." He felt out with his boot, finding the surrounding ground to be relatively flat. No splashes, but the continual sound of his leather sole against damp stone. "Just drop it in the same spot as the rope."

A louder drip echoed behind him, ushering his hand to his sword. He eyed the darkness, trying to determine what he swore moved towards him.

There's nothing living here. It can't.

Even without sensitivity to the Art, Liam couldn't deny the sense of wrongness surrounding Lungaz. He would have much rather turned around and gone the other way.

"Here it comes!" Dani's voice brought his attention back, and the bright spot dropped from the opening above. It plummeted, falling handle-first with her careful release.

The flames blinded him as they fell close, and he lifted an arm to cover his eyes as the handle smacked the ground, the flame guttering as it rolled away.

Squinting, Liam snatched it from the wet ground, lifting it clear. The light broke the darkness, but still limited his vision to a twenty-foot radius.

The end of the rope wiggled, and he looked up, breath catching that Dani had started her descent without warning him. She lowered partway before losing her footing, hanging from her arms as she tried to re-wrap the rope around her leg.

He grabbed the rope, trying to still it to limit the sway and help her reaffirm her grip. "You're all right, just breathe. Twenty more feet."

Dani pinched the rope between her feet again, pausing before continuing her descent. By the time her feet touched the ground, her arms shook. "This is a cruel kind of darkness." Wiping her hands on her pants, she caught her breath.

Before he could think better of it, Liam brushed his hand down her arm in his usual way of telling her where he was.

"Will need more guidance, here. The echo helps, but all my eyes have is a blurry bright spot. I never realized how much of my scent detection was Art-related." Dani frowned. "But it still smells down here."

"It's honestly not that much better being able to see." Liam lifted the torch higher to expand the circle of light, but it only revealed more wet stone. They'd dropped into an open space, no walls or columns within sight. He peered at the opening above again, trying to recall which way was west. "Zelbrali said it'll be further underground, most likely. He said there should be an iron door, and we're supposed to go through that."

Dani clicked her tongue, waited, and then did it again. "There's an opening that way." She motioned behind him. "Not a door, though."

Liam shrugged. "Seems the best direction for now." He tapped his foot, old habits of his minute communications with Dani falling back into place. They'd found many ways for him to help inform her about surroundings without needing to say a word.

She followed him, her fingertip grazing his elbow. "I miss the fresh air already," she whispered.

Her tone evoked a memory of her in the temple while she'd still been his prisoner, when he'd returned to their room and found her with the window open. It made a smile twitch his lips at how far they'd come since then.

The engulfing darkness isolated them within the torchlight. So deep in the world, he felt like they were the only two people who existed.

When was the last time we were alone together?

The question made his heart ache, and he remembered the advice Zaelinstra had given him to try harder. "Dani, I—" His boot struck something solid, and he stumbled, but she caught his arm.

"Role reversal. Interesting." Dani's light tone made him chuckle. "What is it?" She felt forward with her foot, her boot hitting the same object with a tap.

Lowering the torch as she released his arm, he wiped grime off the object's surface. "Rusted to all hell, but It's an iron door." He furrowed his brow, lifting the torch, and spied the open doorway at the edge of his light. "It's not on the hinges, anymore, that's why you could detect the opening. Something... flung it off."

"Flung it off? A little heavy to be flung, is it not?" Dani nudged it, but it didn't budge. "At least we're going the right way."

Again, Liam brushed her wrist before he walked around the mass of disfigured metal. He walked towards the ominous doorway, the thickness of the salt and decay doubling in the air. He lifted his arm to his face, trying to stop himself from gagging. "Might be good that the Art enhances your smell. I wouldn't want any of that extra sense right now."

Dani wrinkled her nose. "Unfortunately, I have plenty without the Art, too." Her next step sounded like it hit something wetter, and she made a disgusted sound. "Just tell me there are no bugs."

"No bugs." He continued through the darkness, studying the walls. Carved patterns depicted symbols he vaguely recognized.

Where did I see this language before?

Understanding hit him like a brick.

Damien's tattoos.

He huffed, shaking his head.

"What is it?" Dani clicked her tongue again and touched the wall, fingers finding the grooves. "Do these mean something?"

"I'm sure they do, if you can read Rahn'ka." Liam slowed as they reached an intersection among the passageways. The further they walked, the more clear the ruins became. This deep, the erosion of the maelstrom had done less damage, preserving more of the ancient structure.

His wife clicked her tongue. "Which way?"

"Left looks like it goes down, so probably the most logical place to start." Each step along the ancient stone felt strange, as if something inside him warned against going further. "We're probably the first people down here in... thousands of years?"

Dani's hand found his arm, and she gripped his bicep. "Not making me feel better."

He paused, slowing to look back at her. "Are you afraid?" Studying her face in the torchlight, Liam tried to read the expressions that had eluded him for the past several weeks.

Her jaw flexed. "Yes," she whispered. "But I can handle it."

"Dani." Liam turned fully to her, touching her waist with the arm she held. "You don't have to put on a brave face with me. We're well beyond that."

She looked up at him, her cloudy eyes moving over his face. "Are we?"

Pain sparked in his chest, followed by a wave of guilt. "We

should be." He chewed the inside of his lip, wishing he knew what to say. "I... miss him, too. You know that, don't you?"

Her eyebrows upturned in the center. "How could I? Before we came to your family's home... You never..." She looked away, taking a quicker breath.

"I couldn't." Liam fought the tightening of his throat. "If I allowed myself, I knew I wouldn't be able to be there for you. For the kids." He swallowed, fighting back the images of his son bleeding out in his arms. Physical pain ruptured through every inch of him as he gritted his jaw. "I would've given anything to trade places with Ryen in those last moments. Wondered if I had expected his throw better, I might have stopped it and saved him. Or if I'd been a better father, if I'd have listened more, then maybe—"

"Stop," Dani's whisper held all the power it needed to silence him. "You are not to blame for his death." She touched his face, her hand shaking as it moved over his temple. "The fault is not yours."

Her fingers left warm trails over his skin, and he leaned into her touch. His heart ached, and he wished he believed her. Sucking in a breath, he tried to hear the words that Rae had also spoken in those moments after Ryen's death. "Isn't it?"

The Dtrüa shook her head, eyes glassy. "No more than it is mine. We made mistakes, but this... this is *Uriel's* fault. And he will pay for what he's done." Her thumb moved over his chin to the underside, her eyelashes fluttering. "I need not your strength, husband. I need your pain so mine may not be alone."

He shook his head. "It's never been alone. I'm sorry I wasn't brave enough to show it." Leaning toward her, he rested his forehead against hers. "Further proof you are the more courageous between us. Always have been."

Dani scoffed but held his face with both hands, shutting her eyes. "I miss him so much, but it's so much worse since I miss you, too."

"I haven't gone anywhere." He breathed, and the foul scent of their surroundings stuck at the back of his throat. "I'm right here with you in these stinking ancient tunnels. And there's nowhere else I'd rather be than at your side, Varadani."

She lifted her chin and kissed him, leaving him suddenly dizzy. The sensation felt foreign, yet like a familiar dream as he returned it.

As she pulled away, she let out a soft exhale and lowered her hands. "We should keep looking."

Liam allowed himself a moment to just look at his wife and marvel at how fortunate he was. Brushing a lock of her hair behind her ear, he nodded. "You're right. Hopefully, it's not much further."

The torch flickered as he turned back to the passageway, eyeing the descent.

Grateful for no more forks, Liam guided them deeper into the ruins. The stench grew more intense, and he wished he had something to cover his face with. Their surroundings kept his mind from whirling at their intimate moment, but he silently swore to have a more extensive conversation with her later.

When we aren't beneath the ocean.

Something shimmered at the end of the tunnel they walked within. Heavily tarnished copper, mostly green with its patina.

"This is it." Liam touched her hand, approaching the cracked double doors.

They sat uneven, the crooked one creating a slim gap between them.

He let go of Dani to push on it, and when it didn't budge, he pulled.

Nothing.

Not even a hint of movement.

"Shit." Liam huffed as he slammed his shoulder into the door. It felt as if he collided with a solid wall.

"Whoa," Dani grabbed his arm before he could try again. "You need to climb a rope, still, remember?" She felt around the doors, finding the narrow opening. "Can you fit through?"

Lifting the torch, he tried to gauge the size. "I don't think Jaxx would fit. There's no way I will."

"Maybe I can." Dani angled herself against the crooked door, squeezing sideways into the crevice. She grunted, cringing as she slid further.

"If you get stuck..." Liam lifted the torch, attempting to see into the darkness of the room over her head. The stench emanating from the room only furthered his dislike of her going in alone.

"I won't. I can make it." Dani spoke through clenched teeth, freeing an arm on the other side and pushing on the door. She huffed and stumbled into the room, breathing deeper as she brushed her hands on her clothes. "See? I'm fine."

Liam pursed his lips. "Take the torch." He reached through the crack and passed it to her. Pushing as far as he could into the opening, he craned his neck to peer into the room beyond. The torchlight shone across the damp stone, trails of water dribbling along the slanted floor.

Dani walked away from him, stepping tentatively over the uneven floor. It shone with lacings of oxidized copper, like the doors, but the sound of rushing water echoed louder beyond the walls.

The awful smell emanated from that space, reeking of dead fish and decay.

His wife clicked her tongue, holding the torch further in front of her to help Liam be her eyes.

"Three more paces, then there's a step up." The flame

flickered off the carved black stone of a monolith at the corner of the step. It refracted off the surface like glass, bouncing to others at the edge of the platform.

Following his guidance, Dani stepped onto the raised platform.

"Lift your feet, there's a collapsed column directly to your right. If it's what I think it is, those broken bits are going to be sharp. So no shuffling either."

Dani clicked her tongue again, maneuvering slowly over the broken obsidian. "Am I near the wall? Where is the lock?"

Liam exhaled, using it to wriggle further into the tight space. "No walls."

She looked back at him. "Stop doing that. You'll get stuck."

Frowning, Liam pulled back, but realized he couldn't move for a moment before his tunic shifted and he slid free again. "I'm fine. You just be careful. There's... a mass of copper in front of you, looks like something tore through it."

Dani lowered the torch, clicking her tongue. "This might be it." She ran a hand over the copper, hissing. She put the torch down, pausing and looking at it. "The water vibrations are strong in here." Her tone almost hid her worry. "I should try to be fast. How do I tell what piece is the lock?" She touched the copper again, her hair orange in the light.

"Are vibrations bad? We are under a maelstrom."

"They're bad when they're worse than other areas. This

room might not be stable." She kept poking at the ancient green mechanism.

Liam tensed, the copper pressing hard against his broad shoulders. "Can you tell what's at the center of that platform? I can't make it out, but if it's a drop into the prison..."

Dani's breathing sped. "There's a gap, yes, but there's something here. Something with... runes or gears or something." She grabbed it and pulled, but nothing budged. "It's stuck in the metal."

"Break down the problem. Are there any weak points?" A rush of air took Liam's breath with the renewed stench.

Dani jerked her head up, staring at the far corner of the room.

The distant roar of the maelstrom shifted, and stones clacked to the copper floor.

Liam's gut knotted as he looked at his wife, isolated at the center of that massive room.

The Dtrüa worked faster, searching around her for anything she could use and finding a piece of obsidian. She slammed it into the copper, grunting with the effort as she repeatedly struck the surface.

Something cracked, a deep sound that shook the floor.

"Come on." Dani hit it again, checked to see if it was loose, then continued her strikes.

"Leave it!" Liam shouted as another shift of pressure in the room made the copper doors around him quake.

Water rushed across the floor, flooding the lower level but not yet reaching her platform.

"I can get it!" Dani huffed as she hit harder, blood oozing down her wrist from the obsidian.

"There's no time." Liam shoved against the door, every muscle in his body screaming as he fought against the unmoving metal. "Get out, now!"

The room groaned, and the entire space tilted to the side. The torch rolled, but she grabbed it, trying again to pull the lock free from the copper. "Just... a little..." It clicked, and she fell back before scrambling to her feet with the lock and torch. Breathing hard, she ran, leaping over the broken black stone and into the water. It rushed past her calves, nearly to her knees.

He reached out to her, and as she held out the tarnished mess of copper towards him, the roar grew deafening. Rocks slammed together, crashing into water somewhere beyond.

The doors around Liam shuddered, vibrating as the crack narrowed, forcing him to withdraw. "No, no." He wedged himself back in, lifting his legs to brace against the metal. A cry escaped his lips as he pushed, but the force of the sea pushed back.

"Take it!" Dani thrust the lock into his chest, making him stumble away from the door. She threw the torch through the gap as the cold copper stung his palm, but he couldn't look away from her.

Her eyes widened as the water rose. The current ripped around her, and she shivered, pressing against the smaller gap. "I can't fit, Liam." Her voice shook, and she grabbed at the doors. But they only narrowed further.

The metal clinked to the ground as Liam threw both his arms out, fighting against the narrowing gap. "Yes, you can. Try, Dani." His heart thundered as he urged more strength into his muscles.

"It's too small," Dani sobbed, shrieking as the water tugged her harder. "I can't—"

Ocean crashed through the room, engulfing the rest of her as it swept sideways. He fell back from the doors and they slammed shut.

Liam stared at the closed copper doors, his whole body shaking. Water dripped from beneath them as the metal groaned. Little trails of seawater crept over the upper edges, weeping down the tarnished facade as he stood, unable to move.

The roar of water mingled with the memory of the last gasp he'd heard from his wife.

Flame guttered on the torch as it struggled to stay lit on the damp ground, a steadily growing puddle making its way towards it.

"Dani…" Liam stared at the doors, wondering if she still stood on the other side. If he'd hear her banging on them, or if the water had swept her away. He looked down at the lock on the floor, panting as he snatched it and the torch.

He glared at the copper mechanism, tempted to heave it at the wall for what it'd cost. The tiny, intricate pieces of metal were tarnished beyond recognition, broken bits at the edges where Dani had freed it from the prison.

Forcing his leaden feet to move, he rushed back the way he'd come, choking on his imagination of Dani drowning. Slowly. Somewhere beyond his reach.

He needed to get back to the water. Back to where he could see the maelstrom's edge where Dani was trapped. Clenching the lock tight in his palm, he forgot about everything except getting to the dragons. They'd be able to do something. To find her somehow.

The tunnels of the ruins blurred, passing in an eternity, wrapped in a single moment. The rope burned his hands as he climbed, the torch abandoned and the lock tucked into the back of his breeches.

As he dragged himself over the edge, Zaelinstra's burgundy body blocked the sky. The dragon huffed at him, her voice tense. "The ground is unstable. We must go." She paused, eyes darting to the opening. "Where is Varadani?"

Liam's vision blurred, the color of Zael's scales tainting the edges of his vision as he turned to the roaring wall of water just beyond the dragon. In the swirling black of the ocean, he saw only Dani's frightened face. He lurched forward, unable to feel his own feet. A sting radiated up his back, and he cursed as he pulled the gnarled copper mass from his pants.

He glared at it before he threw it at Zael's feet. "Here's your fucking lock. Now save her."

Zaelinstra grasped the lock and snarled. "Where is she?"

Liam's arm shook as he held it out towards the water. "Out there, somewhere. The chamber collapsed and she couldn't get out."

Zelbrali cursed in a slithering language Liam didn't understand.

"There is no surviving the water." Zaelinstra growled, a wave of heat emanating from her mouth as she spread her wings and lifted off the ground. She hovered, her fatal words ringing in Liam's ears. Clutched between her claws, the lock glittered like a garish ring.

"You can't just let her die!" Liam rushed to Zelbrali, who crouched to help him climb onto his back.

"She is already dead," Zaelinstra hissed.

Zelbrali pushed off the ground before Liam was fully seated, making him cling to the spikes running down the smaller dragon's back.

"No! She might have survived, we have to—"

"We need to return to—"

"You can't abandon her!" Liam tapped Zelbrali's side to urge him closer to Zael. "Not after all we've been through."

Zaelinstra paused, her great wings drumming the air as she studied Liam. "We will check the shore."

"Can't you… dive into the water or something? With your strength—"

"The depths will crush our wings just as they do your bones." Zael glowered. In a single beat of her wings, she propelled upward before Liam could say another word. Cresting the rim of the maelstrom, Liam squinted at her body hurtling through the mist.

"Go, Zelbrali." Liam urged the dragon beneath him again, but Zelbrali hesitated.

"My friend…"

"Don't." Liam's throat tightened as he leaned forward, his nails scraping over the golden scales. "Don't, please. She's alive."

Zelbrali huffed, surging after Zael, though the larger dragon was no longer in sight.

The water vapor, thick in the air, stung Liam's eyes. But he refused to close them, staring at the swirling ocean below. He watched for any sign of her. Her leather tunic, or a spot of her white hair. But it all blended in with the white caps of the sea.

"There!" Zelbrali's bellow shook Liam to his core.

Zael dove ahead of them, her massive body aimed at the Lungaz shore.

A trail of water and a human form disrupted the ashen stone worn smooth by the sea.

Liam's heart jumped into his throat at the still figure.

Be alive.

AMANDA MURATOFF & KAYLA HANSEN

The larger dragon landed, skidding to a stop on the hard ground just before Zelbrali banked to join her.

Without waiting for the golden dragon to come to a stop, Liam scrambled from his back to the unforgiving ground. His knees wobbled, but he stumbled forward. Falling beside Dani, he sobbed when her eyes flickered to his face.

"Thank the gods." His voice sounded like it wasn't his, broken with relief. "Dani."

She shook, her whole body shivering. Blue tinted her lips and fingers, her skin deathly pale. "She saved me," she whispered.

Zael huffed a breath of heat, scorching the stone to their side to warm it. It glowed orange, radiating heat that almost burned.

Liam raced to unclasp the buttons on Dani's tunic, stripping away the soaked leathers. They hissed as they hit the heated stone, steam rising around them.

Dani shivered in his arms as he methodically removed each piece of clothing, his hands still shaking.

"I thought I lost you." He pushed her hair back from her face after discarding her breeches.

"M-me, too." Her teeth chattered, her jaw flexing on its own accord.

Zaelinstra ceased the fire, having a quiet conversation with Zelbrali.

The smaller dragon shifted closer to the water, his

serpentine head lifted high and peering out at the waves.

"Who saved you, Dani?" Zael lowered her head towards the Dtrüa.

In nothing but her undergarments, Dani rested her head on Liam's chest. "The woman. The woman... in the sea." She lifted an unsteady hand and pointed at the water before touching her own face. "She had... something. I breathed."

Liam touched her cheek, still ice cold. "There's no one here. You must have imagined it when you were under water."

Dani shook her head. "She spoke to me. I should be dead."

"What did she say to you?" Zael had curled around the other side of Dani, crawling low over the glowing stone.

"That they sent her to make sure we succeeded," she murmured. "To make sure... we got what we came for."

Liam looked up at Zael, who lifted her head in a similar direction Zelbrali stared.

"The alcans must understand, then. The importance of what we attempt..." Zael turned back to Dani. "They're not usually known for playing the part of a rescuer."

The elusive underwater dwellers were a people Liam never expected to encounter. "The alcans know about Uriel?"

"The Primeval has engaged with them in the past, but not for millennia. Always a tenuous relationship, just like with the auer. But they understood the importance of imprisoning his evil. Their people were not spared his greed in the past. We're lucky they sent a scout to investigate our visit."

Dani turned her face into his clothing, her shaking easing. A silent sob quaked through her, and he squeezed her. "Did we get it?"

Liam nodded, kissing her damp hair. "We have it. We can go home now."

Chapter 29

KATRIN CENTERED HER BREATHING FOR what felt like the hundredth time that morning. "It's hardly been two weeks. Can't I have more time to consider these kinds of details?"

She walked beside the advisor, a notebook clenched in his hands.

The library had been her destination, seeking more time with the books to research the regions of Isalica that might host Uriel's prison. With Dani and Liam's return home, the vital knowledge of Rahn'ka ruins being required had helped to narrow the ongoing search.

But when Telvesh had spotted her walking past the palace's dining halls, he'd fallen into step beside her. And she walked past the library doors instead.

We don't need people asking questions about what we're trying to do.

Telvesh cleared his throat, quickening his step to keep up with her as she rounded a stone corner. "Unfortunately, my lady, there is much need to make these decisions quickly. It will determine what sections of the temple they will rebuild first."

Katrin sighed, rubbing her brow. "And you're certain we can't just wait for the *entire* temple to be complete?"

The look Telvesh gave her suggested she had just kicked his puppy. "My lady, no. That will take far too long. A year at least, and our city, *our country*, needs a celebration now in these most dire times."

Word of Feyor's declaration of war had spread among the population, reigniting the fear that had reigned before the Midsummer Festival. With the temple's reconstruction having just started, and the progress in the city going well, Isalica couldn't afford any more setbacks in their infrastructure. A wedding would provide ample motivation to continue their efforts with a worthwhile goal in mind.

And it distracts the civilians from the coming war.

But making those decisions now made her stomach flutter. "You want me to determine what section of the temple to host the wedding?"

Telvesh nodded. "Is there a particular god or goddess you feel stronger about?"

The images of the goddess, her face nestled in the trunk of a tree and wreathed in vines, came to Katrin. They were so clear, as if it'd only been days since she'd come to the acolyte in a dream.

"Aedonai." She slowed as they passed in front of a towering window that looked out over the city. "Has Ermine finished her design for her chamber yet?"

They had cracked the window open to allow the warm summer breeze inside, bringing with it the distant taps of hammers hard at work. Along the boulevard that led to the temple, debris had been cleared and pushed into massive piles near the intersections, horse-drawn carts working to take it away. They passed beneath the scaffolding that'd risen overnight, new stone being laid over the charred and broken.

"I will ask. I believe she was meeting this morning with the architects sent by King Martox to assist." Telvesh flipped through a few of the older pages of his notebook, circling something before returning to his blank page that Katrin had done little to help fill.

"And you're resolute that this wedding must take place in a month?" Katrin peered out, following the blue horizon towards the temple ruins. They hardly looked capable of turning into the location for a royal wedding in such a short time.

Her fingers twitched over her dress, carefully tailored to hide the slowly developing bump at her abdomen.

How much will I be showing by then?

"Invitations have already been sent, and several of Pantracia's leaders have committed to attending. It is too late to change the date." Telvesh wrote something down. "We even have a wolf on the guest list."

Katrin couldn't help the smile, turning it gratefully to Telvesh, but it faded. "This all assumes we're not deep at war in the next month."

Telvesh gave her a reassuring look. "All the more reason to focus on happier things. Have you and our king decided on when to announce the..." He sheepishly motioned to her midsection. "The new addition?"

Her spine straightened only briefly, dismissing the surprise because she should have known better. "When the time is right. When the news will help our people the most. Unless the rumor spreads first."

He nodded once. "Of course. I have not heard too many murmurs within the palace, so I believe your secret is safe for now. But times like these certainly are breeding grounds for gossip. It is usually best to get ahead of potentially harmful assumptions."

He broke eye contact as Katrin looked at him. "What assumptions worry you most?"

The advisor hesitated, shrugging as he tucked his notebook beneath his arm. "Save for recent weeks, the king has been seen little with you, and..." He looked ashamed to even be bringing it up. "If gossip spreads before you make the announcement, rumor could follow questioning the child's bloodline."

Unexpected heat rose in Katrin's blood. "The child is Matthias's." She pressed her hand to where she swore her stomach twitched again, the uncomfortable sensation locking her knees. "Without a doubt."

"Forgive my inference. I do not doubt you, Miss Talansiet, but gossip brings out the worst in people." Telvesh sighed and cleared his throat. "Aedonai it is. I can take care of the details, unless you have preferences for the food served, the procession, or the flowers?"

Katrin pursed her lips, patiently placing her hands together in front of her hips. "This is a wedding for Isalica, so let us keep it traditional. And I'd like to see Ermine's drawings for Aedonai's chamber when they're complete."

"Of course." Telvesh bowed his head. "Please excuse me." He opened his notebook, jotting down a few words as he walked away.

The rhythmic tapping of construction in the city beyond seemed to match Katrin's heartbeat. Going to the library for research suddenly felt impossible. She'd left Matthias that morning as the tattoo artist he'd requested had arrived at their private chambers. She didn't mind the work once complete, but watching the needle tapping into his skin had proven too much for her the first time days ago. But now, she only wanted him near.

Turning from the window, she made her way towards one of the blank walls, eyes trained on the stone panel she needed.

Better to not be stopped again.

She slipped into the cool shadows of the hidden passageway before the door had even opened all the way.

Emerging from the passageways near the crown elite quarters, she debated changing direction to seek Dani. The Dtrüa had elaborated little on their journey to the maelstrom, but she and Liam seemed eager to hide in their chambers. She was fairly certain the only reason they even had food was because their children would frequently venture from the rooms.

What happened in that maelstrom...?

But Katrin wouldn't push. They'd never done so to her after she'd woken from Slumber. She walked to the doorway of the king's chambers—their shared chambers—and strode through the unlocked door flanked by two crown guards who gave her an acknowledging salute.

Entering the large sitting room, the recent memories of Geroth's advisors and friends gathered in the room before his death made her heart clench. Matthias had restored it to resemble what it'd been before Uriel had taken his body, truly reminiscent of the days Katrin remembered before losing him.

The faint smell of blood hovered in the air, emanating from the stuffed chair where Matthias sat. He watched the artist work over his forearm with the needle.

Linens piled on the small table next to the artist, blotted with ink and blood. A day and a half ago, they'd finished the king's left forearm and bandaged it. Now, it lay exposed on the arm rest, light glimmering off the healing skin.

The artist, Pirina, worked on his right forearm, likely only a few hours away from finishing it.

Matthias's expression radiated a new calm Katrin hadn't seen since before Uriel.

Katrin approached, getting her first look at his finished left forearm. Black and grey designs covered his skin from his elbow to his wrist, depicting an abstract sun, moon, and intricate line work patterns between them. The sun's rays stretched onto the back of his hand, rimmed with red from his skin's healing.

"My queen," he murmured, his voice gruff as he nodded at Pirina. "Let's take a break."

The artist nodded, adding a few quick touches. She set aside her tools, wiping her hands on a clean piece of linen, and stood. "I will return shortly, your majesty." Bowing her head, she turned and gave Katrin the same acknowledgement before exiting the chambers.

Matthias blinked, clearing his eyes of the haze of pain as he focused on her. "What brings you? I didn't expect to see you until dinner." He tilted his head. "Is something wrong?" He winced as he stood, but it came with a satisfied smile.

She looked again to the new ink on his arm, studying the now permanent fine lines.

They somehow made him seem different, yet still the same.

She resisted running her hand up along his forearm, knowing it would still be tender and that he wouldn't want her to heal it. "Nothing wrong, exactly." She stepped to him, touching his jaw before placing a kiss on his cheek. "Telvesh was just asking for details about the wedding again. Apparently there's no changing the date."

"Nah, probably not, but I can tell him to bug someone else for guidance, if you want?" Matthias glanced at the partially completed design on his right forearm, turning his wrist to inspect the claws of the tattooed dragon.

She shook her head, moving to the couch that looked out the windows at the mountains and the south edge of the city.

The buildings there remained intact from before Uriel's attack. Clothing lines ran between them, dense with stained and drying laundry, suggesting how overcrowded the area of the city was. The palace could only support so many, and those whose homes had been destroyed were forced to relocate to the untouched portions of the city. Beyond the city wall, the meadows boasted the tents of even more Isalicans. Many who had arrived from the southern half of the country to assist in the rebuilding of their capital.

The support was in full force, and pride swelled in Katrin's chest. She swallowed, touching her abdomen. "Telvesh suggested rumors could surface that the baby isn't yours."

Matthias's gaze shot to her. "He *what*?" A threat laced his tone.

She'd had time to grapple with the suggestion during her walk through the tunnels. "Relax, my love, it's not completely unfounded when you look at the situation from the people's perspective. Besides, I think he was merely trying to suggest that we make the announcement sooner rather than later." She looked down, pressing the fabric of her dress against the rounding so she could see it.

The king's expression hardly softened. "Sounds like I need to speak with him."

"It's a serious concern, and I don't blame him for bringing it up. I've kept this secret as close as I could, but somehow Telvesh still knew. Others will find out, too, if he did." She let out a breath as she settled onto the couch, patting the cushion beside her to urge him over.

Matthias sighed and sat. "I have nothing against announcing the pregnancy to the entire kingdom today, if you wish." He faced her, taking her hands. "It will only give our people another reason to celebrate. And your family already knows, so at least they won't be surprised."

"I..." She gripped his hands, pulling them to her stomach and placing them on her abdomen. "I think a small part of me still doubts he's really in there."

The king's shoulders relaxed. "I doubt you're simply eating too many pastries." He smiled, and it reached his eyes. "That's our son in there. While I may not be the most optimistic these days, I know he's perfect."

Heat rose in her eyes as she drank in his words, nodding. "I hope you're right." She glanced over her shoulder towards the city.

"I am right. And besides, in a month, our friend can confirm your worries are unnecessary." He grinned, kissing her forehead. "Damien and Rae will attend the wedding, and you know he can..." He gestured his hand in front of her stomach. "Check."

A glimmer of hopefulness ignited, bringing with it the calm she needed. "Then you want to tell the kingdom, now? While we're on the precipice of war with Feyor?"

Matthias pulled her close, burying his face in her hair to kiss her neck. "We're always on the precipice of war with Feyor," he mumbled into her skin, making goosebumps rise on her arms before he withdrew. "Can't hurt to tell everyone now."

She tilted her head, kissing his beard. "Then we will. I trust you."

A knock came at the door, drawing Matthias's attention.

"What is it?" He watched Katrin, even as he responded to the guards.

The door cracked open. "Your majesty, your brother has arrived."

Chapter 30

Matthias's head whipped towards the door, and his gaze met his brother's. "Seiler..." He stood as his brother took a step inside, the door closing behind him.

Seiler eyed him, his temples streaked with grey. He gaped, swallowing with a sheepish, tentative smile. "Reading your letters is... much different than seeing you. It's really you, my... not-so-older brother."

The king huffed a breath of a laugh and nodded. "Still older, even if you look so much more like Dad, now."

His brother grinned and approached the rest of the way, embracing Matthias in a rough hug. "Gods, I hoped for this forever." As he pulled away, his gaze drifted to the fresh ink on the king's forearms. "Never pictured you with tattoos, though."

"Part of my reclamation." Matthias glanced at Katrin, a weight disappearing from his chest. His gaze drifted to his finished left forearm, where the rays of a sun spread over his wrist and onto the back of his hand.

After the ink had spilled, something changed in him. Some recognition sparked, and he'd done it on purpose again before Katrin suggested making it permanent. He'd never pictured himself with tattoos, either, but his soul awakened at the idea.

Looking at it, his body felt like his again. Altered in a way no one could ever take away from him. In a way it never was while Uriel controlled him.

This is what I needed.

Peace settled into his mind as he admired the beautiful, nearly-finished art, and he returned his gaze to his brother. "Your family make it here all right, too?"

Seiler chuckled. "Not without event, but yes, they're here. Kelsara is helping Avery and Ainsley settle into their new rooms."

Matthias turned to Katrin. "They had twin girls, and I think that has contributed to the deterioration of my brother's hair color."

She laughed, embracing Seiler. "Living with three Zionan women. I can only imagine. Must be rewarding to have such strong daughters."

"Oh, it's amazing. You know Avery can shoot a bullseye at ten yards on horseback now? And Ains has memorized more about the countries of Pantracia than I ever knew." Pride shone in his eyes as they trailed down to her belly. "And you. You marvel. You're still..." As his voice trailed off, concern flickered across his expression, and he glanced at Matthias.

"Don't worry. She's as she was all those years ago. We were just discussing making the announcement to the kingdom." The king smiled, wrapping an arm around Katrin's waist. "And the wedding is in a month's time."

"That's wonderful," Seiler breathed, slapping his brother on the shoulder. "Ave and Ains will be so excited to have a little cousin."

"How old are they now?" Matthias remembered receiving word of his brother's twins, but it had been in passing, and it blurred with whatever other events had been happening at the time.

"They're nine. Will be ten this winter."

So much missed time.

Matthias smiled through his regrets, kissing Katrin's head. "I heard you've been having trouble with Zionan headhunters looking for Kelsara? I thought most of the turmoil around the royal family had diminished by now?"

It'd been years since the Pendaverins were forced off the throne. While many worked to restore their right to rule, those in power wanted to eliminate the bloodline. Kelsara's eldest sister and her daughter lived with the most risk, as the rightful queen and heir to the throne. They'd somehow avoided the headhunters, like Kelsara and her family, unless Ziona's general-queen had succeeded and neglected to brag about it. But Kelsara's other sister and her family hadn't been as lucky when the coup began.

"Apparently we're still seen as a threat, which I take as a good sign. It means perhaps the people are not as pleased with military rule as the coup wants us to think. And Halena will be able to reclaim the throne. But Ziona's politics are not the news I bring, but something far closer to home."

A knot formed in Matthias's gut. "What is it, brother? We already know Feyor has declared war."

"Feyor is mobilizing. My personal scouts just caught up to us from the border. They've brought wolves and wyverns right to the south border wall. And another thirty thousand are on their way from Jaspa."

Katrin's nails bit into Matthias's back. "You'd think they'd forgo the wyverns, considering all of Pantracia must know about the dragons now."

"They..." Seiler glanced between them. "Aren't regular wyverns. At least, that's what I'm hearing. Something is... wrong with them. Different."

The knot pulled tighter, images of the Corrupted swarming Nema's Throne bringing a swell of dread.

Uriel brought the Hollow Ones.

"How soon?" Katrin looked back at Seiler. "When do your scouts predict they'll attack?"

"A couple weeks at most. Maybe sooner if that troop from Jaspa arrives." The prince caught Matthias's gaze. "Where are our soldiers?"

"Now that all our troops have come together, I have forty thousand ready at the south border wall. Helgath is sending ten more to that location. I've kept eight thousand close to the capital." The king had avoided talking numbers in front of Katrin, mostly because they'd lost a large number of their soldiers in the attack months prior, and Feyor still had a good thirty thousand soldiers on them. He'd requested aid from the dragons, but aside from agreeing to use their authority to call off Feyor's draconi, they'd decided to stay out of the war.

I wonder how they'll feel about Corrupted versions of their brethren.

Seiler grimaced, shaking his head.

"How many of Feyor's soldiers are at the border already?" Katrin's tone held her reluctance.

Matthias let out a slow breath. "Approximately fifty thousand."

Her body tensed, pushing closer to him. They'd already discussed the reality of him needing to go to the border should the war begin, and this would only deepen her resolution to keep him in Nema's Throne. "Maybe Dani and Liam will speak to the dragons again?" She looked at him, her dark eyes haunted. "They wouldn't let Feyor destroy us."

"I'm sure they could hole up in their mountain for some

time." Seiler crossed his arms. "In reality, they probably hardly need us. It's just more convenient to be friends with the humans living around you."

"I will speak to them again." Matthias touched her shoulder. "And I will send a message to Helgath, but I doubt they have time to send more."

The room fell silent, the horrible reality settling in.

"I should probably check on Kelsara and the kids." Seiler smiled at Katrin and embraced his brother again, whispering, "It will work out. You always find a way."

Matthias nodded as he released the prince, watching him leave. Letting out a deep breath, he looked at Katrin. "I know it seems dire, but I'm still working on solutions."

She nodded, turning from him towards the window. As she stared out, he wondered what she focused on.

Wind whipped through the distant cerulean flags atop the tents outside the southern border of the city, identifying the troops from Mecora that had just arrived to finish forming the eight thousand who would protect the capital. While the soldiers at the border fight a war.

How many more will die? Haven't my people already suffered enough?

Katrin shrugged as she wrapped her arms around herself. "You have to go, too, don't you?" Her whisper made his heart crack.

Matthias lowered his gaze. "I can't ask my people to fight

for this country and not fight for it myself." He looked at her profile again, hoping she'd understand.

"They're my people, too, yet I already know the answer if I suggested going with you."

His jaw flexed. "You're not just carrying our child, Kat. You're carrying the future king of Isalica. Our people need you safe. I need you safe."

Her head bowed, shoulders sagging. "But I just got you back."

"And you will have me back again." The king took her hand, and it drew her gaze. "I must lead this war, but I will come back to you."

Her grip tightened. "But thirty thousand." Silver lined her dark eyes. "And if the dragons won't help. Uriel will..." Her voice broke as she pushed into him, wrapping her arms tightly around his middle as she buried her face against his chest.

He kissed the top of her head, holding her. "Don't give up. We've beaten worse odds before."

The door to the sitting room burst open, and his shoulders tensed as Dani walked into the room, Liam close behind her.

"Something wrong?" Matthias squeezed Katrin.

"No, but we need to talk." Dani blinked, her cloudy eyes brighter than they'd been for weeks.

"I need to tell you both some things, too. Reports have come back from the border, and it looks like Uriel is testing out his new toys that Alana made." The king frowned, remembering the inhuman language the soulless beings used to communicate with their summoner.

"Well, that sounds ominous." Liam crossed his arms as he glanced at Dani. "You first, then."

"Think Corrupted, but with the bodies of soldiers." Matthias ground his teeth. "Alana calls them the Hollow Ones."

"And you think these things are going to be used at the border?" Liam tensed, but remained far calmer than Matthias expected, only proving he didn't fully understand.

"Along with their Corrupted wyvern mounts. Killing them is the same tactic... Sever the spine. But they'll be armored. You must not underestimate them. We'll need to brief the commanders." Matthias rolled his shoulders.

Katrin's hand closed around Matthias's wrist, her nails biting into his skin. "If these things will be there on wyverns, and with how outnumbered we are... Matthias..." Her voice cracked, her eyes glassy.

"Wait. Let us share our idea before you believe all is lost." Dani smiled, touching Katrin's forearm.

Katrin didn't let go of Matthias, turning her head to look at her friend. "Better be a good one. Unless you can somehow conjure thirty thousand soldiers out of thin air."

The Dtrüa's smile turned wicked. "That's exactly what we're going to do. You and I need to go to Helgath."

Chapter 31

Two weeks later...
Autumn, 2618 R.T.

THE SUN CRESTED THE EASTERN horizon, warming Dani's cheeks and brightening the scents of seawater and damp wood.

The ship creaked, listing gently with each wave crashing against the bow. Wind billowed in the sails, flapping the canvas while Dani's hair danced around her face.

She touched her wedding ring, wishing Liam was with her. But she understood his need to remain at the king's side. He'd be at the border by now, and the thought sparked nerves in her gut.

I'll be with him again soon.

They hadn't been apart for so long in years, and it reminded her of the time before they'd loved each other. She exhaled and returned to a moment years prior when she'd been his prisoner.

Standing in the snow, wrists chained.

Listening.

She could almost smell his teal scent.

A time before her heartbreak. Before the greatest loves she knew. Her friends. Her husband. Her children.

I miss you, Ry.

She wondered if he could see her. Look down on her from wherever he was and be proud of what they worked to accomplish. Her chest still ached with the loss, but her heart swelled as she allowed memories to fully form in her senses.

"I love you too, mom," he'd laughed as he ran away, chasing Varin through the snow.

It'd been the first time he'd called her mom, and she'd never forget that moment.

When Layla was sick, she had insisted he return to the house during the freezing winter night. But he'd snuck out, and she found him in the barn sleeping with the beast.

His fierce spirit had never dimmed. Only grown with him.

I'll always love you.

Warmth echoed through her, like her son reciprocated the feeling. Wind embraced her like it was his arms. A hug he complained about, yet always initiated.

You're with me. I can feel you.

Tears wet her eyes, but they didn't fall. Her son had

perished, but he hadn't been alone in those final moments. Liam had been with him, and she knew without a doubt that he'd made sure Ryen understood how much they loved him. How proud they were. He'd live forever in their minds. In their souls.

But for the time she'd had with him, gratitude filled her.

Near death, deep within the ocean under the maelstrom, Dani had thought she'd heard his voice.

Heard him plead with her to stay awake. Stay alive while the alcan rescued her.

Death had been a certainty. Yet, she didn't want it.

She wasn't ready to join Ryen, even if she yearned to hold him. The cold had been unbearable, but her son's voice kept her conscious. She still struggled to process those events, unsure how much reality they held.

Maybe that's the beauty of it, though. That there is no explanation.

Footsteps approached behind her, and she recognized the gait.

"Early morning for you." She breathed deeper, catching Micah's scent as he leaned on the banister next to her.

"The closer we get, the harder it is to sleep." His gruff voiced sounded almost like Matthias's in his groggy state. "And Stefan is already up, so you know what that means."

Dani cringed. "He still sick?"

"The waves aren't his friend." Micah paused, watching the

sunrise with her. "It will be done, soon, at least. I can see Helgath's coast. It's not far, now."

Each time the Isalican ship maneuvered closer to the coast, the oppressive southern heat had filled the sails, making Dani sweat in the afternoons.

"Remind me next time we go to Helgath to plan for the winter months." Dani ran her hand over her brow, already dreading the sun without the sea breeze to cool her. "This is inhumane and we haven't even made port." She'd abandoned her furs and most of her layers, content to exist in a strapless leather tunic and knee-length shorts.

"And this is the non-desert side of the country." Micah grinned in his tone. "Imagine if we had to go to Xaxos to meet the king."

"No, thank you," Dani muttered, leaning on his shoulder. "What does it look like?"

As he described the rolling hills of Helgath's coast to her, she tried to calm her nerves. Even though her husband hadn't come with them on the journey, she was grateful for the two other crown elites Matthias had sent with them. It had surprised her he'd let Katrin out of the capital at all, but he trusted Micah and Stefan.

And he trusts me. Besides, here is probably safer than Isalica, anyway.

One of the ship's crew let out a sharp whistle, and the sound of the wind in the sails shifted as ropes and wood creaked in response to the crew. Seagulls cawed above them, and the distant rumble of a city peaked in Dani's senses.

"Do you think King Martox got Matthias's message? And will help?" Her stomach roiled at the thought that their only ally might not be willing to provide the military support they desperately needed.

"I don't know. But we'll soon find out."

Katrin's golden scent drifted from the center deck as she emerged from their cabin. She didn't approach them, making her way to the helm where the ship's captain usually presided. Through the duration of their journey to Helgath, the future queen had remained rather solitary, and Dani had decided not to press it. She'd eagerly agreed to the journey, despite that it might very well all be in vain.

If Feyor pushed the border before Dani and Katrin even arrived in Helgath, Isalica could fall before they had a chance to save it. And there'd been no word from Matthias in days. But crossing the Dul'Idur sea that lay between Isalica and Helgath was not an easy journey for one of their messenger owls. They just needed to hope that it was all going to be in time.

Another whistle sounded, this one answered by a similar tone from somewhere off the ship's port side. A dockhand guided the Isalican ship into dock as the crew hoisted her sails.

Dani leaned against the banister as she waited for the ship to knock against the dock, the gangplank grinding into position before a familiar scent drifted from the ramp.

"Permission to come aboard?" Damien's voice seemed far too calm, considering all that weighed on the answer he and his king would give them.

"I think it is us who should seek permission to disembark?" Dani smiled as she approached him, surprised by the amount of comfort his presence granted her.

"That permission is always granted to you, Varadani. You are always welcome in Helgath." A flicker of Damien's power touched her, as if forming his own kind of greeting that no one else would ever notice.

"I'd be more inclined to visit again if it wasn't so hot." Dani huffed as Micah approached next to her and shook Damien's hand.

"Seeing as you're here, I suspect that means you got our king's message." The other crown elite kept his grip with Damien for an extended time, as if another conversation also took place within it.

"We did, and I think you'll be pleased. However, we're a bit fuzzy on what the next steps are. And my king would like to speak with you."

A weight lifted off Dani's chest, and she nodded as Stefan and Katrin joined them. "Lead the way."

Damien guided them through the port of Rylorn, which wrinkled Dani's nose at the smell of fish and seaweed. The heat grew more oppressive the further from the sea they walked.

Katrin strode beside Micah while a small Helgathian force fell into step behind them. Their escort through the markets elicited whispers from the populace, blurred colors and people all around her.

The stench of fish traded for the smoke of chimneys and muck of alleyways, and Dani couldn't decide which was worse.

I miss the smell of snow.

The city noise, which once would have sent her running, came in a commotion without unsettling her, and she silently told herself Liam would be proud.

The chatter of the market shifted as the space in front of them opened to a stone road, horses' hooves clacking. A latch clicked, and the smell of linen and cool air invited Dani into the darkness of the carriage.

"If you're amenable, I'd like to ride with you, Dani." Damien's voice held an uncertain quality in it that hardly suited him. "Just the two of us."

Dani nodded, her stomach flopping over. "Of course." She'd been looking forward to a chance to speak with him privately, but hadn't expected it to be so quick.

Katrin caught her hand as Dani stepped to enter the carriage, squeezing briefly in a comforting gesture, as if the acolyte knew she needed it.

The Dtrüa smiled and nodded, squeezing back before letting go and climbing inside.

Silence settled as Damien joined her before the carriage door closed, bringing sweet relief from the sun and noise of Rylorn.

As it lurched into motion a moment later, he chuckled. "I suppose it's never quite this warm in Isalica or Feyor's north, is it?"

Dani bowed her head, unable to respond to his comment as her mind whirled with all the things she needed to say to him since the attack on Nema's Throne. "I'm sorry," she whispered, clasping her hands on her lap.

Damien quieted, pausing, and the wheels of the carriage clattered against the stone, jostling them. "You don't owe me any apologies. I'm the one who owes you the greatest of them all."

She looked up, but could see little more than his faint outline in the dim carriage. "I was so unfair in what I asked of you. And what I said. I know now that if you could have saved him... you would have."

"Without hesitation." The seat beneath Damien creaked as he leaned forward. "I wish aspects of that day would have gone much differently. But it certainly could have gone far worse."

He was right. Damien's barrier failing and Corrupted swarming the palace would have ended all hope they had of imprisoning Uriel.

We were fortunate.

She swallowed, nodding. "I know. And I know that most of our success hinged on the part you played. I want you to know that I *am* grateful. To you and your wife."

"We have asked plenty of you and your friends in return, but I appreciate it."

"I think we may have unbalanced the favors with this latest one." Dani motioned with her head sideways, wondering how many soldiers they'd gathered to face Feyor's army.

To face Uriel's army.

"I think my brother considered throwing a party to celebrate an excuse to mobilize our military." Damien's tone lightened for the first time. "Not much point in being master of war with no wars to partake in. Though, Helgath has enjoyed the peace of the last several years. But this... this battle is far more than simply protecting Isalica's borders. We all know the truth, even if our soldiers might not fully comprehend."

Dani's pulse quickened as the urgency of the situation returned to her mind, but she let out a breath. "And what of you? Will you remain here or join the bloody festivities?"

"I will remain beside my king, as duty dictates."

She nodded. "I understand that."

"He is looking forward to meeting you, actually."

"He is?"

"Absolutely. Though your bond with animals differs greatly from the one he shares with Neco." Damien leaned back, making the carriage shift slightly as they rounded a corner.

"Yes, I've been wanting to meet him, too, since I learned of Helgath's wolf king."

A silence settled between them, though it didn't feel strained.

Damien sucked in a breath before he lowered his tone. "How goes the search for a prison site?"

The Dtrüa shuddered as memories of icy water snapped through her. "We have one in mind, actually. Isalica uncovered some ruins in an abandoned city that should work well. It's far away from Feyor, unknown to Uriel, and one of the few Rahn'ka sanctums within Isalica's borders. We've yet to visit it, but—"

"I'm sorry, did you say a Rahn'ka sanctum? Why would you choose that for a location?"

Dani stilled before letting out her breath. "Because it *must* be built within a sanctum."

Damien huffed. "You'd think that'd be information Sindré would have mentioned. Of course, I don't know why I'd ever expect them to be forthcoming."

"We learned the location's necessity when we visited the previous prison." Her back straightened, and she fought the urge to wrap her arms around her middle.

"You went to Lungaz?" Surprise echoed in his voice.

Dani nodded and told Damien what had happened, down to the last detail of her being taken by the sea and rescued by an alcan. Her voice trembled at the retelling, but she clenched her jaw and reminded herself she need never return there.

The Rahn'ka gave a low whistle before he reached across the short distance between them and touched Dani's hand. "I'm sorry. I... didn't think about what complications might come with my request to watch over the construction of the prison. So little detail of it is recorded by the Rahn'ka. They were... more focused on the actual spell to lock it rather than the device itself."

She shook her head. "We all have a role to play, and if I'd died that day, it wouldn't have been your fault."

The carriage lurched to a stop, and the curtains rustled as Damien drew them aside.

"Regardless, I'm glad to see you again. I would hate to ask more of any of you in this silent war with Uriel. Matthias, alone, has given enough." The handle of the carriage door clicked as he opened it, and a warm salty wind blew through the door. But it was quieter here, and birdsong rustled through the leaves with the breeze.

Dani lowered her voice. "You needn't ask, Rahn'ka, for

you are merely one piece of the puzzle and the burden of ridding this world of his wickedness isn't yours alone to bear." She raised an eyebrow and stepped from the carriage.

She could feel his smile in a flicker of his power.

"Best be careful with that title here. To Helgath, I am merely personal advisor to the king. I'd like to avoid the complication of anyone else learning of my other responsibilities."

She smirked, shaking her head. "Don't worry, your secrets are safe with me."

Katrin emerged from the carriage ahead, with Micah and Stefan at her side.

Footsteps approached from her right, descending stairs towards them in an unfamiliar cadence. "At ease." The rough voice came with the hint of an amber scent. "I assume time is of the essence, with war brewing at your borders?"

He must be King Martox.

Gentle paws followed behind him, the canine smell standing out among the two other humans who followed. Rae and someone else.

Katrin's skirts brushed along the stone as she bowed before the foreign king. "Very much so, your majesty."

"Please, the formalities aren't necessary. Come, let's go someplace we may speak freely." Martox's attention lingered on Dani, and her cheeks heated.

Should I have bowed?

Before she could think further on it, the others began ascending the steps, with Rae coming to walk next to Damien. "The Hawks within the capital are assembled and on high alert."

"Hawks?" Dani hit each step with her toe before climbing. "You prepared Ashen Hawks, too?" She'd heard of the criminal guild that'd risen to power with Helgath's new king, and how they'd become one of the most prestigious forces within the southern country, now operating within the law.

"Precautionary." Damien placed a kiss on his wife's head. "In case Uriel gets any ideas and tries something while we're away."

"Braka and Meeka will stick with me." Rae's clothing made little noise, reminding Dani of her own war attire. "Can't wait to hear the plan."

Doors clicked open, swinging on squealing hinges. Dots of light dappled the interior from sconces on the wall, bringing the scent of burning oil.

Micah caught up next to her and nudged her subtly with his elbow. "Here if you need it."

"Thank you." Dani didn't reach for him, but her confidence increased with having him there to be her eyes if she needed.

The group rounded a corner before funneling into a room, and Dani touched the back of Micah's arm to keep herself grounded while everyone shuffled around her.

Katrin and Stefan joined her on her other side, but she lost track of Damien and Rae.

The door to the room shut, and a hush fell over everyone before King Martox spoke. "Feel free to sit if you feel so inclined. We received the letter from your king and immediately began assembling our military. The last two battalions are arriving this afternoon."

No one seemed to accept the invitation, as none of the chairs moved from their positions in the room.

"Thank you." Katrin's voice shone with gratitude. "Our situation at the border is dire, and the reports from our king only confirm they are growing worse. We appreciate your willingness to help."

"Of course. Where will you need the army when the time comes?"

"Where ever the largest open space they will all fit within is."

Martox paused, and murmurs passed between him and the others before he spoke again. "General Tyner, see that the troops are relocated to the western fields where the battalions from Pruna are waiting. There is plenty of space there."

"Right away, your majesty." While loyal, a hint of confusion remained in the general's tone.

The door opened and several pairs of footsteps exited before it shut.

Damien sighed, and a wooden chair creaked as he leaned

against it. "I'm sorry we don't have time for introductions, but does this crown elite know what's truly at stake?"

"Stefan is aware." Katrin had moved to the other side of the room, and Stefan's stealthy steps kept beside her.

"Then we may speak freely." A flicker of Damien's power encapsulated the room. "Everyone still here knows about Uriel."

"Do you know if Feyor is using Corrupted?" A male voice she didn't know, from near King Martox. "Damien mentioned their presence in Nema's Throne."

Dani nodded. "We've received reports confirming they are." She leaned closer to Micah and whispered, "Who is that?"

"Corin Lanoret Martox, the king's husband and master of war," he whispered back.

"I'll coordinate to ensure that the sixty-sixth is spread throughout the ranks, then." Corin's voice shifted as he turned, evidently looking at his husband. "They'll have to give a quick tutorial to the rest of the troops about the weak spots. It's been awhile since any of the soldiers have seen a Corrupted."

A wolf's whine echoed through the space, and the king chuckled. "Aye, you can come, too." The sudden lack of formality in his voice made Dani's shoulders relax until she realized what he must be referring to.

"You intend to fight beside your armies, King Martox?"

Katrin failed at veiling her surprise.

"Jarrod, please." Martox ruffled his wolf's fur. "And I always fight alongside my soldiers. Now is no time to resist getting my hands dirty."

That must mean Damien is coming, too, since he said he would remain at his king's side.

Pressure mounted back on her shoulders as reality set in with how many important lives were at stake in this battle.

"There is still the matter of transporting our troops, however." Corin's voice held an air of skepticism. "You've been spectacularly vague in your intentions, especially with telling us to gather in a field rather than on the ships."

"There isn't time for you to sail your troops. Feyor will attack soon if they haven't already. We've lost contact with Matthias at the border, which only heightens the need for haste." Her voice remained steady, despite what she implied might already be happening to her beloved.

Dani rolled her shoulders. "I must go check in, so let us provide you with a demonstration."

Chapter 32

A BONE-RATTLING ROAR ECHOED THROUGH the border camp, sparking murmurs between the men gathered near the wall.

While there had been no real movement from the Feyorian troops, their ghastly wyverns made a habit of reminding everyone they were there, just beyond the wooden structure between their countries.

Ready to rip the Isalicans to shreds.

And Dani isn't here to tame them.

Yet something in Liam's gut told him she wouldn't be able to. Not with what Matthias had told him. They'd be like the Corrupted, with what the king called Hollow Ones for riders.

He paced, unable to be still with the looming battle. His feet carried him aimlessly along the wall, their soldiers having constructed a barrier of angled wooden spikes spanning a mile on either side of the south gate.

The tension in the camp was too familiar. Despite the years since he'd served as a first private in this same location, it still felt the same.

Excitement mingled with utter terror.

Among the conflicting emotions was a hole he hadn't felt in some time. Being apart from Dani left him shorter-tempered than usual and kept his comrades steering clear of him most of the time. He'd forgotten how much she calmed him, not having experienced such uncertainty with her whereabouts since she'd traveled alone to Feyor to break the Dtrüa bond.

Ousa chortled as Liam approached where he was staked. No matter the size of the iron nail wedged into the ground, the drake could break free if it came down to it. The sound sent an odd chill down his spine as he ran his hands over Ousa's smooth scales.

"Soon, boy. You ready?"

Ousa shook his head before baring his fangs.

Liam smiled as he patted him harder under the chin. "Good. Where's Matthias?"

He'd lost track of the king that morning after he'd gone to attempt sending another owl. Feyor kept shooting down their messengers, so Matthias had tried to gain some distance by riding Brek east. But it'd been hours, and he'd yet to return.

Another roar of a Corrupted wyvern pierced the air, and Ousa's head swung towards the wall. A low whine rumbled in the drake's chest.

"Me, too." Liam scratched under Ousa's chin, encouraging the drake's eyes away from the wall. Liam's stomach had been in knots all day, and now the sun was beginning its descent.

"Sir?" A soldier's voice sounded tentative as he moved in beside Liam, but deep concern lined the single syllable. "Delphrain has returned."

Liam nodded at the scout's name and met the soldier's eyes. He could already tell that whatever Delphrain had seen, he'd told the young man. And fear shone in the soldier's expression.

Liam straightened, patting the youth's shoulder. "Find the king." He gestured with his head behind him. "It won't—"

A rasping horn thundered through the air, and the roars of the unseen terrors on the other side of the wall rose in a tidal wave. The entire battalion around Liam froze for an instant before the echo of something worse than drums filled the air.

"Positions!" Liam shouted before he allowed himself the moment to consider the lumbering forms taking to the sky. He shoved the soldier beside him. "To the southern line. Now. Find the king and tell him what Delphrain told you."

The soldier nodded frantically, and his clanking armor disappeared among the rest of the battalion moving into position. They hefted shields and spears as shouts from the army's commanders rang down the line.

We just have to hold this ground until Dani gets here.

Shouts rang out as a Corrupted wyvern's screech rattled the air closer to them. Its bulky form blotted out the sky above the parapets of the gate, its sinuous wings broken and webbed. It launched over the heads of the Isalican soldiers faster than they could position the ballistas, its barbed tail smashing through the top of the wall. The debris rained down on those positioned in disciplined rows, prompting their shields to raise.

Several more desiccated wyverns followed, flying dangerously low, but the lines held firm.

"Shit," Liam grumbled and drew his sword.

As the bonfires along the border wall were lit in warning, the raging fire shone on the underbellies of the creatures. The fathomless dark of their scales consumed the light rather than reflect it.

As the soldier on the wall in front of Liam lifted his torch to the brazier, a wyvern banked lower and snatched him off the stone with charred black claws.

The creature didn't keep hold of the man for long, flinging the soldier off the top reaches of the wall with unnatural force. His body crunched into a pine tree behind the second line, bones and wood snapping. The shouts of the commanders vanished beneath the rising commotion as several more hulking black shapes lifted Isalican's into the air.

The deep thunk of the ballista's firing mechanism made Liam's chest vibrate as the men behind him loosed the giant bolt. But the wyvern dodged, and the projectile sank into the thick wood of a stairwell on the wall, cries of surprise echoing from the soldiers closest to where it shattered the structure. Their voices were silenced when a wyvern dropped from above, its serpentine tail lashing.

More bodies flew, launched from the upper levels of the wall into the battalion below meant to secure the door.

"Third line, in!" Liam's body numbed as he touched Ousa. The drake crouched without command, and he pulled himself into the saddle. "Archers, draw."

Maneuvering Ousa behind the line of archers, they shifted at his command. Even those who wouldn't have heard his call hundreds of yards down the curved line moved in a ripple of action.

"Aim!"

More wyverns dove from above, crashing into Isalica's front line like battering rams and sending soldiers flying. Their snarls cut through the air, distorted and monstrous. So different from the wyverns they'd fought before.

One of the cloaked riders looked in Liam's direction, only fathomless holes where his eyes should have been.

Maybe that's why they named them Hollow Ones.

It sent a shudder through him, but he morphed it into rage. "Loose!"

Arrows soared from the rows of archers, but even as many met their mark, none of the horrid beasts fell from the sky. Those who'd landed among the Isalicans took flight again, lashing as they ascended.

Liam opened his mouth to shout the command to draw again when Ousa tensed beneath him, spinning. Something slammed into them, the drake taking most of the blow. The impact expelled the air from Liam's lungs, and he toppled off Ousa, vision blurring as he landed in the mud.

Soldiers around him fell, dropping faster than he ever thought possible, as a rumbling growl shook every muscle in Liam's body.

The wyvern screeched, the sound so loud his head swam and ears rang. The scent of iron filled his nose, and he rushed to his feet, hand on his sword.

Growls emerged from his drake as Ousa rounded to protect Liam, while the wyvern's tail lashed. The drake lunged at the back flank of the unnatural creature, tearing at its flesh. Black oozed to the ground, the wyvern's head swiveling to the drake. The head didn't look entirely like a draconi's, though. It had tufts of fur, and its snout was short like a bear's.

It snapped at Ousa as the drake's powerful limbs carried him up onto the wyvern's back, snarling with each piece of the monster he tore away.

The Hollow One on the back of the wyvern seemed hardly

fazed as the drake shifted his weight, forcing the wyvern's body sideways, its feet staggering. He looked at the struggling creatures with soulless eyes, his face something like a grygurr and a man. Cat-like, and yet... not. The armored collar around his neck, secured to iron pauldrons, hid the lower portion of his face, making his black eyes even less human.

The blast of a horn shook the air, breaking through the ringing in Liam's ears.

We can't have already lost this ground.

But they had, and he knew it.

Liam's grip tightened on his sword. Looking along the front line, he cringed as dread swelled in his gut. So many dead, and all wearing Isalica's colors. Not a single wyvern's body marred the ground.

Feyor hasn't even sent their army in yet.

Ousa cried out in agony, and Liam turned in time to see the wyvern's maw close on his drake's neck. Bucking, Ousa lashed at the creature with his hind legs as it pulled him from its back like a puma with a rabbit in its jaws. Something snapped, and Ousa's kicks ceased. His body hit the ground with a hard thump, blood running across his icy scales.

A scream tore from Liam's throat, fury pushing his feet towards the wyvern before his brain could stop him.

Heavy steps vibrated the ground behind him, and instinct took hold as Liam spun.

Matthias, barely recognizable beneath the blood and filth,

rode Brek right up to him. "Get on!"

The wyvern behind him screeched as a ballista bolt buried deep into its chest, launched from somewhere near the wall. Claws raked at its own chest as it tore the projectile from its body, blood raining down before it charged at its attacker unhindered.

Brek bellowed a grief-laden cry, blood oozing from his chest and a spear protruding from his flank.

"Talansiet, we don't have time!" The king's deep voice pulled Liam's attention from Brek's wounds.

Liam grimaced, shaking his head as if it would clear it. Quickly sheathing his sword, he turned to Brek. He grabbed at the straps of the leather saddle, hoisting himself up despite a twinge in his shoulder.

Ousa's body lay still on the ground, his blood pooling through the ruts in the mud.

The retreat horn rang again, and Matthias raised his voice as it finished. "Fall back! To the third battalion!" The king wheeled Brek around, urging him into a steady run away from the failing wall.

"What happened to the second?" Liam gripped the king's shoulder, steadying himself as the drake beneath them sprinted.

Matthias shook his head, face grim. "Wyverns hit it like the first. We can't seem to kill them."

AMANDA MURATOFF & KAYLA HANSEN

"I counted seven. You?" Liam looked behind them at the break in the trees.

The Isalican flag billowed before the shaft snapped beneath the wing of a Corrupted wyvern launching over the wall. It dove into the retreating soldiers, like a heron diving for fish. Soldiers' bodies flew, and crimson sprayed.

"At least that." Matthias growled as Brek passed over countless bodies. "If this continues, reinforcements will only add more bloodshed."

Liam groaned. "Did you try asking Zael to help again?"

"She refuses to make those kinds of choices without consulting the—"

A deep roar shook the battlefield, drowning out the screams of the soldiers as they fled. The dying sun gleamed ruby off Zaelinstra's scales as she barreled towards the wall, her massive form swift like a hawk. Her wings drummed as they broke through the tops of the trees, her claws closing on a wyvern perched on the wall. The creature couldn't even move before the dragon tore its head from its shoulders. The body flailed before toppling off the back of the wall.

Guess she changed her mind...

Thrusting out her wings, she snapped a wyvern from the sky as it attempted to pass her, and the thing screamed as she broke its body like a sapling. It still fought, razor talons ripping at the dragon's throat, but Zael flung it onto the barricade below.

Black blood coated the sharpened stakes as they pierced the creature and its rider. It flopped like a fish still struggling to breathe above water, but Zaelinstra's fire answered its squeals of pain. She breathed on the thing, lighting the darkening forest around her in a radiant glow.

As Zaelinstra tore into another wyvern, Matthias wove Brek past the third and fourth battalions towards the command tents. "Feyor will send their armies soon." He brought the drake to a stop and dismounted after Liam. "If Zael keeps this up, they'll pull the wyverns back. At least, that's what I would do. When that happens, see if you can talk to her and get some answers to whether we can expect more help from the dragons."

Soldiers saluted as Matthias strode past them without waiting for Liam's reply. His voice didn't even waver as he addressed the generals waiting for him.

The tightness in Liam's stomach doubled. He hadn't even been able to swing his sword before they'd retreated. And Ousa... His arm shook, and he didn't notice until he spied the blade of his sword wobbling, which he didn't remember drawing, either.

Am I still enough of a fighter to be here?

A screech echoed through the valley from somewhere out of sight and beyond the massive pines the Isalicans had retreated into.

Matthias paused, facing west as the enemy wyverns rose into the sky. In unison, they flew away from the battle, growing smaller as they returned to Feyor.

"Do we retake the ground near the wall?" Liam forced his hand to still as he looked at his king.

"No. Forge a new front line at the third battalion." Matthias met his gaze. "We need more dragons. And we need Helgath."

"Then I better figure out what changed Zael's mind. Can't do much about the other. That's on the women." Liam winced at the unintended anger in his tone. He knew Dani and Katrin couldn't help how long it took to travel there. And that assumed Helgath even agreed to fight with them.

"Go. Take Brek." The king huffed, finally acknowledging another commander who stood waiting for further direction.

The drake lowered to the ground beside Liam, a darkness in his opalescent eye that mirrored his grief. The drakes weren't the mindless beasts he once thought they were, and Liam ran his hand over Brek's brow in comfort.

Brek slowly blinked, as if trying to show Liam the same comfort for their shared loss of Ousa.

Clearing his throat, Liam moved to the saddle and mounted. His subtle lean back signaled the drake up, and they turned towards the border wall.

It'd grown eerily quiet. The walls, constructed of solid pine trunks and planks, were shattered. Their jagged edges coated in black and red blood. The sun flashed as it vanished entirely behind the distant mountains on Feyor's side, and the surrounding land suddenly seemed duller. Destroyed.

Zael's fire still burned where she'd used it against the fallen wyvern, a bluish smoke rising around the twisted corpse. The fire danced in the draft from her wings as she took to the air. She looked to be flying to the clouds, but then banked in his direction as Liam encouraged Brek from the rest of the battalion.

He nodded his head at the open meadow to the north, knowing that even at a distance, Zael would see the gesture.

She answered with a flick of her tail through the air beneath her and angled north.

As Liam rode Brek into the clearing, he stared at the gashes running down the length of Zael's neck. The muscle beneath, coated in a thick layer of her dark maroon blood, lay exposed, the scales shredded.

He'd attempted to cut Zaelinstra with his sword before, after much coaxing from the dragon, and his blade had done nothing to her hide. But the Corrupted...

"Gods," Liam muttered as he slid from Brek's back and stepped towards his friend. "Will you be all right?"

"I'll heal." Zael lowered her head, arching her neck as if trying to hide the wounds from his sight. Something Liam had never seen glimmered in her cat-like eyes as she did. Pain.

"Just as all beings of Pantracia do. With time, or help if it is available."

Liam looked at his hands, wishing he had the power like his sister. "How urgent? I can get some healers…"

Zael shook her head. "It can wait until after we have spoken. And one will be sufficient."

Liam pursed his lips, stopping himself from asking more questions. He recalled Katrin commenting so many years ago that it was easier to heal the drakes than humans. He wondered if the same was true of dragons.

"Ask it." Zael sounded tired. And angry. But not at him.

"Why?" Liam blurted. "You said you wouldn't help in this war. But that…"

"I did not understand before what the enemy did to my brethren." That glimmer of pain hardened to anger. "What… chaos and despicable Art has been used to corrupt them. To bring them back as…" Her tongue lashed over her maw, black blood from the wyverns still coating her teeth. "They are not meant to be like that, and I could not stand by and watch those monstrosities embody my brethren's souls. I have sent word back to the Primeval. Zelbrali and Zedren will be here soon."

Something in Liam's stomach loosened. "Thank you." He met Zael's eyes as she looked at him.

The dragon lowered her head to Liam's level, and he pushed his palm over her nose. Her eyes closed with the touch before she pulled back and gave him a subtle nod.

"Zuriellinith will realize the mistake he has made by employing such techniques. He has rallied his own people against him once more. And even if the Primeval continues to refuse to be involved, I will fight beside my friends."

A warmth passed through Liam as he looked at her. "Friends who hardly deserve such loyalties with the secrets we kept from you."

The dragon shook her head, but stopped as her lips curled over her teeth in a snarl of pain. The blood on her throat swelled, dripping to the ground. "Ones you kept in loyalty. Which only further proves I trusted in the correct humans." Her claws flexed within the grass. "But I'd appreciate that healer now."

Chapter 33

Matthias looked up, blocking the horror from affecting his mind as he watched Zaelinstra maneuver in the sky against more wyverns than he could count. They'd regrouped and returned with a strategy that kept the dragon unsteady.

I can't focus on her.

As much as he wanted to ensure her victory over the Corrupted winged creatures, he had to command the ground forces. They were hours away, at most, from being overwhelmed.

If the plan with Helgath doesn't work...

Certain death. Not just his, but all his soldiers. His crown elites and eventually... the capital. His country. Not only did

Feyor have thirty thousand soldiers on them, they had the wyverns. The Corrupted.

Come on Kat.

The snarl of a dire wolf temporarily transported him back to the border fight over twenty-one years prior. He whirled, hurling an axe through the air at the beast. It spun before cracking into the wolf's skull with a crunch.

He stared as it collapsed, blood oozing around the blade. Approaching, he jerked the weapon from its mark and sighed. "How did you make it so far past the third battalion?" he grumbled, shaking his head. Looking up, he met the gazes of concerned soldiers who ran to protect their king. They were the unit assigned to him, though he couldn't blame them for straggling behind with all the chaos. He was easy to lose track of, all covered in grime.

"Get back to the barricade!" The king's chest seized as he took in the battle in the distance.

They'd retreated to gain the higher ground, Isalican soldiers taking up positions behind barricades that lined the incline of a hill. The green grass that had been there the day before was gone, trampled to mud and growing sloppier as the clouds above continued to drip.

In the flatlands below, the third battalion still stood against Feyor's army. Their enemy's numbers were impossible to count, extending until they vanished into the trees near the border. With the wyverns too busy fighting Zael, the ground troops had torn through the border wall.

Ground Corrupted, as large as the drakes, had barreled through ahead of the men. And three of the huge shapes remained spread along the line. They held back, as if hovering behind the human soldiers, to be hideous reminders of what still waited for the Isalicans if they defeated the army.

The smaller Corrupted, agile as forest panthers, didn't share the same role. Instead, they wove through the army and broke the third battalion's shield line like a great sword. And more Isalicans fell.

How did it get so much worse already?

They didn't have hours.

No, they had minutes, and not even a jump could fix it.

Matthias had yet to use his power, saving every drop for a time when things would undoubtedly become dire. Dappled among the bodies of Isalicans were Feyorians and their Corrupted, but the ratio was far from even.

Matthias hadn't seen Liam since he'd given Brek to him, but now he wished he had a mount. Running through the muck towards the fighting, he readied his axe again, sword sheathed at his side.

In the chaos, the unending din of screams and tearing flesh, the discipline of the Isalican army faltered. Men and women used pure instinct to fight the beasts none of them had ever been trained to battle. They didn't have time for the usual organization. All structure in the battalion lines failed. All formations abandoned in desperation.

And without the strategy, Feyor would keep picking them off a hundred at a time.

A horse whinnied to his left, and the king hurried to grab its reins. Blood streaked its dark coat, hinting at the fate of its rider.

Matthias mounted, cantering across the battlefield.

They needed more distance between them and the enemy.

A blur of black fur and scales clawed viciously over the bodies, tearing the helmet from a fallen soldier. Its back legs bunched, and it launched at the horse.

The horse reared with a scream, its hooves striking the Corrupted. The thing yelped, but regained its footing. It snarled as Matthias forced the horse to turn and swept his axe down. It caught the Corrupted's neck just as its claws grazed over the horse's flank. Black blood splattered as its head knocked against Matthias's boot on its way to the ground.

Growling, the king lifted his gaze to the collapsing battalion around him. "Fall back to the fourth!" His command rang out over the noise, and the troops tried to obey.

They retreated without turning, fighting as they backed towards the fresh troops at the top of the hill and the promise of safety.

Except they're the last. Where are you Dani?

A cat's yeowl pierced the night, and his gaze darted to the trees, expecting a new pack of Corrupted to burst from the pines.

But a muddy panther loped from the darkness, tufts of white visible along her coat.

Matthias's heart pounded, and hope suddenly renewed his aching muscles. Straightening in the saddle, he angled his horse towards distant trees and squeezed his calves.

The horse jolted forward, eager to get away from the battle.

As he neared her, he swung from the saddle. His boots slid in the muck before he came to a stop.

The panther shifted, Dani's face emerging beneath the leather hood. She panted, and he wondered how far she'd run. "Where are we?"

"A mile east of the old temple grounds. You remember?" Matthias studied her face, acutely aware of the fighting behind him.

"I remember. We are gathering. Where should we arrive?"

"Just west of here. Bring them through at the temple." Matthias dared not feel the hope that threatened to swell in his chest.

They might not make it in time. And it might not be enough.

Matthias braved the question. "How many?"

"Enough. When should we—"

"Now, Dani."

"Now?"

"*Now!*"

The Dtrüa backed up, shifted, and bolted the way she'd come.

Matthias stared at her disappearing form. "How long?" he whispered the question, knowing she wouldn't hear. It wouldn't matter, anyway. She would move as fast as possible, and only time would tell if it would be enough.

Thunder rippled across the sky, drawing his gaze. Gold glittered in the moonlight as the silhouette of a dragon danced across the glowing clouds. He held his breath, watching in awe as Zelbrali circled around the outer flank of Feyor's army, unfettered by wyverns as Zael was. His scales blazed as he opened his maw and breathed destruction in a wide swath down the back line of the enemy.

"Thank Nymaera," the king muttered.

Another set of enormous wings thrummed in the sky, belonging to a green dragon he didn't recognize.

Zelbrali circled, cutting off his inferno before flying over the Isalicans. He roared, shaking the ground, and landed in a rush next to Matthias. "Despicable heathens." The snarled words made goosebumps rise on the king's arms.

"I could use a better vantage." Matthias abandoned the horse at Zelbrali's nod, and he approached the enormous creature. "Might need a crash course, here."

"Get on. If you fall, I'll catch you."

Matthias scoffed and climbed onto the dragon's neck as he lowered it, maneuvering back to sit between his shoulder blades. It all felt surreal, too fast for him to bother thinking about how obscene it was.

Once he settled, Zelbrali pushed off the ground again, leaving Matthias's stomach behind.

Gripping tightly to the dragon's scales, the king gaped at the vision of the battlefield from the sky. Fires dappled the ground, smoke rising to smother the moon.

The third dragon joined Zaelinstra's fight, plowing through the Corrupted wyverns to rid the larger, bloodied dragon of the two tearing at her wings. The deep green of its scales looked black in the night until Zael's fire erupted. It spun with her, creating a tornado of raging flames as she flung another wyvern from her tail.

In the dim light, Matthias could see the damage the dragon had suffered. Great gashes covered her sides, and her once steady wing beats faltered.

Zelbrali banked sideways, blurring his surroundings as the screech of a Corrupted wyvern rang next to them. The golden dragon snapped, trapping the enemy within his jaws as the wyvern's inhuman rider barked commands in a guttural language Matthias had never heard before, even as Uriel.

Alana's abominations, the Hollow Ones, had only ever been talked about. Hinted at. As if they might not have truly existed. But they'd come to the field, just as he'd predicted.

Zaelinstra's bellow shattered the air. Dark shapes clung to her underbelly, holding strong even as she plummeted from the sky. Crashing into the trees, she disappeared among the broken pines. The jade dragon dove after her falling form, but spread its wings to catch the wyverns pursuing the injured dragon. It tore them to pieces.

Matthias's heart sank when Zaelinstra didn't emerge and return to the sky, but he averted his attention to the wyvern only feet away.

Zelbrali crunched, and the struggling ceased, but the Hollow One didn't flinch. Not even when the dragon released his kill, rider and wyvern falling to the ground.

"Should I aid the front line with more fire?" Zelbrali's voice rumbled beneath Matthias.

The king scanned the landscape, finally able to see the expanse of the war zone. "Wait."

I need a plan.

The line of fire Zelbrali had run up the back of the Feyorian troops helped illuminate the field. Several troops were rerouting to get around the wall of flame, leaving the battalion in the front exposed from behind. But the large Corrupted at the back advanced.

Another curve in the Feyorian line drew Matthias's attention north, towards the shallow end of the hill closest to the temple. A line of soldiers encircled a less sinister looking group of carts and wagons.

They attacked head on, but left their Art users and healers undefended from the northwest.

He stared at the spot, wishing he'd told Dani to bring the Helgathians there. But it was close enough to the temple.

Maybe I can meet her there.

Matthias glared at the monsters charging across the field at his soldiers. "Now. Light them up, my friend."

Chapter 34

LIGHT FLICKERED IN A RAINBOW spectrum at the edge of the portal as Katrin stared at it, waiting. She already felt the drain from working to open the one passage with Dani, but there were so many more to go.

One for each regiment.

Damien stepped into her peripheral vision. His armor shone in the moonlight, the dark etched patterns along the edges a symbol of his country. They weren't hiding where they came from, which both encouraged and frightened Katrin. Their families would be at risk now, too. Yet, the Rahn'ka still hid his tattoos.

"So the dragons taught you this?" Damien glanced at her.

She nodded, looking at him.

Micah and Stefan stood twenty yards away, keeping an eye on her while discussing something with low tones.

Probably making plans in case I'm crazy enough to follow this army.

King Martox's voice carried over the air from the near side of the field where he addressed the troops, but specific words were lost in the distance. His husband rode a horse on the opposite side, likely giving a similar motivational speech.

"She's taking too long." Katrin grimaced as she wrapped her arms around her roiling stomach. Something deep within her suggested things were already going horribly back home.

Movement to her left made her jump, but it was only Rae. "My crew is stationed throughout Veralian, and Meeka and Braka are ready to go." She warily eyed the prismatic display of the portal before looking at Katrin. "You can't... you know... get *stuck* somewhere in the middle, can you?"

She pursed her lips, knowing the truth wouldn't help. "No one will get stuck. And if they do, Dani and I can pull them back out."

Better not to mention that we haven't tried that yet.

Rae narrowed her eyes, but only glanced at her husband.

The portal sparked, and a big, dark mass barreled out of it.

The Helgathian soldiers in the vicinity drew their weapons in a surge of movement, and Katrin swore she saw a glitter of pale blue power as Damien's hand darted to his sword.

The two crown elites rushed closer, blades ready.

Only Rae hardly reacted to Dani's panther form.

"Gods, whiskers," Stefan muttered, sheathing his sword as Micah chuckled.

The Dtrüa shifted, breathing hard as she regained her bearings. She froze, cloudy eyes flickering from the crown elites to Katrin. "Sorry. We need to do this. Now."

Damien and Rae moved in tandem, the former mounting a large grey horse that stood nearby. He looked back at his king as Rae let out a sharp whistle, and King Martox turned to them in acknowledgement. He nodded once and lightly kicked the sides of his horse to push it into a gallop down the field.

"We need to send them to the old temple grounds." Dani approached Katrin, blood splattered all over her face and clothing. "I can only hope we aren't too late."

Nausea flashed through her at the sight, but she fought for the healer's calm drilled into her. She gripped Dani's hand before she reached out to the portal that the Dtrüa had returned through. The contact brought comfort as her fingers caught the edges of the invisible fabric's power, and she tugged it closed.

Katrin remembered the temple grounds clearly as she shut her eyes to imagine a destination. "By the old herb gardens. Do you know where they were?"

"I remember the smell. And each one, we'll open ten feet from the previous?" Dani still struggled to catch her breath.

"Twenty, to be safe. Working north from the herb garden towards the forest." Katrin reached for Dani's wrists, tightening her grip as she guided her friend to the front of the first line of Helgathian soldiers.

In the night, it was impossible to see the mass of what the king had assembled. But torches blazed at the head of the twenty battalions they planned to open portals for.

"All right. Ready? We'll open it wide." Dani's hands heated.

Katrin's mind whirled to Matthias, stealing her focus. "Dani, is he..." Her hands shook.

"Matthias is alive." Dani blurted the words. "I spoke to him. But I..." She inhaled deeper and shook her head. "I never saw Liam."

Katrin tightened her hold. "He's too stubborn to die." She controlled the worry in her voice. "We both know that's the truth."

Dani nodded, closing her eyes as she let go of Katrin's hands to draw on her Art, and the acolyte did the same.

The energy between them tingled against Katrin's skin as it seized the invisible threads of the Art hovering in the surrounding air. The fabric split, tangled in their grips as the women stepped apart from each other.

It glimmered and vibrated as they pulled the doorway wider, the surface rippling like a soap bubble. As she concentrated, Katrin swore she could see the Yandarin

Mountains, their peaks still tipped with snow despite the summer. A cool wind rushed through, but the sounds...

When she could hardly breathe, she released her hold of the portal, and it snapped into place. All the horrible sensations from the other side of the portal vanished.

Dani blinked faster, and they hurried to the next line of soldiers as the first charged through the new opening.

Repeating the process at each regiment of soldiers, Dani and Katrin struggled to keep up their pace.

Damien lingered behind, even after Rae and the king consort disappeared through, to channel energy to the women. It refreshed them enough to finish the last five portals for the soldiers, before they would create a final one for the acolyte.

The Rahn'ka crossed into Isalica with his king, war cries of the Helgathian soldiers filling the night as Katrin and Dani stretched open the portal to the king's palace chambers in Nema's Throne.

It popped into place, only big enough for a single person to pass through at a time.

Micah stood on her right side with Stefan, arms crossed.

"I'm not going back to the border until you pass through and close that portal." Dani motioned to the newest one and heaved a deeper breath. "I'll make sure nothing can accidentally follow you."

"Ladies first." Stefan motioned to the portal, his voice barely more than a whisper.

Katrin stepped towards it but paused, eyeing her friend. Her exhausted friend, about to join the battle. She rolled her lips together, unsure what she could possibly say.

"I'll be fine." Dani must have felt her worry. "We got this."

The acolyte nodded, a lump in her throat. "Be safe."

"I will."

Katrin sighed and launched herself at her friend, embracing her hard before letting go. "You better be. Send word as soon as it's over." As Dani nodded her agreement, she steeled her nerves and strode through the portal to Nema's Throne.

Her ears popped, and pressure in her head built before she felt the familiar carpet beneath her thin shoes.

Micah came through quickly after her, Stefan close behind.

The former lookalike pulled at his collar. "Gods, that's a better temperature."

Katrin gazed at the portal capable of taking her back to Helgath, where another led to Isalica's front line. But she'd never endanger her child. She waved a hand, dismantling the energy maintaining the opening, and it dissolved like prismatic ash.

Stefan stretched his jaw, shaking his head before grunting.

With only a few candles flickering, the sitting room of

Matthias's chambers looked too put together, too unused, for her liking. She glanced at the cracked bedroom door and wondered how she'd sleep knowing the man she loved fought a war. Fought for far more than just his own life.

The lantern beside the sitting area sprang to life in Stefan's hands, and he set the small fire starter aside. It cast an eerie glow through the empty room, the looming silence of the palace making Katrin's stomach tighten even more. She pressed her hand to her abdomen, reminding herself of the small life within it that would be affected by the outcome of the day. No matter which way it went.

Micah moved to the windows, sliding his sword onto the table. He paused, touching the sill. "Stefan, do you remember that time Matty surprised Seiler?"

Stefan's eyes narrowed, and he braced one hand around the hilt of his sword to silence its draw. "Mhmm."

Quietly picking up his sword, Micah met Katrin's eyes and motioned with his gaze to the exit. "You probably want some tea before bed, yes?"

She stared at Micah, trying to read the look in his eyes as her heart pounded.

Someone is here.

"That sounds like a wise idea." Katrin slipped her hand to her side, fingers grazing over the hilt of the dagger she kept there. She followed the crown elite's eyes to the bedroom door, slightly ajar.

Stefan faced the bedroom, but backed towards the door to the hallway. He reached behind him, turning the knob before sidestepping. Jerking it open with practiced stealth, he looked both ways outside the room before nodding at Katrin.

She glared at him and shook her head, pressing her back against the wall beside the door instead.

Micah huffed, shifting his grip on the leather-wrapped hilt before advancing towards the bedroom.

Understanding in his eyes, Stefan closed the hallway door and mouthed the word 'stay' to her before following his friend. They moved in silent steps to the cracked doorway, their weapons poised and ready.

Micah exchanged a glance with Stefan before he reached for the door handle.

The door crashed outward, colliding with Micah and throwing him back with the unexpected force.

A black-clad figure swept low through the doorway, slamming into Stefan and tackling him to the floor.

Micah found his feet an instant later, lunging for a second intruder who emerged from behind the door. He dodged a swing and kicked, but the figure spun in a sideways flip, a dagger flashing in their grip. The crown elite growled as the enemy blade slashed his shoulder, but he returned the advance with a diagonal blow.

The hood fell back from the attacker's face, revealing her pale blond hair braided tight to her head in rows. A black smear of paint ran across her eyes and over her brow, and she bared her teeth as she drew another blade from the sheath on her back.

"Kat, run!" Micah dodged another stab, his movements slower than the woman's as she flowed into the next attack.

Stefan rolled out from under the first assassin and landed a hit that threw her sideways with a cry of pain.

Katrin's hand closed on the doorknob as panic flooded her veins. Flinging it open, she rushed into the narrow foyer of the king's chambers, and all but threw herself against the elaborate double doors to the main hallway.

The bright light of the high-ceilinged hall left her nearly blinded, and she gasped as the guards on either side of the hallway reacted. They lowered their spears, only to lift them again as they saw her face.

"Lady Katrin." The younger of the two looked past her at the doors.

"Summon the guard. Assassins." She wondered how she was already out of breath after such a quick dash, but then remembered the portals she and Dani had labored over. Her head spun as the two guards exchanged a glance. Without another word, the one who'd spoken took off at a run down the hall, his armor clanking.

The other guard took her arm, leading her away. "Stay with me, my lady. We must get you somewhere safe."

Micah's shout of pain echoed from down the hallway, setting her nerves alight.

"They don't have time to wait. Help them. I'll be fine." She pushed the guard's chest back towards the door.

The guard eyed her, hesitating. "I have orders from King Ray—"

"This is a new order from your soon-to-be queen. Go, now!" She pointed at the chambers, her heart thundering in her chest.

His jaw flexed. "Get out of here." Turning, he raced towards the king's chambers.

Katrin stared down the empty hallway ahead, trying to comprehend what was happening as multiple sets of footsteps rushed towards her. The moment the royal guard arrived, they would order several to protect her and not let her out of their sight. Despite the comfort such realities should have brought, it only made her frustrated. She was an acolyte of the Isalican temples, and perfectly capable of defending herself, yet here she felt so much less competent with how they all treated her.

But there is more to protect than just myself right now.

She thought about slipping into the secret passages of the palace, knowing they were likely the safest place for her to hide.

Katrin replayed the moments before the assassins' attack, the comment Micah made, and the way Stefan had cleared the hallway for her to escape. The dark figure she'd thought a man at first. But a woman. Two women. Female assassins with ice-blond hair. She'd never seen such a thing from Feyor.

And the curved daggers they used...

Realization struck her like a brick to the stomach.

Why would Zionan assassins attack the palace?

She'd seen pictures of the unique blades Ziona's elite murderers used during her research, inspired by the offers Kelsara had made to train her in the battle styles.

Fear coursed through her, remembering her conversation with Seiler.

They're here to kill Kelsara and her children.

Katrin jolted towards the wall beside her, and felt wildly for the loose tile that would open the passage behind it. The small piece of wall depressed beneath her frantic touch, and the grind of the doorway had only just begun when she slipped through, closing it before the royal guards rushed past to help Micah and Stefan.

They'll be all right.

Katrin didn't bother with the lantern on the dusty floor of the passageway, running her fingers along the wall to keep her oriented. Her mind already planned the route, fear for Seiler and his family hurrying her steps. Dust kicked up, tickling her nose as she ran.

Turning a corner towards the hall she was fairly certain would lead to Seiler's chambers, she paused, blinking into the darkness.

If they're here to kill Kelsara, why hide in the king's bedroom?

Her fingertips were raw from running along the stone wall, and she rubbed the pad of her thumb against them. The twinge of pain happened at the same time as a roil in her stomach.

Ziona's presence in Nema's Throne, during a time of declared war, was a dangerous gamble for the country's military leaders to take. Even if they attempted to write the entire thing off as an internal matter that would excuse their defiance of Isalica's borders, it risked enraging the king and starting another war. It was a foolish move, unless Ziona meant for it to be an official alliance with Feyor.

The thought forced Katrin to lean against the wall as her head spun. If Ziona and Feyor allied... Isalica would be cut off from the rest of Pantracia.

Except Dani and I already changed that.

Resolve encouraged her steps towards the doorway that'd lead into the hallway. She didn't know the way to Seiler's chambers through the passages, and would need to risk the open. And hope she wasn't the actual target of any of the assassins.

Her knuckles popped as she grasped the handle of the

knife at her side. Side stepping through the panel in the wall, she barely allowed it to open before it closed again.

The grandiose hallway was empty, and she ran.

She caught the scent of blood before she rounded the corner near Seiler's chambers. Her soft soles skidded on the carpet, stopping a mere inch from the dark pools of blood soaking the blue fabric.

Two guards lay dead, their eyes open and throats slit. Neither seemed to have put up any kind of a struggle, suggesting they hadn't seen their killers coming.

Metal clashed within Seiler's rooms, mixed with the sound of grinding furniture. The door sat a few inches ajar, and light flickered from the opening.

She spun, staring down the long hallway, and calculated how long it would take her to run for help. The truth sank into her gut like a stone.

Aedonai, give me strength.

Hopping over the corpses, she winced as her shoe squelched on the rug. She crouched, peeking through the gap into the room.

Seiler stood beside Kelsara, both their blades bloodied. A chair lay on its side in front of him, doing little to block the pacing assassins. They'd been backed near the far wall, crimson splattered over their clothing and a dark window behind them. The narrow balcony beyond boasted a three-story drop into the palace's moat, dry this time of year. No escape.

The only sign of their children were the smaller shoes strewn by the door, and a compact recurve bow fallen to the floor with its quiver of arrows.

Thank you, Goddess.

Her eyes darted around the room as she evaluated how quickly she could nock an arrow once she entered the room. Despite how silly it'd felt at the time, she'd practiced rapid drawing during her hours in the range. Seiler had insisted, because if she truly was in a situation to use a bow in battle, it'd likely require speed.

She watched the two assassins creep forward, forcing Kelsara and Seiler to take another step towards the window. The Zionan princess stepped between the two black-clad figures and her husband, blood dripping from Seiler's fingers.

The prince's gaze flickered to Katrin and quickly away, his chest heaving. "Whatever Ziona is paying you, we'll double it."

One assassin spun her blade and laughed. "They pay us in honor, fool. This is why the Pendaverin's no longer rule. Too weak. Too obsessed with gold." She slashed the air, driving the two royals back another step.

Something flashed in the darkness beyond the double glass doors, and a dark shape blotted out the moon beyond.

Katrin sucked in a silent breath, not allowing herself to

consider what hitting her target would mean. When she'd first learned to shoot, Seiler had tried to take her hunting. But the prospect of killing a deer had made her queasy.

Her feet didn't make a sound as she slipped into the room, snatching the bow and drawing an arrow from the quiver in a smooth movement. She didn't have time to consider the thunk the quiver made as it fell to the floor. Her muscles quaked as she drew the bow back to its full range and aimed.

The arrow flew as the assassins whirled to face her.

Katrin looked past their kohl-clouded eyes and watched her arrow pierce the window. It sank into the third assassin on the balcony, hitting the center of their chest. The force propelled the assassin backward, their body toppling over the railing.

Kelsara shot forward in the same instant, burying her short sword into her attacker, while Seiler handled the other.

The bodies flopped to the floor, blood spewing over the lush ivory carpet.

Katrin's hands shook as she dropped the bow, staring at it for a moment before she focused on the perfect hole in the window where her arrow had flown. And the empty balcony beyond. Even without the arrow in the chest, there was no surviving the fall.

Seiler huffed, running across the room to push in a panel of wall. He slid it to the side, revealing the nine-year-old twins hiding inside. They lunged at their father, who turned them so they wouldn't see the carnage.

The Zionan princess crossed the room to Katrin, taking her hands and squeezing. "Thank you." She spoke through clenched teeth, her eyelashes fluttering. "Thank you."

Katrin urged her hands to steady as she squeezed back. She met the princess's gaze for a moment before the window drew her attention again. But Seiler blocked her line of sight, herding the children towards the door.

"The guards outside are dead." Katrin meant for it to be a warning to protect the children from the sight, but she winced. Her muddled mind failed to consider the words could accomplish worse in their imaginations than the actual vision.

"Close your eyes, girls," Seiler murmured, his tone warm with comfort. "Everything will be all right. Just close your eyes." He nodded at Katrin and guided his daughters out of the room, steering them carefully around the fallen guards.

Katrin forced herself to stare at Kelsara's shoulder, where a blade had ripped through the fabric and grazed the woman's skin. Instinctively, she reached for it, seeking her power. But it seemed defiant, and she already knew it was because of how ill she felt.

"I..." Katrin swallowed, closing her eyes rather than look at the window again. She tried to find the words, but bile rose. "I've never taken a life before."

"It is never easy," Kelsara whispered.

"How do you..." She saw the assassin's body toppling over the railing on the back of her eyelids and grimaced. Opening her eyes, she met Kelsara's intense stare and steadied her breathing. "I took a *life*."

"Yes." Kelsara gave her a half-hearted smile. "But you saved four."

Chapter 35

LOW BRANCHES SMACKED LIAM IN the face as he raced through the forest towards where Zaelinstra fell. His heart thundered, as if about to erupt from his chest, the exhaustion of his body vanishing in the panic.

A gurgling roar rose, then faded like being washed down a stream.

Zedren's wings thrummed above as his emerald form blotted out the moon, a low rumble vibrating through the air. The sound turned into a raging bellow as he turned on a darting black shape, catching a wyvern in his jaws just as another rammed his flank.

The tang of blood filled Liam's nostrils when he saw the first of the shattered trees, their snapped trunks pale in the night.

A hiss chittered, accompanied by the snap of jaws from movement somewhere to his left.

Another rumble, like massive stones crumbling, from ahead where he could make out the dark shape of a wyvern. Its claws lashed into an unmoving mound beneath it, pulling itself up over the larger creature's scales, rending as it went.

Patiently accommodating the wyvern's destruction, the dark-faced rider seemed bored as his Corrupted mount surveyed their fallen foe.

The silhouette of another fluttered onto Zaelinstra's body, and the creatures so irreverently stepping on her made bile rise in Liam's throat.

He couldn't wait for Zedren to finish breaking the wave in the air. Blindly, his hands found the crossbow at his hip, and he aimed with a steadying breath.

The bolt gave a low whistle as it split the air, and the wyvern howled. It rose, whipping its head back and forth, little claws on the bend of its wing struggling to reach the bolt now sticking out of its eye socket. The thing thrashed, exposing the underside of its jaw as Liam loosed a second. It struck the tender flesh, burying deep into the base of the creature's skull from beneath. It fell forward over Zaelinstra's battered shoulder, landing awkwardly across her once powerful wings.

The dragon didn't stir, and Liam's gut sank deeper into rage.

The Hollow One on the wyvern spat something out in a guttural language, leaping from the saddle. His boots thunked onto Zaelinstra's scales, metal chiming as he drew a broadsword from his back. The weapon looked too thick for a human to wield, yet he lifted it with terrifying ease. His black, eyeless depths locked on Liam, and more unrecognizable words came from his mouth.

Moonlight shone off the black metal collar around his neck, curved horns curling over his jaw.

Liam loaded another bolt and hefted the crossbow back to his shoulder to take aim. Something about the rider's unnatural gaze bored into him as he stepped calmly forward and dropped to the forest floor beside the dragon's neck.

Liam shot his bolt the moment the rider's feet touched the ground.

The bolt flew, and the rider lifted his hand in a swift movement.

For a moment, Liam thought he'd snatched the bolt from the air, but as he lowered the hand back down, the bolt protruded from it. He thrust his hand across the armor at his hip, and the bolt's wooden shaft snapped. Black blood oozed down the Hollow One's arm as he lifted the fletching to his mouth and pulled it from his flesh.

He didn't lose a single step, his giant sword still ready at his side.

Shit.

Liam ignored the ache in his shoulder as he dropped the crossbow and reached for the dual swords at his back. The edges of his vision blurred, only the Corrupted man advancing on him crystalline clear.

Movement to his left stole Liam's attention, his eyes darting to the side as he maneuvered into an open gap in the trees.

The Hollow One lunged with unnatural speed, swinging his massive blade at Liam's neck.

Liam's swords shot up, catching the attacking blade by pure reflex. Sparks danced along their steel as he lifted his together, trapping the larger sword between them. He twisted with the natural step back, a familiar disarm he'd used time and time again.

Only the rider's grip didn't waver. He flowed with the attempt, spinning to use his sword to vault a wide kick into Liam's ribs.

He braced for the blow, stumbling back before he swung a sword down at his enemy's thigh. But the Hollow One's sword was already there. And already back up when Liam's other sword lanced for his throat. The blows continued, each attempt at catching him off guard thwarted.

His muscles protested the repeated movements, but each surge of adrenaline encouraged the next attack, anyway. Liam didn't realize he'd been backing the rider towards Zaelinstra's unmoving form until he bumped her awkwardly positioned wing.

The Hollow One whirled, an armor clad hand raking iron claws over the dragon's hide as he hoisted himself onto her body.

Liam braced himself to follow, shifting to the gradual rise near the dragon's spine, but the rider launched off the dragon and threw a wild punch. The blow made the world spin and knocked the crown elite clear off his feet. His secondary sword slipped from his grip, the other clenched awkwardly as he tried to catch himself.

Landing in the dirt, he blinked wider, but the ground kept tilting.

The rider grasped the back of his armor and hoisted him off the ground with one arm, flinging him into a wide pine.

Something crunched and white flashed across Liam's vision, ears ringing as rough laughter echoed around him. Copper flooded over his tongue, and he fumbled to find his sword, but only patted cold ground.

Groaning, he looked up in time to see the broadsword falling towards his head. He gasped, rolling out of the way as it buried into the forest floor. A boot struck his midsection, sending him sprawling away again.

I need to get up.

The stars above rotated around him like fireworks falling from the sky.

Before Liam could rise, a steel grip clamped down on his throat. The rider's face lowered to his, eyeless yet all-seeing. He squeezed, and Liam kicked, grasping the armored wrist. His swords lay out of reach, useless against the Corrupted foe.

He struggled against the rider's grip, wrenching his armored fingers away from his throat for a single sweet breath. The steel bit into his skin, catching on the leather thong he always kept around his neck. Dani's pendant she'd gifted him so many years ago.

Liam's vision clouded at the edges, a choking breath all he could manage as his fingers fumbled for the panther tooth. Its smooth surface felt cool as he tightened his grip on it. He abandoned his fight to free himself, breaking the necklace off and slamming the tooth at the Hollow One's face.

It sank only slightly into the Corrupted's eye, but he let go and rammed his palm against the end of the tooth, hard enough to break his own skin.

The rider howled, jerking away and clawing at his face. He twitched, body shaking as he lifted the broadsword with his other hand.

Liam hit the ground with a gasp, sucking in air as he rolled back through the underbrush. His boot slipped against his sword's steel.

The leather of the necklace swayed, catching on the spikes of the Hollow One's strange armored collar.

The rider's glove finally found it, ripping it out of his eye socket, but Liam's sword was already moving. It sliced through the air, sinking into the Corrupted's skull.

The enemy's head lurched, and Liam growled before yanking the blade free for a second swing. It severed the top half of the Hollow One's head, and the soulless man collapsed. Black blood and brains oozed as he thudded to the forest floor.

Liam panted, grimacing, before leaning forward and snatching the leather thong and tooth pendant. He gripped it in a fist, blood trickling down his forehead to tint his vision red.

Thank you, Dani.

He'd tried not to think of her, knowing she fought somewhere alongside him without him ever seeing her.

Wings drummed above him, and he opened his mouth to speak to Zedren, but talons closed on his shoulder. Claws sank into his flesh, and he shouted as his feet left the ground. Agony ripped through him, but he dared not pry the talons off as the forest floor grew further and further away.

Reaching up, he grasped the wyverns scales, trying to find purchase as Dani's necklace slipped from his fingers. His heart twinged as it fell, disappearing into the darkness of the trees rushing by far below.

As wind whipped through his hair, Liam latched a gloved hand around one of the wyvern's claws and swung his legs. With each swing, he held his breath, fearing any moment the wyvern would release him. His eyes trained on the cinch's loop, touching it with his toe before needing to swing again.

The wyvern's grip on his shoulder disappeared.

Air soared past him, making breathing impossible as he plummeted through the open sky.

A flash of green, and it was as if the ground had rushed up to greet him. But the hardness of Zedren's scales scraped across his armor, and he clasped the spikes that ran down the dragon's back.

He heaved upward, wedging himself uncomfortably between the smaller gaps of spine ridges near the base of the dragon's back.

Zedren surged forward, catching up to the Corrupted wyvern who'd carried Liam into the sky. His body curled in a sweeping arch to the left as he severed the creature's head with his jaws, and a spray of fiery black blood coated Liam's face. The dragon caught the Corrupted's body as it fell, one of his front claws plucking the rider from the saddle before driving through his armor as if it were made of paper. His body split in two before Zedren dropped it to fall to the battlefield below.

Liam collapsed forward as Zedren turned towards the temple grounds, and he caught his first glance of the Helgathian army.

The portals, crafted by his wife and sister, glowed eerily in the night. They flashed with a pale spectrum of color as the first of the Helgathians passed through.

Zedren chuffed, a low whine of a growl passing through his body as he banked towards the trees where Zaelinstra had fallen. His wing beats slowed, and he bellowed a great breath of fire, leaving the remaining wyverns to Zelbrali.

Liam couldn't blame the dragon for his rage, nor for his desire to return to his élanvital. The link for the two dragons had been different than Dani and Katrin's. Instead of sisters, they'd been mates. Forever linked by the Art and their dedication. And now...

Zedren's scales heated as Liam ran his hand over them in a silent attempt to convey what sorrow he could.

This shouldn't have happened. But if the dragons hadn't come...

Liam cringed as he leaned against Zedren's back, letting the rumble of emotion from the creature fill every fiber of his body. His eyes burned as he thought of the death on the field below, of more than just Zael, but Ryen, too.

"We'll keep fighting," Liam whispered, not knowing if the dragon would hear him. "For them, now."

Chapter 36

FIRES DAPPLED THE WAR-TORN GROUND, the brightest spots in the night.

They'd lost more ground, but the battalions had retaken their defensive formations. Soldiers fell at a slower pace, holding the retreating line.

Time. They just need a little more time.

Matthias caught his breath, having encouraged Zelbrali back to Feyor's front line for another rain of fire. But he needed to watch for the Helgathian army.

"Let's get higher." He looked again towards the temple they'd been forced to fall back from, and a spark of color sped his heart. "They're here. We should meet them."

Zelbrali chuffed his agreement and banked towards the arriving troops. The smaller dragon found a clearing near the portals and landed, drawing the wide-eyed gazes of the maroon-clad soldiers.

A man on a dark horse, followed closely by another, rode closer.

The horse balked, but quickly calmed, even with a wolf at its side.

Matthias slid from Zelbrali's back, climbing down his outstretched wing until his boots found solid ground. "King Martox." He approached the amber-eyed man, hope rising in his chest.

"King Rayeht." The Helgathian leader smiled. "I don't believe we've properly met." He dismounted and held out a hand.

Matthias accepted the grip, shaking it once. "No, we haven't, but it is an honor."

The king's husband exchanged a glance with him, a silent conversation followed by a quick nod before Corin spurred his horse towards the emerging troops. His shouts blended into the night as he began ordering battalions onto the field.

Releasing Martox's hand, Matthias let out a breath. "I don't mean to cut to the chase, but Feyor's healers and artisans are holed up in a camp a quarter-mile north of here. If you circle in behind them, they'll never see you coming. Their ballistas can down Zelbrali with the right hit and I don't want to take that chance."

Jarrod nodded. "We can take them out first. Use your dragon for the front line."

Zelbrali gave an annoyed huff. "I'll do that without direction."

King Martox's gaze shot to the dragon, and he lifted his hands. "And you'll do it better than we ever could. I meant no offense."

The portal light glittered off Zelbrali's scales as he shook his body like a shrug. "No offense taken, human king. I realize your knowledge of my kin is limited. But we fight today of our own will and desire. For offenses against our own. It just happens to align with your war."

"I speak for my entire military when I say we are grateful to have you on our side." Jarrod smiled, and the wolf at his side barked.

Zelbrali snorted again, but nodded as his eyes slid to the wolf. They narrowed slightly, as if the two had a conversation.

The Helgathian king refocused on Matthias. "Have your armies push from the east, and we'll meet in the middle."

"Show the healers some mercy, if you can." Matthias clenched his jaw, imagining Katrin among the acolytes striving to do their job.

"Aye." The Helgathian king's eyes shone with understanding. "Our soldiers never kill those they don't need to. Where is the major conflict happening now?"

"East about a half-mile. We're losing ground." Admitting

it out loud almost made him cringe, but there was no time for anything but honesty. "Feyor has some... substantial Corrupted that are giving us a hell of a time."

"Not for long." King Martox looked at his wolf before mounting his horse. He glanced sideways as soldiers moved out to make room for more coming through the portals. "Feyor won't know what hit them." He wheeled his horse around, rejoining his master of war to relay information.

Matthias watched a few moments longer, eyes drifting to the portals.

Katrin is on the other side.

His jaw flexed, and he resisted the urge to pass through and check on her as another portal materialized in the distance.

Dani can't make them alone, so she must be fine.

He wondered how long before the Dtrüa would pass through, but he didn't have time to wait for her.

Zelbrali moved closer to Matthias, hunkering down and maneuvering his wing in the now familiar invitation.

The king eyed the dragon and pushed up his sleeves, revealing the intricate tattoo work finished over both his forearms. "I will forever owe you a debt for your actions today." He climbed the scales, returning to his seat on the beast's spine. Looking down at the black and grey ink, his resolve hardened.

This night isn't over yet. Isalica is mine to protect.

Zelbrali stretched his wings and chuffed. "While I do not

know all the legends of Zuriellinith, imprisoning him will more than repay that debt."

Matthias nodded, determination pulsing through him.

As Zelbrali rose in the sky, Matthias breathed deeper as he took in the additional forces spreading over Isalica.

Helgathian cavalry thundered north, making a grand arc through the backside of the Feyorian forces. They gouged great holes in the enemy's line, and one of the massive Corrupted beasts lay in a heap, shafts of weapons sticking out like a porcupine.

Another battalion moved on the caravans that housed Feyor's healers and artisans, but he held hope they would spare the innocent.

Several dark Corrupted turned on the field, rushing back into trees as their leashes to their summoners broke. But the few wyverns that remained didn't turn, nor did their riders.

Matthias could now count on one hand how many remained, each with a Hollow One on its back. "We need to eliminate the rest of the threat in the sky."

Zelbrali's final attack on the remaining Corrupted wyverns blurred into a craze of shrieks and snarls. The dragon limited his maneuvers, keeping the king on his back as he snapped each unnatural enemy from the sky. Despite his smaller size, Zelbrali proved his smooth movements were even more effective. Jets of fire blasted from the golden dragon's jaws with precision that avoided the Isalican and Helgathian troops by inches, incinerating the enemy.

A roar, different from those of the Corrupted wyverns, split the air.

A blur of blood red streaked beneath Zelbrali as his claws tore through the underbelly of the last winged Corrupted.

Matthias leaned sideways, eyes pinned on the red wyvern's rider. He'd learned the mount's name during the Feyor prince's many visits to Uriel.

He wouldn't be foolish enough to...

But Jarac's eyes met his.

Matthias's chest clenched as he gaped at Feyor's new Shade king, a wicked smirk on his face.

The surrounding night darkened as shadow whips rose from beneath his wyvern. Keleshna slowed, wings spreading wide with the tendrils of Jarac's power, like legs of a spider.

"Zel, on your left!" Matthias gripped the dragon's scales tighter, bracing as Zelbrali banked to the right.

The shadows lashed past, clipping the dragon's side before losing range.

Zelbrali bellowed, spewing fire in an arc past the red wyvern.

Matthias's heart raced, and he peered down at the damage.

Where the shadow had struck with Uriel's necrotic power, Zelbrali's scales blackened, crumbling like ash. Infected veins radiated from the wound, the damage cracking through more of the dragon's flesh and turning his golden scales grey. His wings faltered, and they plummeted towards the ground while the dragon struggled to recover.

Gritting his teeth, Matthias embraced the Art for the first time that night.

Matthias sucked in a breath as Zelbrali killed the last Corrupted wyvern. "Jarac is coming for me. You need to land!"

The dragon's head turned back to the king in confusion as the red blur of Keleshna soared beneath them.

Matthias pointed sharply to the ground, in the opposite direction they flew. "Turn, now!"

The dragon listened, and with a spread of his wing, banked so sharply that Matthias's knuckles whitened with his grip.

"Find a clearing." The king raised his voice to be heard above the rushing wind. "I need to fight him on the ground, his power will kill you."

As they barreled towards a clearing to the south, Matthias braced himself for the hurried landing.

Jarac and Keleshna were on their tail. While Zelbrali could end them with one bite or blast of fire, it wasn't worth the risk if the Shade king hit the dragon with Uriel's power again.

Why is it so much worse on the dragons?

Matthias had little time to think before he released his hold on Zelbrali's spine and scaled the beast to the forest floor. "Don't let him near you." He pulled his axe free of his belt, leaving his sword still in its sheath. "But if you can get rid of the wyvern, that would be helpful."

Zelbrali huffed, curling his body to follow the clearing edge, his attention centered on the descending wyvern.

Keleshna landed on the other side of the grass, talons digging into the terrain as she snarled. Jarac guided her forward, but she balked. Her head swung towards Zelbrali, lowering. She wouldn't meet his eyes, jaws clicking anxiously as she curled into a smaller ball at Zelbrali's commanding growl.

The Shade cursed and dismounted his wyvern, muttering something under his breath at her. His gaze altered to Matthias, and the smirk returned to his face. "I don't need my wyvern to kill you."

Matthias stared at the man he'd confused with Kin so many times as Zelbrali took to the air, still focused on the wyvern.

"Prove it." Isalica's king spun his axe, readying his stance as the Shade grew closer.

Tendrils erupted from the forest floor and flew at him, slithering like great snakes before rising to strike.

Dodging sideways, Matthias lifted his axe to meet the Art-laden shadows, deflecting their physical blow. He looked sideways at Jarac, shaking his head. "Your brother was a stronger Shade than you. You'll never be Uriel's favorite. Just a sad replacement."

Jarac's face contorted, his frown deepening as his eyes glinted silver in the moonlight. "But I am king. And my brother is dead." The shade rolled his shoulder, bringing his hand up. With it, new tangles of shadow exploded from the ground behind Matthias.

The king stepped sideways, memories of his time as Uriel flooding through him at the stench of rot rising around them. It mingled with his imagination, adding the blood of innocents to the mix. His stomach lurched, and he stared at the shadow.

"Look at you. You miss it, don't you?" Jarac laughed. "Maybe if you ask nicely, he'll take you back as his puppet."

Matthias shuddered. "Not a chance, kid." His skin crawled as he tried to even his breathing. Holding out his axe, his gaze dropped again to the ink embedded in his skin.

This is me. I am nothing like Uriel.

Gritting his teeth, Matthias spun his axe and refocused on the Shade.

If I can defeat him...

"Did you say your brother is dead?"

Jarac sneered. "Nothing gets by you, does it?"

Matthias ignored the sarcasm, chuckling. Avoiding the tendrils, he charged at Jarac, axe ready. As he swung it down to hit the Shade, a shadow burst up and blocked the weapon.

Matthias met the man's eyes, memory flashing to moments Kin had suffered at Uriel's hands. "If Kin is dead, did you see his body?"

Steel flashed from behind the veil of darkness, forcing Matthias to bring his weapon up to catch Jarac's sword. The demented power curled up his arms, gliding over the armored bracers the Feyorian king wore and continuing up his sword as Matthias held against him.

Lifting a boot, Matthias kicked Jarac in the knee, pushing back with his axe until he could put some distance between them.

The Shade snarled, grimacing as he straightened his leg again. "You can't avoid my power forever. How many jumps have you taken so far?"

Matthias let out a single-breathed laugh. "One. And it wasn't while fighting you."

Jarac growled as he lunged, bringing his sword down at the king's head, only to be deflected. The forest floor beneath him boiled with black as the Shade's power coalesced beneath his boots. It arced towards Jarac first, coiling around his wrist like a familiar pet. With a gesture, it launched at Matthias.

Jumping back, Matthias lifted an arm to take the brunt of the attack and braced himself for the burn of the necrotic power.

The black wrapped around his forearm like a whip. But the burn didn't come.

Matthias watched the shadow snaked around his bare arm, disbelief radiating through him. He gaped, looking at Jarac, a mirrored expression on the Shade king's face. Seizing his opportunity, Matthias grabbed the shadow and yanked.

Jarac stumbled forward, barely catching himself in time to untangle the power from his wrist. Swinging low with his sword, Jarac attacked again, but Matthias used the unbalanced momentum to move past him, catching his shoulder in a shove.

The Shade sprawled with Matthias's push, but rolled and came to his feet at the edge of the clearing.

"What are you going to do, little Shade?" Matthias advanced, swapping his axe to his left hand and drawing his sword. "Your power is useless."

Jarac roared in defiance. Without aid from his power, he lashed at Matthias, only to have his blade parried each time. The Feyorian moved with the grace of a trained fighter, but couldn't penetrate Matthias's guard.

Using the back of his axe, Matthias pinned Jarac's sword and glared down at him as he forced him to hunch. "And you dare call yourself a *king*."

"I am a king." Jarac threw Matthias back only for a moment before his sword was caught again. The two men glowered at each other, Jarac's face red in anger as he tried and failed to pull his sword loose. "And I have earned the title."

"You've earned *nothing*," Matthias hissed. "A spoiled brat who killed his own father. For what? Power that you can't even hide behind now. All for a monster who kept the truth of your brother from you."

A dry laugh boiled from Jarac. "Kin doesn't matter, not in any of this"

"To Uriel, he does. He thinks of Kin whenever he sees you." Matthias held his weapons tighter when the Shade jerked his sword. "You'll never be enough."

Jarac yelled and pushed, letting go of his sword to stride backward from Matthias. He stood there, empty-handed, and bared his teeth. "Still better than the husk left behind by a superior being."

Matthias chuckled, sheathing his sword to take up Jarac's. "You realize insulting me only speaks to your own incompetence to best me?"

Jarac sniffed, wrinkling his nose. "You haven't won anything. This battle means nothing." He backed towards his still cowering wyvern. He glanced at her before focusing on Matthias.

"Are you running from me?" Matthias spun his grip on his axe and strode after him.

Jarac frowned as his body shifted. The shadows at his feet crept upward, consuming him in a rippling wave. He vanished into the ground like a drop of water, leaving behind a ring of dead grass.

"Coward!" Matthias threw his axe, and it thunked into the ground where the shadow had been a breath before.

Keleshna let out a whine before she spun and launched into the air just as Zelbrali touched down beside Matthias again.

The dragon chuffed, offering his wing without a word.

The king retrieved his axe and climbed onto the dragon. "We should probably—"

A blast pierced the air. A horn not belonging to Isalica, but to Feyor.

Matthias breathed faster. "That's their signal to retreat." Disbelief hung in his tone. "Let's take a look, shall we?"

Chapter 37

DANI SNARLED, CHARGING THROUGH THE underbrush at the running Feyorian archer who would have killed her with his last shot had she not ducked. He'd taken one look at her panther form coming at him and made a run for it, and her heart pounded with the chase.

He banked around a wide tree, taking his ochre scent with him, and she swerved around it the other way to cut him off. Leaping, she tackled him before he could lift his bow. Her teeth sank into his throat, even as he tried to stab her with an arrow. It barely pierced her hide, but the sting made her clench her jaw, ceasing his struggle.

Dani waited, panting, until the flow of copper over tongue slowed. Releasing him, she huffed and caught a familiar scent that didn't belong. The familiarity brought anxiety rather than relief. Breathing deeper, she followed the tiny tinge of teal through the grass until her nose hit a smooth bone.

Rousing the Art, she shifted to her human form and patted the ground. Finding a leather thong, she lifted it and touched the panther tooth. It was covered in a thick substance, which she rubbed between her fingers before lifting it to her nose.

Corrupted blood.

Fear rushed through her, heating her eyes. "Liam?" She shouted his name as she stood, not caring if an enemy heard her. "Liam!"

Silence, except for the distant battle, filled her ears.

Pulling the necklace over her head, she dropped it under her tunic. Taking a deep breath, she retook her panther form and breathed deeper.

No other hint of Liam's scent lingered in the forest.

How did it get here?

She hadn't seen him since returning from Helgath, but had assumed he'd been fighting with Matthias.

What if they captured him?

Dani darted through the forest, running aimlessly west until a Feyorian horn broke the air. The signal to retreat.

We won?

The knowledge couldn't defeat her fear for her husband, and she kept running.

As she dodged through the woods, the black scent of

smoke rose, weaving through the trees. Her gut tightened, as she considered if Feyor would set fire to the forest to cover their backs as they retreated.

Sniffing, she tried to orient to the direction of the flames, and teal flooded her senses. Accompanied by heavy footsteps through the brush moving in her direction.

Forcing her tired muscles faster, Dani leapt over a fallen log, her surroundings alive in a haze of smells.

"Nymaera's breath!" Liam's swords scraped from the sheaths on his back as Dani rounded a tree onto an old game trail. His breath released in a sigh and one of the swords tapped on the armor of his shin. "Good gods, Dani. Don't charge at me like that in a war zone."

Relief scorched through her as she shifted to her human form, launching herself at him. "You're alive." She wrapped her arms around him, burying her face in his neck to submerge herself in his scent.

His arms closed around her, pulling her tight against his body. He kissed her hair, despite how filthy they both were. Pulling back, he took her cheeks in his hands, thumbs brushing away the muck. "You made it. And brought Helgath."

Dani nodded. "They assembled their military before we even got there without question. Even their king came here to fight. Damien and Rae, too."

"Then we have much to thank them for, and Feyor would

be fools to attack again. But it cost a lot of lives." Liam brushed a hand through her hair, and she recognized the hitch of grief in his breath. "One of the first was Ousa."

Dani winced, her heart clenching. She closed her eyes, remembering the excited sounds Ousa had always made at meal time, or when his hatchlings were introduced to him. They'd shared a lot with the creature, and she steadied herself against Liam as the grief welled. "But he died fighting?"

"Saving me. Before the dragons joined the battle. They... don't like what Uriel has made of the wyverns. We'll have their full support from now on, I suspect." There was a heaviness to his words as he ran his hands down her arms to take her hands between them. "Zael..."

"I knew she would fight with us." Dani tried to smile, but his tone caused a bubble of dread in her stomach.

"She's the sole reason our army survived until support arrived when you came with the Helgathians." Liam squeezed. "She destroyed so many of their wyverns, but there were too many before Zedren and Zelbrali could help."

Dani's breathing slowed, and she squeezed his hands. "What are you telling me? Where is she?"

"She sacrificed herself for us. For Isalica. She fell for us."

Blinking back tears, Dani swallowed. She bowed her head, closing her eyes as the events in Helgath replayed in her mind. "Opening the portals took so long..."

"No, even if Helgath had been here in the beginning, it

wouldn't have helped. It was the Hollow Ones and their wyverns. Helgath would have fallen beside Isalica if you'd come sooner."

Dani's shoulders slumped as tears wetted her cheeks. "Isalica would have fallen months ago to Uriel without Zael. She always had our backs." Her throat tightened, and she leaned her forehead against Liam's chest. The blow of Ousa's death mingled with the new grief, making her knees weak.

The air vibrated with a dragon's call, rumbling mournfully through the trees. Zedren's cries coming from the direction of the smoke.

Liam slid a hand up into Dani's hair, holding her close as he kissed her head again. "Zedren believes that with one of their own fallen, the Primeval won't avoid the human wars anymore."

Closing her eyes, Dani remembered all the advice the dragon had given her on dealing with her grief. Her loss, and how she understood it.

She's with her hatchling now.

"I wish it hadn't taken losing Zaelinstra," she whispered. "I will miss her."

Liam nodded, his cheek rubbing against her temple as he did. He sucked in a deep breath, as if clearing whatever other thoughts remained as he pulled away. "We should get back to the barricade."

"Wait." She pressed her palm to his chest where the tooth

necklace normally rested. "You lost something."

Liam grunted, placing his hand over hers. "Only after it saved my life."

Her brow twitched, but she shook her head. "Then you should have it back, in case such an occasion happens again." Pulling the pendant from beneath her tunic, she drew it from her head to place it over his.

"That nose of yours is pretty amazing." Liam took her hand and held it against the pendant with his. "Thank you. I won't worry you with the story about how it ended up in the middle of the forest."

Dani narrowed her eyes, swiping a tear from her cheek. "I have you here, now, and I plan to keep it that way for quite some time, regardless of your story. So you may as well tell me, but perhaps tomorrow."

"Tomorrow." Liam pushed his forehead to hers before he placed a tender kiss on her lips. "I love you."

Dani pulled him back to her for another kiss, closing her eyes and pressing harder against him. "And I love you, my husband."

Chapter 38

Two weeks later...

MATTHIAS FLUNG HIMSELF OFF HIS decorative warhorse as soon as he reached the base of the palace steps. Ignoring protocol to salute the soldiers waiting for him, he locked eyes with Katrin, who stood midway up on the landing. He took the stairs two at a time, deaf to the crowd at the palace gates as he reached her.

She let out a surprised squeak as he lifted her from the ground.

His heart thundered in his ears, and he spun her in a circle before holding her tighter.

Burying her face against his neck, Katrin squeezed him with a strength he didn't know she had. Her breath hitched as he lowered her back to her feet, her touch encouraging him to further damn protocol.

Their mouths met in a fiery kiss, Katrin humming against his lips as she draped her arms around his neck. As he began to break away, her arms tensed and held him close as she renewed the affection once again.

Cheers grew into a cacophonous roar in the distance behind him, and he laughed into the kiss. They parted only enough to form words, lips still touching.

"It's so damn good to be home," the king murmured, running his hands over her hair and studying her face.

Her eyes shone with tears, but she smiled and nodded. "If you don't acknowledge the crowds at all, Loryena will have your head."

Matthias's brow furrowed. "Loryena? What are you talking about?" He took the cue and turned, waving to his people.

"She came out of retirement to plan the wedding." Katrin grinned with him, waving at the cheering Isalicans. Pink tinted her cheeks, and he admired it.

The king chuckled. "I should have predicted she might want to be involved." His gaze drifted to her again, everything else blurring. "Gods, I missed you."

Her hand slid into his as she lifted her chin. "And I, you." She stepped closer, leaning against his arm and tilting her head against his bicep as she continued waving.

"Where are Micah and Stefan?"

"Micah is having his *hopefully* last healing session right

now to repair a tendon in his arm. It's been a slow process, and Stefan goes with him each time." Katrin's attention shifted to the two crown elites dismounting, and her body relaxed on seeing Liam and Dani. "Stefan figured you'd forgive his absence."

"Of course."

"Aunt Katrin?" Varin drew their attention behind them, closer to the palace's front doors.

The young woman wore a fine rose colored linen, looking ready to rush down the stairs. She held tight to Jaxx's arm, as if holding him back, too. Her eyes darted towards her parents at the base of the stairs, uncertainty in her face.

"Don't worry about formalities." Katrin waved a hand before placing it on Matthias's chest again. "Go."

The king nodded, gesturing with a smile.

The teenagers needed no further encouragement as both barreled down the stairs.

"Mom!" Jaxx reached Dani first, and she opened her arms, catching his hug.

"Oh, I missed you both so much." The Dtrüa kissed the top of her son's head. "Thank you for staying safe."

Varin joined them, though with fewer dramatics, and wrapped her arms around Liam. "We *are* capable of following directions, you know."

"Zionan assassins." Jaxx pulled away, excitement in his tone. "They were right here in the palace. But we didn't even know," he grumbled, joy turning to disappointment. "Slept through the whole thing."

Dani lifted an eyebrow. "Followed directions, huh?"

Varin chuckled. "Well, Aunt Katrin did tell us to go to sleep." She glanced up the stairs at the king and her aunt.

The Helgathian royal family were next to arrive, dismounting near the crown elites. King Martox's wolf wagged his tail, nudging Dani's hand until she scratched between his ears.

Ships from Rylorn met the Helgathian military in Omensea to take them home, but the royals continued to Isalica's capital, eager to attend a wedding celebration after their victory.

Matthias tugged Katrin's hand to descend the stairs together. "Come. I'm supposed to welcome them here."

Jaxx's attention shifted as he pulled back from his mother, pausing as he took in the massive black wolf.

"This is Neco." Dani scratched the wolf harder, and the beast let out a groan. "He's a good wolf."

The boy's eyes moved beyond to the two men who stood a few steps back, dressed in maroon and black formal jackets with silver stitching. The king and his consort exchanged a glance before meeting Matthias's gaze.

"Welcome." The Isalican king let go of Katrin and offered his hand to Jarrod, who took it. "I am honored to have you and your family as my guests for the duration of your stay in Isalica."

"We are most pleased to be here." Martox released his grip and smiled at Jaxx, who pulled from his mother and tugged at the bottom of his tunic to straighten it.

Dani leaned close to her son and whispered something.

Color rose to his cheeks, and the Dtrüa laughed.

Corin lowered his head in a respectful acknowledgement as Katrin dipped into a curtsy. "Pleasure to see you again, too." The consort spoke with a half smile. "I understand we will soon be able to commiserate together about being married to kings. Though you neglected to mention that while visiting Veralian."

"More pressing matters." Katrin looped her arm into Matthias's again. "But please be welcome. The staff will show you to your quarters so you can rest after your journey."

Damien and Rae joined the group, and everyone turned to climb the stairs into the palace.

Matthias pulled Katrin into another embrace, finally alone with her in their chambers. "Gods, when I read your letter about the Zionan assassins... I'm so sorry you had to face that without me, but I'm damn thankful I left Micah and Stefan with you."

"They saved my life," she murmured into his chest, wrapping her arms around his waist.

Matthias closed his eyes, breathing in the flowery smell of her hair. "From what I heard, you did your fair share of *saving* that night, too. What were you thinking, giving the guards the slip and then rushing to Seiler's defense all by yourself?" He drew away from her and looked at her face.

"I don't know." Katrin shook her head. "All I could think about was how the guards would just *protect* me, and not listen. Kelsara and Seiler didn't have that kind of time. I didn't really think it through. And I..."

Tilting his head, the king studied the regret in her expression. "What is it? Did they hurt you? You said they didn't, but—"

"No, no. I wasn't injured. But I did... kill one of them." Her words came as a breath, barely audible even so close.

"I know." Matthias furrowed his brow. "Seiler told me what happened."

"Matthias, I *killed* someone," she whispered.

"Oh." He pulled her into him again, understanding settling. "I hadn't really thought... You've never killed anyone before."

She buried her face harder into his tunic, a shudder passing through her body. "I didn't even see her face. I didn't even stop to think about what the arrow would actually do, I just... let go."

His heart cracked at her tone. "I'm sorry, Kat. It shouldn't have happened. You shouldn't have had to." He took her face in both hands and drew her away to meet her gaze. "But I am so proud of you. Terrified, too, of the thought of you in danger, but mostly just proud."

Katrin blinked faster, eyes glassy. "Proud?"

"Of course. That was crazy, stupid, brave. I am marrying an amazing woman." Matthias kissed her forehead. "My brother and his family still live because of you."

Katrin shuddered again, but her shoulders rose with a deep inhale. "That's what I keep telling myself. That I saved more than I took. But I was lucky. And the only reason I even had the shot I did was because they didn't see me. If Micah and Stefan hadn't noticed the footprint on the window sill..." She paused, running her fingers along the stitching of his tunic. "I still don't know why they were even in our chambers. Micah's been unusually tight-lipped about it." She looked up at him with narrowed eyes, pressing her chin to his chest. "So are you going to tell me?"

Matthias hesitated, jaw flexing. He let out a breath, rolling his shoulders. "After the border battle, we intercepted a letter between Feyor and Ziona. Feyor provided information to aid Ziona's assassination attempt, and it looks like they requested your death in exchange for that information." He swallowed the bile in his throat. "It was Uriel trying to get to us, and using Ziona to do it."

Katrin frowned, averting her gaze. "I suppose we all have targets on our backs as long as Uriel is still out there."

The king nodded. "But he won't succeed. I know this isn't the end, but maybe next time they'll think twice about sending assassins into our home." He touched the bottom of her chin, lifting it. "And, for now, the war is over. Which means I'll be here, with you, and we can face things together."

A weak smile crossed her lips as she took his hand from her chin and lifted it to her lips. "I like the sound of that." Her smile grew more genuine as she inched closer, and they fell naturally into another embrace. She sighed, her breath rustling against his tunic. "We were never meant for normal lives though, were we?"

Matthias chuckled. "I could have told you that the moment I set eyes on the fiery acolyte who went toe to toe with me in a courtyard. But I regret none of it."

"Except for that part when you didn't tell me you were a prince for several weeks, I hope." Her voice lightened for the first time as she poked his gut.

He grinned. "Well... *technically* it worked out, so..."

She poked harder but laughed. "That's when you were the lucky one."

Matthias shook his head, kissing the top of her hair. "Nah. I was always the lucky one."

Chapter 39

KATRIN SMOOTHED THE ICE-BLUE SATIN over her extended belly again, turning sideways in the mirror as the tailor looked her up and down. Sighing, she let go of the fabric. "I guess the entire kingdom knows already anyway, I don't need to be so worried about it." Her back twinged, and she rubbed at the knots of the corset on the back. "Maybe a little looser, Sorelis?"

The woman smiled at her through the mirror and nodded as she loosened the ties once more. "You look beautiful, your majesty."

"Katrin, please." The acolyte met the tailor's eyes. "I'm not your queen yet."

"But you will be in... oh, about an hour." Liam's voice came from the doorway, and Katrin looked up to see him and

Dani stroll into the room together. They both looked like they belonged in one of the storybooks Katrin used to read when she was a child, rather than firmly in reality.

Liam had cleaned up perfectly, and the silver in his hair made him even more refined with the buttoned up formal attire.

Dani draped her arm through his, looking more comfortable in her formal white gown than the last royal wedding they attended. Her neckline dipped in a low curve, sleeves off the shoulder ending at her elbows. While it had a petticoat, the width of her skirt was half of Katrin's full ball gown.

A smile formed on Katrin's lips before she forced it into a disapproving scowl. "Aren't you supposed to be with Matthias right now?" She lifted her brow at her brother.

"Oh, he's fine. Not flustered at all." Liam smirked. "Can't I visit my sister?"

"Does it look the same as your last fitting?" Dani let go of her husband and strode closer with a click of her tongue.

"More or less." Katrin turned back to the mirror, running her hands over her abdomen again. The child within kicked hard enough to make her flinch, and she pushed back on the spot. "You better not kick my bladder in the middle of the ceremony," she grumbled to her stomach.

Dani laughed. "Oh, you better bet he will. They always have wonderful timing."

Katrin's stomach fluttered as the baby rolled, and she gave Sorelis a pitiful glance. "I should pee again."

"And that is my cue to exit." Liam gave her a smile. "Good luck."

She smiled at her departing brother as Sorelis lifted the train of her dress.

Katrin looked at Dani once the door had shut with Liam's exit. "How is Matthias really?" She'd worried about him all day. If the pressure would be too much. If he would change his mind.

"He's good," Dani whispered. "Really. He's excited. A little nervous, I think, but he seems like his old self today more than ever. He's sharing a drink with Jarrod and his wolf right now."

"Now I have an image of the wolf drinking whisky from a glass." Katrin stepped carefully from the pedestal and made her way with the tailor's help towards the bathing chambers.

The Dtrüa shrugged and waved a hand in front of own eyes. "I have no idea what the wolf drinks whisky from."

Katrin snorted and quickly lifted her hand over her mouth. She paused in the doorway, scooping the train from the tailor's hands. Giving Sorelis a brief nod, she looked back at her best friend as the tailor took her leave. She considered the Dtrüa carefully for a moment. She could still see the faint lines on her arms where battle wounds hadn't quite healed.

Memories of the war at the border. Of the price paid for Isalica to still be standing.

And while the sound of hammers throughout the city had quieted for the day so all could celebrate, the skeletons of scaffolds still daunted most of the view.

Reminders of what they had overcome. What they had lost.

They had commissioned a new statue for the courtyard, replacing what had once been an ostentatious fountain. Once complete, Zaelinstra's likeness would overlook the city, her maw open in a roar towards the sky in defiance against any who would challenge the palace. The rough hewn frame of the sculpture still served as a place for the people to remember the dragon's sacrifice. Last Katrin had seen, the cobblestones before it were covered in autumn blossoms and woven wreaths.

"You all right?" Dani's voice softened. "What are you thinking about?"

Katrin wished she could compose all the thoughts that had been plaguing her into a single statement, but sighed. "How long do you think this peace will last?" She tried not to sound as worried as she felt. But with Uriel in control of Feyor and still so much to do to construct the prison...

"It will last as long as it lasts," Dani murmured, tilting her head. "But that is nothing new. For all we know, it will last decades."

Katrin's hand ran over her belly, her son giving an answering kick. "I'd rather not leave problems like Uriel for our children to battle."

A weak smile twitched Dani's lips. "If not Uriel, there will be other problems. Other battles. We must raise them the best we can and hope... hope it's enough." Her jaw flexed, but it was her only outward show of emotion.

Katrin grimaced and chewed her lip, knowing precisely who Dani thought of.

The Dtrüa stepped closer. "Our children will be all right. The ones who walk Pantracia and the ones who look over us. And today... Today you're giving hope to a country." She smiled, eyes glistening. "And I'm so happy for you both."

"Hope." Katrin smiled, closing the distance between them. She took Dani's hand tightly. "You sound like I used to. But you're right. Today is about my marriage to a good man, and my dedication to our people." She bobbed Dani's hand up and down a few times. "I do have another favor to ask of you, though."

"Anything." Dani squeezed.

Heat rose in Katrin's cheeks. "I... need you to help hold my skirt... while I..."

Dani laughed. "Yes. I will hold your skirt."

Crowds spanned the other side of the courtyard, held back at the gates as they cheered for their wedded king and new queen. A whole procession waited at the base of the stairs. Five carriages, each with four white horses. Riders surrounded them, crown guards on all sides.

Katrin's heart still pounded. It'd hardly slowed throughout the entire event. Not in the marriage ceremony, and certainly not throughout the banquet. Both had been longer than she predicted, but the evening was full of joyous dancing. Speeches, food, and laughter.

The sun had already set, great torches on the stairs lighting their path.

Matthias took the first two steps down the front stairs of the palace before looking back at Katrin, holding out his hand. His eyes glimmered, a grin brightening his face. "Your carriage awaits, my queen."

Beneath his sleeve, his tattoo poked up near his wrist, the edge of a dragon's claw.

Placing her hand in his, she fought back the nervous butterflies that still hadn't left her gut. "I think I'll miss you calling me priestess." She smiled, and it felt perfect.

"All right, Priestess." The king escorted her down the stairs to the rising cheers of their people. His eyes never left her, though, his expression strangely relaxed amid the excitement. "Isalica hasn't had a queen in thirty years, and they think you're perfect. I agree with them. Are you ready to be adored by a nation? "

"Gods, I hope so. Otherwise what was that whole ceremony about?" She squeezed his hand as they reached the flat of the courtyard, and the carriage door swung open with the bow of the coachman.

Matthias held her hand as she lifted her skirt and stepped into the open-top carriage. The white wood contrasted the deep blue upholstered seats with silver stitching.

Still in the nation's eye for a little longer.

Katrin settled her procession dress around her hips, already sweating beneath the long sleeves intended to keep her warm in the autumn air.

Matthias sat beside her, giving a nod to the driver that they were ready. "Have I mentioned you're gorgeous?"

"Only like a hundred times."

The king laughed as the carriage eased forward, the other carriages full with the royal family, the Talansiet family, and visiting diplomats.

Katrin watched her mother swipe a nervous hand over the side of her hair, as she'd done all night, to ensure it was in place. Her father's gaze met hers, a twinkle in his eye as he grinned at his daughter. Then he looked back to his wife, wrapping an arm around her. Yez scowled and straightened her dress but shifted closer to her husband, anyway.

"This is the first day in a long time where I've used my power for frivolous reasons," Matthias murmured near her ear. "But I doubt anyone would blame me."

Katrin turned to him, pulling his hands into her lap with a teasing smile. "And what moments did you feel necessary to use it in?"

He kissed her temple as they neared the gates to the city. "The ceremony. I married you twice, Katrin Rayeht."

"Shame I wasn't there to confirm such things." She let out a little gasp as their son did what had to be a somersault in her womb. The surprise turned into a laugh as she pulled Matthias's hands against her swollen belly, holding them tight to where the child kicked. "He hasn't stopped moving all day. I think he can sense all the excitement out here."

The gates to the city swung wide, and flower petals showered over them in all shades of white and blue. Horseback guards kept the crowds at a distance, but even they smiled at the cheers.

"Maybe he will actually let you sleep tonight, then." Matthias caressed her stomach, his smile as genuine as ever.

"One can only hope, though sleep seems hardly something to be concerned about with all the other things we're facing." Katrin frowned, disappointment boiling up as she brought up the one topic she'd sworn to avoid.

The king wrapped an arm around her shoulders. "No sleep will drive you mad," he whispered. "I would know." Her unimpressed look made him chuckle, and he shook his head. "I have no doubt that we have not faced the end of our trying times, but I am certain that for those to come, we can overcome them together."

Katrin gripped his hand harder, unable to stop the glance behind them once again. Their new allies sat in the carriage beyond her family. Damien's hair glowed as gold as the clouds in the dying sunlight, his arm around his wife's shoulders. One would never have guessed what all depended on the couple, or the rest of them.

"Sometimes I still wonder what more we could have accomplished with the time we lost." She turned back to her husband. "How much more prepared we could have been."

Matthias kissed her temple. "That is true, Priestess. But, more importantly, what do you wonder we might accomplish with the time we've got now?"

Epilogue

Thirteen years, nine months, and six days later...
Summer, 2632 R.T.

"HAPPY BIRTHDAY, BROTHER." MATTHIAS LIFTED his goblet in a playful toast, smirking. "What are you, sixty?"

Liam groaned but smiled, causing the crow's feet at the corners of his eyes to deepen. "No, that's you, old man."

The king scoffed. "Hey, twenty of those years don't count, remember?" He crossed his ankles, reclined in a low chair overlooking the Dul'Idur Sea.

The summer sun heated his skin, but nerves rumbled in his gut despite the wine.

Rays of afternoon light reflected off the water, its gentle crash against the cliff face below lulling the visitors of the estate into relaxation, despite the dire truth of what was about to happen.

They'd decided to spend Liam's birthday at Seiler's estate in the southern Isalican city, making sure plenty of witnesses could vouch for their whereabouts during the prison's completion. The dragons weren't sure if humans would sense the moment it happened, but having the king and his companions far away from Orvalinon when it did made sense.

The Rahn'ka ruins at the abandoned city had proven a worthy location. And while Matthias had constructed a barracks over the buried sanctum, he'd constructed five more at other locations across Isalica. Just in case Uriel noticed.

Katrin strode onto the balcony, wiping her hands on an apron. "Have either of you seen Gerry?"

Matthias laughed. "No, but he had a serious talk with me yesterday about calling him that. I should have mentioned it." He grinned up at his wife, admiring the flour dappling her face and hair.

Still can't get it all in her baking.

Katrin rolled her eyes. "Of course, thirteen and suddenly wants to be Geroth."

"Can't blame him. Geroth sounds much more manly than *Gerry*." Liam smirked around the rim of his drink. "Poor kid."

The queen scowled, but only to hide her smile. "It's hardly midday and you're already drinking."

Matthias gave her a sheepish shrug. "We're under a lot of pressure today... and besides, we're celebrating."

"Birthday." Liam pointed at himself. "Or did you forget?"

"Doubtful, considering I've been in the kitchen working on *your* birthday cake." Katrin walked to Matthias, leaning over him to kiss his hair. "If you see *Geroth,* can you tell him that his little brother would appreciate some of his attention today? Zael has been horribly bored and is making my baking infinitely more difficult."

"Tell him to come out here." Matthias patted an empty seat on his other side. "He can tell Uncle Liam about our rabbit hunt yesterday."

Dani walked up behind Katrin. "I finished sifting the powdered sugar." She clicked her tongue and took Liam's goblet to steal a sip.

"Thank you, I—"

Katrin's eyes widened in tandem with a sudden invisible shock wave.

Everything in Matthias's body tensed, responding to the pulse of power coursing through the fabric of the Art blanketing the world.

The three Art-users on the balcony let out an exhale together in answer to the altered flow of energies. It radiated from the north, but none of them expected it to be a directional ripple.

The deep pressure rumbled through the king's veins before it vanished, and the usual light hum of power returned to normal.

"What just happened?" Liam's gaze darted between the other three.

Matthias looked at Katrin, his heart racing. "I think it's done."

"The prison?" Liam sat straighter.

Katrin took Dani's hand, nodding. "It's complete."

Rae gasped and reached for Damien, steadying herself as their gazes met. "Was that what I think it was?"

"Fuck." Damien pulled her into a side room in the Veralian palace, his tattoos brightening beneath his linen tunic. He shut the door, and she watched as the glow subsided.

"The prison?" Rae murmured.

"We need to make that trip back to Eralas. It's time to wake them." Worry glinted in his hazel eyes, even as he tried to hide it.

The Mira'wyld huffed. "Kynis will be so happy to see us."

He gasped, and the cold air burned in his throat. Coughing, he grabbed at his aching chest as he pushed up from the hard stone surface. Grimacing, he touched his head where pain reacted to an encroaching wave, but abruptly subsided.

Beside him, a woman rose from a stone slab that matched his, pale green light reflecting in her long hair. "Who are you?"

He rubbed his face, finding stubble along his jaw. "I..." His voice echoed like hers through the chamber. "I don't know."

Rage. Pure and seething erupted from Uriel's chest. His black shadows flipped the table before him, wriggling like angry vipers.

Alana drew her feet up from the floor, tucking them under herself in a smooth motion. Her nearly black eyes widened as she ducked the flung furniture. "Master?"

The look on her face confirmed she'd felt it, too. She just didn't know. And her ignorance only further infuriated him.

The auer shrank in the large armchair she occupied, casting her gaze down.

Uriel snarled. "Find Mister Rayeht, and find him now. I want to know exactly where he is."

"She's got the Art, seize her!" One guard lunged as the other drew her blade.

Ahria stared at the guards, wide-eyed. "What? I don't..." She leapt to the side, pulling the dagger from her belt.

Why do they think I have power?

Her back hit the wall, and as one guard closed in on her, she dropped to a crouch and rolled out of the way. Looking at the window she'd broken into the palace from, she sucked in a deep breath. More running footsteps pounded outside the doorway beside her, eliminating her other option of escape.

I need to get out of here.

"That was far stronger than we expected the wave might be." Panic tainted Katrin's eyes as she looked at her husband.

"Uriel will have felt that." Matthias clenched his jaw. "But he still won't know where, even with a vague direction."

"Shit." Liam leaned closer to his king. "What do we do?"

The king shook his head. "There's nothing we can do, other than maintain secrecy over the location."

The door to the chamber ricocheted off the wall.

Zael sprinted across the room before he barreled into his mother, wrapping his arms around her hips. "Something just happened, Mom. I don't know what it was."

Matthias stood, approaching his youngest son. "You felt that?"

Katrin looked up at him, running her hand through her son's black hair before she crouched, becoming shorter than the eight-year-old. She pulled him into a hug. "It's all right. We felt it, too."

The king took a deep breath, unable to focus on what it meant that Zael held potential for the Art. "I will write to Damien. He must be planning to wake our other pieces soon." He patted Liam's shoulder. "There isn't enough security here, so it looks like we'll have to finish your birthday celebrations at home."

"You think Uriel will renew his attempts to get to you?" Liam glanced at his sister and nephew before all attention focused on the king.

Matthias scoffed, dread pooling in his chest. "Without a doubt."

The story will continue with...

DAUGHTER OF THE STOLEN PRINCE

www.Pantracia.com

AS LONG AS THE KEY SLEEPS, HER DAUGHTER IS FREE.

Ahria left home in search of her missing father, putting all the skills he taught her to the test. But when she stows away on a ship with her sailor boyfriend's help—and gets caught— she ends up at the captain's mercy.

Conrad's love has always belonged to the sea, yet when Ahria is found on his ship and brought before him, an ember in his heart warms. But with the presence of another man and a quest that will take her far from a life at sea, getting close could be a mistake.

After Ahria has a slip of the tongue, a rival ship corners them, causing problems she can only guess at. In a drastic play, she tries to right her wrong, leaving both Conrad and her boyfriend scrambling to get her back.

Daughter of the Stolen Prince is Part 1 of *The Vanguard Legacy* and Book 11 in the *Pantracia Chronicles*.

Made in the USA
Columbia, SC
07 February 2025

52695266R00309